SHADOW DANCERS

HERBERT LIEBERMAN

SMP

ST. MARTIN'S PAPERBACKS

To Kit Kitzmiller

*For the wise words, the warm counsel,
and all the laughs. Especially the laughs.*

Published by arrangement with Little, Brown

SHADOW DANCERS

Copyright © 1989 by Herbert Lieberman.

Library of Congress Catalog Card Number: 88-37332

ISBN: 0-312-92288-4

Printed in the United States of America

Little, Brown hardcover edition/June 1989
St. Martin's Paperbacks edition/May 1990

10 9 8 7 6 5 4 3 2 1

A Terrifying *Danse Macabre* That Will Haunt Your Dreams
SHADOW DANCERS

A ghoulish madman stalks the women of New York. His victims are raped, robbed, savagely murdered. His grisly handiwork is always identified by cryptic graffiti spattered nearby. . . .

Police Lieutenant Frank Mooney is convinced there are two killers: the original—and an uncanny mimic. Mooney thought he had seen it all. Until tracking the "Shadow Dancers" through the city's seamy netherworld traps him in a gruesome triangle of spiraling terror and consummate evil: a nerve-shattering cat-and-mouse more shocking than anyone dared imagine. . . .

"Lieberman plots a splendid chase!"
—*Newsday*

"High-impact prose . . . stunning!"
—*Kirkus Reviews*

"Taut suspense!" —*Forecast*

"Lieberman's ability to make his way through the steamy caverns and unexplored alleyways of the cramped and distorted human psyche is incredible."
—*Jose Quintero*

"As long as I know that you understand," he whispered. "But of course you do. It's a great satisfaction to have got somebody to understand. You seem to have been there on purpose." And in the same whisper, as if we two whenever we talked had to say things to each other which were not fit for the world to hear, he added, "it's very wonderful."

Joseph Conrad
"The Secret Sharer"

PART I

ONE

IT THUNDERED THAT NIGHT. THE RAIN FELL slantwise in sheets outside and it was wet inside the shaft when they got down there. There was no ladder and the only way in was a rope, not exactly the ideal method of descent for a sixty-two-year-old 230 pounder with disc problems and zero notions once he got down there, how he'd ever get back up.

It was about fifteen feet to the bottom, and the closer he got to it, the stronger the smell became. Mostly it smelled like sewage; then something beyond that, something sweet and rotting, unlike any other odor one's likely to smell in the course of an average workday.

The rainwater pelting through the grate above sluiced down with a dull, incessant roar. After being down there awhile, he could hear it inside his head, as though that's where the noise were coming from. Soon he was soaking wet. The inside of his collar felt like a washcloth, and his socks sucked and bubbled inside his shoes.

It was one of those big old trap drains the city installed nearly a hundred years ago. Now mostly plugged with leaves and sediment, none of them supposedly still function. But still they never overflow, and where the water runs off is anyone's guess. Just after the war, in the late forties, the city rebuilt the whole system, thereby rendering the original trap drains superannuated and defunct.

When he found her, she was right there at the bottom,

sort of jackknifed or folded in half and wedged between the stone walls of a conduit that probed farther down into the spongy earth like the neck of a bottle.

She was upside down, her hair fanned out and trailing in a puddle about a foot deep. Leaves and gumwrappers and ice cream sticks skimmed across the surface and lodged in the strands of slowly undulating hair. Except for the wet stocking plastered to her right leg, she wore no clothing. In her left hand she clutched a small rock as if at the end she'd used it to defend herself.

"Find anything?" Pickering clambered down the rope, banging against the wall as he came, then stood there puffing with the beam of his light playing over the body. "Jesus."

"Looks like she's been down here awhile," Mooney said.

Pickering sniffed. "Smells it."

Gazing down from above, the round, grinning moon of McKloskey's face rose above the grating in the beam of Pickering's light. "Well?"

"She's here, all right."

"Dead?"

"What the fuck would you think?"

"Any ID?"

"Nothing. Naked as a jaybird."

Pickering started to laugh, then broke off, startled by the coarse sound of his own laughter echoing through the cold earth.

Above, McKloskey scrambled to his feet, kicking a shower of gravel down the walls of the shaft as he did so. "Don't touch nothing. The M.E.'s coming right over."

They stood there at the bottom, dismal in their wet shoes, huddling off to one side to avoid the splash from the waterfall above. They could hear voices talking overhead, and by that time a few more squad cars had wheeled into the area. The red flicker of their dome lights bounced off the low, rainy sky and shimmered like wet, freshly applied paint on the stone walls inside the drain.

They were at a point just behind the zoo, not far from the big clock with the animated animals — the bronze bears and rabbits and squirrels — that come whirling and spinning and pirouetting out on the hour. During the day the place is crawling with people. Full of tourists and kids and nurses pushing prams. But at night it could be pretty forlorn, particularly around the late winter when the days are short, and the nights cold and damp. The leaves are still down. Just a few stubborn ones cling to the bare branches, shriveled and wasted like the few survivors of a battle that had long ago ended in defeat.

Steam rose out of the softening earth, entangling itself like rags in the bare trees. Even fifteen feet down, they could still see the lights from the Plaza off to the right and those from the Pierre just behind them. They threw a vapory orange diffusion against the rainy sky.

They heard a grunt. Overhead, someone was shoving the grate farther off to the side. It clanged on the pavement walk above, making Mooney think of the ring of horseshoes played on a summer night in the country. Once again, McKloskey's face rose above the grating and peered down at them.

"You want us to try and bring her up?" Pickering shouted above the din of cascading water.

"The M.E. wants to have a look first."

"Tell him not to rush himself. It's dandy down here."

"Hold your water, will you, Mooney? We sent for a ladder."

In a minute or so there was more clanking and scraping. Then, through the mote-filled beam of Pickering's light, the legs of an aluminum extension ladder probed down through the shaft, making grating sounds as it scraped against the walls. In the next minute, the skirts of a trenchcoat swung above the open drain.

"Heads up," a voice boomed. Something dark and heavy from above hurtled past Mooney's shoulder, landing beside his foot with a squishy thud. It was a battered old black leather bag.

"Thanks for the warning," Mooney shouted up. "You nearly skulled me."

"Fancy that. And I wasn't even aiming."

There was the sound of more dirt and gravel showering down from above as the trenchcoated figure descended through the mist-hung shaft.

"Well, looka this," Mooney said, seeing a familiar face in the beam of Pickering's light. "I didn't think you still made house calls."

"What the hell are you doing here, Mooney? Didn't you quit the force ages ago? I heard you married some poor, benighted creature who devotes her life now to cooking your gruel and rinsing out your underwear."

"I never quit. Just a little sick leave. But that was ages ago. You're just not around much anymore."

They stood there grinning at each other in cordial dislike. The beam of Pickering's light made them look like a pair of genial jackals quarreling over a bit of carrion. They'd known each other the better part of thirty years, and there was no love lost between them. Paul Konig was the chief medical examiner of the City of New York. He was roughly sixty-three or sixty-four then — old by M.E. standards.

"What do we have here?" Konig muscled past the detective.

Pickering swung the beam of his light in an arc above their heads, finally pointing it straight down into the narrowing conduit of the drain.

The M.E. stared down at the vague shape at the bottom of the drain. For a fleeting moment, his lips pursed, about to ask a question, but instead he started toward the girl. Rocks and dirt crumbled beneath his slipping feet as he worked his way down to her.

He knelt beside her for a while, not talking, screening the body from the two men above so that all they saw was the feet and head.

"How the hell you find it?" he asked at last.

"Anonymous tip. Someone just phoned headquarters. Said it was here. Told us to come and get it."

"Just like the last time," Pickering offered. "The job out in Flatbush."

"Figure this is the same guy? Your 'Shadow Dancer' chap?"

Pickering flung his light against the far wall of the shaft, illuminating a large phallic drawing scrawled there in green crayon. Flying out of the head of it, a series of numbers spewed — 14, 18, 23, 28, 34, 42, 50, 59 — as if under great force like volcanic debris. "Sure looks like it."

"An artist, we've got here," Konig grumbled.

"Seen better stuff on the wall of a public toilet," Pickering muttered.

"What's it supposed to mean?"

Mooney shrugged. "You tell me. So far we found the same doodlings in about ten of these things. The numbers change, but the pictures are generally pretty much the same."

Konig pondered the drawing a moment longer, then turned. "Hand me my bag, will you? And let's have some more of that light over here."

It wasn't easy dislodging her. She was wedged in tight between the two stone walls at the point where they narrowed. From the look of her head it appeared that her skull had been crushed.

"Nice shiner she's got there," Pickering said.

"That's no shiner." Konig stooped above the body. "It's a heel mark. Son of a bitch stood on her face and ground his shoe into her eye. It's here, too." The M.E. pointed to a blackish welt on her cheek where the mark of a boot sole had been imprinted upon it.

"She's young," Konig said. "Early twenties, I'd say."

"Doesn't look like the sort to wind up naked at the bottom of a drain," Pickering remarked. "Looks like a class piece of goods. Fashion model or an actress, maybe."

To Mooney, she had the drawn, haggard beauty of one of those icons he'd seen in the paintings of old churches. Lady saints tied to stakes, flames licking up about them, eyes raised heavenward as though confronting God. Only this young saint had been martyred in a sewer.

"How long you figure she been down here, Chief?" Pickering asked.

" 'Bout three days, I'd say." Konig's fingers joined behind her head and lifted gently. "Neck's broken."

"Probably busted it being dropped from above," Pickering speculated.

"Nope." Konig slid his finger sideways across the line of her throat. "The neck was broken before. Throttled. See the ligature marks on the throat?" He raised the lid of one eye and peered hard at it. "See the little red dots? Petechial hemorrhages. That all happened before she was dumped down here."

"Where do you think she got it?" Mooney asked.

"Nearby."

"That figures. If it were done elsewhere, he'd have had to drag her all the way down here through the park."

"Probably nabbed her walking one of those footpaths up near the street."

"Or right off the street," Pickering said. "The Sixtieth Street entrance is just a couple of hundred feet up from here."

Konig nodded. "Son of a bitch could've been lurking right up there. Nabbed her when she passed. Dragged her off into the bushes, strangled her, then lugged her down here and tossed her into the drain."

"Then jumped in after her?" Mooney inquired.

"Why would he do that?"

"Beats me, but he had to. There's the pretty drawings down there. Then he climbed back out on those iron rungs set into the wall."

"And that rock," Konig mused.

"What about it?"

"The fact that she's still holding it."

"So?"

"Suggests she was still alive when she got down here."

Silently, they pondered the riddle.

"Well," Konig sighed, "I can't do anything more here now." He'd started to shove his gear back into the bag.

Mooney stirred, brooding about something. "He hadda be awful strong to lift that grate by himself."

Konig gazed up at him in the beam of Pickering's light. "Who says he was by himself?"

"I don't know. I just assumed it. What makes you think he wasn't?"

"That's the difference between you and me, Mooney. I don't assume things." Konig was binding the girl's hands together and bandaging them with a light gauze in order to keep them clean and undamaged until he had a chance to remove the gunk beneath the fingernails and get it under a microscope.

"Any other clothing besides the stocking?" he asked.

"They're scouring the area now."

"I'd be surprised if they didn't find it scattered right around here someplace — in the bushes," Konig said, snapping his bag shut.

"I'd be surprised if they did," Mooney said.

Konig cocked a brow at him.

"If like you say," Mooney went on, "she's been dead three days, the park workers would've turned the stuff up by now."

"Could've been buried," Konig shot back. He had little patience for opinions that failed to coincide with his own.

"I don't think so," Mooney remarked calmly. "But that's the difference between you and me, Chief. I assume things."

Pickering started to laugh, then caught Konig's frown and broke off fast.

The M.E. wobbled to his feet. "Okay — wrap it up and ship it downtown. I should be back to you with something in a few days."

*   *   *

"I'd never bet a filly against a colt," Patsy Duffy said. He raised the shaker above his shoulder and proceeded to bash the mixture inside into pulpy submission.

"How come?" Mooney asked.

"They're the weaker sex. A good filly can't beat a good colt." Duffy drained off the foaming Manhattan into a cocktail glass.

"Who said?" Mooney asked. "You just say that 'cause trainers in the States won't run a filly 'gainst colts. In Europe, fillies beat colts every day. Orchid's a filly and right now she's the best horse in Europe. It's no big deal for a filly to win the Arc de Triomphe. Happens all the time. Gimme another cherry, will you?"

Duffy dropped a pair of maraschino cherries into the detective's glass, then turned to ring up someone's tab seated beside him. Mooney watched the bartenders work for a while, then looked around the room. They were stacked three-deep at the bar that night. All waiting for tables.

Mooney sat at the bar of the Balloon watching the crowds come and go. For him, there was nothing quite like a good New York steak house. Particularly on a Friday night, normally a payday for most. People were relaxed then, or just beginning to get that way about the dinner hour. There's no school in the morning, and even if people are feeling battered and awful from the week's horrors, they're still feeling pretty good.

If Mooney happened to feel a certain proprietary fondness for this place, it was no great surprise. His wife owned it. The Balloon or, more accurately, Fritzi's Balloon, sat up in the East Eighties in a turn-of-the-century brownstone with a bright striped canopy that ran from the entrance right out to the street. On either side of the big glass revolving doors, a pair of wrought-iron jockeys holding flickering lanterns stood guard in their track colors, welcoming the hungry, well-heeled Upper East Side crowd arriving in cabs for dinner. In a matter of a dozen years or so, the place had become a New York institution — right up there with the likes of Keene's, Crist Cella's, and Smith and Wolenski.

Fritzi Mooney had built it from scratch with her first husband, Nick Baumholz, a wealthy contractor who wanted to give his wife something to do. Baumholz died a few years later, leaving Fritzi to run the place by herself. It was her vision and imagination that had turned it into the booming success it eventually became.

Then she met Mooney. He was in his late fifties at the time. A confirmed, unregenerate bachelor, it was his first trip to the altar. All of his buddies on the force laughed. There was a lottery to see if it would last one week, one month, or one year. Defying all the odds, they were still together after four years, embarrassing all of their betting friends who said they'd be lucky if it went two rounds.

The Mooneys shared a mutual passion. That was the ponies. They loved horse racing to distraction. They only went to the flats. They had no use for the trotters. They had a clubhouse box at Belmont and the unlimited use of a close friend's at Aqueduct, as well. They went each weekend to one or the other with near hieratic zeal. For vacations, they went nowhere that could not provide them a fast, first-rate track.

When they got married, as a sort of wedding present, they bought themselves a yearling. They called him Gumshoe, undoubtedly out of some sort of affectionate deference to Mooney. The colt made them a small bundle and, shortly, they purchased a second thoroughbred — Wizard. When either of their "kids," as they called them, were running, they'd both drop work at any time and dash out to the track just to jump and scream and cheer them on.

"You know Sausalito?" Mooney asked Duffy when he returned.

"Sure. The two-year-old."

"Right. Now there's a filly ran six furlongs at Gulf Stream in 1:09⅘. The last stakes for colts was run 1:10⅖. She'd eat up those colts in the Hutcheson."

"What colts in the Hutcheson?"

Mooney turned, and there was Fritzi in a full-length scarlet skirt, a cream silk blouse with a spray of violets at her throat, and glowing as though she'd just stepped from a hot bath. She threw an arm across his shoulder and pecked his cheek. "You smell like a zoo. Where've you been?"

"Down a sewer."

She shrugged and made a queer face at Duffy. "What's he drinking?"

"Just a tot of bourbon, Fritz. It's his first. Honest."

"That's a hundred fifty calories. Don't give him any more."

Mooney groaned. Having suffered a mild heart attack several years before, he was on a fairly strict diet. Still, he couldn't bear having others decide for him what he would eat and what he would drink.

There was a great burst of laughter as a big, splashy crowd wheeled in through the revolving glass doors. It was a crowd Fritzi loathed, but they spent like Arabs and so she was all smiles and gliding toward the door to greet them.

"Hey," Mooney called after her. "When do we eat?"

"Maybe around ten, when it starts to clear out."

"I can't wait to no ten o'clock. I'm starving now."

"Can't be bothered now. Go on in the kitchen and have them fix you something."

"I don't wanna eat in the kitchen."

"Got no tables now. Have Gino set you up at the bar."

She turned and in the next moment she was swallowed up in a swirl of color and motion. There was a great deal of kissing and laughter and bogus hilarity. Fritzi was snapping her fingers and Otto, the maître-d', came rushing toward them, bowing and scraping and flashing his dentures.

Mooney muttered some oath and tossed off the last of his Jack Daniel's Manhattan. The place was going full tilt now. Four bartenders could scarcely keep up with it.

No sooner were they set out than the bowls of chips and the big wheels of cheddar cheese and the platters of fresh, iced crudités disappeared and had to be replaced. Steaks and chops sizzled on the open grates. Big standing rib roasts turned on the spits above them. The great stone hearth in the main room crackled blue and orange flames, filling the air with the tangy scent of hickory and well-cured apple wood. Corks popped. Creaking trolleys of beef and Yorkshire pudding tottered up and down the narrow aisles. On the walls, hung between a series of staggered flambeaux, were portraits of some of the noblest bloods of racing history — Bold Venture, Citation, Northern Dancer, Proud Clarion, Riva Ridge, Secretariat, Foolish Pleasure, Seattle Slew.

People laughed loudly, counting all the money they'd made, or claimed they'd made, in the market that week. It was a pretty sight. Life was sweet, Mooney thought, at least for the moment. The trap drain he'd been rummaging in behind the zoo just a few hours before seemed very far away.

TWO

". . . HEART, 300 GRAMS. MYOCARDIUM PRE-
sents a red-brown homogeneous color. No evidence of
hemorrhage or scar. Valves not remarkable . . ."

The hiss of coffee steamed on an old Bunsen burner.
An old Regulator clock on the wall ticked hollowly
through the vacant shadows.

Konig struck a match and relit the cold, fuming stump
of his cigar. A coil of blue smoke drifted lazily ceilingward. He was hungry, but he had little appetite for
dinner and no one with whom to eat it even if he had. It
was nearly ten P.M. He was ready by then to quit, but the
prospect of the long drive home to Riverdale was dis-
heartening.

He returned to writing his protocols. There were
three left to go. His stubby, graceless fingers fumbled
over the typewriter keyboard. The stump of cigar
planted dead center in his mouth made his eyes squint
in an effort to elude the smoke.

. . . Stomach contains approximately 200 cc's of grayish
fluid. Particles of undigested food within. Gastric mu-
cosa not remarkable. . . . Kidneys weigh 200 grams together and show smooth dark surface. Ureter normal.
Bladder contains approximately 400 cc's of clear yellow
urine. Anus dilated and containing a large amount of
green feces. . . .

Paul Konig had been a New York City medical examiner for slightly more than thirty years. He'd started in

the days of Bancroft and caught the eye of city dignitaries in the period of Eisler, his predecessor, whose somewhat flamboyant reign was prematurely terminated by his penchant for selling medical opinion to the highest bidder. Suddenly Konig, not quite thirty, found himself in a highly visible, highly influential position.

Over the past three decades he'd distinguished not only himself but the office as well. Aside from the fact that he was Chief M.E. in the world's most powerful city, he carried on a notable career as a writer and lecturer. His opinions on criminal matters were eagerly sought by judicial authorities all over the world. He wrote textbooks on the subject of forensic pathology, and his classes at the university were always oversubscribed. Getting into his course was like getting a ticket to the hottest show on Broadway.

His face was seen frequently in the newspapers and on the six P.M. news. His photograph was always being snapped with the mayor. He was greatly admired but not much liked. For a man in a highly political job, he had a well-documented dislike of politicians. He couldn't be wheedled or bamboozled by ambitious district attorneys eager to chalk up a string of impressive convictions against the day they ran for some more exalted office. Konig had no friends in government and liked things that way. In his personal catechism, anyone with too many friends in public office bore watching.

People who knew Konig in the early days when his beloved Ida and his daughter Lolly were still alive maintain that he was lighthearted and fun. But that was before the horrific tragedy that had started with the girl's kidnaping and ended in her death at the hands of her captors. It was a celebrated case, made all the more so by the fact that the chief medical examiner was her father.

But yes, in the early days there'd been that part of him that was lighthearted and fun. In those halcyon times he could recite Shakespeare by the ream and sing Verdi arias in a credible tenor. Not so today. *Morose* and *disagreeable* were some of the more tactful adjectives one was apt to hear now when people spoke of the chief medical examiner.

There was little doubt, however, that he was the best in the business. From the point of view of detective work, which for an M.E. is all that really counts, Konig was right up there with the legends, Spillsbury and Halperin. On a tough job, having him on your team made all the difference. He could read the riddle of a corpse the way most people read a grocery list.

"BRAIN: Chloroform 38.7%." Konig glanced down at the toxicological report, scribbled there in dark, glyptic figures. "Ethanol not detected.

Lung: Chloroform. 3.8% (GC)
Blood: Acidic drugs. Not detected. Spectrophotometry.
Basic drugs. Not detected. Gas Chromotography.
Chloroform. 17.2% (GC)
Bile: Chloroform. 8.65 mg% (GC)
Acidic and basic drugs not detected. (TLC)
Cause of Death: Acute chloroform poisoning. Unintentional suicide.

Konig glanced up at the old Regulator wall clock, still counting its drowsy, monotonous tick into the hollow, dusty vacancies, its gold pendulum drifting behind the glass window. The door to the outside corridor was open. The air of desertion about the place seemed total. The grim daily tide of mortality had rolled past his door for that day, but in Konig's head the clatter of rushing footsteps still rang on the cold tile floors. The unoiled wheels of gurney carts bearing their grisly cargo toward the freight elevators still echoed squeals down the airless, empty hallways. Except for the handful of night porters and attendants on duty somewhere about the building, Konig had the place to himself.

As a younger man he'd enjoyed working there late at night. Mostly it was the solitude he loved, the sense of proprietorship he felt when only he was there. King of the Underworld. Lord Chancellor of the Necropolis sort of thing. When he worked late into the night now, it was scarcely out of love for the job or devotion to duty. Now it was more out of a fear of having to go home, to face the infinitely more terrifying silences of the big old Norman Tudor, with its turrets and arches and towers, planted like a stone fortress high above the banks of the Hudson.

Built by a charming, megalomaniacal broker in the twenties, who went out the window in the thirties, it was later purchased by Konig for a song and a down payment borrowed from his father-in-law, then paid back to the penny in one year's time at 4 percent, considered regal in those days.

He had little heart for it now — to prowl from floor to unlit floor through the far reaches of the night, with nothing but a grail of moonlight illuminating the empty halls and rooms, left precisely as they were when those who'd formerly occupied them were still in residence.

The chairs and beds and settees were all still there, untouched, unused, still breathing some aura of their former occupants. The drawers and wardrobes were still hung with garments not worn for seven years. An air of strange expectancy clung to them as though they awaited some corporeal presence to reanimate them.

In the conservatory, Ida's piano, massive in its shadowed corner, still bore on its stand the music she played in those final, pain-racked days when she could neither sleep nor even lie comfortably in bed. Nights there had been since, when he imagined that fingers swept over the keyboard and he could hear the ghostly plangencies of some sad old Chopin mazurka.

Not far down the corridor was Lolly's room, with the desk where, as a child, she had labored over geometry and Latin. The bookshelves still sagged with every book she'd ever owned — the Babars and Madeleines, cheek by jowl with the Dostoyevskys and Gides, no order or method to any of it; just a joyous tumult of things. Just as she was in life, with that exasperating, endearing air of cheery, whirlwind chaos.

"Christ," Konig muttered and pushed his chair back. Wobbling to his feet, he rocked from one foot to the other as though trying to restore circulation there. He brushed a trail of old cigar ash from his vest and rubbed his eyes where the thin crescent imprint of his glasses rimmed the bottom of the sockets. Reaching back, he started to pour another cup of coffee from the pot on the Bunsen burner. All that it yielded was a tepid trickle of dregs.

"Christ." He yanked his trenchcoat from the hanger and blundered into it like a man fending off an imaginary assailant. Even as he went, barging down the empty halls, something tugged at him, some nagging sense of incompletion. It was no mystery to him, yet try as he did to resist, the strong, familiar undertow drew him down the narrow, winding spiral stair into the basement of the building.

If it had been quiet above, it was virtually cryptlike below, the sort of silence born of cold, municipal green tile and overheated laboratory machinery now stilled and cooling for the night.

A mere several hours before, these same narrow aisles had teemed with humanity — pathologists and students, police reporters and dieners. Gurneys spattered with gore clogged the aisles, waiting to be rolled up to the tables; people shouted at the top of their lungs, outraged at one another, pleading for assistance where none was readily available.

Now, only a single light bathed the scene in an eerie bluish glow. The smell of formalin was suffocating. The still tables were all empty and scrubbed. Stored in the two big purring refrigerated lockers was the daily harvest of man-made carnage, the carcasses of the hapless and itinerant, the criminal and mad, and those whose only blame was being in the wrong place at the wrong time.

The refrigerators hummed softly. Like a bank of mailboxes, each carried on its face a small white identification card bearing the name of the present occupant — a brief, hand-scribbled epitaph: "Dankworth, Charles. Caucasian. Age 32." "Lenz, Mildred. Caucasian. Female. Age 71." "Carver, Thomas. Black. Male. Age 2." "Guzman, Jesus. Male Hispanic. Age 17."

Konig's eyes swept down the white ID tags until at last they fastened on what he'd been seeking. "Female. Caucasian. Identity unknown. Age approx. 22–25 years."

The drawer wheeled out beneath a slight exertion of his fingers, gliding smoothly over rollers. It was the hair he saw first. Thick, luxuriant, chestnut. The motion of the rollers caused it to shift from her face. In life, no doubt, it had descended to a point well below the shoulders, doubtless one of her most striking features. In death it was mud-streaked, plastered hard in stiff clots against the skull from having lain partially submerged in cistern water for several days.

Next came the face. The eyes not fully closed, a glint of irides showing beneath the bruised lids, the young woman appeared to be wincing as if in fretful sleep, the murderous image of her own destroyer still implanted on the retina. A pretty face, Konig thought. Even somewhat more than pretty. The sort of face that is noted and remarked upon where people gather. The features were framed within a soft oval; the nose a thin blade, the cheeks high; the chin tapering to a graceful cleft. There was an icy, rather patrician air about those features, flawed only by a mouth a bit too sumptuous and full. Possibly even a bit coarse.

Lying there in the cold impersonality of that drawer, she seemed to him smaller than she had several hours before at the bottom of the drain. Diminutive and doll-like, she was a child tucked in safely for the night.

Konig's practiced eye quickly picked out the purplish lividity creeping outward from beneath the shoulders and back where the still, unpumped blood had succumbed to the pull of gravity. The inexorability of nature's laws triumphed over all. Air pressure, fluid pressure, pounds per square inch will have their way. Only some persistent fiction of man himself still bothers to deny that simple autonomy, still pretending he can manipulate the basic physics to his own advantage. The gods know better.

To the large white toe, looking grotesque and a trifle comical, another white tag was affixed. This one was typed in square black capital letters bearing the words IDENTITY UNKNOWN. Tomorrow, when she'd be wheeled into one of the suites and hoisted onto the table, the sheets unceremoniously withdrawn to reveal the frail, battered nakedness below, they would know more. With several deft strokes, the scalpel would rise to flay the body open. In that moment, whatever semblance of a living, sentient being once inhabitating that fragile shell would quickly vanish. Something else would appear in its place. An abstraction reduced to the cold scrutiny of parts and mere function. The terminology of an auto shop.

Scanning the cadaver, Konig's eye quite unexpectedly picked up something it had missed during the initial examination. In the sewer it had been dark and he'd missed the thick clot of dried gore in the vicinity of the right temple. But where the hair had displaced itself with the sliding motion of the opening drawer, the ear now stood exposed. The whole lower half of it had been neatly scissored off.

THREE

March 17, 1986. Crider, Dale, 33. Stabbed to death in her Richmond Hills home on Village Drive. Was studying flower arrangement. Killed approximately 2 A.M. Bite marks on breasts, abdomen, and inner thighs. Numbers and pornographic doodles scrawled on walls. Sizable amount of cash and jewelry taken. Dark-haired youth, medium height, medium weight, age early twenties, seen fleeing site. Murder weapon not recovered.

April 18, 1986. Pillari, Mario, 64, and wife, Maxine, 59. Both found dead in their semi-detached home on Case Street, Flatbush section of Brooklyn. Pillari, retired investment counselor. Liked to garden. Wife was an attorney. Sang in a choir. Bite marks on breasts and buttocks. Pornographic drawings and numbers found on walls. Murder weapon, knife. Probably six-inch blade, serrated. Not recovered. Cash and silver service taken. No witnesses.

May 19, 1986. Katz, William, 52. Wife, Marilyn, 49. Stabbed to death at their home on Stevens Street, Forest Hills Gardens. He was a retired sales manager. She worked for a bank. Drawings and number series scrawled on walls. Died between 4 and 5 A.M. Bite marks on breasts and inner thighs of wife. Cash and various hi-fi and computer equipment taken. No weapon recovered. Dark-haired youth, approximate age 22–25, seen loitering about earlier in evening.

June 1, 1986. Bell, Mabel, 52. Widow. Lived alone in her home on Kappock Street, Riverdale section of Bronx. Knife wounds found about the body. Death attributed to strangulation by ligature. Usual pornographic doodles and numbers. Bite marks found at usual sites. Jewelry and cash taken. Robbery apparent motive, preceded by sexual attack. No weapon recovered. No eyewitnesses.

June 30, 1986. Wheatley, Gail, 32. Special education teacher for the retarded. Found dead from slashed throat in her home on Dell Place, Manhasset. Attack occurred between midnight and two A.M. Sexual attack preceded killing. Small child of approximately two years old also found dead in home. Personal computer, digital tapes, and VCR taken. Usual drawings and numbers. Usual bite marks. No weapon recovered. No eyewitnesses.

Mooney's eyes grew heavy. His cramped, aching legs stretched beneath the sheets. He glanced down at the drowsy figure lying there beside him, a warm emanation of soap and skin, the scent of moisturizers rising all about her. It was near midnight. Unable to sleep, he'd whiled away the restless hours reading from the small ringed notebook he used to record pertinent data for all the cases in which he was involved. The one he was presently engrossed in appeared under the single heading SHADOW DANCER, actually his sole preoccupation these days, since the case during the past six months had been elevated to priority status.

What followed was a chronology of capsule descriptions for a series of particularly grisly crimes. All had been committed over a period of the last nine months and showed little sign of abating.

The police believed that these murders were the work of two different men — one the original architect of the crime spree, the other a copycat who went about assiduously aping him. But the police were by no means certain. Initially, they'd believed just as firmly that this was the work of a single individual, working alone, and with slight variations creeping in from time to time to his basic M.O.

Because of the unmistakably imitative aspect apparent in these brutal acts, the police had come to identify them by the operation code name Shadow Dancer. The name seemed particularly apt since the reality of a single murderer was self-evident, while the reality of the other was somewhat more moot. But over the past months as the body count continued to rise, the copycat two-man theory assumed a position of clear ascendency over the notion of a single operative. The biggest problem detectives faced, however, was the fact that the type of outrages committed by these two individuals merged so closely in appearance and style that the police were often uncertain which was the work of the original and which that of the pretender to the throne.

August 10, 1986. Greeley, Joyce, 31. Divorcée. Production line worker in a bottling plant. Stabbed to death at her home, Springfield Gardens, Queens. Died between 2:45 and 6 A.M. Sexual attack preceded killing. Usual pornographic doodles but no number series. No weapon recovered. No evidence of anything taken. Motive apparently sexual. Fair-haired young man, early twenties, medium height and size, seen fleeing murder site.

September 9, 1986. Weldon, Max, 43, and wife, Leila, 41. Both killed at their home on Brady Avenue, Pelham Parkway section of the Bronx. Mr. Weldon, a service station operator, was a deacon of the Allerton Avenue Seventh Day Adventist Church. Mrs. W. worked as a security guard at Macy's Parkchester. Usual doodles and numbers. Usual bite marks on wife. Jewelry, electronic equipment, and other valuables taken. Signs of mutilation on body. Tip of right index finger apparently missing. No weapon recovered. No eyewitnesses.

October 9, 1986. Mukherjee, Samkid, 27. Sexually assaulted but survived beating in her home in Bayside,

Queens. Bite marks on right cheek, throat, and buttocks. Usual wall scribblings. Attacker fled with an esti-
mated $30,000 in money and jewels. Mrs. Mukherjee's
husband, Chainarang, an importer, was traveling in Far
East at the time. She described dark-haired young man,
early twenties, average weight and height, crooked, off-
center smile, as her assailant.

November 5, 1986. Winton, Elias, 35, stabbed to death
in his Orchard Beach home in the Bronx. His 28-year-
old wife, Darlene, was raped and her throat slashed
during the 3 A.M. attack. Silverware and jewelry taken.
Usual drawings and numbers. Bite marks at usual sites.
No weapon recovered but wounds consistent with six-
inch serrated blade seen in other attacks. No eyewitnesses.

December 11, 1986. Buchwald, Francine, 39. Recent
divorcée. Lived alone in detached brownstone, 580 West
101st Street. Innumerable knife wounds, but death attributed to strangulation. Sexually assaulted before she
died. One eye gouged out during attack. Usual pornographic doodles, but no numbers. Nothing taken. Motive apparently sexual. Fair-haired young man, early
twenties, average height and weight, seen loitering in
the area just prior to assault.

"When are you going to turn off the lights?" Fritzi's
voice mumbled from beneath the counterpane.
"I've just got a couple more pages to go."
"You said that an hour ago."
"Go to sleep."
"I can't with the lights on."
"Can I read you something?"
"Sure. Go ahead." Fritzi turned on her side to face
him, snoring faintly into her pillow.
Mooney adjusted the eyeglasses on his nose and pro-
ceeded to read aloud the M.O.'s for each of the attacks
he had scribbled into his pad.

"Sounds like Cousin Merwin," Fritzi mumbled after he'd finished.

"Occasionally mutilates his victim. Takes a digit of a finger or an ear. Gouges an eye . . ."

"Check out Merwin."

An angry stream of epithets sounded from somewhere out in the darkened apartment.

"What the hell's he yapping about now?" Mooney fumed.

"Light's keeping him up. He wants to go to sleep. You blame him?"

"Balls," the voice intoned, low and sepulchral, from the area of the kitchen. "Balls." It wafted across the living room and into the bedroom. The source of it was a raucous five-year-old mynah bird called Sanchez, a scruffy, garrulous black creature who resided in a tall, bell-shaped cage and appeared to thrive in a state of perpetual molt.

"Just listen to that fool," Mooney grumbled.

"You teach him dirty words, he'll say them for you," Fritzi chastened him.

Mooney glared down at the tumbled mane of red hair spilling across the pillow. He sighed as though in defeat and snapped closed his pad.

"Just try and forget all this for a few hours," Fritzi mumbled into her pillow.

"I try. Believe me, I try. Trouble's Mulvaney. He won't let me. 'Did you do this?' 'Did you do that?' 'Why haven't you checked out so and so?' . . ." Mooney's voice trailed off into smothered exasperation.

"You're getting closer to these nutsos every day. Eventually one of them is bound to make a mistake. That's when you'll nab them both."

"Yesterday I might've believed that. Today I'm as far from a solution as I was last March when I first started. Just when I figure I've got hold of something tangible, it all goes up in smoke. Tonight we pulled this kid out of a sewer. Now that's outdoors. That's not indoors. That's never happened before. That's a whole new wrinkle. That's not a detached or semi-detached dwelling. But it sure looks like one of our two guys again. There was the usual sex stuff, and the naughty little boy scribblings on the walls. There were the bite marks on the body, too. That's consistent. But this little girl was younger than any of the previous victims. Early twenties. The others run from the late twenties on up into the fifties and sometimes the sixties. You see, it's like that. Consistent, but not consistent. I don't know who I'm looking for anymore. One description has him medium height, dark hair, with a crooked smile. Another has him fair-haired and above average height, with a sweet baby face."

"So you know you've got two different guys," Fritzi mumbled sleepily.

"Sure. Classic copycat situation. That's easy." Mooney huffed. "The tough part is trying to tell the one from the other. I keep confusing them. I used to think I could tell the styles apart. Now I can't anymore."

Outside on the street below an ambulance whooped like a stricken creature, beating its way up into some troubled northern precinct.

"What these two guys do is probably ninety-five, ninety-six percent identical." Mooney fretted. "But then there's those two or three few percentage points of deviation where the copycat guy goes off and does his own little number."

"You always do everything one hundred percent the same?" Fritzi asked drowsily. "Brush your teeth the same every morning? Sign your name the same?" Fritzi gathered the blankets up around her shoulders. "You know any horse that runs the same race twice?"

"Sure. They do all the time. Just check the P.P.'s."

"You think you can tell what a horse will do one day just from looking at his P.P.'s? If that were true, how come you're not a millionaire?"

Lying on his back, staring at the ceiling, Mooney grew indignant. "Well, you can damn well pretty much tell how a horse is gonna run if you've got his past performance charts in front of you."

"P.P.'s are just numbers. Weight of horse. Weight of jockey. Speed over a given distance. Where the horse finished last three times out. Numbers. Just numbers."

Mooney flung his hands up in despair. "How did we get into this? Weren't we just talking homicide a minute ago?"

"Same thing. You're giving me M.O.'s and I say they're just P.P.'s. You need something more. For the full story, you need the IP's."

That brought the detective to an abrupt stop. "IP's?"

"The Imponderables. The stuff you can't describe with numbers. How does the horse feel? Is he rested? Does he hurt anywhere? Does he like his jockey? What's his mental attitude? Don't you think that goes into the equation too?"

"Okay. Okay. I get your point," Mooney grumbled. "But how does all this apply to the matter at hand?"

"I'm coming to that." Fritzi lay with a coyly angelic smile on her face. "All I'm asking you now is to acknowledge the fact that you have an incomplete picture with these eleven M.O.'s because they don't take into consideration the little normal variations in human behavior from one day to the next."

"Granted. Okay? Granted." Mooney had started to swell dangerously. "But that's all I have to go on. I don't have the luxury of sitting down with these two nut cases and asking them if they slept well last night and if everything is all perky and rosy with them today."

"Right. That's what separates the truly great handicapper from the merely good one. That's what I call the leap of faith."

"Good Christ," Mooney fumed. He snapped off the light. "Now she's into theology. Forget I asked you."

"If you don't care for 'leap of faith,'" Fritzi continued, "call it hunch or educated guess."

Mooney smoldered silently in the dark for a moment.

"Okay. So what's your best educated guess? Who's who? Which is which? Who's the shadow and who's the dancer? Tell me."

"Well, just from what you've been reading me here, far as I can tell it goes something like this." She flopped on her back and clasped her palms on her chest as though she were praying. "We're agreed we've got two guys. Right?"

"Agreed," Mooney fumed.

"We've got two sets of descriptions. One is a dark-haired guy with a crooked smile. Medium height. Medium weight. We'll call him 'Blackie.' The other is a fair-haired boy. Medium height and weight. We'll call him 'Whitey.' "

"Get on with it, will you, for Chrissake?"

Fritzi ignored the tirade and bore down harder on the puzzle. "We know Blackie and Whitey both prefer detached or semi-detached residences, although one of them is not entirely opposed to working out of doors, as we saw."

"Keep going."

"We know both of these boys like sex, because they both appear to make use of the ladies in that way. Both like to draw naughty pictures on the walls, scrawl little messages. But one of them, *only one of them*, adds numbers to the little pictures and messages. Oh, by the way, what about the handwriting?"

"We spoke to a couple of experts."

"And?"

"One says it's two different guys. The other's not so sure."

"That's experts for you."

Mooney sighed. "Keep going. Keep going."

"Both work the early hours of the morning. Generally between two and six A.M. Both claim the knife as weapon of choice but occasionally will strangle their victims."

"Keep going."

"Finally, while sex appears to be a principle motive in

both M.O.'s, theft appears to play a role in just one."

"That's right." Mooney said. "You got it all right. So what do we have so far?"

"So far, that's only the P.P.'s."

"Okay. So what about these IP's of yours? This 'leap of faith' thing? Which of these guys is which?"

She'd lapsed into a silence and for a moment he thought she'd fallen asleep. "You still there?" he asked.

"I'm here. I'm thinking." Again she propped herself up on an elbow and peered at him through the dark. "Where we've got eyewitness descriptions of the guy, it appears it's Blackie who uses both pictures and numbers. Whitey just does the pictures."

"Okay. So what does that say to you?"

"That says to me that Blackie is the hardheaded pragmatist and Whitey is the daydreaming romantic. That says to me that Whitey is the guy who steals nothing. Only some love. Blackie is the entrepreneur. He grabs stuff. He's in it for both fun and profit. How am I doing so far?"

"Okay. Okay," he snapped impatiently. "Keep going." For the first time since she'd started her disquisition, he appeared to be interested. "So of both of these nutsos, which, if you will, is the copycat and which the original?"

Fritzi laughed lightly. "That's easy. Just check the chronology in your notes."

"You mean just because the first entry I've got fingers a dark-haired guy, he's the chief architect?"

"Figures, doesn't it? There's no description of a blond type till you get down to your fifth or sixth M.O."

"Sixth," Mooney confirmed. "I'm afraid that's a bit too easy, Fritzi. How do you know this hasn't been going on long before we observed the similarities of the two M.O.'s and started to track them? We're still carrying unsolved homicides on the books that go back for years and are very similar in type to these. How do we know when they really started and which guy started it?"

"We don't. All we can do is make that educated guess

based on when your record-keeping started. But given what you have now, I'm willing to bet that Blackie is your original. He's the guy who adds numbers to the dirty pictures and the guy who steals after he rapes. Whitey's got no interest in numbers or in trade. He's the dreamer, as I said. The poet. Also, he's passive. He's a follower. Blackie is a trailblazer. He'd just as soon slit your throat as have a cup of tea with you. He's got a plan to beat you every time. Take my word for it, Mooney. Blackie's your Dancer; Whitey's your Shadow."

In the next moment, as though someone had thrown a switch, she'd flipped over on her stomach and was fast asleep.

Long after, Mooney still lay there in the dark, hands clasped behind his neck, thinking about what she'd said. You had to hand it to Fritzi, he thought, with a touch of professional resentment. She had a way of going at problems, a way of absorbing and processing information, then handing it back to you all wrapped up pretty in some condensed and highly ordered way that enabled you to see things there you'd never seen before. She had an unerring eye for sifting the valuable from a swamp of detail and chucking out the dross. She couldn't care less for the old pro cops' reverence for routine and logic. Fritzi was a true longshotter, and as any good handicapper could tell you, over the long haul, longshot players lose. But if that was statistically correct, it had made little impression on Fritzi. In all of the years Mooney had known her, with all of her longshotting, buck for buck wagered, she was way ahead of the game.

From outside in the kitchen, another sharp volley of oaths rattled through the darkened apartment. They came in the clipped, half-swallowed locutions of a bird's voice box. A stream of comic filth to keep the goblins of the night at bay.

FOUR

HE ALWAYS EXPERIENCED HIS GREATEST sense of elation when driving. The sensation of total freedom only occurred for him behind the wheel of a car. At such times a tremendous weight of care lifted from him. He surrendered to a terrifying buoyancy, letting the car take him wherever it chose.

With windows wide open (even in the coldest weather) and the tape deck turned up to maximum volume, he listened to motets and Gregorian chants, alternating with mind-numbing bouts of heavy-metal rock with lyrics spouting easy blasphemies and conjuring the Devil. The one assured him of the indulgence of a kind and loving God; the other, of the delectable enticements of pure abandon.

When off on these jaunts he liked to play a game. It was a sort of fortune-telling game — divination with license-plate numbers. Simply put, he would add up numbers on the plates of cars and watch for patterns to emerge. There were numbers that were good luck and others that were inauspicious. Any combination of numbers adding up to 9, 13, 18, or 22, or those numbers themselves, he considered propitious. Those combinations adding up to 8, 10, or 12 were bad. Sixteen was the most ominous of all. When he saw a frequently repeated series of plates with any combination of 432 or 576, or 112 or 220, he knew that all things were right with the world. The portents were good. The wind was at his tail.

Double numbers were especially propitious . . . 11,

33, 99. But in his curious system of divination, 22 was the best you could get. He well knew that in the Sacred Tree there were ten circles of the Sephiroth, joining 22 lines. Twenty-two was the most sacred number of all. There were 22 cards of Tarot. He was born on the 22nd day of the 9th month, and the difference between the number of the day and the number of the month was 13.

On the other hand, 666, even though it added up to the benevolent 18, was also the number of the Beast in Revelation, and that, under certain circumstances, could be terrifying.

At first, when the game would commence, the numbers would be random, with no particular order. Just lots of numbers banging about before his eyes. He'd have to add them quickly (hard for him because he didn't add numbers well). For the most part, no discernible pattern would emerge. From the start, the pace of it was frantic, like entering into some barely contained madness, the numbers racketing wildly about inside his head. At that point, it would become compulsive and nonselective. He would have to add every group of numbers that came within his purview — not only license plates, but route numbers, numbers glimpsed on passing buildings, and those appearing on roadside billboards. It became a captivity from which he could not escape. A kind of panic commenced. Bombarded with unending numbers, more and more numbers crammed into an ever-decreasing space, his brain would decline to program any more. Yet, he'd be unable to stop. The numbers would simply lunge at him and he would have to add them. It went on and on like that for miles, until mental stupefaction and simple exhaustion brought it to a halt.

At that point, as surely as if a switch were flicked, something inside him would turn off and he would enter a different, a higher plane of consciousness . . . a place of utter calm. The numbers would still be there, but slowed exquisitely, like tiny molecules falling through heavy liquid, and he was suddenly aware of some preternaturally heightened sense within himself. The sensation was that of the keenest excitation, not entirely unlike sex.

In the cascade of numbers falling slowly before his eyes he could see patterns and combinations repeating themselves with startling frequency. But not only this: he could take these sequences and project them out into near infinity. There were, of course, the simple ones like 1, 2, 4, 8, 16, 32 — demonstrating the power of 2; then mindbendingly complex ones like 1, 1, 2, 5, 14, 38, 120, 353 — representing the number of different ways of folding ever-longer strips of postage stamps. There were patterns that consisted of numbers in which each was the sum of the two previous numbers, such as 1, 1, 2, 3, 5, 8, 13, 21, 34, 55. And more complex variations based on the three, or sometimes four, previous numbers. There were series in which one had to double the last term and then add the second to last, and there were beautifully simple prime numbers that were one less than a power of 2, such as 3, 7, 31, etc.

Of course he knew none of these patterns and was unaware that theoretical mathematicians, working with sophisticated computers, had been tracking them for years. He had no training in any of this, and had he been told that men, learned men, devoted whole lifetimes to the study of such things, he would have been baffled and not a little amused. Ironically, in the realm of simple arithmetic, he was nearly illiterate, barely able to add a column of numbers. His peculiar facility was a form of highly developed idiot savantism — although Warren Mars was by no means an idiot. Quite the contrary. On certain levels, he was actually a very clever fellow.

Given the first three or four digits on a typical license plate, say, for example, 467, he would automatically move that out into 9, 10, 11, 12, 14, 16, 17, cracking the inherent code to it at once. Driving along at 55 miles per hour, a 125 would instantly become 12, 29, 70, 169, 408, 985, and so on out into a gray, colorless void where he was flying free.

It was the passion of a madman, with a certain element of whimsy. But at the completion of the exercise, when he would appear to come back to himself, the car still nosing nicely along at 55 mph, he would be scarcely aware that he was limp and exhausted, and that he was bathed in a cold, clammy sweat from head to toe.

He was not aware of what sort of an ordeal he'd been through. He had no idea how his mind had been stretched by the ruthless tyranny of these numbers. For him it was all simply an amusing game at which he was incontestably the unqualified master.

It was in the small border village of Douglaston, just on the line between Queens and Nassau, that Warren saw the woman. He'd been driving up and down the pretty little streets with their small, cookie-cutter homes all set neatly in straight, unwavering rows, each on its own tiny plot of well-tended lawn.

She'd been standing with her back to the street, bending over, working out front in her garden. There was a car parked in the driveway, all shiny and new, a late-model Japanese make. It was something about the way the house sat there, neat, trim, and tidy, separated from its immediate neighbors by tall privet hedges on either side, that told him it was good. The address above the door was 112. Almost from the moment he'd seen that, something in him started to vibrate.

It was roughly 11 A.M., an hour he well knew; husbands were long gone and not expected back until after dark. It was late March and cloudy. Warm weather and much rain had brought an early thaw. The woman had dropped to her knees, cleaning out the debris of winter from a rose bed. It was far too early for anything to be up, save for an anxious crocus or a snowdrop or two. But she was out there all the same.

He pulled up slowly to the front and stopped and watched her for a time. She never looked up when he reached over and lifted the latch of the little picket fence and walked in. The ground was still wet from the morning dew. His feet moving across the soft, spongy grass left the imprint of his shoes.

For a time he stood there behind her, watching her edge and weed, her small trowel turning the barely unfrozen earth. Her back sloped forward and down to the ground, she gave the appearance of someone kneeling and praying there. When he cleared his throat, she turned and gasped, making a funny little hissing sound like air escaping from a tire.

She looked up to see a slight, dark young man with a smiling, agreeable face. There was nothing particularly remarkable in his looks. The expression was thoughtful, and possibly a bit amused. The impression it gave was that of a slightly crooked smile, rather vague and fixed, as if its owner was accustomed to using his lips to hide some defect of his teeth.

"Beg pardon. You s'pose I could use your phone? My car's broke down."

He could see from the way she looked at him that she was looking for reasons to say no.

"Where's your car?" she asked, affecting sternness.

"Out front there. The green one."

She looked out at the car for a while. Above the white picket fence she could see only a shiny bright green roof and just the top of the hood with a Mercedes emblem on it.

She pondered awhile. "I tell you, my husband and I — we make it a practice never to let strangers in."

He laughed quietly. "Things being what they are nowadays, I can't say I blame you."

She kept looking at him, up and down, but never directly in the eye. She was probably forty or so, a pleasant-looking lady who took good care of herself. She probably had children, all grown up and out of the house.

"All I want to do is call a garage," he explained sympathetically. "They'll just come out and tow me in. I'd just be a minute."

There was something boyish and awkward and terribly appealing in the way he presented it. Even as she was saying okay, he could see she was regretting it. She laid her trowel down and stood up. "Okay — follow me. I'll show you where it is."

It was cool and shady inside, the blinds all down and drawn against the sun, and the place smelled of morning coffee and bacon and cigarettes. Someone smoked a great deal in that house. He hated the smell of cigarettes. By that time he had slipped a pair of white rubber surgical gloves neatly over his hands.

In the few moments it took to get from the front door to the kitchen, he'd already staked out the place. He'd seen the Sony Trinitron in the den, the Panasonic PV 5850 video deck on top of it, the KLH speakers high up on the wall, and on a desk in the den stacked with folders and ledgers, an IBM-XT computer with 20MB hard drive, a compatible drive, plus the keyboard. He knew the model well and admired it.

"Phone's right here," she said, turning, and saw the knife pointing at her chest. It was one of those Sicilian fisherman's jobs, used to gut fish and hack bait. It had a bone handle and a six-inch tempered-steel blade with serrations. When she looked at him there was an amused expression on her face, as if she thought he was having a little joke.

"Now, hey — " Her palms rose before her in a funny defensive gesture.

"Just don't say nothing. Just turn around and walk downstairs to the cellar. You won't get hurt."

Her eyes moved helplessly all around the room as though she were listening for something. "Hey, listen . . . my husband . . ."

"I know," he smiled pityingly at her. "He's due home any minute. Right?"

He tucked the knife point up under her breastbone. "Go on," he coaxed. "I won't hurt you. I promise."

*   *   *

He tied her with some laundry line she had down there and dragged her across the floor. There was a washing machine and a dryer off in a corner with a few baskets of fresh laundry waiting to be ironed. He grabbed a stocking off the top of one and stuffed it into her mouth; all the while she made this growling, gagging sound. She didn't struggle at all. Then, with a sudden lurch, he dumped the rest of the basket of laundry on top of her face, because he didn't want to look into her eyes. Her legs and lower torso stuck out from beneath the scattered laundry. Her dress was hiked up above her thighs.

He was quite heated up by then and knew that if he was going to do anything, he'd better do it fast or it would happen by itself of its own accord. That happened to him when he got excited. He'd just sort of lose control. This time it didn't happen and he got to her fast. She never moved once. Not a muscle. Nor did she even make a sound. But all the time it was going on, he could feel her coiled tight as a spring, something inside her cold and trembling, like vibrations.

When he'd finished, she just lay there, her legs splayed wide, never moving. He pulled all the laundry off her face, the sheets and pillowcases, a pair of ludicrous men's pajamas with palm trees waving all about them. Underneath it all she was still there, eyes opened wide, part of the stocking spilling from her mouth with a clot of drool on it and blood at the corners where she'd bitten her tongue trying not to scream.

When he took the knife out again, she fairly well knew what was up. Her eyes followed the knife, up and down, left and right, as though mesmerized by its dreamy motion. He bent over and put the point up against her throat, her eyes watching him all the time. She never once struggled or tried to stop him. For a moment he thought he saw something like pleading flicker in her eyes.

She looked so silly there, disgusting, with her pants

yanked down around her ankles, and the bloody stocking dangling like a tongue outside her mouth. And those big, flat, dumb eyes pleading.

He punched the blade in hard and gave a sharp half-twist. She made a gagging sound like someone clearing her throat and started to squirm. He gave the blade a second twist and yanked sharp right. This time he must have severed an artery. A stream of blood squirted up about three inches under his hand and suddenly her throat opened and something white yawned from beneath it like a flower blooming. It was rather beautiful, he thought.

When he finished he stood up, feeling a rush of dizziness, as though all the blood had emptied from his head. For a moment he thought he was going to black out. It was over in a minute and then he felt fine. Nearby was a shelf above a wash sink with a lot of paint cans and rags and brushes. He found a spray can of Red Devil, and on the wall right above her head he sprayed a large phallus and wrote beneath it the words *I am the Monster of Chaos*. Directly following that he scrawled the numbers, 2, 6, 14, 38, 52, 79. When he'd finished, he rinsed the blood from his gloved hands in the sink and went upstairs.

FIVE

"CAUSE OF DEATH, ACUTE HEMORRHAGIC pancreatitis . . ."

"Cause of death, hypoglycaemic coma due to Islet-cell adenoma . . ."

". . . Girl, seventeen. Self-abortion by syringing. Vaginal exudations contain bacillus coli and staphylococcus. Post-mortem examination demonstrated peritonitis and septicemia due to perforation of the uterus. Cause of death . . ."

Konig flicked irritably through the stack of recent protocols on his desk, his eye ranging from top to bottom, correcting here and there in red crayon the execrable grammar of his deputies, then moved quickly on as if he were seeking something in particular.

From time to time a detail or a phrase or a combination of words would leap out at him from the page, slowing the fevered race of his eyes: ". . . track of bullet traveled right to left . . . downward inclination of roughly 5 degrees. Base of skull shattered. Gas present between dura mater and skull. Carotid arteries, Circle of Willis, and dural sinuses destroyed. Hind portions of brain detached from pons. No exit wound. No sign of natural disease. Cause of death . . ."

"Specify point of bullet entry," he scrawled in large red crayon letters along the margins. "Any bleeding at nostrils or ears?" He initialed his note, flinging the report aside to be returned to the pathologist who'd prepared it.

His fingers raked hectically through his sparse hair until at last his eye lighted on the words he'd been seeking. "Unidentified female. Caucasian. Age 23–27. Cause of death, strangulation. Left great horn of thyroid cartilage broken. Cricoid cartilage shattered. Central anterior post displaced backward for a distance of about 0.1 inch. Considerable force exerted on front of neck by a broad, ridged, and firm object. A shod foot, probably a boot from evidence of heel marks about the face. Evidence of deep incisor marks in area of . . ."

Even as he read, his lips moving rapidly over the words, he reached behind his desk and buzzed his secretary on the intercom. Instantly the buzz was returned. Without taking his eyes from the report before him, he lifted the phone. "Jonesy — would you ask Dr. Winger to come in here?"

He banged the phone down and drummed the table with his fingers. It was a matter of minutes until she came, but in that time he'd reread the report and virtually committed it to memory.

When the door opened he didn't bother looking up, but continued to glance up and down the protocol as though it were the first time he was reading it. "About this one, the cricoid, hyoid rupture . . ."

"Which one is that?"

"You oughta know. You did the P.M."

"I've signed out on about twenty in the last two days."

"It's the nameless lady." Konig tried to contain his impatience. "The dark lady of the sonnets."

"Oh, her. The pretty one."

"If you like the type." Konig looked up, his eyes settling on the young woman standing there before him. He didn't know why he resented her and would have exploded at anyone who'd had the temerity to tell him it was simply the fact that she was a woman. Small, pert, somewhat boyish features, she looked to him as though she were scarcely out of high school. With her fair Nordic coloring and clean, regular features, she would have been attractive had she cared enough to do anything about it. But clearly she didn't, and there was about her manner something intractable and sullen, as if in her mind she'd concluded there was very little she might expect from this man (possibly any man) but the worst.

"You say here, 'death by strangulation,' " Konig pursued the point.

"That's right. What about it?"

"Well, for one thing, it's different from these other Dancer jobs. Those were mostly throat slashings."

The young woman made a pained face. "With a few strangulations tossed in for good measure. If you'd seen the thyroid and cricoid cartilages . . ."

"You said displaced, didn't you?"

"Backward. About one tenth of an inch. It's in the protocol."

"I know. I saw it."

"Then why did you ask?"

Konig frowned, disregarding the impertinence. "Any sexual stuff?"

"There was some bruising on the external genitalia. Probably digital."

"Did you do swabs?"

"Vaginal and rectal. No semen."

"Ah." Konig sat back, clasping his hands above his ample paunch.

The young woman was silent, observing him for a time. "What's that supposed to mean?"

Konig reflected a moment. "Odd, isn't it? What does it mean to you?"

"Incomplete coitus. Impotence. Could mean any of a half-dozen things. Maybe there just wasn't any time for it. How am I supposed to know?"

Konig removed his glasses and rubbed his eyes. "Have you thought any more about pediatrics?" he asked her.

"Are we going to start that again?"

"Or GYN. What's wrong with GYN?"

"Are you trying to say I'm a lousy pathologist?"

"You're okay."

"Then this must have something to do with the fact that I'm a woman." She said it to him just as though she'd said it to him a thousand times and always in precisely the same manner.

"You're never going to get anyplace here."

"I could bring you up on charges for even suggesting that."

"I'd deny I'd ever said it."

"Anyone who'd ever worked with you would know damned well you said it. It fits you like a glove."

"Pediatrics is where you belong."

"Spend the rest of my life pushing rubella vaccine and baby aspirin? Christ. *You* go into pediatrics. Look, I'm busy. Is there anything wrong with that report?"

"Not at all," Konig said, his voice hoarse and weary. His eyes studied the vivid pattern of blood spattered up and down her white surgical smock. "I'm only saying it would be more appropriate for a lady than spending her life in this goddamned abattoir."

"First of all, Doctor, don't say *lady*. Say *woman*. And second of all, I like abattoirs. I'm at home in abattoirs. I find them exhilarating. I'm not a gynecologist. I'm not a pediatrician. Frankly, I loathe little folk."

"You must be abnormal. What woman doesn't love kids?"

"This woman." Her voice was close to a shout. "So kindly have the decency to permit me to be my own abnormal self. At least, in this line of medicine I can't hurt anyone."

Konig sighed and raised his hands like a man defeated. "I hate to see a good baby doctor go to waste."

The remark, for all of its typical condescension, astonished her. All she could manage by way of response was to stare at him and shake her head despairingly.

He watched impassively the small, wiry frame as it marched toward the door. She moved stiffly erect, struggling to keep her shoulders back. "Oh, Winger," he called somewhat tauntingly, "one other thing. On that new Torrelson job out in Douglaston. What about those bite marks?"

"It's all in the protocol, Doctor. We've seen those same bite marks before."

Konig's face was full of the kind of strained forbearance he would never have sat still for at the hands of a male subaltern. "I'm aware we've seen bite marks before," his voice croaked wearily. "What I'm asking is, did you take an impression of these?"

"No, I didn't."

"You didn't?" There was an edge to his voice that gave her pause.

"There didn't appear to be any reason. I — "

Konig lowered his head into his palms and slowly rubbed his eyes. "It was an incisor, wasn't it?"

"The left lateral."

"Notice anything unusual in those bite marks around the breast?" He continued to rub his eyes but looked up when it appeared no answer was forthcoming. "Something different from the other bites we've seen?" The first thing he saw was her staring down at him, a startled, wary look in her eye, as if he'd reminded her of something she, too, had noted but had been lax enough to forget.

"Now that you mention it, there was. The skin around the bite marks was . . ."

"Jagged? Shredded?"

"For Chrissake, you don't have to lead me by the hand." Her voice dropped with contrition. "It was shredded, as if . . ."

"The incisor that made the marks was . . ."

"Broken, okay?" she snapped crossly. "Will you please let me come to my own conclusions?"

"Well, good God then, stop dancing around it. Come to the point instead of standing there, hemming and hawing. Right. Those incisor impressions around the aureoles were abraded and broken. Very astute observation, Doctor." He beamed at her with an air of triumphant spite. "Now will you kindly go get an impression made? And I'll lay you odds that when you get the prints back from Odontology, you'll find that at least a third of that left incisor is gone."

Rumpled and depleted in her bloodied smock, the young woman stared back at him dismally, then turned abruptly and left.

SIX

(1) Hank of laundry rope, 7 feet, 6 inches.
(2) Can of Red Devil spray paint. Alizarin Crimson.
(3) No prints. Assailant probably wore gloves.
(4) Bloodstains.

Mooney scribbled hastily into his note pad, then glanced down at the long jagged line of spattered blood not far from his feet. Surrounding it nearly completely was a police artist's chalk drawing scrawled on the concrete basement floor. It showed a rudimentary outline of where a body had lain three days before. The chalk outline had the crude look of a petrograph drawing found on a cave wall. It was situated a foot or two from a washer-dryer arrangement where the assault had taken place. The bloodstains, absorbed now into the whitish concrete, had bleached out to a pale orange. Unlike the vivid shapeless splashes characteristic of typical assaults with knives, these were composed of a series of jagged peaks and troughs.

This was arterial bleeding from a thin slash made by a long razorlike blade that had not only severed the carotid artery but nearly severed the head as well.

Whoever wielded that blade, Mooney thought, did it with impressive skill. No newcomer to the art. And that red, unbroken, sawtooth signature of blood suggested that all the while the victim was bleeding to death on the basement floor, her assailant had subjected her dying body to some final horrific outrage.

". . . Broken central and left lateral incisors," Konig had bawled at him over the phone earlier that morning so that he had to hold the receiver away from his ear. "Look for some creep with broken teeth. Central and left lateral incisors."

"What else?"

"What else?" There was a stunned pause. "Isn't that enough? What the hell you want me to do? Come down there and draw you a picture?"

Mooney ignored the tirade. "Those footprints all over her face . . ."

"What about them?"

"There were bootprints all over the face and chest. Like he used her face for a doormat."

Mooney listened to the agitated breathing on the other end, attributing the momentary pause to a cigar being lit. "We've got bootprints with the girl up in the park too." The reply came at last without much enthusiasm. "Could be the same guy."

"Any identification on her yet?"

"We've X-rayed the skull and we're running fingerprints and dentition through the computer."

"So far no one's come in lookin' for anyone sounds like her," Mooney said. Konig muttered something incomprehensible, his thoughts already moving elsewhere. "I've got to go now."

"Listen — I need — "

"Not now," Konig bawled. "I'm busy."

"These broken teeth. I could use — "

"In a day or two. I'll call you when I've got something." The phone banged down, leaving in its wake the dying thunder of the M.E.'s voice ringing in his ear. "Fuck off, old gas bag," Mooney muttered and smashed the phone down.

He looked up, startled to see Pickering standing there watching him with an odd expression. He wondered if the younger man had caught him muttering to himself. "Well?"

"Nothing, Frank. Not a trace of it."

"You look out back?"

"Out back. Out front. In between. Even across the street. There's an empty lot there. Lotta rubble and junk, but no knife, no razor. Nothing you'd imagine could cut a head off."

Mooney stared down at the little pad he'd been scribbling notes in. "Swell. What about the neighbors?"

"Lady next door thinks she saw a car parked out front that morning around eleven A.M."

The pencil ceased. "What kind of car?"

"Green, she thinks."

"Green, she thinks." Mooney shook his head despairingly.

"Saw it from the front window. Doesn't know the make. Wasn't close enough to catch a plate number."

"She didn't happen to see the guy?"

"Nope."

"Course not," Mooney muttered. "Why would she?" He enjoyed magnifying the hopelessness of everything. "I'll talk to her."

"I wouldn't advise it, Frank. Least, not now. She's blubbering too much."

"Good. I'll give her more to blubber about."

She was a diminutive, dried-out little creature of sixty or so, with a pinched, anxious face and an overbite. She had a way of looking almost chronically fretful. Eyes red, a handkerchief wadded into one fist, she sat slumped at her kitchen table, fidgeting with a salt cellar. Mooney sat across from her before a cup of untouched coffee she'd poured him while Pickering hovered about somewhere over his shoulder in the shadows behind them. Rolling the salt cellar back and forth in her hand, she gave the impression of a squirrel rolling nuts in its tiny, prehensile claws.

"Please. Please don't ask me any more about it. I can't bear to . . ." She crammed the crumpled handkerchief against her mouth and made a wet, whimpering sound.

"I appreciate that, Mrs. . . ."

"Wisdo," she whimpered.

"Mrs. Wisdo. But if you could just think back. Try to remember."

She shook her head at the shadowy outline of Pickering in the corner. "I've already told the other gentleman."

"I realize you don't know the make of the car or any of the numbers on the plates. You say it was green?"

"That's right. Green."

"Light or dark?"

"Light."

Mooney started to write in his pad.

"No, wait." She stopped him. "Maybe not exactly light."

"Dark, then?"

"No, not dark."

Mooney felt a flush of heat rise from beneath his collar. Only ten A.M. on a crisp spring morning and already his shirt was damp. He tried to engage her again, but his mind was not entirely there. It was about sixteen miles south and east of there, out at Belmont in the paddocks where he knew Fritzi to be.

"Any special detail about the car you might recall?" Mooney persisted with stiff civility. "Like, was it a two-door or a four-door? Maybe it was a convertible."

"A convertible?" Mrs. Wisdo looked at him as though he'd asked her to state some arcane formula in quantum mechanics. "No . . . I don't . . . I don't think so."

"Did it look new or old, this car? Was it banged up or in good condition?"

"I don't know," she wailed. "I don't know what it was.
I told the other man — "

"Yes, I know what you told him."

She broke off wailing, something sparking in her eye.
"But it did look shiny and bright."

"It did?"

"Yes. It did."

Pen poised, Mooney regarded her with cautious hope.
"You're sure?"

Her nods momentarily ceased their frantic motion.
The salt cellar dangled in midair. "Yes, I'm sure. It was
bright and sunny that morning. I have a distinct impression of sunlight flashing off all of this chrome. There was
a great deal of bright shiny chrome."

Mooney's ears cocked. "Where? The bumper? The
fenders? The grille? Where?"

"The grille." Finally involved, Mrs. Wisdo had forgotten to whimper. "That's right. It was the grille. I'm sure
now. It was a big grille."

"Big, what way?" Pickering drifted out of the shadows.
"Big horizontal? Or big vertical?"

Baffled, she looked at Mooney.

"What he means is, was it wide this way or tall that
way?" Mooney indicated with his hands what he meant.

"Oh, right. I see." She glowed. "Was it wide or tall?"
She gnawed her thumbnail while she pondered that.
"Well, it was tall. This way. Vertical." She demonstrated
with her hands. "It was a tall, very shiny grille."

"Good." Mooney scribbled the words into his pad. "A
green car. Not necessarily dark or light green. Medium."

"Right." Her head nodded eagerly. "Medium."

"With a shiny, vertical grille."

"Right."

"What about an emblem on top of the grille? A stat-
uette? Maybe a circle or a square or an animal or something?"

It had all been a bit too much for Mrs. Wisdo. She

suddenly remembered to grieve again. Another wail
went up. "I don't know. Please . . . I don't know. Poor
Marie. Poor, dear Marie. Oh, how she loved her garden."

Mooney rose, frowning his displeasure. "Okay. That's
fine, Mrs. Wisdo. You've been very helpful. We'll be in
touch if we need anything more." He shoved the pad
back into his inside pocket, and, snapping the crumpled
fedora back on his head, he started out. Pickering fell
into lock-step behind him. Even as the door closed behind them they could hear a resumption of the terrified,
baleful whimpering.

"Well, at least we know it was a late model," Pickering
said as they moved down the flagged walk.

"Oh, yeah? How do we know that?"

"She said it was shiny and bright."

"Lots of guys have old cars they keep shiny and bright.
And big vertical grilles they hardly make anymore. Not
since the forties, anyway. Too expensive to produce.
Maybe some foreign cars still had 'em as late as the
sixties and early seventies. And who knows if this light
green, dark green, medium car even belonged to the
guy. Most likely he just glommed it for this job."

They'd reached the foot of the walk where a patrol car
with Mooney's old Buick parked behind it waited.
"Check with the M.V.B. when you get back. See what's
been stolen lately that's green, vintage sixties or seventies." Mooney lumbered into the Buick and sank heavily
behind the wheel. Pickering leaned on the sill of the car
window and peered in. "I don't have too much faith in
this old dame, Frank."

"Who would? She's ditsy. Tells me the day was bright
and sunny. I already checked the weather bureau. They
say it was cloudy and overcast all day."

"So wherefore the bright, shiny grille, pray?"

"You tell me. But check it out anyway. Oh — and one
more thing. Pull every mug shot you can find on guys
with broken front teeth and a history of sex offenses."

A soft, piteous moan issued from somewhere deep within the younger man. "Who said anything about broken front teeth?"

"The M.E. saw something funny in those bite marks." Mooney flicked the ignition on and gunned the accelerator. "I'll speak to you tonight. You oughta have something by then."

Pickering made a pained, puzzled face. He sighed, contemplating the deadly hours of search that lay ahead of him in the photo morgue. "Where are you going? The ponies?"

Seeing the resentment in his eyes, Mooney winked. "That's our little secret, isn't it, Rollo?"

"He's got zero victories in twenty-two starts. That's zero. Zip. Zip."

"So, who's counting?"

"Five seconds and four thirds. Take my word for it. He's your quintessential sucker horse."

"That's what you say. I say today he's in the money."

"In your money, pal. Not mine. You know where this horse went last time out?"

"Six lengths out behind the winner. I read the same forms you do, Mooney. But that was a mile-and-a-quarter handicap. Today he's going three quarters of a mile. That's his strong suit."

"His strong suit is sucking dust." Mooney pronounced the phrase with pursed lips and maximum contempt. "I wouldn't touch him with a barge pole."

"Your loss. Don't say I didn't warn you."

Mooney made a clucking sound with his tongue, then hoisted the binoculars to his eyes. He was not a long odds player. Never much on hunches or touts, he scorned them like the plague, preferring instead to study speed figures and focus his attention on the horse with superior numbers who could win the day's race.

Like any first-class handicapper, he could win about four bets out of ten . . . that is, if he was conservative,

bet relatively few races, and favored mostly horses whose
odds averaged about 2 to 1, or who ran with a comfortable margin of overlay. Never much on book reading, he
pored over result charts and past-performance records
with rapacious energy. He supplemented those with periodic tabulations summarizing the success or failure of
jockeys, trainers, and owners. He kept abreast of breed-
ing transactions, livestock sales, and equine injuries. For
a man who could scarcely recall his own phone number,
his memory retrieval system for this sort of information
was nigh unto superhuman.

With Fritzi, on the other hand, it was all mysticism.
She had to hear voices or see something in the animal's
eyes before she'd commit money; if the signs were right
she was perfectly capable of committing big.

Coming Sunday, the horse Fritzi had just bet forty
dollars to win and forty dollars to place, was running at
odds of 38 to 1. What Mooney saw through the glasses
when he looked was a quiet, almost solemn three-year-
old. Except for the tail switching easily behind him, he
stood motionless in the gate. Possibly he was even a little
somnolent. Despite his wretched numbers, in all fair-
ness the horse did have a nice look about him that somehow belied the record of distinguished mediocrity he'd
managed to amass for himself over the past fifteen
months. The aloof imperturbability of the animal suggested an intelligence and self-possession not demonstrated by the majority of other horses lined up at the
post. Mostly they were champing and bucking about in
the gates, tossing their heads, nervous and dissipating
energy before the race. Also, Coming Sunday had an
inside position, and an inside post position represented
advantage. This horse was also known to be a strong mud
runner, another bias in his favor. But today he was
running on a pasteboard track with blinkers and front
bandages, generally a sign of tendon problems, all of
which made Mooney nervous.

He swung his glasses three or four positions down to

the left where Casual Air, his own personal selection, surged and bucked in the confinement of the gate. His tail was up. His ears were forward as if he were trying to hear something. His head lashed from side to side and his neck was straining. Although the day was cool, in the low fifties, through his glasses Mooney could see splotches of kidney sweat between the flanks and along the loins and withers. Not all that casual was Casual Air. But for all of the kicking up, the overall impression was not negative enough to make Mooney discount the solid clout of the horse's charts. This was an all-out contender with plenty of energy, and raring to go.

Casual Air's credentials were impeccable. He'd won five out of his last seven starts and his speed figures were notably impressive. His worst out for the season was a figure of 81, which still looked good enough to beat anything on this field. Even a mere duplicate of his worst performance would demolish anything in sight.

Mooney had few doubts about the horse's current condition. Except for that sweating, which could have just been the result of an overly enthusiastic workout, the animal looked superb. His trainer, A. T. Stoddard, was an old pro out of the Lexington school. The horse had raced and won only twelve days ago. Since that effort, he'd rested nicely but had also worked five furlongs in a blazing :59⅘. Better even, he was being ridden by a jockey who'd won on him before.

Mooney put his glasses down with a sigh of contentment. He was easy in his mind. The fifty dollars to win and fifty dollars to place he'd staked on Casual Air at modest but by no means inconsequential odds of 5 to 1 he'd already counted as money in the bank. To him that worked out to a 17 percent chance of winning — far better than Fritzi's 38 to 1, which gave her little better than a 2½ percent shot at the money. A sucker's bet, but you couldn't tell her that. Besides, she won quite often.

"You might as well scrub this one, Fritz." He handed her the glasses back. "It's a washout."

"For you, my friend." She snatched the binoculars and snapped them to her eyes just as the bell rang and the gates shot open.

There was an explosion of dust as the field of twelve pounded out of the gate. A great roar went up for the first race of the day. Pennants flapped wildly atop the grandstand and clubhouse. The scene below was a dazzling palette of track colors all flowing together in a blurry collage.

By the time the dust had cleared, the field had already pounded past the three-sixteenths pole where Mooney and Fritzi stood at the rail, cheering. Coming Sunday and Casual Air were neck and neck, leading the pack by a full length. They were still neck and neck at the far turn and swinging into the back stretch. At the three-quarter pole, it looked as if both of them would finish in the money.

"Go on, you Casual Air," Mooney bellowed until he was hoarse.

"Come on, Sunday." Fritzi jumped up and down. "Come on, you sweet boy."

"Move it. Move it, Casual Air. You son of a bitch."

Past the clubhouse turn and pounding into the home stretch, both horses, for some inexplicable reason, quit. They simply faded as if they'd lost interest or just run out of gas. A pair of disreputable hayburners, Vagrant and Tollkeeper, flew past them along with another horse. Coming Sunday and Casual Air finished fourth and fifth respectively. Both out of the money.

Mooney and Fritzi went home bumper to bumper on the expressway, both glowering in embattled silence all the way back to Manhattan. The quality of their luck in the first race was indicative of how they fared throughout the rest of the day. They'd lost about a thousand dollars between them, added to which Wizard, their own entry in the fourth race, had hardly covered himself with glory. By the time they reached 83rd Street, neither of them was feeling very kindly disposed toward the world.

Upstairs, there was a message from Mulvaney on their answering machine. "Where the hell have you been?" the chief of detectives snarled when Mooney finally reached him on the phone. "I've had the goddamned M.E. on the phone to me six times this afternoon looking for you."

"It's a sorry thing when a man can't even go to his dentist without —"

"Don't give me that dentist crap, Mooney. You better come up with something better than that. This time he's out for blood, and personally —"

"You hope he gets it, right? What's that old bag of gas blowing off about now?"

"That girl you pulled out of the drain last month?"

"What about her?"

"They've got an ID on her."

"How'd they get it?"

"Someone called the Sixth Precinct this morning. Gave her name and address. Wouldn't leave his own name."

"Would you?" Mooney quipped sarcastically.

"What?"

"Nothing. Just thinking out loud. Probably the same joker who tipped the Forty-fourth and told 'em to go fish her out of the drain in the first place."

"Name's Cara Bailey. Four twenty East Seventy-third. It's a brownstone. She had a second-floor walkthrough. Landlord said she's been missing three weeks."

"Why the hell didn't he notify anyone?"

"Says he figured she was on vacation. We went up there and pulled a set of prints. We matched them downtown with what the M.E.'s got. It's her, all right."

"So what the hell are you so browned off about?"

"What the hell am I browned off about?" Mooney could hear the words gagging in the chief of detectives' throat. "I've had a half-dozen guys up on Seventy-third Street all day, doing your goddamned job, while you're off at the flats."

"So I slipped out for a couple of hours. Big deal."

"Big deal is right. It should've been you up there on Seventy-third Street pulling prints. There's a family up in Great Barrington has to be notified."

Mooney groaned. "Oh, Christ, Mulvaney. Don't give me that job. If you've a shred of decency, I beg you."

"You notify those people tonight, Frank. Get 'em down here first thing in the morning to make an identification. Then get on to the girl's boss."

"Her boss?"

"She worked for some kind of literary agency up on Fifty-seventh Street. Crane, Poole Associates. You get your ass up there tomorrow and—"

By that time Mooney was steaming. "Listen, I'm just sitting down to dinner."

"How swell for you. I'm not. I'm three hours away from dinner. Buried under a mound of turd here. Anything yet on those number scribblings?"

Mooney sighed, resigned to what he knew must follow. "The math professor up at Columbia tells me they looked to him like a fixed series."

"A fixed what?"

"He says they're things called fibonacci numbers, tribonacci numbers . . ."

"Oh, Christ."

"Yeah, I know. He's got a lot of fancy names for it. Integer sequences. Combinatorics. Numbers theory. Solid state physics. It all boils down to the fact that there are repetitions of certain sequences all throughout nature, and these sequences sometimes tie things together which you wouldn't normally think tie together. Get it?"

"No," Mulvaney snapped. "I'm not too big on nature. What the hell does that tell me specifically about these numbers we keep finding?"

Mooney swallowed hard. "Nothing. But you know that string of numbers we found down in the drain on that Bailey job last month, fourteen, twenty-three, twenty-eight, thirty-four, forty-two?"

"What about 'em?"

"Mussacchio over at the Nineteenth swears they're also the local stops on the West Side IRT."

"Terrific. Now we can start patrolling the whole goddamned subway."

"I'm also talking to a linguist guy up at Natural History," Mooney went on with failing courage. "He's sure the numbers have something to do with the alphabet."

"Alphabet?" Mulvaney's voice made a sharp squeal as if he'd been struck.

"The idea being that in standard cryptography you can assign a numerical value for every letter in the alphabet, A being one; B, two; C, three; and so forth."

"Brilliant. And how does that jibe with the numbers we've got?"

"It doesn't. At least not for the Roman alphabet. Now he's checking the Hebrew, the Arabic, the Greek, the Pythagorean, the Phoenician, the Syriac . . ."

"And what's all this supposed to tell us?"

"Who knows? Maybe that our guy is a Syrian math whiz. How the hell should I know?"

"Sounds like a pile of horseshit to me."

"Bingo."

"Anything new on that Torrelson job?"

There wasn't, but Mooney felt it might be prudent to make it appear there was. "Well, maybe."

"Maybe what?"

"The car. It looks like it's green."

"Green what?"

"Just that. That's all we know."

Mulvaney made a strangled sound. "You really outdid yourself, didn't you?"

"We squeezed a little more out of the old dame next door. We're trying to put a make on the car now."

"Take my advice, Frank. You try hard. Real hard. There's a lot of people watching you."

"I'll try not to disappoint them," Mooney remarked sourly and started to hang up.

"And one more thing." Mulvaney's voice took an ominous drop. "I've got something I want to talk to you about."

The sudden transition from rage to that of almost collegial intimacy made Mooney uneasy. "About what?"

"Not on the phone. In my office. Tomorrow."

A long, rather strained pause ensued. "Fine. I'll see you in the morning," Mooney snapped and hung up the phone. When he turned, Fritzi was there, staring hard at him.

"Looks like you lost your best friend."

"Worse, even. I lost three hundred bucks."

"I lost seven hundred," she beamed. "You don't see me down in the mouth."

"That's different. You're rich."

"If I am, sailor, so are you." She gave the flesh above his waist a pinch. "What're you eating tonight?"

"Crow."

"Don't have any. What about pot roast?"

"Pot roast," Sanchez intoned sepulchrally from his perch. "Pot roast."

SEVEN

"THIS IS IT."

Slumped in the backseat of the squad car, Mooney looked up from his *Daily News*.

"Four-thirty West Fifty-seventh."

"What's the name of the guy again?"

Pickering extracted the small sheet of crumpled paper from his pocket, smoothing it out on his knee. "Crane, Poole Associates. Room fourteen oh three. It's Crane we're looking for."

Mooney nodded.

"Mr. Avery Crane."

Grumbling to himself, Mooney lumbered up out of the squad car. "Wait here for us, Lopez," he called over his shoulder at the driver. "We'll be down in twenty minutes."

"And she just stopped coming in?"

"Not like that. Not all at once. She tried coming in for a short time after. She was pretty shaky, so we tried her on half days."

"And?"

"It went okay for a while. But it just got to be too much for her. For one thing, the work suffered. Messed up contracts. Didn't give messages. Didn't return phone calls. Stuff like that. She was distracted. Finally we suggested she take a vacation. With pay," Mr. Crane hastened to add. He was a natty, fastidious man. Manicured and barbered impeccably. A vision in gray sideburns and good British tailoring. About him was an air of expensive cologne and the sort of inflated self-importance that becomes quickly annoyed with any interruption of its normal routine.

They were standing in a stairwell on the thirtieth floor of 430 West 57th Street.

"This the only stairwell on the floor?" Mooney asked.

"That's right. That's the way they built them in nineteen twelve. Nowadays the fire code insists on a fire exit as well."

Mooney gave the doorknob several sharp twists. "And the door's always kept locked on the stairwell side like this?"

"If it wasn't, we'd have every creep on Fifty-seventh Street flitting around up here. As it is . . ." His voice trailed off and he glanced at the two policemen uneasily. "I guess I don't have to tell you people."

Mooney sensed in the small, dapper figure before him another solid citizen, eager to inform a member of the local constabulary how badly they were doing their job.

"That washroom she was going to at the time . . ." He doodled in his pad. "That's the only one on this floor?"

"Only women's room. There's a men's room too. There are just eight tenants on the floor. You can't get into them without a key."

"Then he must've come up on the elevator," Pickering said, "since those stairwell doors are always locked."

Crane nodded. "I'd say so. Must've been just getting off the elevator when she stepped out of the office on her way to the washroom."

"And that's when he grabbed her and pulled her in here?"

"That's essentially it. At least, that's the story she told the police afterward."

"He must've had to go all the way back down the steps, thirty flights to get out, since he couldn't get back into the hall through this door," Pickering added thoughtfully.

Mooney stared upward into the shadowy well soaring thirty more flights above them. "Nobody heard anything?"

"Only after. When he'd left. Then we heard her screaming and pounding on the door to get back into the hall."

"Probably kept her quiet with that knife."

"It was a big knife, she said."

Mooney nodded. "We have a description of it."

"It was awful," Crane said, and for the first time that morning, he appeared shaken. "Clothes torn. Pretty well banged up. Hysterical."

"Anyone else get a look at him besides her?" Mooney asked. "What about the elevator man?"

"We haven't had an elevator operator here for twenty years. These things are all automatic now."

"But you've got a dispatcher downstairs," Pickering said.

"We always have one or two on duty. But they don't notice who comes or goes."

"No strange, odd-looking characters?"

Crane's features formed a funny, pained expression. "Ever get a load of some of these messengers that promenade around the city nowadays?"

"I get your point," Mooney snapped, dismissing the line of questioning.

"She gave a fairly good description to the police, though," Crane added.

Mooney sighed and flicked several pages back in his pad. He started to read aloud. "Blond hair. Caucasian. Average height — five eight, five nine — weight approximately a hundred fifty pounds. Wore a full-length, dark-brown leather coat over jeans. A Basque shirt. Was extremely polite. *Apologetic* was Miss Bailey's word." Mooney snapped the pad shut. "I guess that's about it."

They started back slowly up the steps through the airless, dimly lit stairwell.

"She never did make an identification, did she?"

Crane took out a key and proceeded to unlock the hall door.

"The chief at Midtown South said she came down to a couple of lineups with guys pretty much fitting that general description and with known records for sex offenses. She couldn't recognize anyone. Just too jumpy by then, I guess."

They stepped back out onto the floor and strolled toward a door with Crane, Poole, Inc., and Member SAR, ILAA stenciled in black letters on a frosted glass window.

"Christ, wouldn't you be?" Crane fretted. "Young kid like that. Right out of school. Twenty-two years old. First job in New York. Assaulted in a goddamned stairwell at knife point. Then suddenly she starts seeing this guy in all kinds of places. Outside on the street when she goes out to lunch. Lurking in doorways near her apartment. Clearly following her around. Just waiting for a chance to grab her again. And each time she calls the police they don't do a damned thing."

Mooney sighed. He could see where this was leading. "It's a big city, Mr. Crane. Lot of funny people walking around off the leash, as you say. The police answered her calls three times. Never found anything."

"Well, if it takes them twenty minutes to get over here, of course — "

"They were there inside of five to six minutes each time."

"That isn't what she said."

"I've got the operations reports right here." Mooney spoke with gruff persistence. "The girl herself claimed she'd only get quick glimpses of the guy, then he'd be gone."

"All right," Crane conceded. "All right." His head drooped and he appeared momentarily contrite. "It's just a damned shame when people get into trouble in this city, real trouble, and go to the police. The police don't exactly break their necks to help."

"She could've just been imagining things," Pickering said reasonably. "She was in a pretty bad state of mind by then."

By that time Mr. Crane was grinding his teeth. "I hope you didn't say that to her parents when they came down to identify the body." He yanked open the door to his office. "Has anyone spoken to her family?"

"I did." Mooney's voice was barely a whisper. "Thanks very much for your help." Mooney thrust a hand toward him. Crane stared at the big red paw for a moment as if faintly repelled by it. At last he thrust out his hand begrudgingly.

Mooney shook the limp, bony hand. "Just one more thing, if you don't mind. Miss Bailey — she didn't happen to say anything about this fellow's teeth?"

Crane stared at him, bemused.

"Did she say they were stained or broken? Anything like that?"

He considered that a moment, then shrugged. "No. Nothing like that at all."

EIGHT

I still think of you. Don't be scared. Not in the bad old way, but in the way it was (or in the way I used to think it was) before all that . . . business. I regret it now. My memory of things is shot. Today, for a change, it's okay, and I see your face . . . actually see it. But only when I say your name. Will you believe there are days when I can't get your face into my head? Try as I may to dredge it up . . . use tricks like imagining you the way you looked at certain times, all I can manage is a kind of fuzzy outline, all runny and plugged with light, like a photo over-exposed.

My life is still pretty much the same. I drive around all day and sometimes all night. I eat in the car and sleep in it. I let it take me where it wants. Sometimes we go for hours, up and down the state. All the way to the border on up into Canada. We cruise around up there a bit, then turn back.

We play a game together, Mother and me, in which I try to guess where she's taking me while she tries to keep from me our destination. Sometimes she surprises me, but mostly in the end I figure her out. Sometimes we'll go for hours, stopping maybe just for gas, then start again. No food. No sleep. Happy as larks, we two. Not on pills like in the bad old days. Just on myself. Me and Mother. Mother sends her best. She turned 160,000 miles the other day, and still pretty as when I first saw her. Then it was you and me and her. The Holy Trinity, we used to say. I sometimes think, if things were different, if the past weren't what it was, we could . . . still . . . But no, I'm older now and I know better.

My routine is still . . . well, you know . . . pretty much the same. Like what it was when we were together. I look for places with a window open, or a door half-shut. Like where someone has just gone in, but not yet closed the door. Like maybe someone with packages they haven't yet put down. That's the easiest. I've gotten so I can tell when a window or a door is unlocked, even when it isn't open. I can even tell fifty or a hundred feet off, or whizzing by at sixty in a car on the speedway, if a window is unlatched.

It's gotten to be a kind of instinct with me. I can always tell if something's gonna be good. You look at a place and you can pretty much tell from the condition of things outside what you can expect once you get in. Like, how recent it's been painted, if the lawn's mowed, if the shades are up or down in the middle of the day, or if the mailbox is so jammed that all the mail and newspapers and stuff are scattered on the ground around it.

You'd be amazed what you can tell from the garden, from plants and things. Folks who've got a lot of bread to stick in the ground also have a lot of great stuff sitting around inside, just waiting for someone like me. Tires, VCRs, PCs, cameras, super audio stuff. Stuff like that you can just throw in the trunk of your car and turn over quick for cash, no questions asked.

I don't feel bad about things I've done. I feel good about them. Not everyone could've done those things. Not everyone has the guts for it. I'm no different from all the others. God made me just the way He made them. So He must've had some reason for putting me here. I do what I've been put here to do. Everything is preordained. The pattern is all in the numbers, and I'm as much a victim of that as all those who chance to cross my path.

So I don't apologize for a thing. I'm proud. It's the Lord's work I do. That's what Suki says and I believe her. The Lord chose me to do that work and I'm gonna damned well do it the best way I know how. When He thinks I've gone too far, He'll let me know.

The one thing that still bothers me, Janine, is that you're the only other person on this earth who really understands me. Knows my work and my *special* calling. You and me, Janine, we go back a long ways. I know that if I had trouble. Not just ordinary trouble, but big bad trouble, I know you'd be the only one in this world I could turn to. And even though we haven't spoken to each other in two years (next March 12th will be two years exactly), I know I can still trust you.

But sometimes late at night I can be lying in bed unable to sleep, and my mind running 150 miles an hour. You can't imagine the stuff that flies through your head nights like that. But sometimes, when I'm feeling a little down, and off my mark, the thought does cross my mind . . . what if Janine . . . what if some night with some guy, Janine. . . . Like, you know what I'm saying. Just the thought of it . . .

". . . gets me crazy. And if I ever believed that was the case, long as we've been friends and all that, I'd have to come and do something about it. . . ."

Her voice trailed off. She'd been reading it aloud. Not actually aloud, but with her lips forming each word under her breath, but hearing his voice pronounce them. The voice was inside her head, quiet and slow and slightly singsong, the way he had, with that oddly British inflection of his. She wondered where he got it from. Certainly not that scruffy crowd they ran with in the old days when she first knew him. More probably, it came from watching old British movies. The same ones, over and over again: *David Copperfield, Great Expectations, Pride and Prejudice, The Lavender Hill Mob, Brighton Rock*. He loved *Brighton Rock*, particularly the character of Pinkie. He was a great mimic and could recite by heart most of the major roles in those films. It had got so that he would speak that way without his even knowing he was doing it. There were times, she knew, he would stay up all night, watching those films on a VCR, one after the other. Watching them with some secret solitary

delight, seeing them each time all new and fresh as
though he were just watching them for the first time.

He was no more British than she, of course. That was
just some kind of make-believe in his head. He was a city
rat, like her, right out of one of those unclaimed litters.
They lived in the rubble of basements and condemned
buildings. They ran in packs and battened on refuse and
whatever they found that hadn't been nailed down. They
were a sort of nomadic tribe in those days, roving, predatory, homeless, orphaned, made up chiefly of those
who'd fled domestic situations out of a strong sense of
their own self-preservation. "Bug life," the police in the
station houses used to call them during the periodic
roundups and the appearances in juvenile court, with
the judges and lawyers and social workers and other
functionaries all going through the solemn charade of
administering a system virtually bankrupt of any solution
to their problems.

". . . friends and all that, I'd have to come and do
something about it."

She read the words again. This time more slowly, aware
of the slight breathlessness she felt, and of the cold numb
spot about the size of a quarter that had risen like a moon
on her forehead.

It was his handwriting, all right, a calligraphy such as
one seldom sees in the course of normal daily commerce.
Those small, crimped, penciled figures, looking as
though each had been wrought with a chisel. Each figure
precisely the same height, all slanted at precisely the
same angle, descenders and ascenders all matching perfectly, each with a tiny serif at the bottom and all unat-
tached, but yet close enough to read as a whole.
Marshaled one against the other, they gave the impression of tiny toy soldiers massed in perfect formation.

Holding the paper up to the light, she could see that
each character had been drilled into it under the exertion of a hard, fierce pressure, so that the back of the
paper could have been read like braille. A kind of

barely contained rage seemed to emanate from the tight little whorls and bumpy elevations — a rage that belied the soft, cajoling words indited on them. Looking at the page as a whole, it had the look of something curiously antique, a kind of cuneiform graven on an ancient scroll.

She became slowly aware of an odor rising off the sheet, a rather good piece of heavy, tea-tinted paper. He'd always had a taste for good things. Maybe that was his trouble. It was a faint smell, redolent of earth and roots and cellars — a smell buried deep within her memory. It conjured up in her mind dark, bad images, murky subterranean places where unpleasant things were wont to occur.

Over the past several years, she'd been able to put all of those memories out of her head. Not out entirely. Never that, of course. That, she knew, was impossible. But shunted off to the side, at least, in a way that permitted her to get on with some semblance of a normal life. She might go through days, weeks, even months, without once thinking about it, only to wake some night, sitting bolt upright in bed, bathed in a cold, clammy sweat and trembling all over.

He was right. They had not spoken in two years. But that didn't mean she hadn't seen him. She had. On all those strange occasions. How else could you describe them? Perhaps a half dozen times or so. All were meant to appear fortuitous, but in her mind, knowing him as she did, she was certain they'd been planned. Orchestrated right down to the last detail.

No more than glimpses really. Sudden manifestations in large open areas where he could appear and disappear so quickly, she might well think that what she'd seen was chimerical — a figment of the imagination, or possibly just someone bearing an uncanny resemblance to him. But, of course. Wasn't that the most plausible explanation? Hadn't she buried for so long those features once so omnipresent in her former life? What could be more natural than on occasion they would come boiling to the surface, as unexpected as they were unwanted in the most improbable places? On street corners or subway platforms, in the blue fluorescent glare of large department stores where they would vanish instantly in a throng of other faces.

But wasn't that just like him? Secretive and skulking about, playful in a way that carried with it just some faint, yet unmistakable hint of menace. Intended to amuse as much as to frighten. Letting her see him but not permitting her to approach — not that she would. Keeping her off balance. Showing how he meant her no harm. He wouldn't bother her; just so she knew that anytime he wanted, he could reach out and put his hand on her.

". . . I'd have to come and do something. . . ."

"Oh, shit," she whispered, aware that her mouth was dry and she could smell the staleness of her breath. "Not now. Please, not now."

She started to crumple the paper, intending to wad it in her fist and flush it down the bowl. But her fist wouldn't close. It was as if all the strength within it had failed. Instead, she carefully flattened out the crumpled letter, then folded it first in halves, then in quarters, finally cramming it into the pocket of her skirt.

She had to get back out onto the floor. Mr. Whitborn was waiting and Mr. Whitborn did not suffer tardiness gracefully. He was the sort of individual so full of the marvel of his own personal rectitude, he couldn't bear not to share its wonderful example with others.

She started out from the lounge where she'd gone at once to read the letter. She'd found it that afternoon, sitting on her desk, so tidy and welcoming and seemingly innocuous. Emerging from the lounge at a near run, she almost collided with someone just entering and was suddenly aware that was she nauseous.

*   *   *

SIXTEENTH HOMICIDE IN NEW YORK AREA PERPLEXES POLICE
Believe They Now See Signs of Pattern Emerging

With the brutal slaying of Mrs. Marie Torrelson in the basement of her Douglaston, Queens, home last week, police say they now see a pattern emerging in the string of sixteen homicides that have taken place here in the metropolitan area over the past twelve months.

Chief of Detectives Clare Mulvaney declined to comment on whether the police had any suspects in the string of murders that have bedeviled them since last March, all of which have been noted for their particularly ghoulish and brutal nature.

Responding to questions, Chief Mulvaney would only draw parallels between each incident in order to illustrate the thread of similarities common to all sixteen. He made a point of six such parallels to elucidate the pattern he saw emerging. These were as follows:

(1) With one exception, the crimes have all taken place in quiet residential areas, characterized by the police as "low crime areas." In eleven incidents the murders occurred in small detached or semi-detached one-family houses on quiet streets with easy access to major highways and thoroughfares, presumably to ensure quick escape.

(2) The crimes usually take place during the daylight hours, or in the early morning hours shortly before dawn.

(3) The victims have been mostly women ranging in age from 22 to 64. In one instance, a two-year-old child, the daughter of one of the victims, Mrs. Gail Wheatley, was brutally bludgeoned to death in the same room with the mother.

(4) In each case the motivation for the crimes appears to be robbery with sexual assault generally preceding it, although in several assaults nothing was taken.

(5) In each case the murderer had left behind, usually on the wall directly above the murder victim, messages and pictures in the form of ghoulish graffiti — sometimes a number or series of numbers scrawled in seemingly random fashion. The pictures are generally of a phallic nature, along with bizarre, somewhat self-mocking little captions. In the most recent incident involving Mrs. Torrelson, the message scrawled in vivid red from a can of spray paint read, "I am the Monster of Chaos."

"You read slow, Mooney."

"That's 'cause I'm absorbing every detail."

"Looks from here like you're dozing off. Come on, what d'ya think?"

"I think you said it all right here, Clare." Mooney tossed the newspaper back on the chief of detectives' desk. "I couldn't have stated it better myself." The note of sarcasm in the detective's voice did not escape Mulvaney.

"Why do I bother?" He rose and with fists plunged deep in his pockets, he strode around the smoky squad room in small, lunging little circles. He was a short, stocky man with a hood of close-cropped, tightly curled blond hair and a ruddy complexion that gave the impression of someone perilously close to apoplexy. "I call you in here in the wild hope you may have some small thing to contribute — " He went on flailing his arms at the stale, tired air. "After a year, one would think . . ."

"I think you're doing a great job on this, Clare. I really do. You make some really heavy points in the article."

The chief of detectives was in no mood to be patronized that morning. A spray of angry capillaries throbbed at the side of his nose. "Mooney, I take it that an old hand with as much time on the force as you — eighteen months to retirement, is it?"

"Seventeen, but who's counting?"

"Seventeen. Forgive me." Mulvaney affected contrition. "I take it by now that you grasp the fact that this is a very important case with regard to the reputation of this precinct. Aside from the basic media swine, some very important people are watching us. It's a rare day, indeed, when New York City detectives are given full jurisdiction to coordinate the investigation of a series of crimes taking place throughout the five boroughs and their immediate environs. I take it you grasp all this, Frank."

"I grasp it," Mooney replied with irritating serenity. "I do grasp it."

"I take it, too, that you're not unaware that the commissioner has developed an unnatural sensitivity on this subject. That the mayor, by applying a blowtorch to the commissioner's bottom, has tended to increase that sensitivity. And now, partly because it's his job, and partly because he's no fool and wishes to reduce the discomfort to himself, the commissioner is anxious to deflect that heat to others." Mulvaney's agitated fingers drummed an angry tattoo on the desktop. "Do you know whose bottom has borne the major brunt of the old man's fury these past few weeks?"

"Don't tell me. Let me guess." Mooney put his fingers to his temples and closed his eyes. "Is the individual nearby at this moment? Perhaps even seated right here in this room?"

Storm clouds appeared to lower over the chief of detectives' beetled brow. When he spoke, his voice sounded half-strangled in his swelling chest. "I'm warning you, Frank. Don't be funny with me here today. Not now. We're past the time for little funnies. I've committed sixty men to this thing now, with no end in sight. I've got guys staked out in every borough of this city, and on up into Nassau, Suffolk, and Westchester County. I've got 'em sitting in parked cars in little side streets in the Bronx and Queens. I got 'em out on the avenue dressed as junkies and panhandlers, as housewives all ritzed up in mules and pedal pushers. All just waiting for something to happen. I'm getting no results, see? Zero. Zip.

Goose eggs. I called this little meeting this morning to express my impatience with the general state of things. I am not sleeping well these nights. I do not enjoy my food. I'm suffering what is called generalized and systemic *acidità*."

Mulvaney's large, domed head lowered. His eyes, fixing Mooney, appeared to swell from their sockets. "Am I getting through to you, Frank?"

"You're making a big impression, Clare."

"Good." Mulvaney's face had turned an alarming purple. "Let me tell you why. No less a personage than the mayor himself was on the phone to me this morning." Mulvaney watched his old colleague to see what effect his words were having. Nothing but the most blissful innocence shone in Francis Mooney's eyes. Mulvaney resumed his quiet rant. "Not at nine A.M., mind you, our standard starting time in this office. But at six A.M. at my home as I was just stepping from my shower."

"Not very considerate," Mooney clucked sympathetically.

"The gist of his call was to express his dissatisfaction with the way this investigation is going. As you know, His Honor is not shy about expressing his dissatisfaction."

"On the contrary. Sort of enjoys it, has been my impression," Mooney observed sagely.

The finger drumming sputtered ominously to a halt. "I'm trying to give you some smart advice, Frank. Oddly enough, after twenty-five years of having you abuse my support and friendship, I still hold some small affection for you."

The older man's cragged, ruddy features cracked into an amiable grin. "You're a sucker for punishment, Clare."

"Not much longer, my friend." Mulvaney's voice had dropped to an ominous whisper. "The mayor asked me to consider . . ." He paused, staring hard at Mooney. "Merely consider, mind you, transferring command of this investigation from you to Sylvestri."

If Mulvaney had made little impression on his old friend up until then, the mere mention of the name Sylvestri appeared to have an instant seismic effect. Mooney blanched. "Sylvestri?"

"His very self."

"But why?"

"I'd thought I told you why. I've been trying to tell you for some time. The problem is, you haven't been listening."

Mooney's lips moved, attempting to form words. But in place of words came feckless little puffs of air. When at last he could speak, his voice sounded dry and gravelly as though pebbles rattled in his throat. "I don't believe this."

"Well, you'd better."

A long, troubled pause ensued.

In terms of seniority and rank, Edward Sylvestri stood just behind Mooney. Nearly fifteen years Mooney's junior, his advance on the force had been swift and meteoric, moving from patrolman to lieutenant of detectives in one of the city's crack precincts in record time. He was brash and aggressive. People both hated and feared him. He had few friends on the force, which is sufficient to kill the career of most men. But Sylvestri had a saving gift: he knew how to attract the attention of people in high places. He had even cultivated the commissioner and, so it was said, had his ear. He used that advantage to poison the air around whomever he perceived to be an adversary, chief of whom was Francis Mooney, his immediate superior.

Mooney knew him for a fair-to-middling cop who'd risen largely through self-promotion and by appropriating the hard work of underlings and subsuming it under his own personal credit columns.

"Sylvestri," Mooney murmured again, the taste of ashes in his mouth.

"The very same."

"That wimp. That twerp. That suckass." He spat the words out with slow, gathering momentum.

"Be careful, Frank."

"He's not taking over this investigation."

"Who says?"

"I'll go to the commissioner. I'll go to the mayor myself."

"I told you. The mayor's the one who suggested it."

"And you would sit still for this? Knowing what a fraud that dried-out little stool is?"

The chief of detectives attempted a glower, which crumpled quickly into despair. "There's very little I have to say about it. If the mayor wants it, the commissioner wants it. If the commissioner wants it, I want it, unless I'm looking to end my days in a blaze of glory at some drowsy little precinct house in Staten Island, escorting old ladies across the street." Mulvaney daubed his sweat-beaded forehead with a handkerchief. "The way of the world, my friend. The way of the world."

Mooney sat frozen in his seat, framing in his mind some withering reply. None came. Eloquence was not his strong suit. Instead he bolted to his feet and lumbered toward the door.

"I'm telling you this out of friendship," Mulvaney cried after him. "Because I think you should know it. Make of the information what you will. Get cracking, Frank. The little prick is breathing down your neck. As of now, your days on this case are numbered."

"Oh, yeah? What's the number?" Mooney jeered.

"That's for me to decide and for you to guess. When your time's up, I'll make sure you're the first to know."

The dusty, mote-filled air between them fairly sparked with rage. By that time Mulvaney had recovered something of his old, venomous charm. "Think of it this way, Frank. It's only about another year and a half to go for that pension. How do you want to leave? On wings of glory or on your knees?"

NINE

"OUT ON THE CATWALK IT'S PRETTY NARROW, and if it's windy up there, like today, it sways. Not a lot, but if you're off balance, or a little funny about heights . . . Janine, are you there? Hey, Janine?"

The young man whose name was Michael Mancuso frowned across the table at the girl. She gazed back at him with a look of puzzlement, as if possibly she didn't recognize him.

"Hey, Janine, am I interrupting anything?" The young man sat at the dinner table in a shirt of blue denim, open at the collar. He was thin and fair and radiated the sort of bouyant vitality that comes not merely from a soundness of the body but of the spirit as well. Though his manner was rough, there was a crude nobility to it.

"Are you still with me, or does my dinner conversation put you to sleep?"

"I'm here. I'm here."

"Good. I hate to interrupt anything."

"I'm here, I said."

He cast a long, skeptical look her way. "Then what did I say?"

"Oh, Jesus. Are we gonna have a quiz now?"

"No quiz. Just tell me what I was just talking about."

"Go to hell."

"See?" He gave a triumphant laugh.

"You were saying something about the job up on Seventy-third Street."

"Yeah. What about it?"

The girl grew flustered and angry. She tossed her napkin into her plate and started to rise.

"Hey, forget it," he said, waving her back to her seat.

"I don't have to be cross-examined."

"Who's cross-examining you?"

"Not by you. Not by anybody."

"Forget it," he said, his voice lower and his manner placative. "I was just kidding. Tell me what you did today."

"Nothing special," she snapped. "I did nothing special. And you were just saying something about how you were working high up on the site today. And how the wind was blowing and how there was nothing under you."

His face glowed and he held up his hands as if in defeat. "Okay, okay, I was wrong. So forget about it now. I'm sorry."

"Don't ever try that again, Mickey," she said.

"Try what?"

"Checking up on me like that. Cross-examining me. 'Cause if it's gonna be like that, we can just forget the whole thing."

He stared back at her a moment, still chewing a bit of meat, then finally swallowing it. He put his knife and fork back on his plate with a stiff, rather formal deliberation. When at last he spoke, his voice was almost a whisper. "Forget what?"

Instantly, she caught the wary edge, the sudden darkening of his brow, and saw the unmistakable signs of the squall line moving rapidly toward them.

"Forget what, Janine?"

"Nothing. Forget it, I said. Forget Christmas. Forget the whole thing."

He sat there, elbows on table, hands clasped before him, his tongue playing with a fragment of food lodged between his teeth. "Hey, listen — I'm confused. Could someone tell me, please, what we're fighting about?"

"Who's fighting? I'm not fighting. You're the one doing all the fighting."

He threw up his hands in despair. "I just thought you'd be interested in this experience I had sixty floors above the street. It was sort of spirituallike. I thought you'd be interested."

"I was listening. I told you what you said, didn't I?"

"Sure," he said, puzzled and looking hurt. "Sure you did." He rose and crossed around the table to where she sat, then knelt in front of her with his big laborer's hands placed lightly on the sides of her thighs. "Hey, listen, I'm sorry. You haven't touched your supper. Something's wrong."

"Nothing's wrong."

His hand rose to her cheek. She swatted it aside like a fly.

"You wanna cry?" He could see the tears damming up behind her eyes. "Cry. Go ahead and cry."

That was enough to unbind her. The dam broke. Deep, racking sobs shook the wispy, girlish frame.

He lifted her from the chair like some small, badly damaged thing and led her, docile as a child, across the room to the canvas couch, the only sitting area in the sparsely furnished room. She sat stiff and robotlike, permitting herself to be guided down onto the couch. When at last he'd settled her there, he sat beside her and took her into his big, comforting arms. "Is it me?" he asked. "Is it something I done?"

Still sobbing, her face crushed against his chest, she shook her head back and forth.

"Is it that you don't wanna get married anymore?" He probed gently. "Or maybe, you just wanna think it over a little more? Put it off awhile? That's no big deal. We can still cancel the hall."

Again the head shook no.

"Well, what is it, for Chrissake? Something's wrong. This isn't you."

She lay there sprawled against him, the clean, comforting smell of wood and plaster rising from his clothing and enveloping her.

"It's nothing you did," she said after a while, swiping at her eyes and trying to catch her breath. "Nothing you did."

He regarded her skeptically. "Something's wrong, Janine. Something's up. I can see that. You been jumping down my throat all week. It's like, whatever I say is wrong."

"It's not your fault, I said. It's . . ."

"It's what? What is it? You gotta tell me. If we're gonna be a team, we can't have any secrets. Now tell me, is it . . ." He paused, making an expression of profound distaste. "It's not some other guy, is it?"

She looked at him with the most desolate expression. "It's nothing like that."

His face brightened. Once again his manner was buoyant and cocky. "Well, then, what the hell is it?"

Her wet eyes strayed off, across the room and out the window. Her lips pursed hard, and a fierce, tiny throbbing pumped at her throat. "I can't, Mickey. I can't tell you."

He made a clicking sound with his tongue and started to rise.

"No, wait." She tugged at his sleeve, pulling him back down. "I want to tell you something. But it's . . . hard." Tears spilled down her cheek. "This all happened a long time ago. And when you hear it, I'm sure it'll all sound pretty strange to you." As she spoke, it had very much the sound of the start of a children's fairy tale. There'd be witches and ogres, good fairies and bad. "I've already told you a lot about how it was when I was growing up. I mean, it was no bed of roses. But at least I've been honest about it. I never tried to make it any prettier or no better than it was. But . . ." Her voice trailed off a moment. "There were some parts I left out."

She watched him as she spoke, noting on his features the shift of expression as the intent of her words registered. "Before, when you asked me if it was another guy . . ."

"Oh, jeez. Here it comes." He put up his hands before him as if to ward off a blow.

"Well, it was," she blurted, then hastened to add, "But not the way you think." She pushed the hair out of her eyes. "I'm going to tell you this now and I want you to remember that it was long ago, and I was very young. And stupid. I wanna tell it all to you. Everything. When I'm finished," she swallowed hard, "then you tell me if you still wanna do Christmas."

He started to protest, but she silenced him with two fingers pressed firmly to his lips. "Now just shut up and listen and try to understand."

TEN

CLAIRE PELL TURNED IN HER BED. IN THAT gray, shadowy place between sleep and waking she was vaguely aware of a noise. It seemed to her that it had started to rain and that it was the sharp, sudden impact of an incipient downpour pelting the skylight that had roused her.

It had been unnaturally warm, even for that time of year. An hour or so before, she'd been up to open the glass sliders that led off her bedroom and out onto the deck, so that now a soft, briny wind came soughing in off the gently lapping surf not far beyond, fluttering the sheets about her.

Beside her, her husband lay in profound slumber, his deep, rumbling snores conforming to the quiet rise and fall of the sea outside. Something — she couldn't be sure what — made her dimly aware of a presence. It may have been a movement or, possibly, even a slight upward variation in heat emanating from a source nearby. Not a presence exactly, for even in that drowsy, half-conscious state, her mind discounted such a possibility. What she felt was more a kind of shift of physical conditions within her immediate vicinity. It produced in her a quickening of the senses, akin to the pricking of an animal's ears in the presence of a predator.

She lay on her side, fully still, eyes shut, convinced she'd only imagined something close by. Beside her she could feel the long, withdrawing sighs of her husband, somehow far away. Along with that came the disquieting sense of feeling suddenly very much alone.

There was another movement, barely perceptible, but one in which the cool, uncarpeted floor made a soft, furtive sound, as if a sandal or a slippered foot had whispered across it. When her eyes opened, they didn't open at once. Slowly, the thick, wet gray of predawn crept across her eye and, through the moist cage of her lashes, she was at once aware of a gray shape partially blocking the light between her bed and the deck beyond.

It was the displacement of light, a darkness where she was unaccustomed to seeing one, that made her eyes open fully despite her strong disinclination to do so.

She was not alarmed when she saw the face. It was not remarkable in any way, and even the incongruity of its presence there at that moment did not immediately strike her.

It was a dark, rather Mediterranean face, framed in an aureole of dark, curly hair. The impression it gave was something akin to that of a youthful fisherman one might see on a wharf in Naples. It was only when he saw her staring up at him that he smiled. At that moment, something crooked, off kilter, and vaguely brutal drifted across his features. Still smiling, he stooped over and lay a finger gently on her lips in a silencing gesture. The touch of that finger made her bowel turn.

She lay there mute, unmoving, docile as a child, staring up at him. Eyes now fully open, she could feel the pressure of the finger on her lips slowly increase until at last it started to hurt; until that single finger bearing down hard had the effect of pinning her head to the pillow, while all the time he continued to smile down at her.

Mr. Pell still slept. The long, sighing exhalations of his breathing conveyed a message of profound peace. The figure spoke to her now. That is, the lips moved and formed words, but no sound came.

Lifting his finger from her lips, the person suddenly rose from his slight crouch above her. For a moment he stood there, smiling down at her. Then, still smiling, he turned, and, holding her transfixed with his eyes, he circled around the bed. She could still feel the imprint of his finger on her lips and the cold numbness there after he went. Where it had been, a puffy, bruised welt had appeared, along with a thin crescent of blood where his fingernail had pierced the flesh. She could still smell the finger, too, a strangely feral smell, like a dog wet from the rain.

She lay there on her side, still watching him out of the corner of her eye. With the absence of any variation in its expression, the smile had a fixed, unreal look, a smile painted on the face of a child's doll. His gait as he went had a light, jaunty bounce to it.

Hearing the slow, rattling snores of Mr. Pell behind her, she knew precisely where the stranger was headed. She might have easily cried out at that point, yet so great was her terror, nothing in the world could have compelled her to do so.

In a moment he'd passed beyond her field of vision, leaving in his place the view of a spider tracking sideways up the opposite wall. As it grew lighter, she kept watching the spider with an awful fixity, as though by sheer power of concentration she could nullify the existence of all else taking place about her.

The sudden sag of the mattress at her back coincided with a startled shudder, terminating in a quick, strangled yawp. There was the sense of some brief, feeble flutter behind her, followed by the squeal of compressed bedsprings being released. Then it was quiet.

All of that occurred while she kept her eye fixed on the spider, intent on its sideward peregrinations, first upward, then elaborately reversing itself in a half-turn and starting back down.

She knew that something had happened behind her and that something of a large order was about to happen to her. But she could neither move nor cry out, nor get her mind to bear for long on anything but the movements of the spider on the far wall.

Lying there, listening to the awful absence of any new sound behind her, her body grew rigid as a board while she waited in sickening anticipation for something to happen. Soundlessly as the figure had drifted out of her field of vision, just as soundlessly did it reenter there. It came, neither slow nor fast, but with that jaunty, rather bouncing gait. Like a shadow boxer, the figure appeared to float, swinging its arms loosely as though pummeling the air before it.

She felt him there above her before she actually saw him. It came to her in the form of a terrific heat, an animal heat, radiating out of the figure through its clothing. And then once more the smell — the wet dog smell. And he was there again smiling down at her, that curious, fixed smile in which the whole face smiled except the eyes, which were doing something quite different. And then, too, that crooked, off-kilter cast to the features, which she thought was due to crossed eyes.

He was holding a knife, the blade of which she could see was spattered a vivid red. He laid it down with the most exquisite tenderness beside her head on the pillow, so close that she could feel the heat of its hasp near her cheek. The slightly ferrous odor of blood rose from its blade. The next moment he was unbuckling his belt, smiling down on her that fixed, unsmiling smile. He never spoke once but, stooping slightly, inserted both hands with an odd fastidiousness into her mouth, prying the jaws open.

She didn't actually faint, although the effect of what she did do was comparable to that. She remained fully conscious throughout, but some natural inner safety mechanism, like a fuse cutting off an overload, mercifully withdrew her from the place. Out of the corner of her eye, she became aware of a dark, scything motion, then of an uncomfortable pressure of weight on her chest, and of noises at her ear, fierce guttural grunts, whisperings of half-spoken words — oaths, obscenities, and then numbers, long unbroken series of them, incantatory, like a chant. It seemed to her that she smelled rubber, too. The smell of rubber was inside her mouth, inside her head, but what was happening to her at that moment, mercifully, she had no idea.

Suddenly the oppressive weight on her chest was gone. The figure stood above her again, adjusting his clothing, all the while holding her in his smiling gaze. The knife he'd placed on the pillow beside her head was again back in his hand. The hand holding it had started to move in long, languid, sweeping arcs toward her.

Her scream coincided with the doorbell ringing. More accurately, she had no idea which had triggered which, or if indeed they were simultaneous. She came to believe that it was the doorbell, a loud, brash rattle of a bell, preceding her scream by a millisecond, that had shaken her loose from her terrified trance. The sound tore from her — not actually a scream but something else; something guttural and gagging. It rose from somewhere deep inside her, hurting her throat.

In the end, it saved her life. That cry, and the harsh, rude rattle of the bell clattering through the bird-twittering calm of a Sabbath morning, deflected the intruder.

At last she did faint. It came with a slow diminishment of light, like the iris of a camera closing. Just as the light went out entirely, she saw a dark figure fleeing like some large bird through the open glass sliders, and heard until she could hear no more the frantic, unrelenting racket of the doorbell dying in her head.

"Up to your old games again, eh, sonny? Radio's full of your escapades."

The old lady came padding around the big old nineteen-thirties electric range that sat like a derelict car wreck square in the middle of a space that might have been a kitchen, but could just as well have been anything else. There was about the room more the look of a shabby, somewhat disreputable curio shop than a place in which meals were prepared and served. A big square area crammed with junk and refuse, the room was pervaded with a sour haze of decomposing food and cat smells. Innumerable cat bowls with dry, hardened food littered the linoleum floors. Plates containing the remains of meals consumed weeks ago still littered the sinktop, already mantled over with a lacy green mold.

All about were windows, tall and stately, grimed with the dust of decades. Gazing out on the world through them gave the impression of peering through gauze. The shape of objects beyond the panes was a mottled, formless blur.

Short and stout, compact as a coal stove, with a face beet red, Suki Klink lumbered about the room, weaving her way through the intricate clutter with an agility that belied her sixty-some-odd years.

In truth, you couldn't really tell her age. Her skin had a pink, scrubbed, infant quality, although she seldom washed it. On first glance she gave the impression of something put together out of large quantities of undifferentiated rubbish — jackets, sweaters, long, voluminous skirts layered one atop the other, from beneath which a pair of brand-new boxy, blue-white Nike sneakers showed below the numerous hems.

On her head she wore a toque hat set at a dizzy angle, a prize she'd plucked from a trash bin outside a theatrical costumer's shop on the Upper West Side. Accessorizing the entire ensemble was a pair of Walkman headphones wired to her ears, from which she rarely disconnected herself even when she was sleeping. Yet she seemed oblivious to the incessant din of music blaring in her ears as she went about putting together some semblance of a meal, all the while keeping up a steady stream of reasonably coherent gab. When she spoke, it was through a choking haze of smoke wafting upward from the stubby little cigarillo inevitably screwed more or less dead-center into her mouth.

"I knowed it was you, all right. Minute they said that thing about the nasty pictures on the walls, I said that's Warren, all right." She giggled to herself. "Always did have a taste for nasty pictures, you did. Even when you was a tyke. Used to like to go off by yourself with a pencil and pad and draw naughty things." She winked at him slyly, then burst into peals of shrieking laughter.

"Tell me, sonny, was it a profitable trip?"

Warren Mars frowned and turned away. "It was okay." The reply was curt and sullen, intended to terminate the conversation quickly. The abruptness of the response stopped the old lady momentarily.

She'd been opening a can of soup and now she dumped its contents into a frying pan with a loud plopping sound. She pushed it around in there with a big wooden ladle. A sizable overflow spilled over the rim of the pan and sizzled on the burners. "You wouldn't be keeping things from me, sonny, would you?" There was something of a taunt implied in the question. It came with a smile that opened on a mouth full of ruined, stumpy teeth.

"I told you it was okay."

"Sure, sonny. Sure. Right you are. No need to bite old Suki's head off." Her eyes were full of playful mockery, but beneath that lay an edge of cool, shrewd assessment. "Whatcha so touchy for?"

"Well, for Chrissake. I'm gone four weeks. The minute I'm home, right away you're at me — prying into business doesn't concern you."

She made a clucking sound with her tongue and pushed the soup around again. "Everything about my boy concerns me."

"You'll get your share, don't worry."

She giggled and stirred her soup. "Suki ain't worried about her share, darlin'. She knows she'll get her share." She cocked an eyebrow in his direction. "Any nice little fancies you brung me home?"

Something leaped in his eyes. A frown crossed his dark, brutal good looks and all at once he turned away. "What if I didn't?"

The row of stumpy, brownish teeth leered. "You'd never forget. Not your Suki. All she's been to you."

He whirled and flung his hands at the ceiling. "Okay, okay. Just let's quit it."

The soup bubbled and spattered in the frypan. It started to give off an unpleasant odor, like that of burning metal. She stared at the young man through the smoke of burning soup. He was standing there, half-turned away from her, hands plunged deep into his pockets.

She moved toward him with an air of caution. When she stopped, it was directly before him, tiny beside him and looking up. "If I ask about things, it's only 'cause I love to hear how things are gettin' on with my boy. You're still Suki's boy, ain't you, darlin'?"

She reached up tentatively and with a raw red paw cupped his chin in her palm. She patted it several times, each pat gaining momentum so that at the end they'd become short, hard slaps.

"Radio's full o' you, sonny. You best keep your head down for a while now. They'll be out lookin' for you full force." She grasped him hard at both elbows and shook him slightly. "You understand?"

Annoyed, he looked away. She snatched his chin again and tugged his face around so that he looked down directly into her eyes. There was no longer any playfulness there. Only something rock hard and implacable. "You understand, do you?"

"Get off my ass."

"Say it then. Say 'I understand.' "

The annoyance deepened, along with the flush in his face. "I understand. Okay? I understand."

She giggled and pinched his cheek. "Good. Now what'd you bring home nice for poor old Suki?"

He looked at her, shaking his head, weariness and

despair scoring his features. "Time's coming, old lady."

She waved him off with a laugh.

"Soon. I'm telling you. You better believe it."

"Sure, sure. What'd you bring nice for Suki?"

"Pretty soon. You'll see. I'm going for good. I can't say when, but it'll be soon."

Laughing, she turned back to her soup, which was now sending up noxious vapors. "You've had a busy time, is what you've had. Your nerves are frazzled, is all. Come have a bite now. Suki hardly gets to see her boy no more."

She ladled out a scoop of the thick, gelatinous, lavalike substance from the frypan, splashed it into a cracked blue saucer, and thrust it at him. "There you go, little one. Eat up now."

After he'd left, she continued moving about the kitchen, shuffling over the cracked and faded linoleum, slippers slapping the bare floor behind her as she went about shifting the kettle on the burner and stirring a foul, evil-smelling pot of gizzards for the cats.

Anyone using Grand Central on a daily basis would know Suki Klink at once. She was a fixture there. Especially in the winter. She was that old heap of rags you'd see plunked down in the middle of the treasury of junk she'd scavenged from trash bins. She'd lie there, propped up against the wall just outside the entrance to Track 28, directly opposite Zaro's Bake Shop. Safely out of the drafts and cold. People from the offices in all the surrounding buildings would rush in and out of that bustling food emporium with bags of goodies, their fists crammed with change, and always slip her something. She was a canny old lady and chose her spots well.

The house on Bridge Street she owned free and clear. It had been bequeathed to her by her husband, whom she married when she was fifteen. At that time Mr. Klink was hovering up somewhere about the sixty range. He died approximately seven years later and Suki had owned the place ever since. It was a sore point for the Amalgamated Mercantile Bank of New York, who owned everything else on the block and coveted the property with an eye toward erecting yet another sky-blocking monument to corporate majesty. Doubtless, another bank. Their lawyers had offered Suki pots of money to sell, alternately wheedling and coaxing, then threatening to have the place condemned and seized if she didn't comply.

If they thought they were dealing with a bewildered little old lady, she'd quickly disabused them of that notion. Suki was not greatly impressed with desk thumping and fulminations. She informed the bank through the good offices of her friend, a notary public and cigar-store owner, that she had no intention of selling the property at that time, least of all to them. The only way she'd be leaving number 14 Bridge Street was feet first in a coffin and she didn't anticipate doing that for at least another twenty years. The notary public — Mr. Bloom was his name — then concluded by threatening a countersuit. For some reason plausible only to the arcane minds of bankers and lawyers, Amalgamated Mercantile backed off, at least for the time being, to regroup and rethink their strategy.

Now listening to the slamming of doors and banging of windows overhead, Suki laughed softly to herself. It was one of his tantrums, which he'd often had, even as a small boy, venting his spleen on a variety of inanimate objects. He'd kick and punch and fling them across spaces with such force they'd puncture plaster and burst out windows. Then, as now, she knew that such fiery displays were made as much for her benefit as his; largely for effect and intended to inform her that she'd displeased him. She rattled pots and kettles in noisy defiance, sang out loud mock arias at the ceiling, and laughed merrily to herself.

She'd heard it all before. How he was fed up and ready to clear out. How he hated the old place on Bridge

Street. How it was a "goddamned pigpen," smelling like a "shithouse," with all those "fucking cats." She listened to him stamp overhead and watched the shower of plaster dust drizzle slowly down through a fissure in the ceiling. From his eyrie high up in the cupola, he railed down at her against the old house, this fuming wreck that had been both sanctuary and prison cell to him since childhood.

"Door's open, sonny," Suki would shout back at him cackling gleefully to herself and showing those yellow stumps of teeth. "All you've got to do is walk out."

The words were as much a taunt as they were an invitation. She could afford to be magnanimous. She knew he'd never go. Not now. Not anymore. But when he was a child of six or seven and she'd brought him home and fed him soup, like some wild shivering thing plucked from a forest, then she couldn't be so sure.

In those days she made a point of never leaving him alone in the house. Then there was, indeed, the strong likelihood that if she had, he would bolt. So at night, after their late rounds at the terminal when they came home to Bridge Street and went to bed, she would lock him in the little room upstairs beneath the cupola. Weaning him, gradually, modifying his wild, wandering ways, she'd domesticated him from something untamed into a creature of home and hearth and conventional habits, until at last she felt she could leave him by himself in a house unlocked and trust that when she returned he'd still be there. When he got older he was free to come and go as he pleased. It was then she could begin to expect to see some return on her investment, for he was a talent, this one, her wicked little Sonny with the bright, sly smile. He could walk through the crowds in Grand Central and, with fingers light as air, lift wallets out of pockets and filch food and small change from countertops. She'd taught him all she knew of how to glean and gather the rich droppings of a wasteful, profligate society. She taught him the sort of skills that could make him free, a man of independent means who need never work for anyone in his life, to her mind the most contemptible state of existence imaginable.

Now grown lanky and strong, he was a valuable prize. And she had fashioned him. She'd bred the nomadic street ways out of him so he'd remain by her side, an asset and a defense against a hostile world for the rest of her days. There was no danger now that he would ever leave.

It was odd, she thought, that she understood this dependency, but that he didn't, and doubtless never would. In his mind he was free. He'd lived wild as a child and he fully believed he could do so again.

But, just as oddly, she failed to recognize her own dependency on him. Not financial dependency, for in that regard she needed no one. But in another more subtle yet far more potent way, life for her had become unimaginable without Warren. They'd been together the better part of fifteen years. He was the closest thing to blood to her, the only thing that might be looked upon as family since Mr. Klink's untimely demise. Moreover, he was her sole heir, though he didn't know that and she had no intention of telling him until it became absolutely necessary. There was a paper in an old cardboard shoebox buried under the mound of quilts atop her bed. It was a paper drawn up by her notary-public friend, the proprietor of the small cigar store on Pine Street. Based loosely on a standard form found in a *Good Housekeeping* magazine, it had been composed in language simulating a kind of quasi-legalese, waxing more and more flowery as the notary gained confidence, peppering the document with a dazzling array of *wherefores* and *insofar ases* and *party of the first parts*, and so on. And while the end result was ludicrous, as most such documents generally are, it would certainly pass in most probate courts. The concluding line designated Warren Mars in clear, unequivocal terms as "heir to all of my worldly possessions here and now and for the full term of all his mortal days."

That's why the notion that he might actually go had to be taken seriously. Aside from the void it would leave — and that would be considerable — more disturbing even, there would be no one to whom she could leave her "collections" as well as the old house on Bridge Street. If that were actually to occur, then the bank and lawyer leeches, sensing her vulnerability, would come swarming about like jackals and hyenas at the scent of blood.

More unsettling yet, she knew that if suspicious enough, or provoked, he could do her harm. She knew well his fits of towering rage, but she felt reasonably confident in her ability to control them — at least keep them in check. Regardless of how much he professed to hate the old, crumbling, derelict house, she assured herself that he needed it to come back to after the periodic orgies of self-indulgence and self-loathing.

If things got too bad, if Warren were to become dangerously unmanageable, there was always the law. But in her heart of hearts, Suki knew she could never betray him in that fashion. She despised the legal establishment and all of its lackeys — the police who chased her out of the terminal on cold nights, and the judges and lawyers who even then conspired to swindle her out of all her "earthly possessions," — too much to seriously contemplate such an action. She loved Warren (or whatever it was in Suki that passed for love) far too much ever to surrender him to the jackals and hyenas. If they ever got their hands on him, they would surely lock him away forever. They might possibly even kill him.

On the radio that day she'd heard people clamoring for his head. Community groups were out on the streets, in front of City Hall with placards. The press was railing against the police, and neighborhood surveillance groups were threatening to take the law into their own hands. The "Shadow Dancer," they called him. Suki laughed gleefully over that. Her boy a celebrity.

*   *   *

Upstairs in the little room beneath the cupola, Warren
Mars continued to stamp and fling things and flail about.
The floor was now fairly littered with a variety of debris,
from this and earlier eruptions. It was odd, he thought,
how whenever the old lady was around, he was angry.
Angry and a bit scared. He couldn't say precisely why,
but it had been that way since childhood.

He was, possibly, six or seven when she'd first taken
him in. That was shortly after she'd found him in Grand
Central. He was living down there in the dead of winter
with a band of nomadic adolescents in the labyrinth of
tunnels beneath the tracks. She found him there one
night, shivering and feverish, and took him back with
her to Bridge Street. The child was reluctant to go but
too weak to protest.

He hadn't eaten in several days and so when she asked
him, he went eagerly with her. Assuming that he'd remain with her a night or two, steal what he could when
she wasn't looking, then slip away, he complied with her
wishes. It didn't work out that way. Instead, it turned
into a collaboration, a fifteen-year partnership, and a
comfortable habit he was unable to break.

Of his life before Suki plucked him from the terminal
and brought him home to Bridge Street, Warren recalled little. He could not remember his parents except
for a vague pang of distaste whenever the subject came
up. He had some woozy recollection of a basement
apartment far over in the West Forties where he seemed
to think his father was the janitor. He couldn't be certain
about any of that since, beyond the age of six or seven, he
spent little time there. What he recalled, in mostly
broad, unspecific terms, was that the apartment was
always crowded and dirty and there was never anything
to eat.

Once as a child he came home crying. The other kids
had told him that his name wasn't a real name since he
had no real parents. Suki told him that she was his

"parents" and that he had been named after a brave and powerful "god of war" whom everyone feared and that he must live up to that heroic heritage. After that he felt much better about his name.

With Suki things improved one hundredfold. At least with her he ate regularly and slept in a bed, even if it was just a foul, licey mattress with malodorous, urine-stained ticking resting on the cold floor.

As he grew older, Suki occasionally would toss him some pin money to put in his pocket. It was her way of tendering a bit of independence while still keeping the boy on a tight rein. He was still too young and too much of an innocent to realize that it was his own money she was giving him back — the small sums he'd panhandled, swiped from countertops, scrounged from telephone coin slots in the terminal and dutifully turned over to her. At the close of each "working day," Suki would relieve him of all that, putting it on a lofty moral plane, however, by proclaiming that if he was ever to grow up and take his place in society, he had to learn to pay his fair share, meaning, no doubt, the cost of the exiguous bed and board she provided him on Bridge Street.

In those early days, their routine was simple. Suki and Warren would sleep or sit around all day on Bridge Street. In late afternoon, they'd have a bite of supper and go up to the terminal, planning their arrival to coincide with the great homeward rush of commuters spilling out of all the surrounding offices.

They would take up their position at the entrance of Track 28, Suki perched like some obscene carrion bird atop her many bags of trash, Warren sitting small and appealingly pathetic beside her. As an image of social displacement, it was irresistible. Poster-perfect. People seeing them would, of course, conclude they were homeless and that he was her child, although the disparity of their ages made that biologically unlikely. In no time, the battered hats and small tin cans they put out were filled with coins and bills of small denominations.

When activity in the terminal would start to subside, they'd haul all of their baggage crosstown to the theater district and sit on the ground straddling the warm gratings, waiting for the intermissions and the shows to break. With all the people streaming from the theaters at eleven P.M., she would gently propel the boy forward out of the shadows where he'd been dozing. Waiflike and pathetic, he'd move through the well-heeled crowds, his small hand out, his eyes large and beseeching. Needless to say, they would give him change. A lot of change. It was easy.

There were nights, particularly in spring and summer, they would work the streets till three A.M., then repair to the Night Owl Diner on 11th Avenue, where a lot of nocturnal folk, not unlike themselves, and having no better place to go, would gather for coffee and cake, and talk and laugh and smoke until dawn.

Afterward Suki and the boy would grab the IND at 6th Avenue and take it down to Church Street. They never paid fare at that hour of the morning. They merely ducked the turnstile. The attendants in the change booths knew them and would never say a word.

They'd be back on Bridge Street just as the sun was coming up over the Stock Exchange. Inside, they'd unload their bundles, take inventory of the night's haul, and stash it in a safe place. They would then, like a pride of lions that had hunted all night, sleep for the rest of the day. At four P.M., they would rise again. Suki would prepare some small, makeshift supper and they would make ready to go back up to the terminal.

For a small, practically wild child, unaccustomed to any fixed regimen, it was a lark. It provided a sense of security unfamiliar to him, and, to his delight, he never had to attend school. Suki wouldn't permit it, maintaining that the moment she registered him for classes, some do-gooder social worker would undoubtedly come down to Bridge Street and carry him off. Clap him in an institution or some foster home where they'd bang him around as an

integral part of his rehabilitation. Nevertheless, the old
lady had a high regard for education and insisted that the
boy learn to read and write. Accordingly, she taught him
herself. Her methods were unorthodox, to say the least,
and she was a difficult taskmaster. She made him add sums
and write his alphabet over and over again, banging his
knuckles with a steel ruler until he'd gotten everything
correct. Later on, she brought stacks of scrounged newspapers home with her at night, and he would have to read
them aloud to her.

All in all, it wasn't bad, and the boy didn't seem
unhappy. But still, from time to time, with no apparent
warning and for no evident cause, a profound gloom
would descend upon him. At such times he would grow
listless and remote, withdrawing to his room like a sick
cat, and keep to himself for days on end.

This despondency was invariably attended by a series
of daydreams, no less vivid than they were rambling.
The content of them was always the same. The setting
was a large, rather grand house in some undefined location. Only two people appeared to inhabit the
daydream — himself and an ethereally beautiful lady, all
attired in the pristine white of the fairy godmother in a
book of children's tales. He would be seated on her lap.
She would whisper in his ear and tickle him. They would
giggle and laugh and delight one another all day with
jokes and riddles and drawing pictures with crayons. She
would hug him and mess up his hair and stay with him all
day. Then, just as suddenly and unexpectedly as she'd
appeared, she would go. Shortly, the cloud would lift
and soon he was his old self once more. He would wander downstairs and into the kitchen where Suki puttered
about. She'd be waiting for him there with a bowl of
junket or a small cup of chocolate pudding. So it had
been since childhood, and so it still continued, only now
these sulks would take the form of disappearances from
the house of two to four weeks' duration.

It was therefore not unnatural that over the years

Warren had developed a strong sense of attachment to the old lady. But along with that came a decided edge of resentment. From childhood on, he'd always given her his "fair share" of the night's take. But now, at twenty-two, he was into far more profitable ventures, and her unceasing demand for tithes had begun to rankle.

Aside from the gold-mine property she occupied on Bridge Street, Suki was a rich woman. Warren always said she had the first dime she'd ever stolen. Her instinctive antipathy to banks caused her to keep sizable sums of money in old pots and tins hidden around the house. A great deal of it was hoarded down in the abandoned sewer line beneath the house. The line was part of a network of tunnels, some of them one hundred years old or older, that ran, roughly, from 14th Street south to the tip of Manhattan Island. They were not made of brick like the present-day sewer lines, but of clay. Time and hard use had badly undermined them, so that over the years the city had replaced most of them with modern systems. The old ones, like the one running beneath Bridge Street, had simply been sealed off. That's when they became an ideal spot for Suki to store her rich cache of "collections."

The house on Bridge Street was a queer sort of place. Wedged in between factories and warehouses, grimy, soot-stained commercial buildings, the tiny red-brick Federal was something of an anomaly. "Built during the 1840s," Suki liked to say, "during the Polk administration," as if that carried a great deal of weight with the world.

It was a three-story structure with long, high windows of a noble scale, in perfect proportion with the house. There was a cellar and an attic and a tangled, unattended stretch of garden out back with a statue of Diana with a cracked nose and a missing ear. It leaned off to one side, half in, half out of the ground, looking as if a mere whisper might send it toppling.

At the front of the house and running around one side was a big old porch with crumbling banisters and paint peeling from its ceiling and floor. Several of its original pine planks were sprung. At its corners stood a few cast-iron pots in which Suki at one time had planted flowers. Now they sported little more than weeds and the occasional parched sprig of geranium.

In the back, at the bottom of the garden, was a graveyard where the old lady would bury her cats. All about the house dwelled myriad cats, drawn there by the sweet fetor of fresh garbage Suki strewed about for them.

At the very top of the house, at its apex, was the glass, boxlike cupola. From there one could look out on Battery Park and see the Verrazano Straits, the squat, humped outline of Staten Island slumbering like a whale in the hazy distance. At night there was the Statue of Liberty all lit up. It was up there where Warren retreated after the rigors of his various "enterprises."

There was little in the way of furnishings inside the house. What there was of it was a congeries of abandoned things Suki had plucked out of the dumps or off the streets, where they'd been left for the sanitation people to pick up.

The old lady slept on the second floor in a dark, curtained room that smelled faintly of mushrooms. The curtains were never drawn and sunlight seldom strayed into those dark precincts. In the center of the room, occupying most of the livable space, was a big old dark wood bed with an immense headboard, upon which a bestiary of creatures had been carved. Deer, bear, stags, ferrets, and ravening wolves slinked through a gnarled, twisted forest fashioned out of Bavarian oak.

As a child, left alone for long periods in that house, Warren would steal up to the old lady's bedroom and stare in rapt wonder at those carvings. The bed had been sent over from Germany by Mr. Klink's family on the occasion of his first marriage, some forty years before he'd met and married Suki. Generations of Klinks had slept and procreated and died in that bed.

Now there were at least ten pillows on the bed and Suki slept beneath nearly as many blankets. They gave the appearance of a small, steep slope. Even in the dead of summer when the house was an oven and there was no air to breath, Suki reposed beneath that unwholesome weight. She slept in all of her clothing as well. In fact, rarely did she take her clothing off, except to bathe, and that was none too often. Her reluctance to disrobe had nothing to do with reasons of modesty or laziness. She argued, and with some merit, that if there were ever a fire, being dressed at all times meant that she could get out fast with just about everything she owned, including the stash in the basement, for they had agreed that in the event of such an emergency, they would flee the house from there.

Once, when Warren was about nine or ten, Suki took him down into the cellar. She'd always told him never to go down into the cellar alone. There were bad things there. Evil things. If he went down there himself, they would get him.

But on this particular occasion, she took him down herself. It was a dark, cramped, dirty hole of a place. The only illumination came from two narrow rectangular windows set just above ground in the stone foundation. Years of grime and muddy winters had rendered the glass in those windows nearly opaque. What light filtered through had the gray, lugubrious look of perpetual dusk.

The ceiling was low, with stout old joists and beams projecting downward, so that people, even those of average height, had to stoop in order to pass through safely.

She had taken Warren by the hand (Suki's hands were rough and hot as an oven) and proceeded to lead him far back into the cellar — so far back he couldn't see his hand before him. As she tugged him along, the boy kept bouncing off boxes and cartons, at one point barking his shin painfully on a dilapidated old chifforobe stored below ground for years. Shortly, tears were brimming in his eyes.

He kept stumbling and tripping. He couldn't help thinking that there was something angry in the way she pulled him along. He imagined he'd done something wrong, and now she was going to turn him over to those bad "evil" things she said abided down there. At just about that time, he reasoned, there were one or two things he'd been up to that might make her want to do something like that. He wondered if the old lady had found out about them. The thought of it half-scared the child out of his wits.

Just when he thought they could go no farther, they came on another passage off to the right. This one seemed to plunge back even deeper. Suddenly they stopped. In the next moment he felt her fumbling about beneath her skirts. He heard a quick scratching sound on the wall beside him and suddenly a match flared into vivid illumination. She pulled a candle from inside her copious skirts and lit it, then crammed the light into his tiny fist. "Now you hold that, sonny."

Before them stood a huge hooped barrel, brimming over with colored glass, old bronze and pewter candelabra, cheap bric-a-brac, and a variety of other trash. The barrel weighed well over a hundred pounds.

Grunting like an old sow, Suki wrapped her arms around the middle of it, as though she were hugging someone, and wrestled it off to one side.

"Now hold that candle over here." She yanked his trembling hand and planted it in midair about two feet or so off the ground.

Right under their feet, where the barrel had stood, was a great, heavy iron lid planted in the earth. A manhole cover, it was, just the same sort of thing you see up on the street. This one had a lot of ridges in it, all set in a pattern of concentric circles. In the center of those

ever-diminishing circles, the whiskered, hoary face of a
bearded old patriarch was stamped. That, in turn, was
ringed by the words:

> Baynes Iron Foundry
> Erie County, 1862
> Buffalo, New York

In years to come, all throughout the most turbulent
times of his young adulthood, when it became urgent for
Warren to conjure up the face of God, it was the face of
this bearded patriarch struck on a sewer lid that sprang
most quickly to his mind.

By then Suki had a crowbar, which she kept nearby.
With that she wheezed and puffed and finally prised the
lid out of the earth. Then, with a final heave that made
the ground crumble beneath it, and dry earth spill inward about the hole, she jimmied it off to one side.
Almost at once a puff of something cold and damp, like
someone's bad breath, rose out of the earth. It smelled of
moisture and sewage and something rotting. From somewhere below he could hear the sound of rushing water.
That was followed by a quick scurrying noise like that of
dry leaves rattling over the pavement.

Suki snatched the candle from him and grabbed his
hand. "Come on."

His heart beat wildly. "Where?"

"Down." She pointed with the guttering flame to a
steep ladder descending into the earth.

"No," he whined, imagining the "bad" and "evil"
things awaiting him below there. He dug his heels into
the ground, struggling against her greater strength.

"Never you mind that now," she snapped and yanked
him down into the earth behind her.

PART II

ELEVEN

"WHO SAID THAT?"

"The chief of detectives."

"Mulvaney? Go on. Mulvaney never said that. He made a statement to the press, but he never said we had a make on the car."

"He said you had a green car with 'distinctive features.'"

"'Distinctive features'?" Mooney laughed. "That's a big, vertical grille. Could be any of a half-dozen makes. What else did he say?"

Mooney stood outside on the pavement of East 84th Street in front of Fritzi's Balloon. He'd just stepped out of a squad car that had dropped him off and was instantly besieged by hordes of reporters. A TV mobile unit was double-parked on the street while lines of backed-up, horn-honking Friday night traffic tried to get past.

Cameras and reporters weren't Mooney's strong suit. He did his best to affect a jaunty manner, but as the questions pelted him, he looked increasingly like a large bear treed by a pack of shrieking hounds.

"The car parked in front of the Torrelson residence that morning was green. A neighbor saw it. That's all we know about it. We can't even say for sure that was the vehicle the perpetrator came in." He heard himself say that distinctively police word and felt embarrassed for having said it. "We don't have an operator description. We don't have a plate number, and we sure as hell don't know enough about the grille or any other distinguishing marks to put a make on it. We think that it was an older vintage car in very good shape. We're checking with the Motor Vehicle Bureau and our own records to see if there's any recently stolen vehicle fits that description."

He started to turn to go in but was again besieged by a barrage of new questions. Out of the corner of his eye he could see Fritzi and a bunch of his cronies all gathered at the front window to watch the press put him through his paces. Their presence there made him even more self-conscious.

"What's this business about the assailant's teeth, Frank?" the *Daily News* man asked.

Mooney shrugged and made a "who knows?" expression. "Only that teeth marks were found on some of the victims' bodies."

"The others had no teeth marks?"

"None that we know of."

"So those murders could have been committed by someone else? A copycat maybe?"

"Maybe. Maybe not." Mooney shifted uneasily from one foot to the other.

A disembodied arm to which a CBS microphone was attached appeared out of the crowd and thrust the microphone beneath his nose. "There's a rumor going around that this Shadow Dancer guy you're looking for has two broken front teeth."

"Maybe. Maybe not," Mooney repeated evasively, his head starting to pound. "It's just another possibility we're looking at."

"What about the numbers, Frank?" the ABC man asked him. "Anybody figured out the numbers yet?"

"We've had mathematicians look at them . . . all kinds of experts. Nobody seems to know exactly what they mean. Or, if they mean anything at all."

"They say you've finally got an ID on the girl found up in the park last month," the *Times* reporter said. "Is there enough yet to confirm whether or not she was also a victim of this guy?"

Mooney paused. He felt his mind go blank and his vision momentarily blur. A wall of faces undulated like large underwater ferns before him. He was aware of a sharp impulse to turn and run.

"First of all, we're not sure who we're talking about — the Dancer or the copycat. There are some similarities," he began haltingly, stalling to regain his thread of thought. "But there are dissimilarities, too. The other twelve attacks all took place in the victims' homes. This one happened out-of-doors."

"Who was she, Mooney?" one of the TV reporters asked. The cameras rolled in behind him. "Can you tell us something about her?"

"Only that she was a young woman working for a book agency here. Just out of school. It was her first job."

"What about that Howard Beach job last week? Was that the Dancer, too?" another reporter shouted.

"Could well be. We're looking into that now."

A burst of three more questions, all shouted simultaneously, followed. Mooney flung his hands up in despair. "That's it, guys. I told you all I know. That's it for now."

He swung his large square shoulders around and proceeded to wend his way through the crowd toward the revolving glass doors.

"Shit." Warren Mars slapped his forehead with the palm of his hand. "Son of a bitch." Envy fueled with rage welled up in him as he watched the big detective turn his back on the crowd and swing through the big glass doors of the Balloon.

"Shit," Warren muttered again and banged off the television, nearly dislodging it from the table. Who was this person, this copycat they all talked about? He'd love to get his hands on this slimy weasel who went about imitating him. Stealing his act. No sooner do you have success, he smoldered, than all these second-raters crawl out from under the rocks trying to rip you off. Doing your number. They might as well be in your bank account, for Chrissake.

Warren had been watching this character's activity, whoever he was, for almost a year. He'd been reading about him in the newspapers and following his progress on the TV, and now when they were all starting to talk about a "pattern" and to take Warren seriously, that's when this creep moved in, jealous for a piece of the action himself.

Now, the more attention Warren got, the bolder this copycat character seemed to get; the more he seemed to hover over Warren, following behind him, dogging his footsteps. Sometimes when Warren read about a new crime in the newspapers attributed to the Dancer that he knew he'd had nothing to do with, he'd go nearly crazy with rage.

Warren sprawled on his narrow bed beneath the grimy, rain-streaked cupola. The back of his head started to pound as the thought of this copycat gnawed at him and he tried to imagine ways of ferreting him out.

But shortly he was thinking about the TV news he'd just seen, and his dark mood shifted quickly. He was tickled and flattered by it. "They were talking about me. I'm the star of all this." He laughed out loud. His face flushed with delighted embarrassment, like a person shown old snapshots of someone he didn't recognize and then told it was himself.

He rose from the rumpled bed and prowled restlessly about the tiny room. Still full of the broadcast and the detective and all those reporters asking questions about him, he couldn't get over the thought of the thousands of others glued to their TV screens just to see and hear about him. It wasn't this copycat they were interested in; it was him.

He'd stumbled on the newscast quite by accident. He'd been watching a film, *Private's Progress* with Ian Carmichael and Terry-Thomas — one of his favorites. He'd seen it seven times but had finally grown bored with it. He

flicked the switch and there, suddenly, was this man —
big and disheveled and undoubtedly tough — with all
these reporters swarming like gnats about him. They were
all shouting at once and talking about *him*.

At first it was fright that he felt. He'd imagined they'd
found something. There'd been a break. He'd been
sloppy and had made a mistake. When it became apparent that he hadn't, that they were as much in the dark as
ever, he relaxed and started to enjoy the interview. He
liked to hear all the various theories. Sometimes it made
him laugh out loud. He was greatly flattered that he
could be the focus of so much speculation amongst such
seemingly important people.

About the detective, the man in charge of the investigation, he felt a nagging ambivalence. Initially, he dis-
liked the man. Number one, he was the law, and that
was reason enough to despise him. Number two, he was
Warren's adversary, the man whose principal responsibility was to seek him out, identify him, and ultimately,
put him away where he could no longer harm anyone.

Oddly, however, he wished the man were more impressive. Mooney didn't strike him as somehow important enough. He felt that the job, particularly the
spectacular nature of it, warranted someone more im-
posing than this coarse, unkempt man who answered
questions in a slow, halting way. Warren would have
been happier with someone more suave and better
dressed. Something more along the lines of William
Powell doing his Nick Charles number.

All of this antipathy came at the beginning of the
broadcast and in a great rush. Then gradually, the more
the detective spoke, the more he felt his feelings swing
the other way. He was flattered now to think that this
grizzled old cop whom reporters addressed by his first
name and cameras filmed could be interested in him. He
liked Mooney's sly smile and the low growl of his voice,
that slightly unshaven look, just a tad this side of disrep-
utability. The slow, halting manner of his replies he now

took to be shrewdness and caginess; an angler skillfully playing the fish nibbling at the end of his hook.

Warren suddenly felt an unaccountable rush of affection for the man. He imagined they could find much to talk about together. He was sure they had lots in common. He'd love to sit and talk with the detective about some of his cases. There was a thing or two he could tell him about the way things really worked in this city. Things this cop and all the police never suspected and would give their eyeteeth to know.

It would be fun to know this Mooney. He knew there were things he could tell him in the strictest confidence, at which the cop wouldn't bat an eye or think any the less of him for it.

As he lay back on his pillow, the pounding in his head subsided and he grew drowsy. It occurred to him he hadn't slept in sixty hours. He'd been up and driving and going about his business all that while. Making his way in the world, just like everyone else.

His eyes fluttered and started to droop. He felt a blessed loosening of the limbs and a letting go. The feeling he experienced almost every waking moment of each day, that someone, something, was pursuing him, some faceless, nameless something he could never identify, for he could never glance back over his shoulder in time to see it — that feeling now at least for the time being had begun to subside.

His eyes closed. The sounds of the old woman moving about in the kitchen below wafted upward through the thick, musty attic air.

That night he dreamed of tall buildings, huge, untenanted shafts of steel and glass, with the sun slanting blindingly off them. Amid them, needle-pointed spires soared dizzyingly upward into a vault of cloudless, enamel-blue sky. Across the spangled water of the harbor, Sweet Liberty, with torch-bearing arm raised on high, watched like a *magna mater* over the dreaming city.

He slept all night with the lights on. Warren Mars did not like to go to sleep in the dark.

"You think you could pick him out of a lineup?"

"No."

"I could bring photographs here so you wouldn't have to —"

"No . . . I can't, I said."

"A few minutes ago you told me you had a general impression of the guy." Mooney watched the woman as he spoke. She sat listless and unmoving in a rocking chair, her hands folded in her lap. He'd been at it with her the better part of an hour and felt he'd still not asked a third of the questions he'd intended to. That was because of the long pauses between each of his questions and her answers. Then when the answers finally came, they did so falteringly and with great gaps that he was left to fill in for himself. It was not that she was uncooperative; it was more like disinterest. About her was a frightening apathy reflected in the slow monotone of the voice and the dull gaze of her eyes.

They sat in an unlit room as dusk crept on. A single large picture window looked out over the Rockaway inlet where gulls that had fed for the evening now bobbed on the water. Voices could be heard outside in the corridor, and the sounds of an early-evening television game show came muffled through the walls from the room next door.

Just before entering the room, the floor doctor had told Mooney she was sedated. But this was a far cry from any sedation he'd ever seen. It was more a stupor, induced by powerful drugs that had carried her off to a far place where she could feel secure in the knowledge that no one could pursue her there.

The place was not a hospital but a convalescent home, since Mrs. Pell's injuries were determined to be not of the body — although she'd sustained a number of bruises — but of the mind. Of the morning in Far Rockaway on which her husband had been savagely murdered, then she herself subjected to brutal assault, she could recall little. The doctor had characterized it as a "selective amnesia." She could recall being attacked, but not what had been done to her.

Mooney shook his head wearily. It was the tag end of a doggish, sultry July afternoon. He'd been working nearly sixteen hours tracking down a flurry of fresh leads that had all come to naught.

"You've already told the police he was medium height, slight, dark, nice-looking, but with something off kilter when he smiled." Mooney looked up at her from the pad out of which he'd read to her his scribbled notes. There was something almost touchingly hopeful in his tired, expectant gaze, as if he'd believed that mere repetition of detail might dislodge the blockage in her recall and dispel the protective fog with which she surrounded herself. "You think that smile had something to do with his teeth?"

He waited for her to reply until at last he realized that she hadn't heard. Instead, she continued to sit in her chair, slumped and rather smallish, as if she were shrinking before his eyes.

Mooney gazed over his shoulder at Pickering, a gray, boxy presence slouching against the wall in a shadowy corner behind him. He shrugged and the younger man shrugged back.

"Mrs. Pell," Mooney murmured in a voice unnaturally low, as if he feared he might alarm her. "Mrs. Pell?"

She turned and gazed up at him, on her face a look of startled vacancy. He hovered there in the gathering twilight, uncertain where to go next.

"Mrs. Pell — if you'd like, I could come back when you're feeling more yourself."

"More myself." She repeated the words blankly.

A nurse framed in the orange glow of light from the corridor put her head in to signal their time was up. The doctor was outside as they were leaving. A small, natty man, his manner was curt and bristling with self-importance.

"When do you think she'll snap out of this, Doc?" Mooney asked.

"When she does, it's going to be one hell of a shock for her."

"But you think she will?"

"Eventually."

Eventually was not good enough for Mooney. "She's one of the few live witnesses we have to a series of crimes."

"I'm aware of the case," the doctor replied coldly.

"Then you can appreciate the urgency."

"I can appreciate it. Unfortunately, I can't do anything about it."

"I'd like to take her down to a police lineup."

The doctor frowned. "You must be kidding. This woman's severely traumatized. Her stability, whatever's left of it, is hanging by a thread. Now you want to put her through a grueling business like a police lineup?"

"It doesn't have to be grueling," Mooney protested. "She'll sit behind one-way glass. She'd never have to confront these people. I could send a car, an ambulance, if you'd like. She could have a nurse or a doctor with her, or both." Mooney could hear himself pleading and didn't particularly care for the sound. "She's the only hope we have right now. She can do a service. Make an identification that could possibly prevent additional tragedies."

The doctor looked at him skeptically, all about him the busy, distracted air of one who's already given far more time to something than the matter warranted. "You have any suspects yet?"

The question took the wind out of Mooney's sail. He grinned sheepishly at the young man. "Not yet."

"What are we discussing, then?" The doctor shook his head huffily and walked away.

TWELVE

"WE NOW HAVE A POSITIVE ON SEMINAL fluid for Torrelson, Pell, and the old lady in Flatbush."

"Great."

"Not so great. We found no sperm in two of the samples and not enough in the other to make a blood grouping."

"Wasn't that the same situation with the Bailey girl?"

"With her we found infertile semen around, but not inside her."

Konig cocked a brow and looked at the young woman sidewards. There was a moment of silence in which their mutual dislike of each other grew vividly apparent. "So we're looking for one azoospermia. What about the other?"

"We've got a couple of AB positive blood groupings down on the record. Most of the other semen samples were just too old to take an accurate reading."

"You did a Florence?"

"Twice. And confirmed them with a Barbera. It's semen, all right."

"But no sperm?"

"No sperm."

Konig looked dubious. "Not even nonmotile?"

"Nothing." The young woman shrugged and lit a cigarette. "We're going to try acid phosphatase and gel diffusions just to make sure."

Konig slapped his knees and rose. He started to pace

the length of the cramped office. "Azoospermia. Haven't seen one of those in twenty years."

"You've just been out of general practice too long, Doctor." Joan Winger extinguished her cigarette in a tray full of the cold, reeking stubs of Konig's cheap cigars. "It's all around us now. This is the Golden Age of Vasectomy."

Konig gave a snorting little laugh. "This is no vasectomy. Not with that pattern of assault. Potency is too big a factor in this man's self-esteem to just voluntarily have himself unwired." He resumed his pacing, pausing every now and then to view slides under a microscope. "In all probability, one of these Shadow Dancer boys has no idea he's not producing sperm."

"Probably not. Unless he's had a sperm count done recently."

"Probably urethral. An obstruction of some sort. Seminal vesicles. Sperm ducts. Trauma to the testes, maybe."

The young woman watched him pace stiffly and recognized his sciatic walk. He tended to lean off to the right side and drag the left leg behind him. "Why don't you take some codeine for that?"

He stopped abruptly and turned. "And that girl up in the park last winter . . ."

"The only clothing we ever recovered was a stocking. I already told you: there was semen around, but he'd never penetrated her."

"You never recovered anything? Vaginal? Anal?"

"Negative. All negative. I said then I thought the reason was probably premature ejaculation, or functional impotence. Now, I'm convinced, at least in the Bailey case, one of these guys is an azoospermia."

Konig planted a cold half-smoked cigar between his lips and lit it, then resumed his lame pacing. Suddenly tickled by some thought, he laughed aloud. "Well, if that's the case, it's a nice break for us."

She glanced up at him, momentarily puzzled. "Oh, you mean for purposes of an ID. I suppose so; that is, if we're ever lucky enough to get the azoospermic guy on an examination table and get a semen sample out of him. Then again, it's hard luck, too."

Konig stooped his shoulders and lit his cigar. "Oh, sure, you mean the blood grouping. I forgot."

The young woman nodded. "I thought for sure with the semen specimens we'd gathered off some of the others, we'd have more than just the few firm blood groupings we've got." She shook her head dejectedly. "Where do we go from here?" she asked, in a rare, unguarded moment. Long ago she'd learned never to display doubt or confusion to Konig. Almost certainly he'd use it against her. Sure enough, he did. It came in the form of a taunting little jibe. "Don't ask me. You're the professor."

She caught the tone quickly and felt her color rise. "Let's not do the professor routine again, please."

"Who's doing a routine?"

"And, for God's sake, don't smirk like that, as if you had some dazzlingly brilliant insight about what all this means. At this point, you don't know any more about this than I do. And that is that one of these Dancer guys looks like an AB pos, and the other is probably an azoospermia."

Konig puffed contentedly, making the tip of his cigar glow. He appeared to be immensely pleased with himself. "You've been working hard. A few days off would do you good."

She rose from her seat, swinging her arms from side to side. "When I'm ready to take time off, I will, thank you. And thank you, too, for absolutely zero guidance in this matter." She started out the door, but he called after her. "I'm not here as a house mother for any of my deputies. I don't coddle anyone. We're all grown men — people," he quickly covered the slip.

Now it was her turn to smile tauntingly. "That's better. More like it. I prefer you when you're your genuinely nasty self. I don't know quite how to deal with all that sticky paternal stuff about my health. If you've got anything constructive to add to all this," she went on, "I'm in my office for the next half hour." She flung out, slamming the door with a shattering bang behind her.

"This one looks like an old high school buddy of mine, Eddie Carboy."

"Looks like a road company Sylvester Stallone. Get a load of the sideburns."

"I used to wear sideburns like that."

"You would. You're just the type."

Pickering frowned. He wasn't certain if he'd been insulted or merely joshed. It was late and they were sitting in one of the little back rooms in the police photo library on West 48th Street.

On a table before them were stacks of police mug shots, interspersed with the paper cartons and debris of a send-out Chinese supper.

It was dark and airless in the little room. There were no windows, and the only light came from a fluorescent gooseneck desk lamp clamped to the table at which they worked. An ancient ceiling fan drifted listlessly overhead, pushing stale air from one corner of the cubicle to the other. Occasionally, a bit of loose paper would drift from the table to the floor.

"You're sure all these suckers have busted front teeth?" Mooney asked. Flicking the photographs about the table, he looked dubious.

"Right. Not necessarily the two teeth the M.E. said, but they all have some kind of damaged front teeth."

"You're sure?"

Pickering sighed and let his head slump forward onto his chest. "You feed your data into the computer and hope for the best."

"Computers are often wrong."

"Not the computer, it's the operator."

"So the manufacturers would have us believe," Mooney grumbled. "Hey, geta load o' this monkey: Luccabrava, Anthony. Age, twenty-seven. Height, six one. Weight, two seventy-three. Convicted nineteen eighty-two, sexual assault. Convicted nineteen eighty-three, sexual assault. Nineteen eighty-four, armed robbery, sodomy, sexual assault and battery. Served thirteen months of an eight-year sentence on Rikers. Released, January 'eighty-six. Scary lookin', eh? How'd you like that to come up on you in some dark alley?"

Pickering studied the photo gloomily. "If it was me he wanted, I'd just drop my pants and let him have his way with me. Hey, Frank. It's one in the morning. Let's get the hell out of here."

Mooney disregarded the plaint and continued to flick through mug shots. "Tell me once more what the Motor Vehicle Bureau guys told you."

Pickering's tousled head dropped onto the table. A long, hollow moan echoed from somewhere within him. "Nothing. They got no record of any recent theft of a green automobile, vintage sixties or early seventies, possible Chevy, possible Pontiac, possible Buick, possible anything. Nothing of that general description. *General* being the operative word here."

"So our guy owns the car himself."

"They're checking registrations now for a medium/dark green car of that vintage. They'll have a list for us next week."

"What if it's an out-of-state car?"

"That's tough patooties." Pickering flung his hands up in despair. "I'm not checking out the M.V.B.'s in the other forty-nine states." He rose suddenly, tipping the chair over behind him. The loud crash that followed reverberated through the vacant cavernous library outside.

"Gee, don't bust up the place, will you?"

"You really gonna stick around here?"

"I got work to do, my friend."

Pickering made a pinched, suffering face. "Am I supposed to feel guilty about that?"

"Not at all," Mooney assured him with a most cordial venom. "You run along home to the little lady, Rollo. I'll be just fine."

"I'll be just fine. I'll be just fine." Pickering mimicked the older detective. "Ain't you some piece of business."

Mooney's eyes never left the stack of mug shots. He continued to search for some combination of elements he had fixed firmly in his head. "Run along now."

Pickering stood there, baffled and furious, looking alternately at the door, then back at Mooney. At last, defeated, he shrugged and slumped back down into his chair, his capitulation complete.

Mooney never bothered to acknowledge the concession. The thought of Eddie Sylvestri dogging his tracks was a sharp goad. His hands moved ceaselessly, like a poker dealer's, flicking mug shots into three distinct piles: *probable*, *improbable*, and *impossible*. "So tell me once more," he said after a while. "What exactly do we have on these Shadow Dancer guys?"

Outside on 48th Street, fire engines wailed westward toward some cataclysm on the river. Pickering sighed, pulled out a small pad from his inside pocket, and, in a voice husky with fatigue, proceeded to read. "Suspect A: Dark. Slender. Caucasian. Possible Hispanic. Age, twenty-three to twenty-six. Height, five eight to five ten. Possible broken right front and right lateral incisor. Operates a medium/dark green car. Possible vintage, sixties or early seventies." He flicked the pad shut.

"That all?" Mooney asked.

"That's it."

"What about Suspect B?"

Pickering flicked forward to the next page. "Suspect B: Fair. Slender. Caucasian . . ."

"No busted front teeth?"

"No—that's the dark, slender Caucasian. Possible Hispanic."

"Two different guys with almost identical M.O.'s. One copycatting the other. With the exception of the Bailey kid, all private or semi-detached homes. Residential suburbs. Forced entry through windows or side doors. Sexual assault often followed by theft. Electronic stuff. Audios. Hi-fi's, PC's mostly. Some jewelry. Cash, wherever available."

They stared at each other, grasping for anything possibly overlooked.

"That it?" Mooney asked.

"That's all I got."

Mooney shot a long, disdainful look at his partner. "Add to your list one additional item."

Pickering's brow rose, curiosity sparking his drowsy, crumpled features.

"One of the suspects is sterile. I got that straight from the M.E. today."

Pickering frowned, then laughed as if he suspected a joke. "A sterile rapist."

"That's right, Rollo. Just think how mad that makes him. Hand me that stack of shots, will you?"

Suki Klink bent over in her garden in the rear of the old house on Bridge Street. To call it a "garden" would be perhaps misleading. It was actually a plot, nearly a full square acre with a clean, unimpeded prospect of the Hudson sliding seaward off Battery Park.

The plot was not cultivated in any formal sense of the word. There were no beds of annuals and perennials, no rows of flowers set in some orderly procession, descending in size, or displayed by color. What there was, was simply a tangle of weeds and overgrowth permitted to run rampant. In the midst of it all stood the dung-spattered statue of Diana with a missing nose, and not far from that a cracked birdbath devoid of water. Crickets and grasshoppers darted ceaselessly in and out of the gaping fissures of its cracked basin.

As unlikely a garden as it was, the old woman still

referred to it as the "garden" and insisted on working it as one. On weekend mornings she would rise early and don her gardening clothes: sneakers, a floppy straw bonnet, and a patched and badly faded old denim worksuit.

Bending over nearly in half from the waist, her wimpled head hanging almost perpendicular to the earth, she moved through the tangled clutter like some creature browsing on the forest floor. To the untutored eye, her "garden" was little more than an untidy jumble of weeds and thistles, cockle burrs left to their own devices, and the general chaos of untrammeled nature.

To Suki Klink, however, it was a laboratory of herbs, roots, and rare and exotic medicinal plantings she'd sought out in the wooded parks and open sand lots of the city, then carefully transplanted to her own backyard where they would always be close at hand. An amateur herbalist of considerable skill, she could not only brew salubrious teas with her own chamomile and chickory, but treat warts and chilblains and whip up various decoctions to relieve itching and reduce fevers.

With the tall spikes of purple loosestrife, through which she moved so that they leaned over with the forward motion of her body, she could conjure up muscle relaxants and infusions for diarrhea. There was fumitory for skin eruptions; long, feathery stalks of fairy wand for use as a diuretic; celandine for the treatment of ringworm from which she suffered chronically.

There were clover and moneywort, and moonseed, which she used to compound a root extract for treatment of constipation. There was senna and white mustard and pokeberry, dill and great patches of dodder — a vast and wondrous pharmacopeia. All of this she cultivated and collected in old jam jars and mayonnaise bottles, all carefully labeled and tagged, then cataloged on long yellow legal pads, upon which she'd record the location in her garden and precise therapeutic use. For every specimen, she produced a credible and generally quite attractive hand drawing, also kept in neat files.

Then, too, there were the other roots and herbs, those less talked of but perhaps more carefully attended to. These were the plants Suki liked to think of as those associated with her "dark practices." This latter type were invariably planted along a gentle slope that descended toward the river. Though she prized them highly, she planted them far from the house so that in the event city inspectors or lawyers or even the police came poking about, their discovery or connection with her would not be easy to establish.

Of these there were nightshade and witches' bells, her prize Pareira specimens which she'd procured at the Botanical Gardens and from which she'd learned the relatively simple process of extracting curare from the long woody stems of the vines. She had her own ongoing full-time supply of cannabis and peyote buttons from mescal cactus she grew indoors, both of which she had a fondness for but no dependence on. She was far too clever for that.

At the farthest fringes of the garden several wild plants grew, out of which the old lady could fabricate sleeping potions. There was also a particularly virulent strain of henbane, highly toxic in certain dosages, but in smaller, more measured preparations a powerful hallucinogen of the hyoscyamine family, to which she was particularly drawn.

There were nights, particularly in the winter, when even for her it was too cold to be on the streets. Nights such as that, when the world was too much with her, when the icy blasts of January, aching bones, and simple weariness had brought her to her bed early, when the bleak reality of her situation would press in upon her like unwanted ghosts, she would brew a small infusion of henbane, steeping its leaves into her midnight tea, and carry it back up to bed with her.

In short order a series of bright, multicolored pinwheels would spin before her eyes. The everyday drabness of her surroundings would be transformed from dense mauves and sooty grays to a dazzling kaleidoscope of colors and patterns. The wood bestiary of the headboard above her would proceed to move in a woozy dance. The eyes of the carved beasts would glow like burning coals. The music from her Walkman headphones would amplify itself tenfold until she could experience the sounds as if she were no longer merely just listening to them but curiously inside the sound, peering out.

The high point of such episodes was when the music would take tangible shape before her eyes. It appeared in the form of long, unbroken, undulating threadlike lines. They would hang in midair like brightly colored ribbons, threads and filaments of wavering living matter dancing ceaselessly in ever-shifting patterns before her. These patterns were not superficial but multilayered and of ever-deepening complexity. Like a dark, trackless forest, they lured you into them until you were hopelessly lost. Suki had permitted herself to go just so far into that forest and no farther. By administering her dosages carefully, she held the key to her freedom. She was canny enough to realize that if she succumbed entirely to the strong, dark pull of that forest, followed it down into its very heart, she would find things she didn't care to find. There were few things that terrified Suki. Her own potential for madness was at the top of the list.

Still bent over double in her garden, she moved along, dragging a big old burlap sack behind her. She rambled through the tall, gently nodding canes of horseweed, bullrush, cattails, and Indian pipe, snipping blossoms and leaves with small scissors, rooting up various rhizomes, studying them briefly under a glass, then stuffing them into a mothy canvas sack.

Moving through the tall canes, she made her way down from the house toward the river, followed by a horde of mangy stray cats. They stuck to her heels, gamboling in the tall weeds, lunging at butterflies, and pouncing on the occasional hapless small mice and birds that crossed their paths.

Tonight she would work at her various infusions and medicaments. She'd been away from it too long, and now she felt the need of practicing the old art again. There were things that worried her, things that Warren had said that had unsettled her far more than she was willing to admit.

Krause, Irwin ....Dodge 1961, green
Mercado, Hector ....Pontiac 1963, green
Nudleman, Arthur ....Cadillac 1959, green
Quodomine, Malcolm ....Pontiac 1962, green
Rossman, Betty Jean ....Nash 1959, green
Starr, Mrs. Diane............Chevrolet 1960, green
Teleford, Seton ....Oldsmobile 1976, green

"Scotch that. Seventy-six is too recent."

"How come?"

" 'Cause by then the grilles are all mostly horizontal. Keep going."

Pickering looked up from his list and gazed at the square, rumpled figure seated beside him. They sat in the rear of an unmarked police car, moving through the late-afternoon traffic congestion of Webster Avenue beneath the Elevated in the West Bronx. "Are you listening?"

"Sure," Mooney replied and settled back more deeply in his seat.

"That's funny. I got the impression you were asleep."

"That's odd. What gave you that impression?"

Pickering shrugged. "I don't know. The closed eyes, I guess. And the light snore."

Mooney cocked a brow and stared at his partner out of a single opened eye. "Just keep reading, will you?"

The younger man sighed, appealing to heaven with his eyes. "Frankly, I don't see what for. That car . . . that is, assuming we're ever gonna be able to identify the right green car with a vertical grille . . ."

"Vintage sixties through the early seventies. Looking

all shiny and new," Mooney added. His eyes remained shut. The lids fluttered lightly as the car bounced along over the cobbled street and turned off Webster heading west toward Sedgwick.

"Okay," Pickering conceded. "Assuming you got all that. That car's either been stolen — "

"We already checked that out, dummo, and it hasn't been. At least, no one's come up with a 'stolen' report on it yet. Keep reading."

Pickering grumbled and swatted at a fly that had come along for the ride. "Umberto, Oswaldo . . . Hudson nineteen fifty-seven, green. Hey, remember the Hudson?"

"Sure. Looked like a bathtub upside down. What was the grille like, again?"

"Big. Lotta chrome. I guess you could call it vertical."

"Sedgwick Avenue, Lieutenant," the police driver up front called. "What's your number, again?"

"Seven eighty-four," Mooney said. He sat up, pushing his hands back through his thick, gray hair. "Oughta be right up ahead on the left."

The car cruised slowly up the block of nineteen-thirties six-story apartment buildings. Most of them had been abandoned and gutted by vandals. Trompe l'oeil still lifes of drapery and flower pots had been stenciled onto aluminum sheets and hammered over the gaping, punched-out windows as a neighborhood beautification project. The buildings that were still occupied had gone pretty much to seed. Once it had been a fairly stable middle-class neighborhood, mostly Jewish, with a sprinkling of Irish and Italian congregating on the fringes where it started to spill over into Dyckmans. Now it was a seedy, vaguely disreputable mélange of red and brown brick apartment houses in which residents, primarily black and Hispanic, lived behind barred windows and triple-locked doors, as terrified of thieves as they were of their next-door neighbors.

Jammed in tight between these huddled, crumbling

structures was a patchwork of bodegas, car washes, muffler-repair shops, open-air fruit and vegetable markets, beer and soda discount distributors, and check-cashing establishments where you could cash a check and play a number at the same time.

"That's it, seven eighty-four. Right up there on the left." Mooney thrust his finger over the driver's shoulder to point the way. "Who we looking for here, now?"

Pickering consulted his list of printed names again. "Krause, Irwin. Dodge, nineteen sixty-one. Green."

The squad car slid past a double-parked paneled dry-cleaning van and slipped into an open spot before a fire hydrant in front of the building.

Mooney sighed and straightened his tie. Looking at the clutter of brimming trashcans accumulated at the curb, he made a face of distaste, pushed the door open, and lumbered out onto the street.

"Where'd you find this, Irwin?"

"Got it off a mechanic. Friend of mine in Long Island."

"Oh, yeah? How long ago?"

Irwin Krause scratched his chin and rolled his eyes skyward. "Hadda be a good ten years."

"And it's a sixty-one Dodge?" Mooney asked.

"That's right. One of the best they ever made."

Pickering strolled around to the driver's side. "That the original color?"

"Yeah. That's it."

"Never had it repainted, or anything?"

"Never. That green you see there, that's it. Hey, listen, what's all this about, anyway?"

Pickering cleared his throat. "Like I told you on the phone. We're running this survey for the Motor Vehicle Bureau. They wanna know how many automobiles, twenty-five years or older, are still on the road."

"Oh, yeah?" Irwin Krause made an odd face. "How come?"

"Insurance." Mooney stepped in quickly when Pickering proved too slow on the reply. "We're doing it for the Insurance Institute of America. The IIA, you know?"

"Sure." Krause nodded, appearing too dazed to be sure of anything.

"Statistical study and all that," Mooney rattled on.

"Sure." The expression on Mr. Krause's face remained unchanged, but for the moment he was placated.

He was a short, slight, swarthy young man in his late twenties, with bad skin and a mop of oily hair teased forward into a frisette that drooped on his forehead. He wore sandals and a pair of khaki shorts with a T-shirt that read "I brake for anything."

"How many miles she got on her?" Pickering asked.

" 'Bout a hundred and eighty. Runs like a top. Mechanic says she's good for another fifty."

"You must take pretty good care of her."

"Nothing special." Krause spat into the gutter. "Tune-up twice a year. Oil and lube. Sparks and points. Don't put much mileage on it. Just city driving, you know."

"You keep it on the street?" Mooney asked.

"In this neighborhood? Are you kidding? You keep a car like this on the street overnight, you're lucky you find the cigarette lighter when you come back in the morning. I garage it down on Webster."

"Body's in great shape for a car twenty-six years old," Pickering remarked.

Flattered by the attention, Krause warmed to his subject. "She gets washed once a week, simonize twice a year. I take it to an auto body guy on Sedgwick Avenue cuts out all the rust soon as it appears."

"You married, Irwin?" Mooney asked.

The question caught the young man off guard. "Married?"

"That's right. Are you?"

The smile of moments earlier still lingered, but the young man was flustered. "Who, me? No."

"You go out a lot, Irwin? You like the ladies?"

Krause grew defensive. "What the hell's that got to do with car insurance?"

"Nothing personal." Mooney made a series of calming gestures with his hands. "Just inquiring if you use the car for social purposes. Like going out with the gals. That affects the insurance rates, you know."

A wary, stealthy look crept into the young man's face. "You guys ain't gonna raise my insurance, are you?"

"No, no." Mooney calmed him again. "Nothing like that. We got nothing to do with rates. This is all done on a strictly anonymous basis. No names, or nothing like that. We're just interested in the answers. We don't file your name with the report."

The look of sharp suspicion still lingered about the young man. "Oh, okay," he muttered doubtfully.

"What kind of work you do, Irwin?" Mooney asked.

"I'm a bus driver."

"Bus driver." Pickering laughed. "I would've never taken you for that."

Irwin Krause grew increasingly displeased with the tone of the interview. "Well, that's what I happen to do. I drive a bus for the MTA. I drive six days a week. That's how come my idea of fun is not spending a lot of time driving around in this thing." He indicated the shiny green vintage Dodge with a nod of his head.

"You don't like driving, Irwin?"

"I hate it. How would you like it if you hadda push a bus around Manhattan six days a week?"

"What is your idea of fun?" Mooney asked.

Irwin Krause frowned and shook his head. "This is the funniest damned survey I ever heard."

Mooney sensed the young man's increasing suspicion. "Reason I ask is that since you don't use your car for business but only recreational purposes, it helps us to know the sort of things you do with the car."

Once again, Mooney's quick fix had mollified him somewhat. "Well, I take it out to the beach weekends, and sometimes on a Saturday night I drive it into the

city. Like when I've got a date and all. But otherwise . . ."

"You never take it outta town?" Pickering asked.

"Like I say" — young Krause was beginning to show
signs of exasperation — "I drive a bus all week long. It's
no big pleasure for me getting behind the wheel on a
weekend. Also, this baby breaks down somewhere upstate in the mountains, I can't find no parts for it. I can't
find no mechanic who knows the machine."

Mooney and Pickering exchanged glances.

"You got any criminal record, Irwin?" Mooney asked
suddenly, seeing agitation leap back into the young
man's eye. "This is just for the M.V.B. records. Just a
formality. We try to keep tabs on all criminal types still
on the road."

Krause's look of skepticism had turned to one of hurt.

"It's for your own safety, Irwin," Pickering assured
him.

"Sure. I see," Krause agreed, more mystified than
ever. "No, I got no criminal record."

"Get me a make on this guy, Lopez," Mooney said to the
driver when they'd settled back in the car. He handed
him a small profile card with pertinent data he could
flash instantly over the car's radio to the National Crime
Center in Washington.

"That old Dodge was in beautiful shape," Pickering
said. "The grille was just the sort of thing that old Wisdo
babe was talking about."

"Too pale, though."

"Too what?"

"Too pale," Mooney growled. "The green was too
pale. She was talking about a darker green."

"How do you know?"

"Trust me." Mooney glowered out into the street.

"He's the right physical type, though," Pickering
added hopefully.

"All depends."

"On what?"

"On whether you're talking about the dark-complected character or the fair-haired one. Did you happen to notice Krause's front teeth at all?"

"Straight. Perfectly straight."

"Probably the only thing straight about him."

The police driver up front half-turned in his seat. The action caused his jowly face to redden. "On that Krause guy . . ."

"Yeah?"

"He was jugged a couple of times for driving under the influence. No prior criminal record."

THIRTEEN

FERRIS KOOPS WATCHED THE TRAIN GLIDE slowly over the track, then rock and sway gently into the little station. It was a freight train with an engine and a coal tender, with six cars coupled behind that. There was a boxcar, two flatcars, two oilers, and a caboose tagged on at the end with a Great Northern Railway shield stenciled on its side.

Ferris pressed closer, inching his way forward to a better vantage point. At the station the steam engine hooted. A puff of smoke rose from its stack as an automated delivery arm poked out from inside a baggage room, dropped a sack of mail onto one of the flatcars, then retracted itself. The engine hooted again, a low, wistful moan, the big drive wheels spun slowly, and the train chugged out of the station.

Farther up the track it slowed to permit a five-car passenger train to pass in front of it, then switched onto a shallow elevated track leading into a tunnel that wound its way beneath a papier-mâché mountain.

Ferris watched the tail of the caboose vanish into the dark maw of the tunnel. A smile of near childlike delight transported his features. In his early twenties, he didn't appear to be much beyond some of the older children swarming about him. His presence there at that moment in a crowd comprised mostly of children tended to heighten the impression of extreme youth.

It was 5:45 P.M., fifteen minutes before closing time at the F.A.O. Schwartz toy emporium. Though the sun was still up, it had already swung well to the west and appeared to have gotten itself tangled in the soaring new construction in the vicinity of Columbus Circle. It was at a point that could be described as neither daylight nor dusk, but somewhere just between, when the first few streetlamps have turned on, appearing white and ineffective in the dwindling daylight.

Ferris had wandered into the famous toy shop from the street. Having no place to go and nothing in particular to do, he stood outside the big display windows for twenty minutes or so, watching electric robots blink and lurch about. Beside that was a window full of animated Mother Goose characters reenacting their little tales.

More than he loved toys, Ferris loved children. Among them, he enjoyed a serenity and sense of well being he seldom experienced in the presence of adults. It brought him back to his own childhood. Christmas mornings. Toys beneath a tree. Thanksgiving Day parades. Halloween trick-or-treating. Ice-skating in the park, at the Wollman Memorial Rink. The building he'd grown up in was just across the street from there on upper Fifth Avenue. Standing at the window of his bedroom, he'd had an unimpeded view of the zoo at the south end of the park and of the Delacorte Theater and the ice rink farther north.

The room he had in those years was full of toys. Bookshelves from ceiling to floor were lined with volumes of children's classics sitting side by side with regiments of lead soldiers, kites, model ships and planes, bubble pipes, wind-up gymnasts, model vintage sports cars — all things to delight a child.

Ferris had never been to regular school like other boys and girls. The doctors had said he could never go. In a physical sense, he was perfectly healthy. But early on, in the first or second grade, his teachers had discovered that he was unable to learn at the same rate as other children. Learning what to do with numbers and letters for Ferris, hard as he tried, was an insurmountable task.

Even as he struggled to overcome his deficit, receiving special coaching, his reading level failed to advance at the same rate as other children's.

Concerned, his parents brought him to a special clinic where batteries of tests were administered, and it was quickly discovered that Ferris was largely incapable of any sustained concentration. A learned clinician there had informed the Koopses one gray, icy February morning that the part of Ferris's brain associated with cognitive skills was apparently underdeveloped. This might be due to some longstanding heretofore undiagnosed hormonal dysfunction, or more likely the result of a brief period of oxygen deprivation during birth. This was not retardation in the truly crippling sense, the doctor hastened to add, but all the same, the sad outcome that had to be faced was that Ferris would be afflicted with learning deficits throughout the course of his life.

On the other hand, Ferris had excellent muscle coordination. He was articulate with an extraordinarily large vocabulary (which appeared to fly in the face of the learned clinician's findings), and showed every indication of growing into a charming and comely young man.

But still, the doctors assured Mr. and Mrs. Koops that Ferris would never be normal. As he grew older he would give the appearance of normality. He could dress and wash, feed himself and attend to all his bodily needs, to be sure. He could even learn to read and write. Up to a point. But as for taking his place in the world — marriage, job, family — that, unhappily, seemed doubtful.

Shortly after (Ferris was only seven when that cruel verdict was handed down), the Koopses' fortunes began to founder. Several imprudent investments, coupled with one sizable loss in the market, all but decimated their savings. The need for ready cash compelled Mr. Koops to sell off some extremely valuable real estate holdings and liquidate his once-prosperous importing business, all at prices drastically disadvantageous to him.

Several weeks later Mr. Koops died of a massive coronary, and his wife remarried, many said with indecent haste. Sometime before his demise, however, Koops had set terms in his will to provide, not luxuriously, but more than adequately, for Ferris's needs throughout the remainder of his life.

That would have been all well and good had things gone the way Mr. Koops imagined they would. He didn't count on Mrs. Koops remarrying quite so quickly after his death, nor could he have possibly foreseen that his wife's new husband, a widower in his late fifties with enviable social connections and smart friends in high places, had little room in his life for a seven-year-old slow learner who required tutors and constant supervision.

Never a strong-willed person, Mrs. Koops soon bowed to pressures to institutionalize Ferris. "After all," her new husband assured her, "these people are professionals. They're trained to handle people like Ferris."

Ferris hovered round the Schwartz windows until closing time, then with a few other stragglers drifted out into the pale purple dusk of 57th Street, where the stores were now all lit. Office buildings were disgorging people onto the streets. Crowds brushed past the lagging, meandering youth, scurrying for subways and buses, rushing off to social engagements, family, and friends.

Ferris Koops had no place to go. He had not eaten in seventy-two hours except for occasional fruit drinks taken at outdoor stands. For all that, he was not conscious of being hungry, and even if he were, he had not at that moment the financial wherewithal to attend to the problem. The proceeds from the check that arrived every two weeks from the offices of a law firm on Madison Avenue had a way of disappearing almost the moment it was cashed.

He carried in his pocket some food vouchers entitling him to hot meals at various welfare shelters. The absence of means, coupled with no prospects of obtaining any until the arrival of the next check, held little in the way of fear for him. Since his father's death and his mother's remarriage, he had been largely on his own, working in a desultory fashion at a number of jobs too inconsequential to enumerate. Suffice it to say, he never worried for his next meal, and as for shelter, he had a tiny apartment on the Upper East Side, the rent for which was paid directly by the law firm serving as executors of his small estate.

It was toward the park he walked now, moving along in his wayward, dreamy fashion, destinationless, with an odd little smile curling at the corners of his mouth.

The streetlamps were all lit now along Fifth Avenue. He wended his way north, moving up the west side of the avenue, right along the shallow stone wall enclosing the park. Pausing for a moment to rub the pinkish muzzle of one of the horses from the hansom cabs, he chatted amiably with the driver, then continued up Fifth Avenue. The route took him past the Sherry Netherland, past the Frick, the French Embassy, the Metropolitan, and the Guggenheim, his sneaker-shod feet gliding aimlessly toward a specific place he had in mind but wasn't yet quite aware of.

Several blocks beyond the Guggenheim, his pace finally slackened then came to a halt across from a large, thirty-story, dun-colored, nineteen-fifties apartment house. Just behind him stood a bench against the park wall. He sat there for a while, watching people going in and out of the building. Businessmen returning home from work nodded to a liveried doorman and spun through the revolving front doors. Couples emerged from within on their way to social engagements all around town. The doorman hailed them cabs, doffing his cap when he'd closed the cab door behind them. A young woman emerged with a brace of Afghans on a single leash. A florist's truck double-parked in front while the driver made deliveries.

Lights shone in all the windows of the building, casting a glow of warm radiance down onto the street. There was an air of holiday gaiety and excitement about it all, a sense of some impending joy. He could not say why, but what he felt just then was a curious sort of exultation.

He rose and walked to the edge of the curb and stared up at the building. Eyes scanning the face of the structure, he counted fourteen floors up and eight windows to the right, ending at a corner window. Seventeen years before, he'd stood behind the glass panes of that window and gazed out at the onrushing magical night. It spread like an inkstain across the woody rolling hills of the park.

He knew, of course, that he was staring up at the window of what was once his own bedroom. Four windows to the left of that were the big four-pane casements of his parents' bedroom. The lights in there were on now and the shades drawn. He was aware of a momentary darkening motion drifting behind them and knew that people walked there. He liked to play a game in which he imagined that his own mother and father moved there now behind the drawn shades, and that they were waiting for him. He felt a rush of warmth and love rise fast and hard in him, settling finally in his throat and causing an ache there.

He was aware suddenly of the doorman out front, watching him intently. There was something wary, even slightly belligerent in his gaze. He'd encountered that sort of look from doormen before — and police. He'd always seemed to elicit that same response from uniformed people. It alarmed him and he was about to move off. Just then, a young woman in a flannel jogging outfit emerged from the revolving doors with a small King Charles terrier on a leash.

The doorman tipped his hat to her. Ferris heard her voice carry across the narrow strip of avenue where taxis and buses and private cars rolled endlessly.

There was something warm and friendly in that husky, laughing voice. Ferris watched her with growing fascination as she walked to the end of the block, waited for the light to change, then crossed toward him, the small yipping terrier straining at its leash.

On the west side of the avenue where Ferris stood, thirty or so feet down from him, was an entrance to the park. It was into that entrance that Ferris watched the young woman disappear.

It occurred to him with rather startling urgency that he had to speak with her. He wanted to say hello and tell her that as a small child he'd lived in the same building she lived in now. Possibly even in the same apartment. Was that her window at the corner on the fourteenth floor?

How odd. What a coincidence. How long had she lived there? Maybe they'd all lived there together at the same time. Had she known his parents? Mr. and Mrs. Frederick Koops. He was a tall, dignified-looking gentleman. "My mom was small and pretty."

In the next moment, Ferris was moving off into the park after the gray figure up ahead receding quickly into the gathering dark. By that time, in his surging joy at the prospect of a reunion with someone he might have known as a child, he'd completely forgotten the doorman, who watched him as he struck off after the girl.

FOURTEEN

"YOU'RE GONNA HAVE TO SPEAK LOUDER," Mooney shouted into the phone, but that was only because Konig was shouting at him. "We got a lousy connection."

"Where the hell are you?"

"We just left the park. I'm up on Fifty-eighth and Third."

"Sounds like you're at the bottom of the Hudson Tube."

"I'm on a pay phone. There's a construction job going on right over my head. Speak louder, will you?"

"Was there anything in the drain?"

"What?"

"The drain. The goddamned drain. Did you find anything?"

Mooney held the receiver away from his ear until he'd finished ranting. "Nothing special. Pretty much the same sort of thing as the Bailey job. Only this time the drain wasn't so deep. It was easier locating the body. And the dog —"

"Dog? What dog?" Konig bellowed. "Will you speak up, for Chrissake?"

"She was walking a dog. The doorman found the dog wandering out on the street, trailing his leash. That's how he knew something had happened. He watched her walk into the park with the dog, then saw this guy follow her in."

"He saw the guy?"

"Right." Mooney's head had started to pound just talking to the man. "He'd been standing across the street, watching the building. Looked kind of suspicious, the doorman said. It wasn't dark yet and all the building lights were on. He got a good look at the guy. We have a fairly detailed description."

"Does it match up with any of the others?"

"This one looks like the fair-haired, slender one."

There was a pause and Mooney could hear him breathing heavily. "You got anything for me?"

"She's still on the table now," he snapped. "But I can tell you right now, she's covered with bite marks."

Mooney caught his breath. "Where?"

"Breasts and genitals."

"Sounds familiar."

"That's good news. Here's the bad. We did a couple of quick impressions." Mooney could hear him shuffle some papers on his desk, then start to speak again as though he were reading from a report. "Bite marks in evidence here show no indication of either a broken front or broken left lateral incisor."

Mooney stared bleakly into the black perforations of the speaker.

Konig didn't wait for him to reply. "And something else . . . We took a load of semen samples out of her." He paused, drawing it out for maximum effect while Mooney waited with his head pounding. "Yeah?"

"The samples we took from Torrelson and the Pell woman and a few of the others were deader than old custard. The stuff we sucked out of this gal — what's her name?"

"Bender. Carol Bender."

"Bender. Right. This semen was jumping with live sperm. So all I can say now for sure is you've got two suspects: one with broken front teeth and azoospermia, and another with straight, sound teeth and fertile as a fruit fly. One blood type looks like an AB pos, and I can't say about the other."

"One dark, one fair," Mooney added softly to himself. "We know all that."

"What?"

"Never mind. Doesn't matter."

"Well, there you have it," Konig boomed heartily. Mooney could hear satisfaction brimming over in his voice. "Sounds to me like a couple of lads who are reading each other's press and trying to outdo one another."

Mooney stared at the receiver, then made a face back at a man outside the booth waiting to use it. "This job gets more unpleasant by the minute," he said.

"That's what adds zest to life, my friend. You wouldn't want them all to be too easy, would you?" Konig crowed like a cock and the phone clicked off.

Outside on the street the noise level was like the inside of a boilerworks. They were digging a foundation right outside of the phone booth. The machine-gun rattle of compressor drills banged through Mooney's pounding head. In the squad car Pickering was just signing off on the car radio. "What's up?" Mooney snapped, sliding into the back seat beside Pickering.

"Mulvaney wants us to come in right away."

"Shit."

"Commissioner just had him on the carpet for two hours. CBS ran an editorial last night calling for the old man's resignation."

With Mulvaney, Mooney always looked for the rosy flush of apoplexy. This usually informed him that things were okay, basically normal. That morning when they were brought in to see him, he was ashen. His skin was the color of parchment and he sat slumped over his desk, so limp that if you happened to nudge him he might just topple over.

"Look a bit peaked, Clare," Mooney said with the breeziest insouciance he could muster under the circumstances. "Looks like you et something."

Mulvaney looked up at them, his jaw slack, his eyes

bleary, as though he'd peered too long into a blast furnace. "Sit down."

There was no starch in his voice, no snarl, no four-letter words, all of which would have been customary and welcome and put them at their ease. Instead, there was an ominous quiet, and for the first time since Mooney had known him, Mulvaney looked defeated.

"I've been in with the commissioner this morning," he said. "I don't have to go into details about what it was like. Suffice it to say, he's unhappy about the way things are going."

"I know. You told me all this in April."

"Well, now it's August and I'm telling you again."

He paused to let the solemnity of the event seep in. "Now, listen, Clare — "

"No, you listen. Let me finish. Then we'll hear your side."

He looked at Pickering, then at Mooney, then back and forth for a while. "No doubt, you heard the CBS editorial on the six o'clock news last night. I'm sure you heard they were out beating the drum for the old man's resignation."

"That old devil blowtorch again, eh?" Mooney quipped.

"Right. And you know where it's pointed now, don't you?"

"I noticed you were sitting kind of funny there, Clare — like up on one cheek."

"Spare me the funny stuff, will you, Frank."

"Sorry," Mooney replied, trying not to look too worried.

"Let me finish, please."

There was something so weary and beaten in his voice, Mooney grew genuinely alarmed.

"I'm sure what I have to say is not going to displease you." He poured a glass of water from a carafe on his desk and drank slowly. Mooney watched him while he regained his train of thought. "No one is going to shove a blowtorch under your ass, Frank. Given the fact that you're a little more than a year from retirement, you're perfectly safe. As of this moment, you have ninety days to wind up this investigation on the so-called Shadow Dancer case. That puts you somewheres in the middle of November. If there's nothing tangible by then — "

"Tangible?"

"A suspect, or suspects, fully identified . . ." Mulvaney's eyes narrowed. "Barring that, then Eddie Sylvestri of the Nineteenth will at that time take full charge of the investigation."

Concluding the announcement with a small flick of his upraised wrist, Mulvaney popped several Maalox into his mouth and chewed gloomily. "Oughta make you very happy, Frank. You're back chasing pickpockets and three-card-monte dealers. All roller-coaster, no-sweat duty from here on in."

Mooney sat there, staring at him, feeling as though he'd been kicked in the stomach.

"Why?" he asked, when he'd caught his second breath. "Why dump me just when we're starting to make some real progress?"

"Not real enough, my friend. And not nearly fast enough." Mulvaney shuffled through a stack of night reports on his desk. "The commissioner is not about to sit around and take heat from City Hall and the media without any real progress to show. I don't know whether you've noticed it yet, Frank, but this city has a way of getting very jumpy in emergencies, and ten million people jumping all at once tend to have a seismic effect. Like something of the order of ten megatons."

"But why Sylvestri? Why him?"

A bitter smile flickered at the corners of Mulvaney's lips. "Because everybody knows your great regard for him."

"He's a jerk. He's a mouthbreather. There's ten pounds of suet between his ears where his brain oughta be."

"You've got ninety days, Frank. You just might beat

him out yet. But for now I'd say he's the odds-on favorite." He was smiling again, but it was a tired smile. There was no great cheer in it. Then, rather grimly, he added: "The commissioner authorized him to form a new fifty-man special task force."

That was the breaking straw. "So what you're saying is the decision's already made. Sylvestri will take over in ninety days whether I've got something tangible or not."

Mulvaney sat at his desk staring down at the night reports and doing his best to ignore him. "I'm sorry, Frank. This wasn't my decision. I warned you about this, didn't I? You're out. Sylvestri's in." He glanced at Pickering as if surprised to see him still there. "Rollo, you, of course, will be reassigned to Sylvestri's group for the duration of the investigation."

It was spoken with the kind of finality intended to signal the end of an unsatisfactory interview.

Mooney stood up. "You think that's it?"

"Frank." Mulvaney's voice was tired. "You've already had one coronary."

"I'm still on this job," Mooney shouted.

"You are. For three more months."

"Sylvestri can head it. But I'm still on it."

"Sylvestri doesn't want you on it," Mulvaney said wearily. He could barely look the detective in the eye. "Take my word for it, Frank." His voice was still quiet but this time it had an edge of threat to it. "If after ninety days you continue to mess around in this thing against my authority, the commissioner, who still retains his fondness for you, will find that fondness wearing thin."

"Meaning?" Mooney hovered over his desk glaring down at him. The chief of detectives didn't bat an eye.

"Meaning, butt out — or you're gonna find yourself out on the street thirteen months still shy of that full pension."

"You say he's been up here before?"

"That's right."

"How often?"

"I don't know. But you know how things sometimes come back to you. All of a sudden, like that. Things you think are gone forever."

"Sure. Like something happening today causing a lot of things that happened long ago to become suddenly all related. Like a chain of events. Something like that?"

"Yeah. Exactly. That's right. How nice you put it." The old man laughed lightly. A look of gratitude shone from his rheumy eyes. "That's exactly it. What you described. Excuse me. Good evening, Mr. Wexler." Mr. Carlucci doffed his cap to a portly gentleman in bold plaids just turning into the revolving doors. He smiled and resumed his conversation with the young man who said his name was Hoskins and that he was a reporter for a large newspaper in Houston.

"And I tell you something else, Mr. Hopkins — "

"Hoskins."

"Oh, that's right. Hoskins. I beg your pardon." Mr. Carlucci spoke with a lilting Neopolitan accent. In his green doorman's livery with its gold frogging and epaulets, he looked like a cross between a Stromboli fisherman and a Gilbert and Sullivan vice admiral. "I seen this guy before."

"Well, sure. That's what you've been telling me. You saw him standing out there across the street a couple of times. Right."

"Sure. More than a couple of times. That's right. But I don't mean just that. I mean, long before. I had a good look at this fellow across the way down there on the corner. I know him from somewhere. Don't ask me where. I just can't place it." Mr. Carlucci slapped his head hard, nearly dislodging his doorman's cap. It was his way of jarring loose his impacted memory.

A look of mounting curiosity bloomed in the young man's features. "How long ago?"

"Oh, way back. Way back, Mr. Hoskins."

"How long you been working as doorman here?"

"Forty years." A look of almost childlike pride suffused the old gentleman's face. "I come here forty years ago, last Sunday. They give me a big party, Mr. Rothstein."

"Mr. Rothstein?"

"Mr. Rothstein and his partners. The landlords here. They own the building. They own lotsa buildings in the area. Your finest addresses. All carriage trade. Eight sixty Fifth. Nine seventy-two Madison. Six sixty Park. I mean the best. Your top of the line. Fine gentleman, Mr. Rothstein. They give me a big party here. Champagne. Hors d'oeuvres."

"Forty years is a long time on one job," the young man remarked.

Mr. Carlucci glowed with satisfaction. "How old you think I am?"

"Fifty. Maybe, tops, fifty-five."

"I'm gonna be seventy in another two weeks."

"Seventy?" The young man stood back and reexamined the doorman in the bright warm lights from the lobby. "You don't look any seventy to me."

The doorman flung his chest out and pounded it, attesting to his general soundness. In the next moment he grew suddenly downcast. "Gonna have to retire now. Law says you gotta retire at seventy."

"Did you tell any of this to the police?" the reporter asked, sensing that Mr. Carlucci was on the verge of one of those dizzying flights of circumlocution.

Mr. Carlucci appeared puzzled. "What?"

"That this guy who was here the other night had been around here before, and that you think you recognize him from maybe someplace else? You didn't say that to the police?"

The old man shook his head vehemently. "No — that's just it. Like I told you. None of this ever hit me till maybe two, three days after the police come up here to question me. They questioned me maybe two, three hours."

"And you never called them back to tell them?"

"No. Should I?" Mr. Carlucci was suddenly alarmed as if told he'd violated the law. "I mean, it all come back to me in a kind of flash days later. But I never thought to call the police 'cause I still can't even place the guy. You don't think they could give me trouble?"

"No." Mr. Hoskins waved the possibility aside, banishing all of the old man's anxieties in a trice. "Forget it." But even as he spoke, something shrewd and a bit calculating hardened the young man's dark pleasant features. "As a matter of fact, I'd really appreciate it if you didn't mention any of this to anyone. Like, I mean, other reporters . . . By the way, any other reporters come up here to interview you?"

"Sure. Sure." Mr. Carlucci's eyes widened. "Day after the incident I had four fellas up here, all standing in line just waiting to talk to me. Poor Miss Bender." His eyes suddenly glistened. "I can still hardly believe it. What a lovely young lady. Always smiling. Always laughing. Always give me a hundred dollars at Christmas. Fifty bucks when I go on vacation . . . Didn't you read none of them articles?"

"Course I read them. That's how I got your name and address." The reporter seemed irritated by even the mere suggestion that he hadn't. "But you're certain you never told these reporters or the police anything about recognizing this guy or anything?"

"Nothing. Like I told you, I didn't remember it then. Just like I told my missus the other night — this guy's face keeps flashing through my head. I know him from somewhere."

Mr. Hoskins put his arm around the old man's shoulders and looked around to make certain they were not being overheard. "This could be a big opportunity for me." The reporter's eyes opened wide to emphasize the point. "Very big."

"Sure. Sure." Mr. Carlucci lowered his voice to demonstrate that he grasped the importance of the point.

"You understand?"

"Sure, I understand."

"I mean, what you told me here tonight. This could be a big break. Like a scoop for me over all the other papers."

Mr. Carlucci's excited laugh conveyed an air of conspiracy. He winked. "Sure. This could be your big break. I like to see a young fellow like you get ahead."

"I've got an idea."

"Sure, sure."

"If you say this guy comes back here from time to time . . ."

"That's right." Mr. Carlucci's head nodded with each affirmation.

"How often would you say he comes back?"

"Oh, jeez." The old man drew back, somewhat astonished by the question. "I couldn't say."

Catching the disappointment in the reporter's eye, he grew apologetic. "Nothing regular, see? Just from time to time, is all. He'll just come and stand out there across the street, or sit on the bench, is all."

"You're sure it's the same guy?"

"Oh, sure. Like I tell you, I know the face from somewhere. That drawing the police artist made in the papers: that don't look nothing like him. The artist come up here to talk to me." Mr. Carlucci's chest was swelling again. "I give him the whole description. Perfect." He threw his hands up in a gesture of Italian futility. "It don't look nothing like him, what he drew. How could they go so wrong?"

The reporter's youthful geniality appeared to slip and now he bore down. "This guy . . . does he always come at night, or does he sometimes come in the day?"

"Always dusk," Mr. Carlucci fired back without hesitation. Smiling, he held both hands up to the sky as if to indicate the precise conditions of light. "And he'll sit over there on that bench, third from the corner. Or else he'll stand right out at the curb and stare up at the building. Reason I notice him is 'cause Mr. Rothstein always tells us to be on the watch for people like that — strangers who look like they don't belong here, like they're casing the joint."

"Look," said Mr. Hoskins. "If I were to come up here a couple of nights a week for the next month or so, and just sort of sit out there myself . . ."

"Yeah?"

"Like I was taking the air."

"Sure." Mr. Carlucci winked as he caught the drift of the young man's plan.

"What I need from you . . ."

"Yeah?"

"Is that you just pay no attention to me. Ignore me. Right?"

"Right," said the old man with great enthusiasm, but it was clear that he was slightly puzzled.

"Unless he shows up."

The light went on in the old gentleman's eyes. "Okay. Sure. Now I get you."

"If I'm just sitting there and he shows up, just step off the curb, and wave your hand and whistle sort of like you're hailing a cab for someone. Like that." The reporter did it several times just to show him.

"Sure." Mr. Carlucci giggled gleefully. "Sure."

"Are we in business? Do we have a deal?"

"Sure. You bet, young fella. I wanna get this creep bad as you. Poor Miss Bender. Lovely young lady. Give me a hundred dollars every Christmas." His voice trailed off in a little whine, but Hoskins headed him off before the lamentations could begin anew.

"And not a word to any reporters or the police."

"Not a word."

"This is our little secret." Hoskins pumped the old man's rough, red paw. "I'll be back up here tomorrow around dusk."

"That's right, Mr. Hopkins. You bet. Around dusk."

"Now I want to take a walk through the park along the

same path that young woman walked that evening. See if I can learn something. We're gonna nail this guy, Mr. Carlucci. You and me . . ."

"Oh, I wanna get that son of a bitch, you'll pardon the expression."

"I understand what you're saying. Believe me, I feel that way too. I've got to go now," the young man said and pointed across the brightly lit, heavily trafficked avenue. "You say she walked the dog right through that entrance there?"

"That's right. Right through those two stone columns and started north."

"Okay." Hoskins patted the old man's arm. "Here I go."

The young man started off into the crowded, dazzling night.

"Carlucci," the old man shouted after him. "You remember how to spell it?"

Long after the reporter had left, Mr. Carlucci wondered about him. Something about the young man troubled him — troubled him to the point of distraction. He wondered why in heaven's name a nice-looking young fellow like that, a reporter and all that for a big-time city newspaper, couldn't spend some money and get his teeth fixed.

Warren Mars moved into the darkness of the park where a few joggers and dog walkers straggled home through the quickening shadows. Still smoldering at the impertinence of this person who had the temerity to imitate him, he now felt a sudden elation at what he'd learned from the doorman. His feet trod north up the winding bench-lined walk, along the same fateful course taken by Caroline Bender nearly a week before.

Several days earlier when the TV people and all the press had proclaimed that the infamous Dancer had struck again in Central Park, Warren had flown into a rage.

Oddly enough, he was not half as troubled by the fact

that he'd been wrongly accused of crimes he hadn't committed as he was by the idea that someone out there was imitating him. That infuriated him. He felt personally violated as if someone, some perfect stranger out there, was attempting to steal his identity.

News of the murder of the Bender girl in Central Park, found naked and crammed down a sewer and attributed to him, caused in him something akin to self-righteous indignation. Someone had copied his method in an attempt to cash in on all of the celebrity he'd achieved over the past year or so. Why the police couldn't see how vastly different these crimes were in both style and execution was a mystery to him. An infuriating mystery at that.

He, Warren, had never sexually abused anyone for mere fleshly gratification. The "sexy" stuff for him was secondary. Strictly kid stuff. For him it was the lucre, the potential for sizable financial gain that drew him to the hunt. When he'd done the Bailey girl, he'd taken jewelry and cash. He was a professional. He could never be deflected by kid's play. This stranger, this impostor, never took anything from his victims. He was in it just for kicks. There was no art to what he did, no premeditation prior to execution. All of his actions had a spur-of-the-moment quality about them, sheer impulse. They were artless, whereas he, Warren, gave a good deal of attention and planning to the task at hand. Everything was worked out in advance to the last detail. That's why he'd succeeded so stunningly. He liked to be called the Shadow Dancer. That was poetic and a bit creepy. But this *poseur*, this cheap impostor, grieved him greatly.

He'd brooded about the situation for days after the discovery of the girl in the sewer. And the more he brooded, the more he became convinced that this stranger, whoever he was, had to be eliminated. And if the police were going to be so inept and dim-witted in the matter, he'd have to go out and do something about it himself.

After watching the newscasts and reading all the coverage in the press, the idea of going up to see the doorman struck him as the most obvious way to begin. The thought of getting into a suit and a tie and passing himself off as a reporter from an out-of-town newspaper seemed to him a natural.

It had gone well. Better than he'd hoped for. But he'd never expected the bonus at the end when the old man confided to him that this stranger, this other Shadow Dancer, had visited that same spot, had sat on that very same bench across the way from 860 Fifth Avenue on not one but on frequent occasions. Well, if that were so, wouldn't it also follow that he'd return there again? Obviously, it was some sort of compulsion that drew him there. Some need to return to the same spot again and again. The fact, too, that the old man not only recognized this stranger, but felt certain that he knew him from some earlier period, was luck beyond his wildest dreams.

Striding north up the winding, tree-lined path, Warren still felt anger, but along with that, an exhilaration — the sort of exhilaration hunters feel when they sense they're closing in on their quarry.

Walking that fateful path at dusk now in the park, Warren Mars imagined himself to be that blond stranger. Moving perhaps in that person's very steps, he trod lightly through the heat-muffled darkness of an August night, pursuing some fleeting evanescent shape that receded seductively into the shadows before him. So vivid, in fact, was his impression of the event that it seemed to him that he was now about to reenact it himself.

The small dog straining on the leash tugged the girl forward. Each time the dog would stop to sniff a place, then relieve himself, Warren, too, would stop, and hang back, breathless in the shadows.

Warren could feel excitement rise between his legs as he trod north up the park path, now virtually deserted. He tried to imagine where this stranger first accosted the girl. How did he do it? Did he attempt to strike up casual conversation to disarm her, to overcome whatever apprehension she might have felt at the approach of a stranger on a deserted park path at night? Or, did he merely come up behind her and take her brutally, dragging her off into the bushes, forcibly tearing her clothes from her, then ravishing her as the yapping little terrier, which had broken free during the attack, darted wildly about under the lampposts, dragging his leash behind him?

Warren envisioned all of that. He'd even selected what he thought to be the most likely site for the assault: a small knoll at the top of a shallow acclivity, all bowered in dogwood and twice-blooming crab.

At a certain point he saw with brilliant clarity the two figures suddenly merge in the dark. Instantly, he himself became one of those figures. There was a small startled scream — not a scream actually, but the beginning of it — quickly muffled — and then the stricken sounds of one living thing succumbing to another, while the bushes in the area of the attack swayed and rattled violently back and forth as if driven by wind. Then all was still. There was the awful panicky flutter of wings, and then resignation.

Long before Warren was old enough to know or understand the strange, dark tidal pull between man and woman, he'd watched a cat stalk a bird, capture it, and proceed to devour it while the creature still lived. Within his own unwritten biography, he marked that down as the first time he'd experienced sexual excitement. This was not unlike the bird taken by the cat.

Looking up suddenly, Warren found himself farther north in the park than he would have guessed, moving between a thickly wooded grove, not far from the Wollman Memorial Rink. There, just ahead of him, with blades of grass thrusting up along its rusted rectangular sides, he saw in the pale orange glow from a lamppost the lid of a drain cover atop a sewer. It was odd, he thought, how he knew precisely the spot, as if something had almost guided him there.

FIFTEEN

FIVE O'CLOCK WAS "DEAD" TIME AT THE BAL-
loon, undoubtedly why Mooney liked it so much. It was
the hour when the luncheon rush was over and the staff
had its feet up and was taking a breather before the
onslaught of supper.

He pretty much had the place to himself then. He
could sit there in the cool, air-conditioned quiet, have
a couple of stingers, and gab to his heart's content with
Patsy. Outside, it was pouring — a drenching rain at
the finish of a hazy, steamy, mostly miserable day. Great
claps of summer thunder hammered overhead, making
the dry, cozy peace of the bar all the more enjoyable.
Fritzi hadn't arrived yet and wouldn't for at least another hour, just before dinner when she'd come to make
her final inspection before the charge of the famished
hordes.

Patsy and Mooney talked mainly about the track and
the Mets. Mooney said nothing about his encounter that
afternoon with Mulvaney, but there it was all the same,
gnawing away at his intestinal lining.

For some time after he'd left Mulvaney's office, he'd
told himself he didn't care. He was just biding his time
for a while until he could cut free of the force. So what
did it matter what they took from him or, for that matter,
what they reassigned him to? And as for the Dancer,
he'd never wanted the job in the first place. So why
all the fuss? What was he sitting around for, hiding in

this dark, cool place, sipping stingers and licking his wounds?

"They say Angel Pie's a cinch for the Acorn," Patsy said. He was polishing glasses at the end of the bar.

"That's dumb," Mooney grumbled. "Strictly for chalk players. Never listen to touts. Make your own moves. Angel Pie's a lox." Mooney looked up from the bottom of his stinger, surprised to see Patsy staring at him with a funny expression on his face.

"What the hell are you shouting at me for?" he said. "All I said was Angel Pie's looking good for the Acorn."

The bartender's reaction took him by surprise. He hadn't been conscious of the fact that all the while he'd been gabbing with him, his voice was growing louder and his face redder.

"Sorry, Pats. I guess I got carried away."

"Must've had a sensational day."

"I guess it wasn't what you'd call tops. Gimme another of these." He held up his glass.

"Ah, now look, Frank," Patsy protested. "You know what Fritzi — "

"Never mind what Fritzi says. If I want another stinger, I'm gonna have it."

The phone rang at the end of the bar.

Patsy picked it up. Mooney could hear him talking low, watching him all the while. "Hey, Frank, it's for you. Pickering."

"What the hell does he want?" Patsy slid the phone down the bar in front of his stool.

"Hello, Frank?" The high, fluttery voice came over the lines. "Listen, I'm up here in . . ."

The words got lost in a lot of buzzing and hissing through the wires.

"Speak up, will you, Rollo. I can't hear a word — "

"I'm up here in Dyckmans."

"Where?" Mooney cupped his ear, trying to hear better.

"Dyckmans. Near the Cloisters."

"What the hell you doing up there?" Mooney asked.

"I'm in a radio/ TV repair shop." Pickering sounded a little out of breath. "Listen, we located one of the pieces taken on the Torrelson job. We got the amplifier."

"Yeah?"

"Sansui four hundred."

"The 'seventy-eight model with the twin speakers?"

"That's what the repairman here tells me."

"How'd you find it?" Mooney asked, feeling the dull throb starting up again at the back of his head.

"Some guy brought it in to be repaired. The owner of the shop remembered reading in the papers that this was the same model amplifier that was grabbed on the Torrelson job. They get a lot of fenced goods passing through here and so they're always on the lookout for what don't look kosher. He called the precinct house and they referred him to me."

"Who brought it in?"

"I got the ticket right here. Guy's name is Berrida. Hector Berrida. Three twenty-four West One Hundred Eighty-first."

"Washington Heights."

"Right. I called Torrelson," Pickering rattled on. "I described the set. The color and model numbers. He said it sounded like his. It even has a big nick in the side that his set had."

Mooney's brain started to whirl. "Let's go see Berrida."

"How long will it take you to get up here?"

"Gimme a half hour. That's if I can grab a cab and the rain hasn't flooded the Drive. I'll meet you there."

"Where? Here or Berrida's?"

"Berrida's."

"Swell. That was three twenty-four West — "

"One Hundred Eighty-first," Mooney said. "I scribbled it here on my napkin. So long."

"Hey, Frank . . . wait a minute. Should I call Berrida and tell him we're coming over?"

"No. Better we just walk in on him. You get over there now and wait for me out front."

Mooney slammed the phone down, feeling something like the first jolt of exhilaration he'd felt all day. "Hey, Patsy. Gotta run. Can you call me a cab, real quick?"

Just as he was whirling out the front door, Fritzi was whirling in, backing into the revolving door while closing her umbrella. They waved at each other through the dividing glass. She didn't go into the bar but kept turning and spun back out onto the street. "Where you going?"

"Washington Heights. Gotta run," Mooney said, diving through the downpour to a cab waiting there in the steam rising at the curb.

"You coming back for supper?"

"I don't know. Don't wait for me. I'll talk to you later."

Mooney slammed the door. The cab jolted. A wall of rain from a passing truck hit the windshield with a splat as they lurched off into 84th Street.

"Where did you get it, Hector?"

"I already told you, man. In the street. This guy — "

"He from around here?"

"No. I never seen him before. I already told you."

"What did he look like?"

They were standing in the turmoil of a cramped, low-ceilinged apartment smelling strongly of fish and wet laundry. The single window of the living room faced out on the brick wall of an inner court. The voices of children playing in the courtyard drifted up from below and from a window across the way came the throbbing beat of congas and timbales played on a hi-fi at a mind-numbing volume.

"What did he look like, Hector?"

Mr. Berrida paused. A slight, dark young man, his nervous eyes flashed back and forth from the two detectives to the brick wall looming gray and oppressive beyond the window. Responding to the barrage of questions, he grew increasingly agitated and spoke very fast.

"It's okay. You can tell us, Hector," Mooney coaxed gently. "Nothing's gonna happen to you."

Torn between instinctive fear of the police and the inviolable code of the streets, Mr. Berrida continued to stare out the window, his legs and arms moving, but no sound forthcoming from his mouth.

"Was this a white guy?" Pickering asked.

"Yeah. A white guy."

"How tall?"

Berrida answered by raising his hand to a level several inches above his head.

"Five nine, five ten," Mooney murmured and scribbled figures into his pad. "What else? Hair?"

"Dark," the young man whispered as if afraid to be overheard.

"Long or short?"

"Medium. You know. Wavy, like." His hands fluttered above his own darkly flamboyant locks.

"Like yours?" Mooney was beginning to exhibit impatience.

"Yeah. But shorter. You know."

"Yeah, sure. Were there any distinguishing marks?"

The concept of distinguishing marks appeared to baffle the young man.

"Scars. Disabilities. Anything unusual in his appearance?" Pickering attempted to clarify.

"You notice his teeth, Hector?" Mooney got right to the point. "Anything funny about his teeth?"

"Teeth. I didn't see no teeth, man."

"How come?"

"I didn't look."

"You say he was downstairs in the street?"

"That's right. Right out in front of the building. I come down and see a lot of people standing around this car. The trunk's open and there's a guy selling stuff out the back of it."

"What kind of stuff?"

"Electronic stuff. You know, man? Speakers, amplifiers, tape decks. That kind of stuff." As he spoke, the young man grew increasingly gloomy.

"Anyone else down there you know bought anything?"

Berrida put his hands up before him and started to back away. "Eh — man."

"Okay, okay, forget that," Mooney said. "Tell me about the car."

Berrida's large, dark eyes swerved wildly about the room.

"What kind of car was it? Can you describe it?"

"That car. Yeah, sure. That was a Mercedes, man."

Mooney and Pickering exchanged glances.

"What color Mercedes, Hector?"

"Green."

"What shade green? Light? Dark?"

"Dark. It was dark green."

"You didn't happen to see the plates or catch a number or two on it?" Pickering asked hopefully.

The young man laughed with a tinge of contempt. "See what plates? I'm down there checkin' the goods. I don't see no plates, man."

Mr. Berrida began to work himself up into a lather. "I mean, I guess maybe I saw them but I don't remember no numbers."

"Were they New York plates?"

Something in the question relieved his gloom. "I was standing right in back of the car, staring into the truck. Maybe I remember seeing the plates."

"You happen to notice where they came from?" Mooney remarked wearily.

"You mean like the state and all? No. I didn't see." He sensed their disappointment. "But I can tell you the color. Blue and white. They were blue and white."

"Blue on white or white on blue?" Pickering inquired.

"New York's blue on white."

Mr. Berrida closed his eyes in a conscious effort to

recall. "I think this was maybe blue on white," he said at last.

"You sure, Hector?"

"Yeah. Pretty sure," the young man said, but with sufficient hesitation to unnerve them.

"Connecticut is white on blue," Pickering said. "You're sure it wasn't white on blue?"

"Could've been pale yellow on blue," Mooney grumbled. "Jersey and California are pale yellow on blue. Anyone could make that mistake. Particularly at dusk." He turned back to the young man. "By any chance, you don't happen to know the year of that Mercedes?"

Mr. Berrida glowed with sudden, unaccountable joy. It was as if he'd been waiting for just that question. "It was a nineteen sixty-eight."

Mooney and Pickering exchanged glances.

"What model?"

"A two twenty."

Mooney frowned. "How can you be so sure?"

" 'Cause I asked the guy," Berrida proclaimed with huge pride.

"And he told you it was a 'sixty-eight Mercedes and that it was a two twenty?"

"I could see it was a two twenty for myself, man. It said so right on the trunk." Their skepticism baffled him. "What's wrong with that?"

"Nothing," Mooney said. "Nothing's wrong with that. You asked the guy and the guy told you it was a nineteen sixty-eight. What kind of condition was it in?"

"Great. But I mean this car was fantastic. New tires. Polished. All shiny like new."

"And it was a dark green?"

"Right. He just had it painted."

"Painted?" Mooney and Pickering both answered at once. The sound they made was like a yelp of pain.

"How do you know that?"

Berrida was still smiling. " 'Cause I asked the guy."

"And he told you?"

"Yeah. What's wrong with that? I mean, I'm interested in cars, man. I'm like a car freak. And that car I liked."

"You asked him if the car had just been painted?"

"No. I asked him how come a car nearly twenty years old looks so good."

"And he told you it was just painted?"

Berrida's smile wavered between pleasure and puzzlement. "Yeah."

"He didn't just happen to say what the color was before?"

The young man shook his head from side to side. "Coulda been any color, man. He didn't say."

"Or even the same color," Mooney added, recalling that the car spotted on the Torrelson job also happened to be green.

"Sure. Coulda been the same color." The young man grinned amiably. "Hey, look, you guys ain't gonna run me in or anything?"

Mooney flung an arm out as though swiping a fly. "No, no one's gonna run you in, but you did know these were stolen goods in back of the car."

"Oh, look, man. You don't know this place." Berrida glanced over his shoulder as though he were being watched. "Lots of guys drive into these streets. All times of the day and night. It's commerce, man. See? Simple as that. They pull in here with a van full of stuff. Nobody asks no questions. It's just commerce."

"Commerce," Mooney grumbled.

Outside, the rain had stopped but water continued to splash noisily from a drainpipe down into the courtyard below. There was a rumble of distant thunder moving off to the east.

The three men stood there, shifting their feet. The questions appeared to have run out.

Berrida smiled, flashing a gold tooth at them. "That it?"

Mooney scratched his ear slowly. "I guess so. Just one more thing." He pulled a sheet of paper from his inside pocket and carefully unfolded it. On it was the police artist's composite drawing of the face of at least one of the suspects, reconstructed from versions given by Cara Bailey and two survivors of his assaults. "This look anything like your guy in the green Mercedes?"

Mr. Berrida took the paper from Mooney, squinted down at it, and considered it for a moment or two. At last he shook his head. "No, man. This don't look nothin' like the guy."

"So what do we have now?" Mooney asked when they'd settled back in the squad car waiting below in the street.

"A 'sixty-eight Mercedes. Model two twenty. Green."

"Maybe green," Mooney grunted. "Maybe blue. Maybe pink. Maybe tan. Who knows?"

"I gotta hand it to you, Frank. Your hunch on the age of the car."

"So what? The list we got from the M.V.B. didn't have a single Mercedes that vintage, let alone green. So where are we exactly?"

The ignition turned over and the squad car wheeled slowly out from the curb. At the end of the block they turned right onto Amsterdam Avenue. Outside, in the teeming streets beyond the windows, Mooney's eyes caught the sullen, resentful expressions of pedestrians watching them as they rolled past.

"Could be one of two things," Mooney continued. "One, this car is either registered out of state; or two, and this is the worst possible scenario, it's stolen and unregistered, with stolen New York plates."

"The blue on white plates sort of make it sound like the second to me, Frank."

"If it's blue on white the way Berrida says, it sounds like it could be New York. If it's the other way around, it's Connecticut or also maybe a half dozen other states with the same color combination. Once a stolen alarm goes out on a car, it's in the computer. It's tricky getting it re-registered, but it can be done."

"A guy that changes the color of his car on a fairly regular basis could just as easily be stealing plates and changing them every few months, too."

Pickering had quickly picked up Mooney's line of reasoning. "Meaning, he uses the car on the job and keeps changing the physical appearance and the plates to foil identification."

"Doesn't that sound logical to you?"

They were silent as the car wheeled and bounced through the puddled ruts of the Harlem River Drive, then swung directly onto the FDR Drive.

"Soon as we get down to the station, let's have a check run on all out-of-state plates, colors blue on white. Let's also check the white on blue. Berrida didn't sound too sure exactly what he saw, but I think he was favoring New York. When you get that, let's ask for M.V.B. checks in all those states. See if they've got a registered 'sixty-eight Merc two twenty still running around loose out there, or if they've got a stolen report out on one."

"Green?"

"Any color," Mooney snapped. "I'll give you five-to-three odds what you got here is a stolen vehicle, unregistered with stolen plates. Guy's probably got a set of twenty different stolen plates, all different states, in the trunk."

Pickering whistled beneath his breath.

They pulled off the FDR Drive at the 49th Street exit and rolled up the ramp onto First Avenue. The streetlamps were on and early-evening strollers moved phantomlike through the stagnant mists of puddled streets.

"This color thing, Frank," Pickering fretted. "It still bothers me."

"I'm coming to that." Mooney clapped a mentholated cough drop between his lips. "The more I hear about this guy, the more it sounds like he's some kind of car nut. Not too many guys in his line of business will depend on a twenty-year-old antique, even if it is a Mercedes. He's more into the aesthetics and the image of the thing than its performance. Probably washes it twice a week, tune-ups and oil change every three months."

"And paint jobs . . ."

"I'm comin' to that." Mooney ground the cough drop noisily between his teeth. "Say he paints this car every couple of months. Probably right after he does a job. That's not aesthetics. That's self-preservation. It's dumb enough using the same car over and over again on each new job. Soon as the papers and the TV start shouting about a green getaway car, you can bet that little two twenty is on its way to the paint shop for a rinse and dye."

Pickering brooded awhile, staring out the window at the tawdry jitterbug of lights illuminating the West Forties. "Somehow I get the feeling you're about to ask me to do something distinctly unpleasant."

"You got it, pal."

"Like go through the Yellow Pages . . ."

"Bingo. Clairvoyant, you are. Go through the NYNEX. Check out every auto paint shop. Particularly those that specialize in custom jobs for expensive foreign automobiles. No schlock shops. Ask each of them if they've sprayed a 'sixty-eight Merc in the last couple of months and for who. And tell all of them if a green 'sixty-eight Merc should come in to be sprayed a different color, let us know immediately."

"This guy could be doing his own paint jobs, Frank. All it takes is a spray gun and a can of paint."

"And a lot of know-how not to mess up the chrome and the glass." Mooney waved the thought aside with an abrupt chopping motion of his hand. "No, our guy loves this baby too much to take a chance on messing her up himself."

The car moved west across 49th Street, nosing its way through the heavy theater-hour congestion. Between Ninth and Tenth Avenue, they pulled up at last to the old station house in the middle of the block.

"There are probably a couple of hundred auto body shops in the city, Frank."

"I've only got eighty-one days, pal," Mooney brooded. "Actually, now eighty. I can get us a few extra hands from Mulvaney. We'll split it up between us."

Getting out of the car, he turned and winked at Pickering, slumped there in the shadows. "Not a word of this 'sixty-eight Mercedes business to any of the buzzards upstairs."

SIXTEEN

"PARDON ME. IS THIS SEAT TAKEN?"

"No, it's — "

"Hello, Janine."

At first she didn't recognize him. He wore a suit and tie. His hair (that's what threw her) seemed somewhat shorter than usual. He might have been a junior trainee at a bank or at any one of a dozen or so of the big multinational corporations with headquarters in the area.

"Hello, Warren." She nearly choked trying to say it, then smiled queasily up at him. He was smiling at her, carrying a plastic tray on which sat a plate mounded with salad. In addition, there was a roll and a glass of milk.

They were in a salad bar over in the East Sixties, one of those places where you help yourself to as much salad as you like, choose from any one of a dozen dressings, and grab a seat at any one of the tables available.

"I thought I recognized you," he said. "What are you doing here?"

"I work around the corner."

"Oh, you do?"

His reply was full of surprise, as if he hadn't really known. But, of course, she'd thought she'd seen him on at least three occasions, hovering about outside at six P.M., when she left the building where she worked.

"Gosh, you look great."

"You, too." She smiled dismally, conscious of the tremor in her voice. "What brings you around here?"

"I'm looking for a job."

"A job?" She nearly laughed aloud, then quickly covered her mirth, assuming a more serious air. But it was too late, he'd caught the smile. Something like a frown crossed his face, then he laughed. "I know what you're thinking, Janine. That asshole, looking for a job. A real job. When did he ever work? Right?"

She smiled, wary of all that disarming good humor and self-effacement. "Right."

"Well, you're absolutely right," he said, applying a large dollop of blue cheese dressing to his salad. "Hey, isn't this place great? You eat here a lot?"

He watched her closely, scrutinizing her every mood. "Truth is," he went on cheerily, forking salad into his mouth. "I've changed quite a bit since I saw you last, Janine. Since when you and me were running together. You get my letter?"

"I got it." She nodded uneasily.

He chewed his salad, watching her expression carefully for some indication of what she might be thinking. "Truth is" — he lowered his voice — "I haven't stopped thinking about you for two years, Janine."

"Look, Warren — "

"You and I go back a long ways, Janine. There's a lot of history between us." He smiled. It nearly made her sick to see that smile, so bright, so loving, so ineffably innocent and childlike. So very lethal. She knew that smile all too well. As a child he'd used it to get things he wanted, to disarm unwitting strangers, while she snatched their purses or bags or whatever. She used to love his smile when she was a child because it took away the fear that was with her day and night. He was like a big brother. He made her feel wanted and special and safe. When she was a child, she would do anything for the reward of that smile. But now she distrusted it. It frightened her and made her want to get up and run.

"Warren," she started tentatively, weighing the wisdom of saying what she was about to say. "Warren, tell me I'm not crazy. I have seen you around here, haven't

I? I mean, like a couple of times over the past few months. Right?"

At first he feigned surprise, then appeared to think better of it. He laughed aloud with his mouth filled with salad. "I guess I've been up around this way a few times."

"Looking for me?"

A look of unaccustomed soberness brought his chewing to a sudden stop. "Right. To see you."

The sound of it and the look of him just then made her blood freeze. All of that coyness and fake laughter just dropped from him and he was deadly serious. "I been sick to see you again, Janine."

She had a pretty good idea by then where all of this was leading.

"We should've never busted up," he went on.

She started to shake her head back and forth. "Warren . . ."

"I made a mess of things, Janine. I did some really dumb things. If I'd still been with you, I'd never —"

"Don't say that, Warren. We did plenty of dumb things when we were together."

"No," he said, almost physically pushing back with his hands the inexorable logic of her words. "No."

"We had to split." She heard her voice pleading far away outside herself. "If we hadn't, God knows where we'd be today. In jail or dead." She had a strong impulse to stand up and walk away quickly and never look back. Instead, she sat there glued to her seat, legs leaden, heart banging wildly in her chest, watching him chew his salad while he considered all of her arguments. He wiped a smear of dressing from the corner of his mouth. "Janine, I've been thinking about us. I've been thinking real hard about us." He wadded the napkin in his fist with such sudden force it made her flinch. "I wanna leave Suki."

The full significance of that disclosure came to her slowly, but at last terrifyingly. It was not merely the fact that the old woman represented the only family, hence stability and restraint, in his life; it was more surely the girl's realization that he had reached some juncture in his life where his needs now compelled him to abandon one form of security for another. It was the latter part that froze her blood. There was little doubt she was the alternative he'd chosen.

"Why?" she asked in a dry, slightly choked whisper.

" 'Cause," he said, and his manner was so frighteningly plausible. " 'Cause I don't want to do what I've been doing anymore. I want something normal now." He said the word as though it were a magic incantation. "Suki's crazy. You know that as well as me, Janine. And she makes me crazy. I do crazy things cause of Suki. I mean, she doesn't tell me to do them, but I know she wants me to, and so I just do them. Then after I do them, I can't remember why I did them. It's like she controls me in some way. Just pushes buttons someplace and I start to move. That scares me, Janine. That scares me a lot."

"But why? What's Suki got to do with what you do?"

His brow furrowed and his eyes rose ceilingward, evading hers. He gave the impression that he was reaching far out for something well beyond him. " 'Cause all my life, ever since I was a kid and came to live with Suki, she's always made me feel I owe her something. Like I've got some big debt to pay back. And the only thing Suki wants from me is more stuff. Get my meaning?"

"More stuff she can sell for cash?"

"You got it." He winked slyly at her. "Suki's bad for me, honey." He hadn't called her that in years. He laid his hand, which was cold now, across the back of hers. Instinctively, she recoiled, but still she was afraid to withdraw it. "Now I want to leave her and change my life."

The chill of his hand and the sudden sickening intimacy of his manner revolted her. An image of her past life with Warren flashed in her head. A seedy little room with an unmade bed, an electric coil to cook over, living out of a battered suitcase in some rat-infested, junkie-ridden, single-occupancy dive on the Upper West Side. Bare lightbulbs hanging from extension cords drooping like vines from ceiling outlets. Corridors you wouldn't care to walk down at any time of the day or night. Licey beds, milk containers on a window ledge, flyblown toilets with cracked, leaky commodes ringed with the fecal stains of former occupants. And then the police. Life with Warren meant living in shadows, constantly hiding from the police.

She'd had enough of that. She'd come too far, pulled too hard, sweated blood to leave all that behind and bring some semblance of normalcy to her days. Now suddenly a whole new way of life — not grand by any means, but better by far than anything she'd ever known or even dared to hope for — was almost within her grasp.

"Warren." She struggled to control her voice. "If you're thinking about wanting to move back with me . . ."

He nodded, smiling with almost irrepressible delight.

"Warren, I've got to tell you something."

"I know," he said, still holding her hand. "I've seen him come out of your apartment house."

A fist closed over her heart. But of course he would know where she lived and with whom. He would know everything down to the last detail. "Mickey?"

"Mickey Mancuso. Isn't that his name?" His smile had an edge of triumph to it. She knew it was intended not only to impress her with his cleverness, but to frighten her as well.

"I want to tell you something, Janine. I want you to know I don't blame you. I don't hold a thing against you. Not a bit. We'd split. You were alone. All fair and square. Perfectly natural you'd look around for someone else. But now, honey, I want you to —"

"Warren, please."

" — drop him."

Her jaw fell and she sat there, watching him while he

resumed chewing his salad. "Warren . . ." She could barely get the name out.

"Drop him, Janine," Warren repeated, the smile more angelic than ever. "Tell him it's over now. Done. Finished. Tell him to go."

"Warren . . ."

"You do as I tell you, Janine."

"Warren . . ."

He started to rise.

"Warren. Wait a minute, for Chrissake." She tried to pull him back down in his seat. "Warren. Mickey and I are engaged."

The smile never wavered, but something like a cloud passed across his eyes. It passed quickly, but she was certain she saw there that vulnerable, hurt look she recalled so well from their stormy, wayward past; a clear echo of the same expression he bore as a seven-year-old street arab.

It was gone as quickly as it had come, and there was the smile again, beaming and replete with love. So fast had it shifted that for a moment she thought she'd merely imagined the other.

"Like I say, Janine," he went on. "I'm not angry about any of that. I'm willing to forgive and forget."

"Forgive?" she gasped. "We're getting married Christmas."

"No harm done. Water under the bridge. You just get rid of him now. See?" He was still smiling at her. " 'Cause if you don't, I'm gonna have to do something about it myself."

She sat there long after he'd gone, staring at the tray of salad he'd been eating. Lettuce leaves and bits of carrots and celery were strewn all about the plate and off it, as if some small, wild creature had pastured there.

She was numb. Her mind whirled. The quiet din of people eating about her magnified to a deafening roar. None of what had happened seemed real. It had an air of something dreamlike, from which she had just awakened, confused and unsettled. Where he'd sat, some aura of that smile still persisted in midair above the place; that oddly disturbing smile she had been so fond of as a child. Now it struck her as furtive and sly, as if all kinds of nasty thoughts were going on behind it.

For a woman well into her sixth decade of life, Suki Klink retained remarkable powers of physical dexterity. When she had a mind to, she could move fast. Impelled by instinct, keen as a famished alley cat, she made straight for the little eyrie planted beneath the glass cupola at the top of the house.

Warren was away now, presumably off on one of his little "jaunts," and the need had come urgently over her to have a look about upstairs. Periodically, she did this when he went off and was not expected back for some time. Without closely examining her motives for these periodic searches, she liked to think of them as intelligence-gathering missions. Devoted to him as she was, with a loose cannon like Warren lurching about in one's life, it behooved her to know precisely where he was and what he was about at all times.

She moved now like a small cyclone through the little cupola room at the top of the stairs. With her multitudinous flowing skirts ballooning out behind her, she gave the appearance of being in flight, and while the frantic action of her search appeared to wreak havoc, when she'd finished ransacking a specific area, it was as if nothing, save possibly the most gentle breeze, had ever stirred there.

She tore blankets back, poked beneath mattresses, ran her stubby, grime-streaked fingers along the springs, rifled through the closets and drawers, all with the grim single-mindedness of a hungry ferret.

It was in the ceiling light fixture that she found it. She had not been looking for anything specifically. It was only an instinct, sharp and palpable as a tooth pain, that had informed her that if she looked, she would find something. Instinct in a creature of Suki's somewhat unorthodox lifestyle was an instrument honed to the sharpness of a razor. Once again that instinct had not misled her. It was a small flannel sack you closed and opened with a drawstring. The name of a Forty-seventh Street jewelry shop had been stenciled on it in flowing white cursive.

She tugged the string, slowly pulling it open, tipping it, and letting the contents tumble out into her slightly palsied palm. Gems and pretty baubles held little place in the old lady's scheme of things. It was only what they could be converted to on the open market that earned her true esteem.

Here were clasps and pins, an old cameo brooch rimmed in eighteen-carat gold, along with a rather good Rolex watch apparently in working condition. There was, in addition, a silver pendant with gold putti encircled with baguettes. It was an unusual piece, ornate and fussy, of Italian design. Quite distinctive in its way.

Squinting, she held the pendant up to the sunlight streaming through the cupola glass. Where it struck the baguettes, it broke into prismatic bands of color flashing behind her on the white plaster walls.

"Souvenirs he's got for himself," she murmured while her crooked fingers lifted the pendant and rotated it slowly in the shaft of sunlight, making it flash and sparkle like some living thing. "Souvenirs of all his merry pranks." She laughed softly to herself, but even a creature such as Suki, so inured to the darker side of things, experienced a vague shudder of distaste, thinking of the fate of the former owners of all those glittering little bits of glass fanned out in her palm.

Squeamishness of that sort was generally not long-lived in Suki. She could always rationalize crime, even brutal crime, in terms of some vague, retributive social theory. Everyone had to live, didn't they? What she couldn't dispel quite so easily was the unpleasant aware-ness, growing stronger each day, that Warren was holding out on her, that he was gathering riches all the time, cadging it away and not counting her in for her share. If he had a little sack here, why not in other places as well?

In the past she had only asked her fair share of things. That had been roughly fifty percent. When Warren was a small child and just starting out, it was more like a hundred percent. But that was when he was a mere acolyte, serving his internship at her feet. Then he was still small enough to push around. As he grew older, more wily and adept, and the takes grew more sizable, she'd naturally expected her percentage to drop as the value of his booty increased.

But now it had become increasingly clear that Warren had been cultivating his own garden, picking up riches here and there and storing them like a squirrel preparing for a shift in seasons. What was Warren's shift of seasons to be? Her tawny cat's eyes narrowed to thin slits that sank into the quivering roses in her knobby cheeks. It made her appear like a gypsy before her crystal ball, attempting to pierce the veil of the future.

What she saw there was disquieting. All of his recent talk about "clearing out" she'd rashly discounted. But now with tangible evidence glittering in her palm suggesting that he might be piling up wealth against just such a day, she was forced to reconsider the situation.

He'd been strange over the past several months. There was no denying that. He was not his usual self. Restlessness and dissatisfaction were his daily moods. There was about him the sense of a chapter coming to a close while he waited for another to begin. She knew exactly where she'd figured in the former chapter but had no idea where she fit in the one to come. The possibility that she might not fit in at all had not occurred to her.

Suki had grown so accustomed to Warren's presence over the years that life without him seemed too unlikely a thought to even entertain. They were all the family either of them had. Whatever their life together was, they were at least a unit — a symbiosis of need and circumstance, each nourishing the other. Despite all of Warren's tantrums and threats, she could never permit that to change.

She chuckled softly to herself, replacing the little sack of jewelry in the ceiling fixture. Setting the room back in perfect order, she assured herself that nothing would change. Nothing could ever alter the condition of their lives together, she told herself. But still, far away at the distant rim of her consciousness, something stirred, some faint alteration of light, a hint of something unwanted and unsavory approaching them with no total shape as yet to define it.

When she left the small room in the attic that morning and locked the door behind her, she was a bit unnerved.

"Don't tell me you're getting up again."

"I am."

"Jesus. You've been up and down five times in the last hour."

"I can't sleep."

"Are you sick?"

"I'm fine."

She listened to him lying there in the dark for a while, quiet, as if he'd exhausted their talk. Shortly, he grunted, rolled over, and proceeded to snore.

"Well, I'm not fine," she said. She waited for him to respond. When nothing came, she said it again, but this time louder. "I'm not fine."

He rolled back over, sat halfway up, and peered at her in the dark.

"I'm not fine, Mickey. I'm sick. I'm sick to my stomach."

"Must've been the sausage in the linguini," he murmured drowsily. "Wait a minute. I'll get you an Alka-Seltzer."

He started out of bed but she pulled him back. "I don't need no Alka-Seltzer, Mickey. It's not my stomach. My stomach's fine. It's something else."

She said it with just the right note of portentousness. She felt him turn again in the dark and peer at her. Then the light switched on.

"It's him," she said, looking directly at him.

"It's who?"

"It's him. Warren. The one I told you about."

"Oh, the creep. What about him?"

Her mouth was dry. She felt her jaws moving ponderously, unanchored and uncontrolled, lifting up and down with no sound coming from them. Then came the tears bursting from her eyes, coursing down her cheeks, followed next by the sobs — deep, inconsolable rales that conveyed a sense of profound distress.

He pulled her roughly to him, smothering her face in the coarse cotton of his pajama top. "Hey, what is this? If that guy's done anything . . ."

"I don't want you to do nothing, Mickey." Her fingers fluttered nervously at the buttonholes of his pajama top. "It's nothing he did, see. It's more like what he said."

Then it all came out, bursting from her as though she were regurgitating something. It came in fragments and snatches, seemingly incoherent and disconnected. Meaning only emerged from it toward the very end.

"Hey, wait. Now wait. Just a minute." With his hands he tried physically to slow her tirade. "You're telling me he said you gotta leave me."

The jaws worked fitfully. "That's right." The words emerged at last, followed by another volley of sobs.

"Shhh," he tried to subdue the awful spasms, placing a hand over her mouth. "For Chrissake — shhh. The neighbors'll think I'm whaling the hell out of you."

"Mickey — I'm scared."

"Where is this Warren guy? Tell me. I'll cream him."

She tried to push him back into bed. "No, no. I don't want you going near him. He's crazy."

"I know he's crazy. That's why I'm gonna twist his head off. He didn't touch you, did he?"

"No. I told you he didn't."

"Where does he live?"

She flung her hands up in the air. "I don't know." Another high, keening wail, the sound of pure fright, tore from her. "Somewhere way downtown. I don't know. He lives with this old lady."

"His mother? He lives with his mother?"

"No. Some old bag lady. She raised him. She's crazy, too. The both of them are loons. Right around the bend. I met her once in Grand Central Station. You can't believe what she is."

"You ever been to her place?"

"Never." She was annoyed by the implication. "She doesn't like him to bring anyone around. Particularly girls. So he doesn't. I think he's ashamed to bring friends anyway. I'm telling you, it's crazy."

He thought about it while she watched him, sniffling and fretting. At last he spoke: "I tell you what we're gonna do."

Cold terror stamped her face. "I'm not going to the police, Mickey. I'm not gonna start with that."

"Who said anything about the police?"

"He's crazy. If he ever heard I went to the police . . ."

"Forget about the police," he snapped angrily. "This guy is just blowing hard."

"No, no. This is no bluff. Believe me. When he says — "

"From now on you don't leave or return here alone. I'm gonna take you to work in the morning and I'm gonna bring you back home at night. I'm gonna meet you for lunch at noon. We'll see about this Warren. We'll see if he takes a hint. 'Cause if he don't, I'm gonna cream him."

He brought his palm down flat on the night table with a sharp crack. She lay trembling against him, whimpering into his pajama top.

"Mickey, promise me you won't go near him. You don't know him the way I know him. He's not like anyone else you know. He's nuts. He believes in demons and devils. He reads all kind of crazy stuff on things like magic and numbers. He believes he can tell the future by numbers. He's done stuff . . ." She jammed the knuckle of her fist into her mouth and bit down hard to keep from starting to sob again. "He's done stuff . . . I mean, all kinds of stuff. Stuff you wouldn't believe. I can't tell you. Just don't you go near him, Mickey. Now, I'm telling you. He's dangerous. And he's watching us. He knows this house and where I work. He knows my telephone number at work. He's already called me there."

"He called you there?"

"I'm telling you."

"How did he get the number?"

"I don't know," she moaned. "I don't know. Probably just followed me to the office one morning. Watched me get on the elevator. He knows you, too, Mickey. He knew your name. Don't ask me how. He snoops around. He has his way of finding things out."

"When he calls you, what does he say?"

"Nothing. I just hear him breathing over the phone. I know it's him. He does it to scare me."

"To scare you?" A shrewd smile creased the young man's features. He reached up and turned off the light. "Okay, Janine. You can forget about Warren now. Leave Warren to me."

She was up again at once, pleading with him in the darkness. The lights from the street below pierced through the louvered blinds of the tiny bedroom, throwing bars of vivid white against the walls.

"Mickey, you promised me. You promised."

"I know what I promised." The young man spoke quietly, but with a note of grim resolve in his voice. "I'm not gonna go out lookin' for trouble. But if he comes sucking around here lookin' to bother you, I'm gonna twist his head off."

"Well, our friend Berrida really picked a doozie for a color combination. In all, there are eighteen states with a combo of blue and white."

"Blue on white or white on blue?"

"Both combined."

A weary sigh issued from somewhere deep inside Mooney. "Okay," he growled. "Better start with the blue on white since I think that's what Berrida was leaning toward."

"Blue on white. Okay. Got a pencil?"

"Yeah. Shoot."

"License plates. Blue letters on a white field: South Carolina. Illinois. Tennessee. Alabama. Ohio. Virginia. Kentucky. West Virginia. Georgia. Both Montana and Mississippi are blue on white with red trim. Minnesota is dark blue on a pale gray that reads almost white. And then, of course, there's yours truly, the Empire State, New York."

"Those are all the blue on white?"

"Right."

"Okay. Now give me all the white on blue. Just for the record."

"Right." Pickering attempted a feint at enthusiasm. "License plates. White letters on a blue field: That'd be Connecticut. Nevada. Kansas. Rhode Island. Both Jersey and California are a pale yellow on blue, which might easily be confused for white in a poor light."

"Such as dusk. We already figured that."

Pickering nodded. "Right. We already figured that."

"Is that it?" Mooney's eyes ranged up and down the list. "That's it, Frank."

"Okay. Send out a general all-points to the M.V.B.s for every one of those states. Check to see if any one of them still has a 'sixty-eight Mercedes two twenty active in their files."

"Green?"

"Green. Pink. Orange. Any color. Next, find out if any of those M.V.B.'s has a stolen tag reporting for a 'sixty-eight Mercedes two twenty."

"This is gonna take time, Frank. We're talking eighteen, nineteen states here."

Mooney grinned fiendishly. "Everything takes time, my friend. Time's the key player in the game. Time is what wins the horse races."

Pickering made a faint groaning sound and started for the door.

"Hey," Mooney shouted after him. "What's happening with those auto paint shops?"

"There's only about three hundred fifty of them in the city. What d'ya think's happening? We're checking. Gimme a break. We've got a half-dozen guys out on this thing. We've only just started."

Mooney made a quick computation in his head. "I figure each man oughta be able to cover at least ten shops a day. That comes to sixty shops a day total. I figure you need, maybe, five, six days to cover the field. Get me an answer by Thursday."

Pickering's shoulders drooped in a suit too large for him. It was not yet eight A.M., and he already had the winded, somewhat depleted look of a dog who'd been running hard.

"So long, Rollo." Mooney waved.

Pickering sighed and hobbled out the door.

PART III

SEVENTEEN

WARREN MARS HAD BEEN GOING DUTIFULLY up to 860 Fifth Avenue for nearly three weeks. He went at dusk each day with dogged, uncomplaining regularity. Arriving there, he would nod unobtrusively to Mr. Carlucci, the building doorman, then take up his seat on the bench across from the building. By now it had taken on something of the air of ritual, something he and Mr. Carlucci carried out each evening with a kind of priest-like solemnity.

So far, for all of their persistence, nothing had occurred. No one had appeared on the street near the bench to stare up at the building. For Warren, it was not unpleasant. Nor did the demand on his time appear to annoy him. He liked sitting there in the gathering dusk of upper Fifth Avenue with the thick bank of foliage exhaling its sweet, grassy breath behind him. The sleekly elegant comings and goings of conspicuously privileged people, bustling off in expensive cars to smart parties and expensive restaurants, pleased him. He enjoyed observing the grand, self-important air of opulence on display there. It was a far cry from the sort of life he knew and understood, but he felt no sense of resentment or disadvantage for its being so. Oddly enough, he felt a distinct sense of superiority to these people. His view of them was that of spoiled children, a bit selfish and over-indulged, showy about their possessions, and totally mindless of the deprivation of others. But he bore them no malice. Paradoxically, it all seemed quite familiar to him, as though he himself were, and indeed had always been, very much a part of it.

Three weeks was certainly not a long time to have waited for something tangible to happen. Warren was a reasonable fellow. If life had taught him anything, it was how to wait. He sat on the bench now, legs crossed at the knee, looking relaxed and rather debonair. He had taken to dressing up for the occasion — looking the part, more or less, of a real big-city reporter on a big story. To him it had all the feeling of a mystery film in which he played the hero. As in all good mystery films, he had no doubt that all that was necessary was for him to wait and, inevitably, his quarry would appear. It was virtually guaranteed. Eventually, this stranger would show and Warren would be there to greet him.

At eight-thirty sharp, as dusk succumbed to darkness, Warren rose, stretched his legs, waved to the nervously vigilant Mr. Carlucci, and strolled off into the night.

"And what about the suicide over on the West Side?"

"The cardiologist?"

"Right. The goddamned insurance company's been after me all morning."

"Well, it sure looks like suicide. Blood, urine, brain tissue loaded with pentobarbital. Was there a policy?"

"Huge. And he was up to his ears in debt. Liked to go to the casinos. Leaves a wife and four kids. What about the Ortega job?"

"We lifted a slug out of the parietal lobe. Forty-five caliber. Went to ballistics this morning."

"And Bender?"

Joan Winger smiled oddly, as if there were a tinge of perverse satisfaction in what she had to disclose. "We've got an AB pos."

Something sparked in Paul Konig's bleary, drooping eyes. "You're sure?"

"Course I'm sure. We got it on a semen smear we took off her."

"A week ago you were telling me we had an azoospermia running loose."

"That was last week. This week we don't." She appeared delighted by his puzzlement. "This week we've got Shadow Dancer II, dancing right behind Shadow Dancer I."

He put a sheaf of reports down, folded his arms, and glared at her in expectation.

"Look at it this way," she went on eagerly. "Dancer I is an azoospermia. Dancer II has enough motile sperm zipping around inside him to impregnate the Rockettes. Dancer I is dark, possible Hispanic. Dancer II is fair. From the tooth imprints we've lifted off all these cadavers so far, Dancer I looks like he has broken incisors; II looks to have nice straight, even teeth. II is an AB-pos blood type, and I'm willing to lay odds that I is an AB pos also."

By that time the red flush had spilled over Konig's collar and was surging upward into his cheeks. "You bring me that Dancer I blood type. You show it to me. I want it here."

Ferris Koops drove north on the Hutchinson River Parkway. He'd just passed through the little toll booth at Pelham and was meandering his way through the fringes of Mount Vernon where the pretty little Tudor houses staggered along the service lanes of the Parkway gave the impression of a toy village. It made him think of the little toy towns set up around the model train tracks in the big festive displays at Schwartz's.

It was nearly the end of August. Ferris drove along, enjoying the good, hot feeling of sun beating down on his elbow sticking out the open window. He was going nowhere in particular.

He liked to drive, although he had no license to do so. When he was about seventeen, he took several driving lessons, but he'd never been able to pass the test. It was not the mechanical part of the test that stymied him but the written part. He'd taken it several times, studying hard before each exam and always certain he knew the answers. But then when it came to actually taking the test, something always happened and all the knowledge that he'd committed to memory would flee his head like a flock of startled sparrows.

It was pure chance that he found himself in this car, driving north into Westchester County on this dazzling summer day. Leaving his small efficiency walk-up apartment on East 81st Street that morning, he'd come down into the street wondering how he might occupy his time for the rest of the day. The evening before, he had cashed the check that came to him biweekly from the law firm on Madison Avenue. With money in his pocket and the long day stretching out before him, he had not the vaguest notion of what he would do until it was evening again and he could go home.

Suddenly there was the car. It was double-parked right near the curb in front of the building, its motor running and no one in it, as if the driver had just parked for a moment and dashed in someplace on a quick errand.

He had no recollection of how it happened, but the next thing he knew, he was in the car behind the wheel and driving out onto First Avenue. It scarcely occurred to him that he had done anything illegal. Had anyone proposed such a thing to him, he would have been appalled at the mere thought of it. But it was such a pretty car, deep green and spiffy bright, a late-model Pontiac coupe in spanking good condition. Just the sort of car they talked about on the TV — the green car of that strange fellow who went about doing awful things. He hated that person, whoever he was. He believed that individuals like that ought to be taken off the streets and put away forever so that people would never again be hurt by them.

He'd read all the stories about that person. How he'd cruise about in his green car up and down the highways, ooking for a house, a person, something that looked "easy," and then he'd move in. He would do horrible hings to the people unlucky enough to be found there when he arrived. Then afterward, when he'd finished, he would steal things like televisions and cameras, computers and tape decks.

Driving along up the Hutchinson River, Ferris listened to music on the radio (a Bach fugue) and thought about that man. Deep within the mesmerizing repetitions of the music, he could almost imagine what the fellow looked like and what he might feel just cruising about all by himself, on possibly just such a fine morning as this — driving along, listening to music in just such a spiffy little green car as this. It seemed to him that the more he thought about the man, the more excited he became.

In the area of New Rochelle, he turned off at the Webster Avenue exit, with no idea why he did so, except that, possibly, the pretty little homes in the lightly wooded area looked so cozy and welcoming.

In the next moment he found himself rolling slowly up and down the little secondary road parallel to the Parkway and peering into all the little houses and yards, strangely silent now and devoid of people at that early hour of the day.

"Westchester state troopers said the body had been mutilated. Pathologists at the Valhalla Medical Center had indicated that there were signs that Mrs. Wybnishinski, a forty-three-year-old widow who lived alone in the modest two-story stucco dwelling, had been sexually assaulted. The coroner's office reported evidence of bite marks all over the body, and the throat had been slashed. In addition, she'd been disemboweled with what police believed to be a large kitchen knife with a serrated blade. So far all attempts to turn up such a knife in the area have failed.

"The body was discovered by Mrs. Wybnishinski's

sister, Mrs. Clara Purse, who said she grew suspicious when she was unable to reach her sister by phone for three days. Normally, it was her custom to speak with her sister at least once a day.

"The partially clad body was discovered in the basement. The house had apparently been ransacked but nothing was taken. The car driven by the intruder, a nineteen eighty-five green Pontiac Firebird, was recovered late today on the West Side Drive. In a strikingly similar incident occurring in the Douglaston section of Queens, New York, earlier this year, witnesses also implicated a green car.

"Since early last year, fourteen incidents, each involving breaking and entering with intent to rob, also involving sexual assault, have occurred. Seventeen people have already died, including an infant. One woman, Mrs. Claire Pell of Howard Beach, New York, survived the attack only because a newspaper delivery man showed up at the precise moment of the attack.

"Tying yesterday's brutal slaying of Mrs. Wybnishinski closer to the so-called Shadow Dancer murders was a crude drawing in large pink crayon letters scrawled on the basement wall directly above where the body was discovered. Police described the drawing as phallic in nature and signed, 'The Monster of Chaos.' Similar drawings signed in precisely the same way have been discovered at several murder sites around the New York area earlier this year. New Rochelle and New York City police are coordinating their investigations.

Warren Mars slammed a fist down hard on the top of the TV. The picture shuddered, sending a series of jagged white lines radiating outward in waves from the center of the screen. He snapped off the set and started to prowl about the little room, muttering a low stream of epithets. In the next moment he swung his fist blindly, as if striking some invisible assailant. The wall before him appeared to sag, then buckle inward. Something inside his hand felt as though it had exploded. He yowled with pain.

"Hey, hey." There was a great banging outside. Suki Klink flung open the door, her eyes wide and swiveling wildly about, as if she half-expected to find someone else there. "What the hell's wrong with you? Sounds like you're killing somebody up here."

Ignoring her, Warren sat bent over the edge of the bed, his aching fist cradled in his lap for comfort. "Shit."

"What's ailing you?" Suki snapped, a look of flustered petulance about her.

"Get out of here," he fumed, still bent over, grinding his fist into his lap. "Get the hell out . . ."

She could see he was in pain. "What's wrong, Sonny? You ain't hurt yourself?"

"It's nothing, I said. Get out."

She watched him for a while, writhing and wincing. Her pity quickly waned and sharp disapproval crept across her wizened features. "You in some kind of trouble, I bet."

"No trouble. I'm in no trouble. Get out of here."

He bounded up and started toward her. But the old lady, frightened as she was, stood her ground. Exasperated, Warren wheeled and stomped off.

"Where you going?" she called after him.

"Out. Anywhere, out of here."

"Better not. Better lay low till things cool down."

He wheeled and started back toward her. "Things? What things?"

She grinned at him, showing her yellow stumps of broken teeth.

"What things?" he bellowed again.

She could tell he was frightened. "Oh, come, Sonny. Papers this morning are full of you."

"Papers? What papers? What the hell are you talking about?"

She made that disagreeable sound, somewhere between a screech and a sucking noise, that was intended for a laugh. "What'd you do to that poor lady up in Westchester? So bad, the newspapers wouldn't hardly talk about it." The screech again, high and stridulous, like a broken fiddle. "You are a caution."

He came at her fast, taking her by both arms above the elbows, as if he intended to shake her. His eyes were open wide and he spun his head from side to side. "Hey, listen. That wasn't me. You hear? That wasn't me."

He was near panic and that pleased her. She liked it when he was frightened. He was more manageable then. "You don't have to have secrets with me, Sonny. We got no secrets."

"I didn't do this thing, I tell you. I swear, I had nothing to do with it."

She nodded her old gray head sagely. "It's got all your marks on it, Warren. The naughty pictures on the walls. The funny stuff with the lady." She leered at him merrily. "You better get rid of that car. Police are gonna trace it right to you."

At the mention of the word *car*, his face brightened. "That's right. The car. News said just now it was a green Pontiac they found. You know I don't have no Pontiac."

"What's the difference? They're lookin' for a green car. You got a green car."

"It's not my car." He pounded the top of a battered old chifforobe, then winced. "My car's no crummy Pontiac. You know that."

Doubt passed like a film across her eyes for the first time that morning.

"Don't you see?" he rattled on, bent on his own vindication. His voice half-jeered, half-pleaded. "Can't you see? It's some other guy just imitating me."

She watched him warily for a while, her head cocked to one side like an edgy hound, something spiteful glinting in her eye. "What are you telling me, Sonny?"

"I'm telling you the truth. Some other guy's been out there going around doing my thing. He uses all my stuff. Then the cops hang it on me."

"How do you know? What proof do you have?"

"How do I know?" He gaped at her furiously. "I know it's not me these jokers are talking about on the TV." Suddenly, as if a dam burst, the story of the building on upper Fifth Avenue and the doorman and his nightly twilight vigils all came flooding out. Standing there before her, he had the look of a small boy confessing mischief to a stern mother. When it was all over, he felt an immense sense of relief, almost gratitude. Shortly, he was eating out of her hand like an affectionate but chastened puppy.

"For the next few weeks," Suki went on sternly, "I want no more funny stuff." "Funny stuff" was her euphemism for sexual activity. "Stay here. Lie low. I don't want you going out."

As she laid the law down to him, she felt a surge of confidence return with the reassertion of authority over him. That gnawing sense of uneasiness she'd been feeling over the past several weeks, with all of his talk about "clearing out" — that was over now. She knew he'd never go.

"Don't worry your head no more on this score," she lectured him. "We'll figure out what to do about this other fellow when the time comes. Now come down." She tugged his ear playfully. "Come have a bowl of Suki's good hot soup."

Several nights later, Ferris Koops watched the gray-white figures flicker across the TV screen. The disturbingly graphic accounts of the slaying in Westchester County had sickened him, but he was unable to avert his eyes from the horror of it.

During the almost daily accounts of it, they had flashed on the screen clips of the house and the basement where the grim discovery had been made. The camera had shown splashes of blood on the basement floor, then swung around the walls to show momentarily that ghastly graffiti scrawled in jagged broken letters of pink crayon.

All the while he watched it, he was unaware that beads of sweat had erupted on his forehead and that his heart thumped wildly in his chest. How awful. How horrible. How could people do such things? One human being to another. Ferris tried to imagine the man who'd wreaked such havoc on a poor defenseless individual. What sort of person could be so vicious? So unfeeling?

Ferris again made an effort to conjure up a picture of this person in his mind. Where was he? Far off in some remote northern suburb, or nearby in the city, perhaps only one or two blocks away from where Ferris lay now on the narrow cot of his stifling single-room efficiency apartment just east of First Avenue.

The thought of that sent a chill shuddering through him. He knew there were people like that in the world. His mother had told him all about them. They were crazy, twisted people who did horrific things, sometimes out of desperation, but more often out of a desire for the perverse pleasure they derived from inflicting pain. They were sick people with badly deranged minds who desperately needed help.

Ferris would have liked to help these people. If he could have been a psychologist or a counselor of some sort, he would have happily committed his life to such work. He knew that his natural affection for people afforded him a special affinity for troubled souls. Ferris felt that he had simply to look into a person's eyes to know at once if that individual was troubled or at peace.

It occurred to Ferris that he had an overwhelming need to meet this man the newspapers called the Shadow Dancer. As admittedly repugnant as all of his acts were, Ferris had a desire to sit him down, take him by the hand, and tell him that he was not a beast — not a detestable subcreature, as they liked to call him. He was a human being, like anyone else, with feelings and definite needs. All of his impulses were not destructive. He was capable of kindness and generosity. Even acts of great nobility. If he could just tell this man that, and then share with him whatever he had, in the way of material comforts and friendship, he felt certain that this poor deranged soul would be well on his way to recovery.

Outside in the street it was dark. Ferris's apartment was on the second floor and the light from the streetlamp shined directly in his window. The window was open and he could hear people passing back and forth below in the street. Across the way, the lights from a small fish restaurant twinkled with a vague blur. A large red neon fish in its window blinked bulging eyes on and off in the hazy closeness of the evening. People kept arriving and departing. He could hear their laughter, hear them hailing cabs, and hear car doors slamming, as they pulled away from the curb.

Sometimes he liked to draw a chair up to the window, and with the lights out in his room and his elbows resting on the concrete sill, he would watch the comings and goings with a sense of quiet joy — these trivial, wholly unremarkable daily transactions of mortal affairs.

What of that poor man, the Shadow Dancer? he thought once more. He imagined the poor creature crouching somewhere in darkness, hungry, frightened, cowering in some rank corner from his pursuers whom he could not hope to elude much longer.

It was nearly eleven P.M. Shortly there would be more news. He had an urgent need to hear more about the Shadow Dancer. Ever since those ghastly murders had started over a year ago, Ferris had read everything that had been written. He'd watched each news account on TV. He kept a scrapbook of clippings and knew by heart almost everything down to the most minute details of the case.

When he flicked the late news on, they were already discussing the murder in Westchester. A mob of reporters swarmed around the chief of detectives and a big, hulking gray-haired man, a lieutenant, who was in charge of the case. They had just come down from New Rochelle where they'd been conferring with the police.

Ferris knew the lieutenant. His name was Mooney. He'd seen him several times before on TV. He had even written his name down someplace. Beside him stood the chief of detectives. His name was Mulvaney. He looked tired and harried. Ferris could tell he was nervous, trying to respond to the barrage of reporters' questions fired at him from every direction.

"Mooney?"

"Uh huh."

"You still up?"

"If I wasn't, I am now." The voice came muffled from beneath the covers.

"Come on. You know I didn't wake you."

"If you're so sure, then why bother asking?"

The question gave her pause but not for long. "You've been tossing and thrashing for the last three hours."

"Something I ate."

"You hardly ate a bite all day."

"Then maybe it's something I didn't eat." He ground his head deeper into the pillows.

"I don't like the way you're looking these days. What's bothering you? This Shadow Dancer business?"

"How come you always ask questions if you know the answers to them? That's how you pick horses, too. You ask me who I like in the fifth someplace. Then after I tell you, you go out and bet some other nag."

Fritzi flicked on the light, then slipped from beneath the sheets and into a robe. "How about some eggs?"

"Eggs? It's three A.M., for God's sake."

"Come on. We'll have an early breakfast."

"An early breakfast? We just had supper."

She yanked the bedsheets down, exposing the sprawling, tangled dishevelment of the figure below. "Come on, Mooney. Get up. I'm starved."

She hauled him to his feet, bundled his big, hulking shape into a robe, then steered him out like a small tug guiding a liner through the obstacles and hidden perils of some treacherous shoals. In the kitchen, she sat him down at the long white slab of marble that served as their breakfast table. She put up a pot of coffee and proceeded to melt margarine in a skillet. She prepared bacon and toast, all the while maintaining a virtually unbroken line of breezy chatter. She talked about their horses, their trainer, races coming up in which they planned to participate. She talked about an aunt in Milwaukee, her father's ancient sister, Em, whom she'd been thinking about and wanted to visit before "anything happened."

She broke off abruptly at that point as if all of the foregoing chat had been nothing but a prelude to more pressing matters. "Mulvaney's been at you pretty hard, I guess."

Mooney's drowsy eyes rose from the depths of his coffee mug. "He threatened to pull me off the case couple of weeks ago. Gave me ninety days to finish the job."

"You didn't tell me."

"What's to tell?"

Fritzi slid a plate of bacon and eggs before him. "Be the best thing."

He glared down into his plate and shook his head despairingly. "Look at this now. Fake yolkless rubber eggs and vegetarian bacon." His tongue slipped queasily between his lips.

"I didn't give you high cholesterol and a coronary. I'm just here to make sure you don't get another."

Mooney groaned and picked up his fork. She sat down across from him and proceeded to spread margarine on his toast.

"Papers say this thing up in Westchester was pretty foul."

Mooney made a sour face and forked egg into his mouth.

"Sure looks a lot like all the others though," Fritzi continued. "All that biting stuff. And the funny pictures and numbers on the walls."

Mooney bit down on a corner of jellied toast and proceeded to chew thoughtfully. "Not the car though. That's the only thing that don't fit. This latest was a green Pontiac. They found it on the West Side Drive."

"How come they're so sure it was the same one used in New Rochelle?"

"One of the neighbors identified it. Saw it in front of the house. Even remembered part of the plate number. Got any more of that carrot bacon?"

"It's not carrots." She speared several pieces onto his plate. "It's made of — "

"Don't tell me. I'd rather not know."

"What's wrong with Pontiacs? You don't think the real Shadow Dancer drove a Pontiac?"

"We've already got a make on his car. Got if off a pretty reliable source. It's a Mercedes. A 'sixty-eight. That's why I say the cars are the only thing that don't fit."

"Did it ever occur to you the same guy might change cars for each job?"

Mooney pushed his empty plate away and rubbed his sleepless eyes. "It never occurred to me." His eyes drooped and he appeared to doze off.

"Okay. It's just a suggestion."

"Don't ask dumb questions. Of course we figured that. Any guy in his right mind, knocking off a different dame every five, six weeks, is not gonna use the same car each time."

"But this guy isn't in his right mind."

"Bingo," Mooney mumbled and patted his stomach. The sky outside the kitchen window above East 78th Street had begun to glow with faint streaks of pink. Fritzi rose and started to carry dishes from the table to the sink. "So what are you chaps doing about all this?"

Mooney's eyes had closed and he was drowsing once more at the table.

"Mooney? Did you hear me?"

"Oh, Fritz. For God's sake, it's four-thirty in the

morning." He wobbled to his feet and flicked out the kitchen light. "Let's go to bed. It's getting early."

Mooney slipped back beneath the cool sheets and turned on his stomach. Almost at once he began to snore. Fritzi lay frowning and agitated, propped on a pair of goosedown pillows. She stared disapprovingly down at the slumbering form beside her.

"Hey, Mooney. I almost forgot." She elbowed his ribs. The gray tousled head rose sleepily. "Hey, Mooney."

He moaned. "Is this because you want me to die, Fritzi?"

"I just remembered. Some guy came in tonight. Sat at the bar awhile."

"Wonderful."

"Said he was looking for you."

"He didn't find me." Mooney burrowed his face into the pillows.

"Said he saw you a couple of times on TV, out in front of the place. Said he wanted to talk to you."

"About what?"

"He didn't say."

"Good." Mooney began to snore.

"Nice-looking young guy. Kind of cute in that sort of dark, Latino way."

"Hope you didn't do nothin' to embarrass me," Mooney croaked feebly.

She punched him lightly on the back. "He said he wanted to talk to you about the case."

Sprawled beneath the sheets, the pillow planted atop his head, Mooney appeared to have dropped back off. Fritzi sat there for a while, propped against the headboard, watching him. There was a troubled, somewhat baleful look on her face.

In the next moment, she felt stirrings and grumblings rising from the mattress beside her. It was Mooney, struggling to disentangle himself from the entrapment of twisted bedding. At last, he sat halfway up, propped on one elbow. "What else did he say?"

"I already told you. Said he wanted to talk to you about the case."

"What case?"

"What case?" Fritzi slapped her forehead. "This thing we're discussing for the last hour. The Shadow Dancer, naturally."

"Oh?" Mooney flopped back down.

"Said he had a theory about all this."

"Just what we need. Another theoretician. He leave his name?"

"Nope. Said he'd drop back some other time."

Mooney started to snore again.

"He might have something useful to say. You never can tell."

"Sure. You bet."

"Aren't you even a little curious?"

"I've had hundreds of calls from people, all with some cockamamie theory about this case. They're all sure they know the guy."

"Did I say he said that?" Fritzi protested. "He just said he wanted to talk to you about the case."

"I can't wait to hear."

She watched him slip off to sleep again, or seem to, until suddenly he bolted back up into a sitting position. As he spoke, rapidly and out of breath, he started to shake her. "Listen, that thing I told you about our having a make on this Mercedes, and all. Don't breathe a word of that to a soul. You hear? That's not for public consumption."

EIGHTEEN

Female. Age 14. Attempted self-abortion by syringing. Perforated uterus. Extensive abdominal septicemia. Tenderness in Pouch of Douglass. Blood urea 256 mg percent. Death by . . .

Victim. Male child. Age 2. Poorly nourished but not emaciated. Numerous contusions on body including nine on forehead. Back of knee joints, outer side of right thigh marked by patterned bruises in the form of small circles arranged in equilateral triangles. Mother admitted having 'chastised' the child with leather belt, roughly 1½" wide, studded with brass cones set in form of equilateral triangles. Cause of death, compression of brain as a result of bilateral subdural hemorrhage . . .

Konig glanced up into the musty stillness of his office. There was a look of puzzlement on his face as if surprised to find himself there so early on a Sunday morning. A shaft of mote-filled sunlight crossed his desk and fell against his back like a warm hand. Before him in a sloping pile was a stack of protocols awaiting his review — the chronicles of last week's carnage in the city. Some two hundred or so reports, all illuminated in meticulous and grisly detail. After thirty years of service in the medical examiner's office, he was sometimes tempted to conclude that all the methodology of homicide (and he knew it intimately and by heart) was repetitive and even boring. But every now and then, something would come along so breathtakingly original in approach, so ingenious in cruelty, in its sheer nastiness, as to renew his faith in man's unflagging creativity in this area.

He rose, rubbing his eyes and prowling the perimeter of his cluttered office, restless as a penned horse, as if seeking something he couldn't quite recall. He moved slowly, placing one foot gingerly before the other to avert as much as possible the daggers of chronic sciatica stabbing up and down the length of his leg. It gave him the appearance of a man walking uphill into a strong wind.

Everything about his dress that morning was clean and fresh, yet he conveyed an impression of dishevelment. There was about him the weariness of eons, along with the resignation of those who'd long ago abandoned all hope. But in spite of that, there remained that air of angry intransigence about him that suggested something approaching dignity.

In the clutterment of his bookshelves, with an order discernible only to him, the bleached skulls of seabirds sat amid musty old tomes of long-out-of-print textbooks he had authored; human organs and small appendages floated in formalin in rows of glass canisters like the canopic jars of the ancient Egyptians. His eyes scoured the shelves until at last they lighted on the small article he'd been seeking, an electric coil upon which he could brew one of the endless cups of black powdered coffee that kept him galvanized throughout the day.

Puttering about in the debris of the drawers, he fished out a plastic spoon and a cracked mug ringed with the brownish patina of decades. He heated water in a small alembic over his coil and drummed his desk distractedly as he waited.

Part of the morning ritual was the first cigar, which he unwrapped from its cellophane, bit off its tip with a deft, fastidious snap, then lit. Not eager to return to protocols, he dallied instead over the weekend mail, reading half-heartedly as he stirred freeze-dried coffee into the mug of boiling water. Shortly he rose, and with the cigar screwed tightly into the center of his mouth, he wandered forth into the corridor outside his office.

It was slightly past ten A.M. on an early September Sunday. The light streaming in from 31st Street outside had the sort of dazzling clarity that comes only with lowered temperatures and little humidity. The tops of trees visible from the corridor windows were still in leaf, still green but brightly tinged with red and russet hues. The muted sounds of street traffic drifted up from the world below.

Above the corridors where he walked there hovered the sort of silence that bespeaks eternity and all final things. Even the sound of one's own breathing seemed intrusive there. Walking down the corridor, he was slightly appalled at the sound of his own slurred footsteps ricocheting off the tiled walls and vinyl floors. Limping stiffly, he carried his cup awkwardly before him like a libation bearer. As well as he knew those corridors, at that moment he felt a curious estrangement from them. The solitary look of his appearance in that large and seemingly empty building imparted to his movements the stilted, rather dreamy quality of the somnambulist.

His way took him past the spectroscopy labs, the toxicology and ballistics departments, then on into an intersecting corridor containing a row of additional office suites in which colleagues, deputies, and young assistants had their offices. Had anyone stopped him then and asked where he was going, he would, doubtless, have been at a loss to say.

Paul Konig was a man given to walking as a form of problem solving. Desk work, to his way of thinking, was the place to execute mechanical chores. Locomotion, however, was reserved for the intuitive part of his job, the truly inspired part, although he himself would never have agreed to such a distinction. He was a trained scientist and as such had an unyielding reverence for hard scientific method. Observation. Quantification. Trial and error. Verification. Those were his watch words. He hammered them hard at his students three days a week at the university. He professed a strong antipathy for intuition along with the current rage for gurus within the scientific community who'd built up a following by practicing it.

Yet, whenever the chief medical examiner was prowling the labyrinthine corridors of the New York City Coroner's Office, it was generally when the scientific method had all but exhausted itself, and he had no recourse but to revert to some "less reliable mode." It was here where some of his best work was done.

Just about to end his prowl and turn back to the gloomy prospect of writing protocols, a scattering of faint, indeterminate sounds caught his attention.

At first he thought it was a stray cat or, possibly, mice foraging brazenly in one of the offices. Rodents were not at all uncommon in the medical examiner's office. These noises, however, consisted of tappings and the tentative clicks of a hard object being pushed or rolled along a desktop.

The noises seemed to be coming from a point down the corridor and nearly fifty feet directly ahead of him. He paused, straining his ears. The more he listened to the noises, the more they seemed the work of some human agency. Prudence urged that he return to his office and notify the security people down front, then bar himself behind his door and wait there until help arrived.

Prudence, however, had never been the chief medical examiner's strong suit. Dismissing all danger, he plunged forward, grasping his coffee mug, brandishing it slightly above his head as though it were a weapon. The closer he came, the more insistent grew the noises. From where he stood they gave the distinct impression of someone rifling through files or a drawer.

Six feet from the opened door of the last office at the end of the corridor, he stopped again in a half-crouch, craning his neck, gathering strength for the final push. He took a deep breath and proceeded to count inwardly to ten. At six, he could contain himself no longer and lunged forward. Eyes blazing, he wheeled into the office.

There was no light on inside. Sun streamed into the office from a large picture window facing the rear of the building. Momentarily blinded by the light, he saw nothing but a whirr of black spots flying before his eyes. With a slight change of physical position, the glare dissolved and suddenly he could see the blurred outline of a person, seated faceless, at the desk.

There was a shriek and the squeal of a chair skidding violently backward. The sound of it rent the quiet, Sabbath hush of the building. Everything suddenly exploded into wild, frenetic motion.

"Good God!"

Konig gaped at the figure, half-seated, half up on its feet, shouting at him. The hand brandishing the mug dripped hot, spilled coffee over his wrist. "What the hell are you doing here?"

"I work here!" Joan Winger shouted. The chair behind her had toppled and she was backing perilously toward it. She looked at him as though he were possessed by demons. "Will you kindly put that mug down. I don't relish the thought of being skulled by it."

He glanced at the mug above his head. The sight of it poised there suddenly embarrassed him. His wrist and shirt cuff dripped coffee. He was overcome with a sense of ludicrousness, like some overly sober and upright citizen inadvertently caught in a beer hall with a party hat tilted askew on his head. "You scared the hell out of me," he blustered.

"I'm not exactly enchanted by your sudden appearance, either."

"I'm working here."

"Well, so am I, for Chrissake."

"This is Sunday," he thundered at her as though it were an accusation.

"For you, too, right?" she shot back. "I've just as much right to come in here on a Sunday as you, don't I?"

The reasonableness of the question appeared to baffle him. He grumbled something and cleared his throat. His hand and shirt sleeve continued to drip coffee. "Well, of course . . ."

"Now, if you'd be so kind as to permit me to get back . . ."

"Sure," he mumbled. "Go ahead." He half-turned, then turned back. Suddenly he was all curiosity. "What are you doing, anyway?"

Something vulgar leapt to her tongue but then died there. Instead she frowned. "If you must know, I'm running a second battery of tests on those semen smears we took off of Bender and Torrelson."

He appeared troubled. "Why?"

"Because I'm not entirely satisfied with the reliability of the Florence technique."

"I told you to try the gel diffusion, didn't I?"

"Okay — I'm trying it. Now if I can just get the one to corroborate the other . . ."

Konig gazed at her, looking somewhat crazed. Wisps of hair stuck out from the side of his head. His tie was askew and his shirt collar poked above his jacket lapels. "What grouping systems are you using?"

"Both the ABO and the GM," she fired back at him, curt to the point of rudeness. She wanted to get back to work and she didn't bother to conceal the fact that she considered him an intrusion.

"Fine," he murmured, starting to back out. "Fine. All right, then."

She stooped to pick up her chair, then watched him collide with the corner of a table.

He winced as the pain stabbed up his aching leg.

"Are you all right?" she asked, more exasperated than concerned.

"Fine. I'm fine." He brushed the incident aside with a sweep of his arm. At the door, he still appeared baffled, casting about with a fretful air for some reason to remain. "What reagents are you using?" he resumed the interrogation.

"Iodine and potassium iodide."

"And distilled water?"

"I didn't intend to take it from the tap," she snapped, regretting at once the sarcasm. "I'm sorry. I really didn't mean . . ."

"Fine. Perfectly all right. I shouldn't have . . . I suppose you've heard?"

"What?"

"They got the car used in the Wybnishinski job."

"Yes. I know. On the West Side Drive. I heard." By that time she was bristling with impatience. "Did they get prints?"

"Mooney doesn't think so. And certainly not if it's like any of the others. We should know in a day or so. I've got a preliminary report from the Westchester Coroner's Office."

"Anything there?" She displayed no real curiosity, but in point of fact, she was listening keenly.

"Looks like our boy, all right. Bite marks. Wall doodles."

"Semen?"

"Plenty — and the stuff they got from the vaginal aspirate was live."

"They make a blood type?" she asked, still cool and incurious.

"AB pos," he replied, watching her intently. "If you care to see the report, it's on my desk." He gazed around the office, somewhat at a loss. "I'd be happy to help you run those gel diffusions."

The long, weighty pause telegraphed the answer that followed. "If it's all the same to you, I'd prefer to run them off myself."

"Fine. Right you are." He laughed feebly, wondering

why he felt so whipped and hangdog. He hovered at the threshold, his gnarled, freckled hand patting the doorjamb. "Sorry the way I busted in on you like that. I thought you were a . . ."

"Thief," she finished the sentence for him. "Yes. I imagine you would."

Anger flashed in his eye, then receded abjectly. "Well, if you need me, I'm just down the hall." He turned and started out, half-expecting her to call him back. But she didn't.

NINETEEN

HE'D BEEN WATCHING HIM FOR SEVERAL MINutes before he realized who it was. Thirty or forty-someodd feet away at the corner of the street, throngs of people brushed past him, moving up and down in a blur of motion. He stood at the center of that blur of motion, distinct yet very much a part of it. In that peculiar half-light of dusk, amid all the swirl of people, Warren never had a clear, unimpeded view of him, but only caught glimpses of him in the momentary voids caused by the ever-shifting crowds. But simply from the way he stood, rigid and fixed, staring up at the window across the way, Warren knew without having to be told that here, at last, was his man.

He was young, from what Warren could see, approximately his own age, pallid and wispy, just as old Mr. Carlucci had described him, and doing precisely what the old man had said he always did on those evenings, along about dusk when he came to stand across the way from 860 Fifth and gaze up at the windows as if in silent homage at some shrine.

But as luck would have it, old Mr. Carlucci wasn't even there. When Warren had reached the bench that evening, just a tad under an hour or so before, to take up his nightly vigil, he was surprised to see another uniformed man out front of 860, opening car doors, flagging cabs, doffing his cap, and greeting people. But that didn't matter. Not one bit. Warren didn't need Mr. Carlucci to confirm for him the identity of the slight, wispy character, staring up at the building at the end of the block.

Warren rose from the bench and moved slowly forward — not toward the person, but toward the curb, until at last he stood roughly abreast of him, nearly twenty feet off. From that vantage point, he had a shadowy view of the face in three-quarter profile. At that distance and in that light, what he could make of it was a boyish, slightly epicene face, just a bit too pretty. Buffeted by waves of people, crowds disgorged from buses, he stood there, staring up at the window, seemingly oblivious to everything about him. His white tennis sneakers half on, half off the lip of the curb, gave him the look of a diver on a board poised to take flight.

Warren stood motionless, waiting to see what his mysterious counterpart would do next. Periodically, he would lose visual contact with him entirely. During those brief moments a surge of panic would overtake him and he would inch forward trying to spot him again. Then, when the buses pulled away and the crowd thinned, the figure would reappear, standing beneath a streetlamp in the moth-haunted twilight of early fall, still staring fixedly up at the window across the way.

Warren had moved up within ten feet of the fellow, standing roughly parallel to him. Affecting lack of interest, he acted out his own little role, checking his watch frequently and staring up and down the avenue as if he were expecting someone. Outwardly calm, what he was actually experiencing just then was an explosion of not entirely unpleasant emotions. First and foremost, he thought it would be all anger. Here at last he stood virtually face to face with the man who'd had the gall (or was it more likely the imprudence?) to imitate him. As if he, Warren, could be imitated by anyone.

But then there was also the sheer exhilaration of having found him, of having rooted out the little bug from a city of millions, of having set snares with an unwitting doorman that had finally sprung. It was the one-in-a-million needle-in-the-haystack story, and he, Warren Mars, had brought it off.

All the while his brain raced with a dozen schemes for dealing with this upstart, Warren suddenly lost sight of him in a flurry of activity as several buses discharged passengers at the corner. Then just as suddenly, he picked him out again, just stepping from the curb as the light changed and starting east across Fifth Avenue.

Warren watched him go. He waited a minute beneath the shadowy overhang of ginkgo branches, time enough for the light to change and change back again. Then, with an eye fixed on the figure slouching slowly east, he dashed across the avenue and fell quickly into step behind him.

Darkness came on swiftly. The light of bistros and store fronts transformed the drab streets into gaudy bazaars where milling crowds pulsed, people shopped and marketed. Warren kept his eye riveted to the back of the fellow, moving east across town.

He was on his way home, Warren imagined, but the path he took was like the flight of a butterfly, random and impulsive.

Moving slowly, he loitered at shop windows here and there. Several times he circled around blocks, only to return to where he'd been only minutes before. Then, crossing the street and reversing himself, he'd emerge onto an avenue he'd already traversed.

With each ensuing zig and zag Warren's fury mounted. A faint buzz had started in his ears, a familiar precursor of an old affliction of his. Then, all the tawdry colors of the night seemed to bleach into gray-white monotones. Funny things happened with his eyes. Objects grew small and distant the way they do when looking through the wrong end of binoculars.

They were now somewhere in the vicinity of York Avenue around 81st Street, moving east toward the river. The night was cool and a haze, fine and wet like

something sprayed from an atomizer, heightened Warren's discomfort. The fellow's gait, which had been languid up until then, now quickened. He made a sudden,
unexpected turn down 90th Street toward East End
Avenue.

Fearing he might lose him inside the maze of buildings, Warren rushed to the corner only to see the back,
then the heels of his quarry disappear into the entryway
of an apartment house halfway down the block. He
paused long enough to regain his composure. Then, he
was pounding down the street, slowing as he approached
the entryway, just in time to see the object of the chase
locking a mailbox in the outer vestibule then turning to
enter a narrow, dimly lit hallway.

Instead of following, Warren backed away from the
entrance into a narrow alley, a thin gash between two
buildings. He waited there, breathless in the fetid gloom
where trashcans brimming with refuse suffused the air
with a dank sweetness. In the next moment, he stepped
back out into the street and peered up at the facade of
the building, where lights glowed invitingly from within.

It was an old building, hard by the river, built in the
late thirties or early forties — a six-story anachronism
crammed in between a phalanx of glass/steel shafts of
thirty stories or more.

There was no lock on the outer door to prevent anyone
from entering freely, and Warren did so, a trifle tentatively, as if half-expecting his way to be barred by a
doorman or some other impediment. At last, confident
there was nothing of the sort there to stop him, he
bustled forward with the brusque authority of someone
who'd lived on the premises all of his life.

He had a perfect visual memory of the mailbox he'd
watched his quarry unlock through the glass doors of the
entryway. He went directly to it and read the name
posted on the little card in the name slot. It was written
in ink and had been smudged. Still, it was legible enough
to make out. F. KOOPS, it read.

"Koops." Warren nearly laughed aloud. He read it again just to be certain. It sounded like a joke to him. When he was a child, he used to read a comic strip about a cat called Koops. The apartment number assigned that name was 2G.

Up until that moment, Warren had no specific idea of what he had in mind. He had set out at first to trail a man to his home. It seemed to him that the mission was now completed and successful. He'd located his man (if Mr. Carlucci's tip was right, and he had no reason to assume it wasn't), so he could now assign both a name and an address to him. Without knowing precisely why, Warren moved into the shabby, airless little hallway, its walls splotched and peeling where large sections of plaster had broken away, and started up the stairs.

Apartment 2G was at the head of the corridor. It was a steel sheet door painted green and full of scratch marks carved into it by generations of marauding adolescents. Warren came to a halt before it. Again he read the name. F. KOOPS. This time it appeared just beneath the doorbell, written in precisely the same untidy fashion as on the mailbox, scrawled in ballpoint ink on a little ragged white card.

Somewhere down the hall (or was it merely in his head?) came the sound of a radio playing old forties big-band music. Permeating the hallway was the rank odor of meals cooked and consumed over four decades. It repelled him. Yet he continued to stand there, staring down at the tops of his shoes outlined against the broken black-and-white terrazzo floor, listening to the sounds of life inside. Why didn't he leave before someone saw him there? He couldn't say exactly. All he knew was that he'd enjoyed the hunt and now that it was over, he couldn't quite bring himself to depart it.

Something remained to be done.

The big band music coming from somewhere down the hall was an old Tommy Dorsey recording of "Getting Sentimental Over You." Without knowing the name of it, Warren recognized it at once. He'd heard it often as a child. It was one of his mother's favorites. She'd played it over and over again on an old RCA Victrola and sometimes danced to it by herself. It was odd, he suddenly thought, that he could remember the song and the old phonograph and his mother dancing, but of her he had no visual memory at all.

In the next moment, he thrust a finger out. Then, leaning slightly forward from the waist, he poked the doorbell. It wasn't a bell, actually, but something between a bell and a buzzer. When activated, it clattered like a dried bean inside a hollow gourd. Warren heard its brash rattle echo through the apartment. It made a hollow sound, suggesting vacancy beyond the door. Tommy Dorsey had stopped playing and a curious abrupt silence fell over the hall as if a switch had suddenly been thrown.

Warren waited, his ears strained, every muscle in his body coiled as if to spring, but on his face a vague smile flickered strangely. He had a keen image of the life on the other side of the door. It seemed to him that he could feel every nerve fiber of the person there, vibrating in perfect resonance with his own.

Warren pushed the bell again, this time less tentatively. The gourdlike sound rattled back at him from inside. Then he heard footsteps start, approaching at uneven speeds. A rustling, susurrant sound followed as of slippered feet across an uncarpeted floor. The footsteps came to a halt on the other side of the door; then he could hear someone breathing there. The exhalations, slow and regular, conveyed a sense of wariness. They were now less than a foot apart, with only the thin sheet of metal separating them.

In the next moment, Warren saw a disc in the center of the door slide upward. A thin pencil of light streamed through the tiny aperture. Then the light beam was suddenly eclipsed and Warren was aware of the movement of an iris and pupil regarding him from the other side. There was a pause and Warren heard a lock slip the bolt.

The door opened a crack and a chainlock stretched across the gap. Into that gap Warren jammed his foot and held it there, an action intended to be threatening. But if that were the case, the person on the other side of the door scarcely appeared to take note of it.

Warren had a glimpse of blond hair and a face in profile staring down at the floor. The face never once looked up or out at him. Nor did either of them attempt to speak. It was as though they were both content merely to remain that way, listening to each other's breathing and take in, as it were, the measure of one another.

There was nothing more. They remained that way a few moments longer, Warren with his foot jammed in the door, the blond figure on the other side still staring down at the floor, the tinny, scratchy sound of the old Tommy Dorsey recording, which had started up again, wafting out from somewhere inside.

When Warren left, a few moments later, they had still not looked directly at each other, nor had they even exchanged one word. But none of that mattered, for by that time, their communion was complete.

Outside in front of the building Warren stood for a moment, cooling off under a streetlamp, the buzzing in his ears dying. Where moments before he could see only bleached-out grays and white, all the gaudy colors of the night now came flooding back into his eyes. He felt more himself. His head darted right and left, glaring up and down the street. Though it was cool, even chilly out, he was drenched in sweat. He felt dizzy and sick. After all the thrill of the hunt, the meeting itself had been a dismal disappointment. Nothing had been resolved. He'd been left with a gnawing sense of incompletion. He had not done what he was supposed to do, but in point of fact, he had no idea what he was supposed to do.

Fists clenched and plunged deep into his pockets, Warren lurched off into the night. With no particular destination in mind, he swung west. Moving slowly at first, then gradually gaining speed, he moved back crosstown. It was going on nine P.M. Moving west on 81st Street, Warren's footsteps were slurred and halting. Occasionally, he'd stop dead in the street, mulling over the confusing events of the evening and his queer confrontation with Ferris Koops.

With the shank of the night still before him, Warren had nothing to do. He had no place to go and no one who expected him anywhere. He wasn't at all tired. He had been before, while he trekked mile after mile after the fleeting will-o'-the-wisp figure of Koops receding into the waves of teeming crowds before him. He'd been exhausted then. But now he was wide awake. Agitation and adrenaline had transformed weariness into raw, twitching nerves. There was now a bounce to his lagging gait, and while he was going nowhere in particular, he went there at a fairly brisk clip.

At a news kiosk at 86th and Lexington, he stopped to read details from a *New York Post* headline story, boasting of new clues uncovered in the Shadow Dancer case. He was relieved to learn that the new clues were really old hat and that the police were as stymied as ever. But, now more than ever, he was infuriated to see that the murders of the Bender girl and the woman in New Rochelle had been attributed to him. When he glanced up, he saw the kiosk manager, a Pakistani gentleman with a frozen smile, glaring at him. He replaced the newspaper on its stack and skulked off.

In his confused, strangely elevated state, he had started east again, now striding down Second Avenue in the Eighties, full of dark ruminations, when his gaze was deflected by a blaze of red lights floating above a canopy. The seven large letters flashing the name *Fritzi's* throbbed like a red pulse into the moist, vapory night air, while the word *Balloon* floated in a smaller discreet calligraphy beneath it.

He knew the place at once. He'd seen it often enough

on the television and recalled the big, gray-haired detective standing out in front, being interviewed by the press. He'd gone there once before looking for the detective (whose name he now forgot). He hadn't found him there on that occasion but had spoken to a woman he'd presumed to be the manager and who told him when the detective might be expected.

He crossed the street and loitered for a time beneath the canopy, watching people departing and cabs pulling up to the door. Through big leaded bottle-green saloon windows he could make out a cluster of night-owl New Yorkers gathered at the bar. He saw it through the blurry distortion of the old glass.

Each time the revolving doors spun round, a faint din of activity from within drifted out. An air of festivity hovered over the low-ceilinged, flame-lit rooms. For some reason the sound of it filled him with a fleeting sense of unaccountable sadness.

He waited for a while outside, peering through the windows, aware of the doorman's sharp, disapproving gaze. With a hand above his eyes to reduce the street glare, he scanned the bar. Smartly attired, well-heeled individuals lingered about there in small clusters of noisy, after-dinner affability.

He recognized the detective the moment he saw him. He loomed like a church steeple above all the rest. The thatch of thick, unruly white hair flashed like a beacon, guiding Warren's searching eye. A circle of people surrounded him and occasionally Warren could hear bursts of muted laughter flow outward onto the street from behind the thick green panes.

"What time's closing?" Warren asked the doorman over his shoulder.

"Eleven o'clock. Kitchen's closed, but if it's just a nightcap you want, you'd better go now."

Warren nodded and stepped into the whirl of swinging doors just as a laughing young couple spun out the other side.

In the next moment he'd left the din of traffic and the chill, wet night behind him. Before him lay a pleasure dome of roaring hearths, thick carpets, and flaming sconces. The air reeked of sizzling fat and savory meats. The soft lighting and quiet understatement of the interior bespoke a world of taste and privilege.

The dinner hour was clearly over. The maître d' stood at a small podium reviewing his guest lists for the night and the chef's proposed luncheon menu for tomorrow. In the main dining room a handful of late-night diners lingered over coffee and liqueurs. But it was at the bar where activity was at its height, and it was in that direction Warren was drawn.

It was hardly the sort of place he was accustomed to. Far too tony and pricy for his tastes, he felt scorn and at the same time a bit of intimidation. Warren preferred the seedy little neighborhood saloons along the Bowery and lower Broadway, with their large, watery drinks and coarse, inexpensive food. There, one could wear his anonymity with something bordering on defiance. In places like this, the ground rules virtually demanded that you be "somebody."

He found a spot at the end of the bar almost directly opposite where Mooney stood surrounded by friends. From where he positioned himself, Warren had a clear view of the detective. The peculiar acoustics of the room made it possible for him to hear everything that was being said.

Warren ordered a beer, munched a few chips, and listened. The talk was animated, sprinkled liberally with the argot of the street and the lore of the race tracks. There was talk of champions past and present, of jockeys and trainers, the clowns and princes of the circuit.

". . . No comparing Swale with Danzig Connection."

". . . Apples and oranges."

". . . Give Swale five lengths. He'd eat him up alive."

"You're mad. Danzig's already won the Peter Pan and

the Belmont by a length and a quarter over John's Treasure."

"He still don't have Swale's stuff. Swale was a prince on turf."

The talk was noisy and heated. Warren understood little of it, but he listened with the rapt attention of the spellbound. Though they all spoke at one time, it was the big man with the white hair who dominated the flow of chatter.

Warren drank his beer and studied the detective across the way. The fact that this man who'd been searching high and low for him for more than a year and didn't realize that the object of his search was now seated no more than twenty feet from him, sipping a beer, tickled him mightily. He wanted to laugh out loud. Several times he had to stifle an urge to shout across the bar, "It's me. Hey, look. Over here. It's me. Here I am. Come get me. I'm your guy. Forget about that faggoty wimp, Koops. I'm the real Dancer. This is me, Warren Mars. Here I am."

Like a child in possession of a wonderful secret, Warren felt little shocks of dangerous mirth quaking upward into his throat where he swallowed them, sitting there listening to the noisy blare of Mooney and his crowd, his own face a mask of stony impassivity.

Curiously, Warren felt no dislike for this man, his hunter and, conceivably, executioner. Quite the contrary, and just as before, it was admiration, even a sort of affection that he felt. There was a part of him that actually wished Mooney well and wanted the detective to succeed. Still, another part, wholly more realistic, was more determined than ever that that would never happen.

For Warren, the game of cat-and-mouse had become irresistible. Suddenly he was seized with a strange desire to make Mooney notice him. Possibly he might even speak to the detective. To Warren, that would have been sublime — sending up the world as very few had ever done. And the secret would have been his and his alone. He'd never share it with another soul.

The more he toyed with the idea, the more the cautious, realistic side of him retreated into the background. Despite all the obvious reasons for fearing the detective, giving him as wide a berth as possible, the more he was impelled to thrust himself at him. He was unaware that a small, foolish grin had begun to dart across his features.

For all of his efforts, he was having little luck attracting Mooney. The detective was too preoccupied just then to take note of the dark young stranger seated across the way, grinning at him. The talk was lively and heated. Another round of drinks was being served.

Warren tried again to catch Mooney's eye. By that time the grin on his face had shifted from amiability to something bordering on either insolence or dementia. He had no way of knowing that until, suddenly, the big man, encircled by friends, reached for a drink. He turned and their gazes met.

Mooney had the sort of face that reveals everything at once, and Warren had a clear view of it the moment he turned — the startlement and then the frown as though the detective had confused the grin for ridicule. Was he being laughed at? Mooney scowled back at him. There was a question in his eye as if he were trying to recall whether or not he knew the person grinning at him across the bar or possibly whether this person was just grinning at someone else nearby.

Warren was about to rise and go over and introduce himself. He would tell the detective that he'd seen him several times on television and how much he admired him, and wished him the best of luck on that Dancer job. He was about to stand, but just then Mooney was distracted by a tall, attractive lady with red hair. Warren recognized her at once as the woman he'd spoken to that first night he'd come into the Balloon.

She'd appeared now from the main dining room and

greeted friends at the bar. She never noticed Warren, and even if she had, chances are she'd not have recognized him, so fleeting had their contact been.

She was busy at the moment, saying goodnight to guests. Most of them she knew by name. They appeared to be regulars of the restaurant. She looked around, waving and nodding and smiling here and there.

Warren waited for her to recognize him, but to no avail. Once her eyes even lighted on him. She smiled directly at him and for a moment he imagined she was about to come over and say hello. He half-rose to greet her in anticipation, only to suddenly realize she was smiling at someone else just behind him. She glided past him and beyond with not even a glimmer of recognition. It hurt and even angered him that she seemed not to recall him.

People were clustered around the front doors. Outside, an endless succession of taxis kept rolling up beside the canopy. Warren turned slightly, only to have his field of vision suddenly darkened by a huge looming object bearing down on him. The speed with which it came made Warren lean back as if to step aside. It was Mooney. Several people trailed at his heels, all chatting animatedly at one time, still talking horses.

At a certain point Mooney passed so close that Warren felt the heat of his body, radiating outward from his clothing. As he lumbered past, the sleeve of the detective's jacket brushed Warren's arm. The sensation was exquisite, too giddy and unreal to believe. It was imperative now that he talk to Mooney. Actually, his arm half-rose, as if to stop him before he bustled past. But something stayed him. In the next moment his arm dropped. He kept his place instead, lapping like a thirsty dog at the last of his warmish beer.

Mooney was now standing beside the tall, handsome lady.

"Hey, Fritz," the detective boomed. "What d'ya say we go home?"

"When we get all cleaned up here."

"I'm dead on my feet. I've got a busy day tomorrow."

"That's what you get for marrying a saloon keeper," someone chided.

"Go on ahead," the lady said. "I'll be along in a half hour."

Mooney grumbled. Several of his friends laughed.

So they're married, Warren thought to himself. He rose quickly, oddly annoyed, and made for the door. So they're married.

Outside on the street he could barely contain himself. He breathed deeply, gulping at the cold, wet air as if he were snapping at it with his teeth.

He started to walk. The annoyance he'd felt was now past. The laughter he'd managed to suppress inside the bar he now gave full rein to. Laughing to himself, his walk was nearly a sprint. To a passing couple he appeared demented, and they gave him a wide berth.

He had no idea what he'd found so funny. Only moments before he was angry. Now all he knew was that something tickled him immensely. He touched the place on his arm where Mooney had grazed it. Feeling a surge of elation, he bustled down the street, his feet fairly flying over the pavements.

He had no wish to go home to Bridge Street. After the Balloon, the gloomy house with the dirt and rank smells, the unventilated garret he slept in under the grimy, rain-spattered cupola, struck him as more of an offense than ever. Finding Koops, his *Doppelgänger*, picking him out of a city of millions, then finding Mooney, his pursuer, with whom he'd made actual physical contact that night, had left him feverish with excitement.

He would take care of Koops. He would eliminate that problem in his own way. But for now, he was hungry. Ferociously hungry. He would eat. It occurred to him that he wanted meat more than anything. The savory smell of roasts and thick steaks broiled on the open charcoal pits of the Balloon still lingered in his nostrils.

He could taste meat at the back of his throat. The roof of his mouth tingled for it.

He wheeled sharply, heading suddenly north and farther west. His course took him up past the Nineties and on to 103rd Street and Madison, where Janine lived.

Though he was famished, he wanted to go to Janine first. He longed to tell her about his encounter with Koops and then the detective. He had a need to be near her. It wasn't necessary to see her; just to be within some reasonable proximity to her. To drink in the closeness of her. Even though her "friend" was there, sleeping by her side, no matter. He would not be there much longer. Warren would see to that too.

He had plans for Janine's friend. He'd thought it all out. It wasn't pleasant, but it had to be done, just as Koops had to be done. And, in the end, Janine would understand. Even be grateful. He would make it all up to her. He had the power to do so. It was purely a matter of will and concentration. Once he set his mind to something, there was nothing in the world that could deflect him.

It was just past midnight when he reached the modest little walk-up where Janine and Michael Mancuso lived. He knew the location of their apartment from his many nocturnal visits to the area. Several times he'd seen Janine through the windows fronting the street.

Those windows were dark now, as were most of the others in the building. Only a single set of apartment lights at the northeast corner of the building still glowed, suggesting insomnia or sickness behind them. The streets were deserted. He leaned against a streetlamp across the way, and, with a sigh of enormous contentment, he gazed up at her darkened windows.

TWENTY

"AND YOU'RE SURE THIS WAS A SIXTY-EIGHT Mercedes?"

"In mint condition. Positive."

"How come he wanted to paint it?"

"He had some rust going on around the headlights and fenders. So while I was taking care of that, he said I should also paint it."

They were in the cramped little space that served as Mr. Anthony Pagano's office. A glass partition separated them from the big floodlit paint shop where just then an old Coupe de Ville was being sprayed.

Mr. Pagano sat behind a desk stacked with little hills of invoices, paper coffee cups, and unemptied ashtrays reeking of dead cigar stumps.

"And it was a two twenty," Pickering went on.

"Right. A two twenty."

"You're sure?"

"Course I'm sure," Mr. Pagano snapped. "Pretty sure, anyway."

"What color did you paint it?"

Mr. Pagano's eyes closed and his head tilted back slightly. "Lemme see. It was green when he brought it in."

"What shade of green?"

Pickering tried to control his excitement. This was the ninth auto body shop he'd been to that morning. He'd visited nearly a hundred over the past several days, with no luck whatsoever.

By that time he was tired, and there was a conviction deep in his bones, going back to boyhood, that over-enthusiasm for anything leads inevitably to disappointment.

"It was dark green." Mr. Pagano snatched some color swatches down from the pegboard and pointed his paint-stained finger at one. "That's a basic Mercedes color. What we call your basic forest green." Beyond the glass wall, masked and suited figures drifted phantomlike through steamy clouds of vaporized paint hissing under great pressure.

"And the color you painted it?"

Pagano's head rolled backward again. The eyes closed. "Now, you gotta remember this is like four, five weeks ago. I paint maybe a hundred cars a week."

Pickering's brow started to lower.

"But this one," Mr. Pagano continued, "I got a distinct impression we sprayed gray."

"Yeah. How come?"

"How come we sprayed it gray?"

"No. How come you remember this one especially? What was so special about this one?"

Pagano turned to watch the ghostlike figures of his painters drifting beyond the glass partition. " 'Cause of the guy," he remarked distractedly. "It was the guy. Something about him."

"Strange?"

"Not at all. Friendly. Pleasant. Chatty, you know. Spoke in a low voice. Kind of dignified. Knew a lot about cars."

"Did he say why he wanted it painted?"

"There was this rust, I told you. And I guess he figured if he was gonna spring for that, he might as well go all the way with a paint job. Car's nearly twenty years old, don't forget."

"This was the first paint job it's had in twenty years?"

"I didn't say that, did I?" Mr. Pagano was irritated by the question. "As a matter of fact, when we scraped it down, there must've been four, five layers of paint. All different colors. A regular fucking rainbow." Pagano beamed amiably. "That's how come I recall this car. You don't see that too often. People spray a car, they generally spray it the same color."

Pickering had been sitting there spinning his thumbs. Over the past several minutes the speed of his rotations had steadily increased. "If your memory's so great," he taunted, "I bet you don't recall this guy's name."

Mr. Pagano's caterpillar brows furrowed. For the first time during the course of questioning, he appeared distressed. "What d'ya want him for? What'd the guy do?"

"Maybe something. Maybe nothing," Pickering replied evasively. "Who knows? That's what we're trying to find out."

"Look," Mr. Pagano proclaimed, "I run a respectable place here. Everything on the up and up. Never had no trouble with the law. I'm a good neighbor. Ask anyone on the block."

"Who's talkin' about you?" Pickering shot back. "You're clean. We know that. I'm just asking, do you know this guy's name, is all."

Mr. Pagano seemed offended. "Sure I know his name. Not off the top of my head. But right here in my file."

Pickering waited, slowly tapping the arm of his chair, scarcely breathing as the boxy little Italian man rummaged through his file. It was no ordinary file, not the sort of thing one finds in a well-organized, well-run office. Items here were filed according to no discernible system — not alphabetical by name, not by category, or by date in time, but rather by some system, internal and mysterious, consisting wholly of a series of tiny abstruse symbols known only to Mr. Pagano himself.

Even from where Pickering sat across the desk from the file, he could view the turmoil within those drawers. They bulged and spilled over with stacks of tatty, dog-eared invoices, yellow and dusty with age.

From beyond the plate glass, a figure like a fish in an

quarium tank floated up to the glass pane and peered
out at them incuriously through goggles. Great gusts of
hissing air whirled all about him. The haze of paint
fumes hovering above the outer office made Pickering's
eyes burn and his head throb.

"I got it right here somewhere." Mr. Pagano ransacked his drawers, waxing more furious by the moment.
He could sense the growing skepticism of the detective
sitting, waiting there, before him.

Several times he pulled out invoices, apparently forgetting what it was he'd been looking for, then proceeded to read them to himself. Then he would place
them carefully off to the side as if he intended to return
to them at some future date. Then he'd turn back to the
chaos of his files. "Don't worry. It's here. It's right here."

Pickering's burning eyes rolled heavenward in silent,
long-suffering despair.

"Now where the hell is that invoice, anyway?" Mr.
Pagano banged the file drawer shut and started to rum-
mage through the wire out box on his littered desk.
"Let's see now. What do we got here? Mercedes. Mercedes. Everybody owns a fucking Mercedes . . ." He
whistled breathily while papers flew through his hands.
"Mercedes." He plucked an invoice out of the pile.
"Here's one." His eyes scanned quickly over the yellow
sheet, the smile on his face fading as quickly as it had
appeared. "Forget it. It's a four fifty SL. A nineteen
eighty-five. Foster. I remember that guy, all right. A
stiff. Still ain't got my money."

The harried, overworked man pressed on. "Jesus, I
know I got it. It's right here someplace."

"I can come back," Pickering said, anxious by then to
depart the place himself.

"No, no. You stay right there. It's right here, I tell
you. Right under my nose. I can almost smell it. It's
right . . . " Suddenly his face lit up and he was flapping
a yellow carbon sheet about over his head. "Briggs.
Donald Briggs."

Pickering rose and moved quickly around the desk. "You got it?"

"Sure I got it. I told you, didn't I? Nothing in these files I don't keep a record of right up here." His thick, paint-spattered fingers tapped the side of his head for emphasis.

"Briggs. Donald. I even got a copy of the registration, if you want."

Pickering gaped back at him. Can this be me? Rollo Pickering? he thought. Can I be so lucky? "You've actually got a copy of the registration?"

"Course I do. I always make a copy of the registration. Specially with these fancy cars. Most of 'em are hot, you know."

"Briggs, Donald." Pickering's eyes swarmed over the invoice. The pale Xerox letters wavered like objects under water beneath his burning eyes. The registration number was perfectly clear, but some of the computer-generated letters and numbers of the address were either faded or had not reproduced at all. He held the sheet away from his eyes, squinting to decipher the address. "Hey, what's this look like to you?"

Mr. Pagano craned his neck and peered over the detective's shoulder. "What's that, a *b*?"

"Yeah. But the next letter is missing. Then you got an *i*. Then the next two letters are missing."

"What's that at the end? Looks like an *e*."

"Yeah. That's an *e*, all right. Can you make out the number?"

"Looks like a fourteen."

Pickering looked at him skeptically. "You could've fooled me."

"Zip's pretty clear, though: one-oh-oh-one-four. That's way downtown, ain't it?"

"From the Village on south," Pickering said to himself. "It figures then he'd pick your place to have his car sprayed. Must live right around here somewhere." Pickering had scribbled out onto his pad a diagram of the letters he had available to him with a series of short dashes in between to indicate those letters that were missing.

B — I — — E   Street
New York, N.Y. 10014

Together the two men puzzled over the acrostic . . . to no avail. Nothing whatever came to mind. Mr. Pagano slapped his knees and sighed ruefully. "Listen, I gotta get back out there." He indicated with his head the two priestlike figures floating behind the glass partition.

Pickering regarded him with sympathy. "Can I borrow this here?" He held up the invoice.

"Be my guest."

"Thanks. I'll send it back. Oh, listen. One more thing. Is it okay I use your phone for a minute?"

"Sure," Mr. Pagano mumbled sadly. "Just don't call China." In the next moment he passed through a side door and suddenly reappeared as one of the rubber-shawled moonwalkers on the other side.

Pickering snapped up a nearby telephone directory and flipped quickly through the pages. Under the section devoted to federal departments, he quickly located the number for central headquarters of the New York City Post Office. He dialed and asked to be connected with their special tracking unit. He identified himself to a Mrs. Sternhagen, informed her that he was a New York City detective, and gave her his shield number. Then he explained his problem, provided her with the letters he had, and gave her the zip code.

Mrs. Sternhagen sounded maternal and concerned. "Will you be there a few minutes?" she asked.

"If you say so."

"Give me your number. I'll get right back to you."

She was as good as her word. In five minutes she rang back. "The only thing we've got in that postal zone with six letters looking like what you've got is either Beaver or

Bridge Street. Both are down around the financial district. But since Beaver ends with an *r*, not an *e*, offhand, I'd say what you've got looks more like Bridge."

"Offhand, I'd say you were right." The detective scribbled both street names on a scrap of paper before him. "God bless," he said and hung up.

In the next moment he was lunging for the front door. Half in, half out, he stood straddling the threshold, peering back into the shop as if he'd forgotten something. He lunged back into the shop and tore open the door leading into the painting area. He poked his head in, then snatched it back at once. It was like entering Hell. Gales of atomized paint drove him backward, leaving behind a thick dusting of gray spray on his collar and sleeves. He ducked back quickly, closing the door partially for protection. "Hey, Pagano," he shouted above the roaring compressors.

Attired in overalls, mask, and goggles, the beleaguered Italian shuffled toward him, ghostlike, seemingly from out of nowhere.

"It's Bridge Street," Pickering bellowed at him, his voice rising above the gale from within. "Fourteen Bridge Street."

TWENTY-ONE

THE MOMENT SHE SAW THE UNMARKED CAR turn the corner and cruise into the street, Suki Klink knew it was the police. Years of staying out of the path of the law gave her long antennae and keen instincts. She watched the car from her kitchen window and knew that something was up. Even unmarked cars driven by the police had a certain unmistakable swagger to them. They never had much chrome on them, either.

The car crept slowly down the street so that she could see the people inside, their heads swiveling about, as if they were looking for something in particular. An address. She didn't have to be told. She knew it was 14 Bridge Street. She had that sort of prescience one associates with the old, the deranged, and the persistently hunted.

Even before the car drew to a halt at the foot of the weedy old brick walk, she was up the stairs, skirts flying behind her, flinging into Warren's room and shaking him wildly. He'd come in early that morning and had slept through most of the day.

"Get up. Get up," she hissed, spittle flying from between her teeth. "They're here, for Chrissake. They're here."

Wound in his sheets, Warren turned, cocking a bleary eye up at her. "What?"

"They're here, for Chrissake. The cops. The goddamn cops."

She started to haul him up and had him halfway out of bed before he came fully awake.

"Who?"

"The cops. I told you to lay low, didn't I? Christ, you never listen, do you? You always know better than anyone. Go down now. Quick. Quick, goddamn it. Into the tunnel."

By then he was wide awake, grabbing trousers and struggling into shoes. He stumbled as she pushed him out the bedroom door and down the stairs. Outside, she could hear voices on the walk as she whirled backwards into the little turret room, bowing, stooping, lunging, and whisking away every sign of its occupant strewn carelessly about.

The way down to the basement was through a small door behind the stairs. No sooner had it closed behind Warren than the rusty old cast-iron knocker clanked hard against the front door.

Suki stood at the cellar door, her back to it, half-crouched in the shadows, waiting several moments until she heard the sound of Warren's scurrying steps receding back into the farthest reaches of the cellar.

"Coming. Coming," she hollered at the knocker as it sounded again. Even as she approached the door, her step slowed and her shoulders stooped as she underwent the miraculous transformation of aging in the course of a few moments.

The two plainclothesmen standing out front on the porch were detectives. She knew that at once. They were of a type she knew all too well. This was no social call. She knew that, too. They were not out there raising money for the policeman's ball. "This fourteen Bridge Street?" the younger man asked, but she was looking at the tall, white-haired one, peering down at her disapprovingly.

"Says so right out front on the mailbox, don't it?" she snapped back.

"You Mrs. Klink?"

"I go by that name."

One of them flashed a shield. "My name's Sergeant Pickering. This here is Detective Lieutenant Mooney."

Suki's gaze traveled slowly up the big, steeple-like figure. Its shoulders blocked the sunlight from her doorway. The face she saw at the top of the shoulders wore a pinched expression, as if its owner smelled something disagreeable.

"May we come in?" Pickering asked.

She chewed on her tongue, stalling for time and hoping that Warren was already out and into the abandoned sewer line beneath the house. "Suit yourself," she muttered, none too graciously, and stood aside.

The two detectives moved on the step outside, each deferring to the other, until finally Mooney mumbled something and stepped into the rank shadows.

"Not used to strangers comin' through here." Suki led them in through the front hallway. She dragged a foot behind her as though she were lame. In the last several minutes she'd grown more stooped than ever.

"I'll bet," Mooney replied. He trod cautiously around the dried cat stools and assorted mess littered over the floors. A fetor of something sweet and rotten hung in a haze above the little sitting room into which the old woman led them.

With a crooked, trembling finger, she indicated a pair of frayed Morris chairs, their seats sprung and the gray horsehair innards spilling out. "Have a seat."

Mooney scowled down at the chair and waved the suggestion aside. "How long you been here, mother?"

Suki let herself slowly down with a groan onto a four-foot bundle of old *Life* magazines trussed up with clothesline. "Maybe forty-five years now. Come here with my husband, nineteen forty-two."

Pickering consulted his pad. "His name was Klink?"

"Fred Klink. Friends called him Freddy. Left me this place when he died so's I'd never be out on the street. I own it free and clear." The old lady's back stiffened as she proclaimed this and she glowered straight at Mooney. "Bank'd just love to take it from me. Let 'em try. They'll rue the day."

Something in the way she'd said it made Mooney believe they would. Even though the sun was shining outside, it was dark in the room. One of the windows was cracked and had been covered over with a sheet of corrugated cardboard. The other three were grimed, almost glazed hard with a coating of soot.

"How old's this place?" Mooney gazed up at the wormy timbered beams that braced the sagging ceiling.

" 'Bout a hundred and fifty years. Built during the Polk administration."

"Didn't think there were too many more of these around," Pickering said.

"There aren't," the old lady snapped back with that edge of pride and defiance. "President Polk took tea here once," she boasted.

"How much land you sitting on, mother?" Mooney inquired.

"Near three acres."

Pickering whistled. "Three acres in the financial district. No wonder the bank wants it. You must be some kind of millionaire."

"If I am, sonny, I sure got nothin' to show for it." She made a short, gruff noise that might have been a laugh.

"That's for sure," Mooney mumbled.

"Beg pardon?"

"Nothing. Just thinking aloud. You here all by yourself?"

"That's right. Been that way since Mr. Klink, God rest him, passed on."

"The name Donald Briggs mean anything to you?"

"Who?"

"Briggs. Donald Briggs."

She cocked an eye at him, her tongue darting across her lips. "Briggs? No. Can't say it does. Should it?"

Mooney moved across to the window and peered out through the grimy panes. "You got a garage here? A car?"

She started to laugh, then broke off suddenly as

though she'd thought better of it. "Do I look like the sort drives a car?"

Mooney regarded her through the dim, rancid air. "I get your point. . . . Mind if we have a look around?"

She looked back and forth from one to the other of them, wariness gathering itself about her like a cloak. "Wouldn't make no difference if I did, would it?"

"You've got a right to insist on a warrant," Pickering said. "We don't have one with us now, but we can get one in twenty-four hours."

"Don't bother on my score, sonny." She groaned and rose creaking to her feet. "Just don't make a mess of things," she said and hobbled out.

The two men stood alone in the room, gazing about in dismay at the filth and disorder.

By then Mooney had given up all real hope of finding anything there. Driving up to the house that day, they'd scoured Bridge Street for a vintage Mercedes of any color and found no sign of one. There was no garage to the house, not even a driveway. Nor was there anyplace around back where a car might be driven and concealed from the street.

Pickering was discouraged, too. You could see it in the young man's face, lined and tired — looking a bit sheepish and contrite. Though he'd not discussed it with Mooney, he'd already come to many of the same conclusions regarding the house and its peculiar owner. Their "look around" was just that. Perfunctory and glum, as though they were merely going through the motions in order to file a report. They prowled through the lower floor, peering into rooms, skirting litter and cartons, opening closets reeking of camphor and mold that hadn't been opened for years.

Their way took them through the old lady's kitchen where, amidst the yowling of hungry cats, Suki was sorting foliage and botanical specimens, tagging each and dropping them into canisters and old jam jars, their

contents identified in spidery ballpoint letters on dirty
strips of adhesive tape.

On the stovetop, a huge old dented caldron simmered
with a thick vapory fluid. It had formed a frothy scum at
the top, lapping at the pot rim like a crater full of lava
about to blow. The haze above the room was choking,
causing the two detectives to seek relief in the upper
reaches of the house. They found nothing on the second
floor more controversial than the dusty old room beneath the eves where Suki dwelled in awesome disarray.
His big pawlike hand covering his mouth and nose,
Mooney pondered the massive wooden headboard of the
bed, with its grotesque gargoyles staring down at him
like demon totems. They moved through the room like
swimmers breaststroking, pushing aside cobwebs, making their way to the door.

There were two additional rooms on the second floor
and a dank privy with a cracked commode and a ring of
filth at its bottom. At the place where it was anchored to
the floor, water leaked out, a brownish, lackadaisical
trickle.

The doors to the other two rooms were closed. When
opened, they revealed no more than additional storage
space used to warehouse cartons and boxes of clothes,
stacks of old newspapers, some dating back to the forties.
Life magazine with the smiling ghostly portraits of the
great and near-great leaped up at them out of the shadows. Charles Lindbergh. Pierpont Morgan scowling
above his huge red, tumid nose. Franklin Delano
Roosevelt in three-quarter profile, dapper in a soft gray
fedora, a cigarette holder clenched between his teeth.
Winston Churchill, cigar in mouth, a pug dog on his
arm, a twinkly curmudgeon. Marilyn Monroe and Joe
DiMaggio in the blissful first blush of early matrimony.

There was electricity but no lamps, only some ceiling
fixtures, mostly without bulbs, to illuminate the upper
stories. They groped about in the dense shadows, col-
liding with boxes and strips of flypaper dangling from the

ceiling, still covered with the dried husks of their hapless victims.

"Let's get the hell out of this." Mooney swatted a lacy cobweb draped in his path.

Out on the landing, just before they were about to go down, they saw the little extension ladder leading up to the cupola room.

Pickering glowered up through a mote-filled sunbeam. "What do you suppose that is?"

"More shit."

"Better have a look, anyway."

Because of the glass cupola and the lack of a window to ventilate the area, the room above was nearly twenty degrees warmer than those on the first and second stories.

Covering their mouths and noses from the dust and smell of sour bedding, they stepped in. Mooney's eyes ranged up the walls and ceiling, then dropped to the bed. "Who the hell sleeps here?"

"The old dame, probably."

"I thought she slept in the bedroom downstairs." Mooney opened the closet and gazed at the clothing hanging there. "Don't look like old lady's clothes to me."

Pickering gazed blankly back at him. They stood there a moment pondering the question.

"Let's get out of here before we're cooked alive." Mooney started to back down the extension ladder, which swayed ominously beneath his weight.

Down in the kitchen again, Mooney asked the old lady, "Who sleeps in the little room up under the dome?"

"I do," Suki replied instantly.

"Then who sleeps in the big bedroom on the second floor?"

"I do. Used to be Mr. Klink's room and mine before he died. I still use it from time to time. When the mood suits me."

"Whose clothing was that hanging in the closet up there?" Mooney asked.

"Mr. Klink's — I keep everything of his just as he left it." She looked at them smiling as though pleased with the facility of her reply, then changed the subject quickly. "You boys find what you're lookin' for?"

"There a cellar here?" Mooney asked, ignoring her question.

"Sure."

"Where's it at?"

"Under your feet, just like any other."

Mooney scowled at her. "How do we get to it?"

"Little door just under the stairs."

"Anything down there?" Pickering asked.

"Just the same as up here."

"Oh?" Mooney grumbled. By that time he was smoldering. "We'll have a look, anyway."

"No lights down there," Suki said. "Better take this."

She took a candle and a holder from the shelf above the stove and lit the wick from the gas flame. Then she led them out to the cellar stair.

The two men had to stoop beneath the shallow lintel of the little doorway, then trundled down the narrow stone stairs.

Once at the bottom, they stood in the damp, strangely icy air with the candle flame guttering before them. Mooney held it above his head and peered into the cluttered murkiness. A thin veil of light filtered down from the grimy little half-windows set in the stone foundation above them. "God," the detective muttered, "would you believe this?"

Pickering kicked disconsolately at something on the floor.

"Cold as a crypt down here." Mooney started to edge his way between a pair of broken old chifforobes, one listing dangerously on only three legs. At the sound of something scurrying over the dirt floor, he lunged back. "Rats," he snarled at the unwelcoming shadows. "I've had it. Let's blow this joint."

Upstairs, the old lady was still puttering about with

her phials and canisters when the two detectives reappeared. She made a point of ignoring them as she went about pouring a sticky amber philtre from one beakered vessel into another.

"You've got no garage around the back?" Mooney asked.

"I said I didn't before."

Mooney whisked cinder dust from his shoulders.

"You sure you don't know no Donald Briggs?" Pickering asked a little hopelessly.

"Name means nothin' to me."

The two men hovered there uncertainly as though unsure where to proceed next.

"That all?" Suki helped them along.

Mooney shrugged his shoulders. "I guess so. By the way, you've got rats in your cellar."

"Always had," Suki replied phlegmatically. "They don't bother no one. Besides, they nourish the cats."

There seemed little more to say. Abject, the two detectives skulked out and down the weedy brick walk to where the unmarked squad car awaited them.

"Ditsy," Pickering muttered when they'd settled back in their seats.

Mooney sat grim and unspeaking, watching the sooty, humped skyline of Bridge Street roll past the window.

"Never saw nothin' like that," Pickering went on, full of childish wonder.

"What the hell was she cooking in that pot?"

"Looked like a mess of grass to me."

"Did you get a whiff of it?" Mooney asked.

"All I could smell was cat piss all over the place."

Mooney stared out the window, watching the tide of life teeming up and down Pine Street. "I smelled it, all right." His voice was quiet, expressionless. "Smelled medicinal. Earthy. Herbal. I've smelled something like that before. Can't quite put my finger on it."

Pickering was unimpressed. Mooney went on ruminating aloud. "She took the lid of that pot off to stir it.

That's when I got a blast of it. Made me a little dizzy for a second."

The car moved north, through the choked and snarling late-afternoon traffic.

"You didn't happen to get a look at her eyes, did you?" Mooney asked suddenly.

The question brought Pickering up. "Looked like curdled cheese to me."

"I bet that old dame is on something. She was flying."

"On a broomstick, if you ask me."

"Looked like she was brewing a mess of pot there. Whatever kind of junk it is, she's on it, too."

"Did you believe her?" Pickering asked.

"About this Briggs character?" Mooney reflected. "I don't know. Could be. Sure as hell wasn't no Mercedes parked out front. The clothes in that attic closet didn't look like her old man's clothes, either."

They were moving up Chambers Street toward Nassau, making their way to Police Plaza.

"What am I supposed to tell Mulvaney?" Mooney asked. He appeared uneasy at the prospect of reporting another "no progress" to the chief of detectives. He was sorely aware that by then, he'd used up nearly half of the ninety days allotted to him to close the case, and that Eddie Sylvestri, hot and eager, was waiting in the wings.

"Tell him about the auto body shop and the line we got on the car," Pickering suggested. "Tell him about Berrida and the description we got on the guy who sold him the software components. Tell him to hold his water, is what I say."

"You tell him that." Mooney scowled out the window. "What about the old lady just now?"

"Sure. Tell him all that. Sounds like progress, even if it's not. What about the stuff we got from the M.E.?"

Mooney made a disparaging sound with his lips. "He knows all of that by now. The broken front teeth. The fix on the blood types. The conflicting descriptions."

"And still he's not satisfied?"

"What's to be satisfied? We've known all that for weeks."

They sat there smoldering in stalled traffic while horns blared all about them. "How do you like that old dame?" Mooney asked suddenly. "Living like a hedgehog in that dump. Owns three acres of New York's financial district."

"Rich as Croesus." Pickering laughed. "Living in a shit house."

"Let's run a check on that registration you got from the body shop."

"We already did. How d'ya think we got to Bridge Street?"

"Check it again. But this time for any stolen 'sixty-eight Merce two twenty. Any color. Not just green. Look for a name sounds anything like Donald Briggs."

Pickering looked at him gloomily.

"You heard me, Rollo. Check it again."

Pickering flung his hands up in despair.

The squad car wheeled left and swung down the ramp into the garage below Number One Police Plaza.

"You heard?"

"Most of it. They came down the cellar."

"Where were you?"

"Top of the tunnel. Just pulled the lid down over me." Warren's eyes shone large and white in the kitchen shadows. "What'd they want?"

"They wanted you, sonny." There was a note of spiteful glee in her voice. "Kept asking for Briggs, though."

"How'd they find out about him?"

"You tell me, Mr. Smart Guy," she jeered. "Better go ask those fancy auto body guys you like to give your money to. You just better hope they don't go checking up on Mr. Griggs and find out what a sticky finish he come to."

Comprehension dawned on Warren's face. Pounding his fist on the side of the stove, he turned suddenly and started out, then rushed back. "You didn't tell them about Griggs. I swear, Suki, if you opened your yap . . ."

"If you were listening like you said you were, you know I said nothing."

"Jesus." He slammed his head with his fist. "That car. That goddamned car."

"Didn't you just have it painted?"

Warren gaped at her. "I had to. They'd been looking for a dark green car. I painted it gray."

"Did they take your registration at the paint shop?"

An expression like that of a hurt child crept over Warren's agitated features.

"That's where they got Briggs from," Suki went on harshly. "And that's where they got this address from." She seemed to be enjoying his fright. "Now you listen to me. I don't know what they saw in your closet up there, but you best clear out of here for a while, sonny," she panted heavily. "They'll be back. Mark my words. They're a little confused right now, but once they get a chance to sort it all out, they'll put two and two together. Didn't I tell you that car would be your undoing? A man in your line of work doesn't want fancy cars."

Warren stared around the kitchen wildly, as if he were seeking exits for hasty getaways. "What do I do now?" He was angry and frightened. For a moment she thought he was about to strike her, but he could just as easily have fallen into her arms like a terrified child and wept. "What am I supposed to do now?"

She started to pull cans of food out of the cupboard: tuna fish and soup. Little bags of greasy snacks, cramming it all in a bag with a kind of wild, scything motion.

Outside dark had fallen. Through the grimy windows the lights from offices, factories, and warehouses twinkled with an almost festive heartlessness.

"Where's that car now?"

"Over on Pine Street. In the garage."

"Go get it. Drive it somewhere far away. Up north maybe. Then dump it."

He gaped at her. "Dump it?"

"Ain't that what I just said? Drive it into the woods and just dump it. Or better yet, drive it off a pier." She cocked an eye at him. "You got another registration?"

"I got four, five others."

"Then make use of them." She tossed a package of store-bought cupcakes into the bag and crammed the whole thing into his arms. The next moment she turned away and, with a curious modesty, hiked her copious skirts so he couldn't see her spindly legs. She fumbled about in the enormous folds of ragged material, finally extracting from there a thick wad of bills. She peeled off a sizable number of them, all of one-hundred-dollar denomination, and jammed them into his pockets. "Now get out of here before they come back."

He hovered there, helplessly, until she started pushing him out of the kitchen back toward the cellar door.

"Where do I go?"

"How do I know? Where you always go. North. Buffalo. Canada, maybe. You can cross the border at Niagara. They never ask for identification. But first get rid of that car. Chances are they're out lookin' for that car right now."

All the while she spoke, firing instructions at him, she kept crowding him toward the cellar door. When they reached the small alcove beneath the stairs in which it was recessed, she reached around him and yanked the door open. "Now you get. Right through the tunnel and out."

He was already on the first step down when he started back up. "First I've got to — "

"Never mind." She blocked his reentry. "You go now, sonny. Fast. Those good old boys meant business. They're not so dumb they won't catch on soon."

Warren stumbled back down three more steps. If she'd asked him to stay at that moment, he would've come right back. "How long do I have to stay away?"

She could see the fright in his eyes. There was something sad and desperate about them, like someone trapped.

"Three, four weeks. Not less. Now you get goin', sonny."

"Shit." Warren Mars staggered to his feet, clutching his knee where he'd scraped it when he'd fallen. The moment he was up again, his legs started scrambling somewhat in advance of the rest of his body. He'd already banged his head on the tunnel roof. It was no higher than four and a half feet and he had to run in a half crouch. When his head hit the clay roof, a shower of multicolored scintilla bloomed behind his eyes. The groceries Suki had given him scattered all over the tunnel floor, but he had no intention of stopping to retrieve them.

It was inky dark in the tunnel. There was, however, only one way to go, so there was little chance of his losing his way. He knew himself to be inside a narrow, semicircular ditch with clay siding.

Though the tunnel was dry, there was a brackish, low-tide smell about it. Warren thought of the dangers of methane gas and ran faster toward the fresh air. He imagined he could almost feel it up ahead where the tunnel ended at a sewer grating near the edge of Battery Park.

He stumbled again and plunged forward, feeling the warm, sticky sensation of blood seeping down the inside of his trousers from where he'd scraped his knee.

He didn't care much for this tunnel, or, for that matter, any tunnel. All small cramped areas in general, without windows through which you could see to the outside, tended to make him nervous. Nor did the feeling of being underground with tons of earth and concrete bearing down on him from above do much to lift his spirits. Even if there was sufficient ventilation about, he felt he was suffocating. Having to run doubled over in a crouch only served to compound the anxiety, and it made him short of breath. The steady rumble of traffic he could hear overhead and feel vibrating in his stomach made him certain that the thin sheet of roadway above was about to give way and bury him alive.

Warren tried to imagine what might happen in that event. He'd be crushed to death, of course. But would it be instantaneous or prolonged and agonizing, with him pinned beneath tons of macadam and dirt, still alive but slowly expiring for lack of air, like a hooked fish whomping out its final moments on the floor of a boat? As a way of dying, suffocation to him was undoubtedly the most horrifying.

He had no way of knowing in that moment where he was in relation to the duct opening at the edge of the river. He'd been through this tunnel countless times, mostly as a child, then later as a young boy, but not recently, and never after dark. In the past, when he was younger, Suki would lead him down there and walk him through with a large battery lantern. She wanted him to be prepared, she said, for any and all emergencies. Regarding what form these emergencies might take, she was none too specific. As a child he had only a vague idea of what constituted an emergency. Now suddenly, the reality of one was all too clear.

The tunnel was approximately a mile long from where he entered it beneath the house on Bridge Street to where he intended to emerge, somewhere on the Hudson River.

Running doubled over for nearly three-quarters of a mile had cramped his stomach and winded him badly. He had to stop every several minutes to catch his breath. He slumped now against the clay walls and slid slowly down to the dank floor of the duct, using his hands to guide him and gauge distance. At last, sitting there panting like some winded creature chased by hounds, he felt the sharp abrasive sensation of pebble and dirt piercing up into the seat of his trousers.

The discomfort didn't matter that much to him. He

knew it would pass the moment he stood up. It was rather the steady, unrelenting rumble of traffic banging overhead, sending waves of vibration through the old clay duct, that unnerved him. Tiny shards of stone and dirt drizzled down on his head and into the tunnel, making him virtually certain that the roof of the duct was about to crumble.

While he crouched there against the wall, waiting for his breath to return, something curious occurred. For a moment he was six years old again. He was a little child in a damp, black hole, hiding from someone. He was cold and frightened, not at all certain what he was doing there, or how he'd come to be in that place. He was either hiding from someone or he'd been put there as punishment for something he'd done.

It was not simple recollection, however. It went quite beyond mere memory, for as he squatted there in the close, almost palpable dark, he had the strange sensation of being half his size. His head and torso, his limbs and hands were no longer those of an adult. They'd shrunk to childlike proportions. He felt very small and alone, and from somewhere outside himself, he could hear a faint, high whimpering. In the next moment, he felt a rush of warmth between his legs and felt the front of his trousers sag and grow heavy with wet.

He was on his feet the next moment, running again, stooped over, careening headlong through the dark, narrow tube, the unpleasant itchy feeling of wet woolen pants clinging to his leg. Up ahead a fresh breeze blew. From where he was he could feel it gusting through the tunnel, making a low, buffeting sound. Lunging toward it, his head preceding his body, he gulped air, filling his lungs like a diver who'd been submerged too long.

Another fifty feet or so and he'd reached the grating. It was a heavy, reticulated square of cast iron set over the opening. Beyond it he could see the lights of buildings twinkling across the water on the Weehawken docks and hear the flow of the river, a steady lapping sound of small, angry waves chopping at the shoreline as they made their sullen way out to sea.

The moment he reached the grating, he seized it with both hands, nearly swamped by a rush of panic born of the fear that he was trapped. The grating was not above him but at eye level so that it didn't have to be lifted so much as pushed out. When he first tried, it wouldn't budge. There was no play in it as there would be if it were separate from the earth. This was more like a part of the earth in which the grating was embedded. For several minutes he struggled with it, to no avail, the rush of panic mounting in him by the minute. To have to return the way he'd come, all the way back through the tunnel to Bridge Street, was unthinkable. By then, distraught, his imagination running rampant, he was convinced the police were swarming through the duct toward him.

He put his shoulder against the grating and brought the full weight of his body to bear against it. He felt it give grudgingly, but only enough so that he could rock it back and forth, loosening the dry, packed earth that came spilling out from around it.

Through the mesh he could see sky and stars wheeling overhead. On the shimmering dark water of the river the hulking silhouette of a garbage scow running out to sea loomed dark and immense.

The sense of entrapment, first in the tunnel and then there behind the grating, freedom only inches away, was unbearable. In the next moment he flung himself back on the grating, with renewed ferocity, clawing at it with his fingers. He kicked and spat at it as though it were something alive and malign. Finally, with the last bit of strength he had, he braced his back against the duct wall, jammed a foot hard up against the grating, and heaved.

What followed was a sucking sound, followed by a sharp clang. A cascade of gravel and earth came next, followed by a dark, hurtling figure emerging as though propelled by something from behind. Warren found himself standing hip high in marsh grass and cattails at the river's edge, coughing and beating the dust off his jacket.

The strong wind chilled him and ballooned his sodden trousers. Staring up at the starlit firmament, he looked like nothing human, but rather like some throwback to the dawn of time.

PART IV

TWENTY-TWO

FERRIS KOOPS STOOD IN THE SHADOWS OF A furniture warehouse just across the way from 14 Bridge Street. He stood watching the blurred shape of a figure moving back and forth behind the curtained windows, trying to make out its identity. He assumed the figure was that of the young man he'd followed there from his own apartment several days before, all the way down from 81st Street. But he couldn't be sure.

The shadowing had taken time and a certain kind of dogged patience. But it wasn't difficult. It was made easy by the fact that the young man who'd come to Ferris's door that evening had decided to walk all the way home. Had he chosen to take a taxi or some public conveyance instead, the job would have been vastly more complicated.

The fact that there were people on the street, as there invariably are in New York at all hours, also helped. He had tailed him all the way from the Upper East Side down to the tip of Manhattan, where he disappeared finally into a side door of an old house hard by Battery Park.

Why had he done so was the question. The trail was long, the way arduous. What compelled Ferris to leave the comfort of his tiny apartment on such a problematic, even risky, venture?

The answer is that it was neither problematic nor risky to Ferris. Quite the contrary. Once it had started and was fully under way, nothing could have stopped him.

As they'd stood there together, the door between them slightly ajar, and listening to each other's breathing, it had occurred to Ferris who this person actually was. Nothing had been said. Ferris simply divined it with that strange sort of prescience he had been graced with from childhood. The revelation came to him complete and unqualified, just as if he'd had it on highest authority. Though he'd not even seen his face, this person Ferris knew perfectly well was the man they called the Shadow Dancer.

How curious that this individual who had occupied so much of Ferris's waking thoughts should now come to him, to his door. Even more curious, Ferris felt none of the fear or revulsion the fellow's activities had inspired in others. He felt, instead, a strangely unaccountable affection for him, as if he saw within him some profound calling or mission for himself.

Ferris had found the Dancer without even trying. The Dancer had come to him, and Ferris had had the uncanny insight to recognize him for who he was. It was providential. It could be nothing less. Whatever forces of fate controlled human destinies had now contrived to put Ferris and this lethal stranger in touch. Having found him at last, Ferris had no intention of ever losing him again. He had been singled out by the gods, charged with a responsibility to prevent further slaughter, and to save this star-crossed man from his own destruction. And for this he was grateful.

TWENTY-THREE

"WHERE DID YOU SAY YOU WERE?"

"Pawling. Know where that is?"

"I'm in no mood for mysteries."

It was 4:40 P.M. Mooney had just had an abusive phone call from the chief of detectives and had also crossed swords at midday with the medical examiner. One had again threatened his job and the other his sanity. He had little heart for games. "What the hell are you doing up there, anyway?"

"You asked me to run a check on the Briggs registration we got from the auto body shop."

"Oh — right. What's up?"

"This town happens to be where the Briggs trail ends."

A flutter of interest elevated Mooney's mood. "You find him?"

"Not exactly. I found his wife instead."

Outside the sooty windows of Manhattan South, the quick dusk of autumn had descended. Where drab, gray daylight had hovered moments before, there was now the harsh white glare of neon contrasted starkly against the urban night.

"Where is *he*?" Mooney snapped.

"I'm getting to that." Crammed into a tiny, airless phone booth on the main street in downtown Pawling, Pickering ground his teeth and struggled to keep his voice under control. "I ran that Briggs registration back through the M.V.B. like you told me."

"So?

"So, the closest thing the computer had to a Donald Briggs was a Donald Griggs, Ten Porter Road, Pawling, New York."

"With a stolen 'sixty-eight Merce two twenty."

"Color, sky blue."

"Hmm," Mooney reflected. "What about the ID number?"

"That's what's interesting. It's exactly the same as Briggs except for one digit."

"Don't tell me. Let me guess. It's the last digit. Right?"

"You got it, Frank." Pickering felt the excitement rising. "The final digit in Griggs's registration was a one. With Briggs it was a seven. All the other numbers are identical."

"See that," Mooney gloated. "Was I so dumb, after all?"

"I gotta hand it to you, Frank. If nothing else, we got us a car thief."

"You been over to this Griggs already?"

"Over and back."

"And you met the wife?"

"I already told you I did."

"What's the story on this guy?" Mooney snarled.

"That's just it. I can't tell you. Nor can his wife. He disappeared six years ago, along with the Mercedes. Neither of them has been heard from since. His wife still has a reward posted for ten grand to anyone with information leading to his whereabouts."

"What about the law?" Mooney asked. "What do they say?"

"I spoke to the Putnam County sheriff about an hour ago. They closed the books on Griggs last year."

Mooney frowned into the receiver. He waited for an ambulance siren to wail past his window before responding. "What's he look like, this Griggs?"

"I thought that for a minute, too, Frank. You're barking up the wrong tree. His wife showed me a photo.

Griggs was a big, shaggy, dopey-looking character with a soft face and a double chin. If he were alive today, and nobody up here thinks he is, he'd be fifty-one. Not exactly our dark, young romantic poet or our fair-haired lad, either."

"You talk to the state up there?"

"I spoke with the chief at the troopers barracks in Brewster. They never found the car. They never found a trace of the guy. Griggs was a paint and hardware salesman. Used to travel Putnam, Westchester, and Dutchess. The chief told me he knew him pretty well. Nice, easygoing sort of guy. Family man. Church deacon. A regular Mr. Responsibility. One fatal flaw."

"Yeah?" Mooney hung there, waiting.

"Griggs had a penchant for picking up hitchhikers. Just for company on the territory. No kinky stuff. Least none that they're talkin' about."

"And the chief figures one day he stopped for the wrong guy?"

"More or less."

"More more than less." Mooney pushed for clarification.

"You got it the first time, Frank."

Feet up on the desk, Mooney stared out the window where theater marquees glared out into the tawdry night. "Maybe we got ourselves a bit more than a car thief."

"Maybe." Pickering paused. "What I can't figure, though, is the registration part. Griggs's registration was never renewed after 'seventy-six, when he disappeared. The Briggs registration I picked up in the auto body shop was current. Up to date with the Bridge Street address."

"But the name was changed from Griggs to Briggs. Just a one-letter change. Like the one-digit change on the V.I.N. Don't that suggest something to you?"

"Sure," Pickering snapped back, but he wasn't at all sure what it was. "I can see that. You change just one letter or a number on the registration, you throw the whole computer off . . ."

"Smart, Rollo. Now, why would somebody want to do that?"

"Well, like if you wanted to re-register a stolen car . . ."

"Very good. Excellent. I'm impressed," Mooney taunted his young partner heartlessly. "Now, if you intended to re-register this so-called stolen car, why would you do it in a name that sounds almost like the original owner's name?"

An icy wind soughed around the phone booth, a pale, orange beacon of illumination in an otherwise darkened street. "I don't know," Pickering sighed dismally. "Tell me."

Mooney held the phone in the crook of his shoulder and doodled on a pad. "Okay. I'll tell you what our guy's done. Could be one of three things: (A) Either he's driving round in a stolen, unregistered car. We know that's not so because we've got a copy of an up-to-date, legit registration on that car from the auto body shop."

"Besides, that would be dumb," Pickering added. "He couldn't get new plates or inspection stickers, or insurance. Sooner or later they'd pick him up."

"Right. So now we've got alternative (B). He's re-registered the car in a different name. That's tricky and risky, but it's possible. You go find yourself a new ID number, maybe off a wreck or from a legit car with no stolen tag out on it, preferably the same make and model as the one you glommed. Next, you go find yourself some phony papers. Fraudulent documents. A title sheet. Importation papers. That's easy. They're all over the street. Or, you go to a shady printer or some guy with a copying machine. Tell 'em what you want. They'll make it up for you. Then, go find yourself some inspection stickers for the window. Easy again. Go to a gas station where they know you. When you got all that together, go down to your local M.V.B. and re-register the car in whatever name you want. You still there, Rollo?"

"I'm still here," Pickering shivered, feeling the cold seeping upward through the soles of his shoes.

"But if you're really clever," Mooney went on, warming to his subject, "if you really got some smarts, you do what our boy here did."

"Alternative (C)?" Pickering could barely suppress the excitement in his voice.

"Right. First off, when you steal the car, you manage to steal the registration along with it."

"Okay. Then what?"

"Then, instead of going the risky route of trying to re-register a stolen vehicle in person, you just mail the registration in to your local M.V.B. Tell them they've misspelled your name and would they be good enough to correct it. Griggs to Briggs. Brown to Crown. Whatever. One letter. Easy enough. A computer error. Happens all the time. And, oh, by the way, while they're correcting that little error, would they also be good enough to change the address on the registration. You're moving down from Pawling to the city. Fourteen Bridge Street. Please make all necessary changes. They even include a couple of blank lines for you to correct any mistakes they've made on the spelling of your name or address. You send along your phony title of ownership or your fake importation documents just so's everything looks legit. Three weeks later they send you back your corrected registration, with a new name and a new address."

"But you've still got the same ID number as the stolen car."

"You wouldn't want to ask them to change that or else they would start asking questions. What you do there is change the ID number yourself. With a Mercedes the ID's on the pillar doorpost on the driver's side. Take it into a machine shop where, once again, maybe they know you, and ask them to change the V.I.N. That's where the last digit comes in. That's the easiest one to file off and restamp with a new number. In this case, it

was a snap. All they had to do was stamp the little
horizontal bar onto the one. Lo and behold, you've got a
seven where there used to be a one, and also now you've
got a whole new ID number. You give your machinist
pal fifty bucks. He winks and looks the other way and
you're in business. Now when the M.V.B. sends you
back your corrected registration, you make that little
change yourself on the last digit with a ballpoint that has
the same color ink as your registration. It's so tiny maybe
one cop in a hundred would catch it, if you happened to
get stopped."

"Clever." Pickering nodded wearily. "So now you've
got a new registration with a new ID number, a new
address and a new name with just one small change."

"Right. And that one small change is enough to throw
off the computer if it just happens to be looking for the
car you're driving. And now, without having had to actually re-register the car, you've got the computer re-
registering it for you automatically, sending you an
updated registration, new plates. The insurance company can't wait to insure you. They're panting after your
premiums. You're legit."

The process had gradually become clear to Pickering,
but still there were loose ends that nagged at him.
"Okay. Okay. But I still can't figure how come Griggs's
car didn't show up on the M.V.B. list they furnished us
of stolen vehicles, vintage late sixties or early seventies.
Mrs. Griggs assured me they reported it stolen."

Mooney sighed wearily. "I don't know what I'm gonna
do with you, Rollo. All my efforts to make you a savvy
first-class detective seem futile. Number one, we asked
them to look for cars that were dark green. This one, you
tell me, was baby blue. Number two, and most importantly, the NYSPIN computer doesn't carry stolen data
indefinitely. After about five years it spits it out like old
chewing gum and the matter is forgotten. Griggs, you
say, disappeared six years ago."

Pickering gnawed the inside of his lip. His feet hurt.

and he was cold. Having felt elated before his call to Mooney, what he now felt was dismay. "I don't know, Frank. It's plausible, I guess. But I still don't get it. Why would a supercautious guy like this Dancer provide a legitimate address on his registration?"

" 'Cause it's not his address."

"No," Pickering unhappily conceded. "I guess not. Not with that old broad. That'd be too spooky."

"Could be one of two things," Mooney went on. "He either pulled the address out of the phone book, or he lives someplace else and just uses the address as a mail drop."

"With the consent of the old broad?"

"Would have to be, wouldn't you say?" Mooney hesitated. "Or, could be he lives there off and on. Just uses the place as a crash. She said the clothing in that upstairs closet had belonged to her old man who died twenty years ago, but the clothes I saw there, even the quick glance I had, didn't look no twenty years old."

There was a lengthy pause as each of them listened to the other's breathing.

"So," — Pickering continued to spin his hypothesis out to its logical conclusion — "when the old dame told us there's no Donald Briggs living there, she was telling the truth."

"In a manner of speaking," Mooney smiled slyly. "No Briggs and no Griggs, either. The guy who crashes there from time to time has another name entirely. And that one he's not sticking on no car registration and leaving around at auto body shops."

"Clever old babe."

"Not clever enough," Mooney snapped. "Now we watch that place like hawks."

"Four nine three two . . . five one seven eight . . . six four three four . . . four six two five . . . four three one . . ."

The numbers rose like incantations with a faint humming sound and moved through the room, which smelled of mushrooms and damp earth. Suki lay in the big old oak bed beneath the wood headboard with animals, predatory and grotesque, grinning down upon her like illustrations in an old edition of Grimm.

She lay at the bottom of a mound of blankets (not blankets really, more just a hill of undifferentiated rags). There was no illumination in the room other than a stump of tallow mounted in a jam jar with a wick of flame that guttered from the currents of icy air that crept in over the sill and through the cracked window panes that rattled and whistled in their frames.

The temperature in the room was only several degrees above that of the outside. A wind buffeting in off the river gnashed about the eaves. Periodically, a loose shutter banged at the rear of the house.

Insulated with several coats and dresses, Suki lay drowsy from long draughts of one of her herbal infusions, mumbling numbers to herself of some arcane and mystical origin. Plugged into her ears were the Walkman earphones. Planted like a root dead center in her mouth was a stump of fuming weed that smelled vaguely of punk. A cup of something hot and pitchy black beside the tallow and the toothglass on her night table sent wisps of steam curling ceilingward.

Balanced on the old woman's chest was a thickish volume with a ragged antique binding out of which she read by means of a pair of eyeglasses she'd found in a trashcan in the Bowery and used as a magnifying glass. One of the lenses was cracked and one of the temple cables was held on by a wad of dirty adhesive. The lens refraction combined with the black smoke from her cigarette made her squint as she alternately read and mumbled numbers from which she believed she could divine the future. That was the way she'd taught Warren to add and prophesy the future, too.

"Nine three two four . . . one eight oh one . . . one

seven two five . . . " Her voice trailed off in little gasps and wheezes as the narcotic properties of her herbal brew took a slow but commanding hold of her.

The numbers she mumbled came from the book she'd been reading — one of her *grimoires,* as she liked to call them, one of the cherished volumes she used in order to penetrate the mysteries she believed governed all life. These mysteries were the spirits dwelling on some elevated plane that could be reached only by means of the powerful draughts she confected nightly out of herbs grown in her own garden and compounded in accordance with some ancient formula.

The numbers stumbling off her tongue were interchanged with letters that would form words that translated into messages from the spirits dwelling in the higher plane. This was the technique of the tetragrammaton taught to her by Mr. Klink, who had been a third order Rosicrucian. She, in turn, had passed it on to Warren when she'd first brought him to Bridge Street as a homeless waif.

At seven years he could not add a column of numbers or sign his name. It was by means of this system that she taught him, imbuing him, as she did, with her own obsession for an unseen world. He was an eager pupil and learned his lessons well.

Barely audible, the numbers spilled from her lips along with tiny bubbles of saliva. The voice droning through her earphones was that of a late-night talk-show host who made a specialty of putting on the air what he called "night people." They came there to share with others of like predilections their strange and mostly bizarre encounters in the realm of the extrasensory.

The flickering candle beside her bed cast gloomy undulating shapes on the walls and ceilings of her room. She had by then succumbed to the effects of her "tea." It coursed through her limbs, exerting in her a tide with a strong pull. It moved from the extremities into her legs and arms, and from there into her head, which had begun to spin pleasantly, changing the focus of her eyes and distorting whatever she looked at.

One of the properties of her "tea" — one she counted most salubrious — was the power of the brew to transform her immediate surroundings; to disorient her to the point where she was transported to some place, far away and far above the drab, prosaic setting of her daily life.

The feeling was pleasant. Even beyond pleasant. But the psychic journey she had to make in order to reach there was terrifying, full of peril and risk that lay in the vast, twilight landscape stretching between one realm and the other.

The voice inside her earphones droned on somewhat louder. Its point of origin seemed to be inside her head. Its resonance seemed to vibrate in the bones of her skull. It carried with it the terrifying, yet oddly pleasurable, sensation that the bones of her skull were about to shatter.

The flame beside her bed transformed itself magically from a small, lambent shaft to the point where it loomed large as a wall oven. It was full of crevices and fissures, hues of purple and green, into which one might walk without fear of injury. Beyond there, she could enter into some cavernous place, vast and silent, fashioned of ice like a frozen waste. It was there in those labyrinthine, tunneled corridors, noiseless and unpeopled, that she liked to wander endlessly, seemingly directionless, but drawn irresistibly as if by a magnet to some specific destination.

Soon there would be a buoyancy to her step as if the leaden weight of her legs were suddenly freed of the force of gravity. A blaze of light somewhere up ahead emitted a peculiar glow, an unearthly effulgence coming from no human agency or recognizable source.

It was toward that light she walked, free of all the encumbrances of daily life. She went barefoot in a plain dress of white cotton. She was neither cold nor hot. Temperature appeared to be no factor here. Gazing at ordinary objects — rocks, water, the foliage of trees — her perceptions of things were magnified a hundredfold. She would see objects as though they were beneath the lens of a microscope, in infinite detail. A molecule of dust would divulge within itself a universe of intricate detail.

Noises heard could be anatomized as though their component parts would split and divide, each then listened to individually. The most simple, scarcely audible sound — the falling of a sheet of paper onto the floor or the passage of air in a corridor — took on exquisite proportions. All sights, sounds, odors of things were immense yet simple, quickly revealing their structural composition. And all the while, something inside her continued to open and expand. She could feel herself filling like a vessel with an awareness of things she could have scarcely imagined. The gnawing rat of daily worry, the ceaseless scramble and grubbing about for sustenance was shed like an old skin, and, for that time at least, she was at peace.

But then, just as suddenly and abruptly as if a switch were thrown, the sensation of transcendence ceased and she found herself standing in the darkened, stuffy little cubicle upstairs beneath the cupola in Warren's room. The air was close and smelled of sour bedding. Outside, the wind howling up and down Bridge Street rattled the glass of the cupola in its frames. Beyond the glass, the light from the Statue of Liberty glowed with an unearthly golden sheen in the harbor.

Half crouching there in the dark, swathed in coats and robes and layers of outer wear, she slowly regained an awareness of her surroundings. Still resonating from the intensity of her "experience," she tingled with excitement. She'd been exhausted, bone weary and feverish, when she'd taken to her bed that evening. Now she could feel a current of new vitality surging through her. With her finger she touched tentatively the flesh of her cheek and found it warm and glowing.

For days, ever since he'd left, she'd had no contact with Warren. That didn't alarm her. With the police poking about as they had, she was glad there hadn't been any. In the past she'd known him to disappear for months on end, making virtually no contact with home. Then, just as suddenly he would reappear, with not so much as a word about where he'd been or what he'd been up to.

Knowing that the police had traced him to Bridge Street (even though the police themselves didn't yet quite realize it) and for a time were even watching the house (several times she'd seen the unmarked cars parked with their lights out at the head of the street), she scarcely expected Warren to be so rash as to try and make any sort of contact. He'd be an awful fool if he did, and whatever one might say about Warren Mars, in matters of the police he was nobody's fool.

Now something had told her that Warren would soon be returning. She no longer had anything to fear about his threats of breaking away. Feelings of imminent good fortune suffused her. Things would go well now. She'd had an inkling while under the influence of her nightly infusion and those inklings were always reliable. Once again, there would be the old closeness between her and Warren. Just like the old days, when he was a slip of a thing seated at her side, his tiny child's hand in hers and learning the trade.

An angry blast of wind leaned hard up against the cupola glass. The noise of its creaking jolted her rudely from her reverie. Suddenly, she was keenly aware of things to do if Warren was to be returning soon.

Although she was reasonably certain the police still continued their surveillance of Bridge Street, she was not uneasy. Even if Warren did return while they were still about, she knew he was canny enough not to march brazenly up the gravel walk and knock on the front door. The night he'd left Bridge Street in near panic, he'd left through the tunnel. She was certain that if he came back now, it would be by precisely the same route.

As a matter of additional precaution, she moved more of his things out of the little room in the attic, boxed them, and hauled them down into the far reaches of the cellar. As a final gesture, she pulled a chair beneath the light fixture hanging overhead, reached up, unscrewing the small brass crown ringing the bulb, and lifted down from there the little velvet jeweler's sack of rings and bracelets and brooches of precious and semi-precious stones comprising Warren's own personal cache. These she would stash away out of sight until such time that any danger of the police re-searching the house would have faded entirely.

Even at that late hour (two A.M., at least), she carried the small sack down into the cellar. She made her hobbling, lurching way into the distant reaches of the icy, subterranean vault. With the fat knob of tallow flickering before her, she found the cast-iron lid marking the entrance to the sewer line, wrestled it off by means of a crowbar, and descended.

Not more than fifty or so feet from the bottom of the stone stair stood the half-dozen assorted barrels and crates that contained the cream of her "collections." Before tucking Warren's sack deep into one of those containers, she spilled its contents into her ruddy, callused palm and rummaged through them once again. Several she hefted separately, holding them up to the sputtering candle for closer inspection.

As always, when she handled valuables, something rapt overcame her. She never perceived such objects in terms of pure, simple beauty, but rather as a source of powerful "magic" to be hoarded up against the bad days she was always certain were coming. The sense of physically possessing them produced in her a joy that was oddly sexual. Merely handling them, the sensations in her were nearly identical. In her mind she'd already forgotten that they were Warren's prizes. Had someone confronted her with that unpleasant fact, she would have said she was merely holding them for safekeeping against his return.

She was protecting him in the event the police might return and search the room again. She had his interest at heart, she told herself, without pushing self-analysis of her motives too far.

She didn't covet anything of his, she assured herself. But what if he were to return to the house at a time when she wasn't there and discover that his little cache was missing? What then? The consequences might be dire.

On reflection, however, she concluded that such an outcome was improbable. When the time came for him to return, she would be there to explain. Having pushed all such unpleasantness from her mind, she turned her attention to the fistful of pretty baubles gleaming in her palm — the little bits of colored stone, the chunks of silver and gold shimmering in the murky gloom of the candlelit tunnel.

"Hey, Briggs."

"Beg pardon?"

"That's right. I'm talking to you. You're Briggs, aren't you?"

Ferris Koops hovered in the shadows beneath the scaffolding of a construction site on Bridge Street. The voice he heard came from the inside of a four-door Dodge sedan parked nearly opposite him at the curb. He couldn't see the face of the person addressing him, only the featureless silhouette of a disembodied head poised above the driver's seat.

"You're Donald Briggs, aren't you?"

Koops stared blankly at the dark square of the car window, where the disembodied head appeared to be nodding at him. In the next moment, both front doors opened simultaneously. Two men emerged from either side of the car. The doors slammed hollowly through the empty street. Koops could see a pair of dark, boxy forms approaching him, their footsteps ringing on the cold cobblestone of the street.

They approached him quickly from either side, one

swooping down on him from the left, the other on the right. The one approaching from the left, a stoutish man with a bull neck and a bristly, well-trimmed mustache adorning his upper lip, flicked open a wallet. A silver badge flashed like a gash of lightning. "My name is Officer Borelli, N.Y.P.D. This is Officer Carpenter." He tilted his head at a sullen black man in a houndstooth suit of imitation British cut.

"Your name is Briggs, isn't it?"

"My name?" There was a smile of pleasant bemusement on Koops's face. "My name's not Briggs. My name's Koops."

"Koops?"

"Right. Ferris Koops."

The officer calling himself Borelli frowned. "What the hell kind of name is that?"

"Dutch. My ancestors were Dutch. On my father's side, that is," Ferris hastened to explain just in case it was not immediately apparent to the officer.

Borelli stared him up and down skeptically. "What are you doing out here this hour, Koops?"

"Out here?"

"That's right. You been out here the last three nights. What's the big attraction? This ain't exactly Broadway and Forty-third."

"You been starin' at that house a lot, Koops," the black officer chimed in. "Something about that house interest you?"

"I've been out here the last three nights?" Ferris replied in the form of a question. The ingenuous smile, the good-natured perplexity gave the impression of someone vaguely distracted but altogether likable.

"That's right. I can vouch for it, 'cause we been out here the past three nights watching you," Officer Borelli said. "You got some identification on you, Ferris?"

"Identification?" The word appeared to elude him. He wavered there beneath the streetlamp, his eyes smiling off into space.

The officers exchanged quick glances. "Driver's license. Social Security. A credit card," the black officer said. "Anything with your name on it?"

"Oh, sure. With my name. I get it," Ferris yelped like an overexcited puppy. Fumbling in his back pocket, he withdrew a wallet. He flipped it open, revealing a swollen compartment of leather, crammed full with cards, scraps of paper, and assorted debris.

From out of that turmoil, he produced several cards. One was a Social Security card and the other a pass with his photograph on it, issued by the Department of Welfare, entitling him to eat in various shelters around the city.

"This your address, Ferris?" Officer Borelli read from an address card inside a plastic window. "Four twenty East Eighty-first Street."

"That's where I live. That's my address," Ferris proclaimed with boyish eager pleasure. Borelli and Carpenter exchanged more meaningful glances.

"You're a bit off your beat, aren't you, my man?" the black officer remarked.

"I guess so."

"What brings you down here, three nights in a row?"

"Down here." Ferris pointed with his finger at the ground as if to clarify the question. "Oh, you mean down here?" A radiance illuminated his youthful features. "I used to live down here. Right there in that house." His longish finger waved excitedly at the ramshackle brick Federal nearly eclipsed by the shadows of the encroaching warehouses and factories.

Borelli stared doubtfully across at the crumbling, near-derelict structure. "You lived over there?"

"Right. With my mom and dad. Lived there the first seven years of my life." Ferris beamed with pride.

"Then what happened?" Borelli inquired.

"My dad died and my mom remarried."

"That's when you moved up to Eighty-first?"

"There were some other places before that," Ferris

said. "Not so nice." The smile on his face never wavered as he recited a litany of woe.

"Where were some of these other places?" Borelli asked while he flipped incuriously through the grimy wad of papers Ferris had provided him.

The young man closed his eyes in an effort to recall. When he opened them again he looked apologetic.

"You don't recall?" Borelli regarded him skeptically. "People don't usually forget where they lived."

"It's not that far back, Ferris," Officer Carpenter pressed him. "Try and remember."

Ferris stared blankly down at his shoes as if stalling for time. The two plainclothesmen waited patiently.

"Tell you what we're gonna do, Ferris." Officer Borelli's voice rang with hearty goodwill. "This area's not exactly the best area to stroll around in after dark, recapturing boyhood memories. What d'ya say we run you up to Eighty-first Street?"

"I'd sure appreciate that," Ferris replied full of earnest gratitude. He was excited at the prospect of riding in the unmarked police car with the two plainclothesmen.

"But first, we gotta make a little stop at the precinct house. Want to ask you a few more questions. Check a few things out."

"Sure. Great."

"Just routine stuff." Borelli patted him on the arm and opened the back door. "Hop in."

"He says he lived there as a kid."

"You check it out?"

"At the Bureau of Deeds . . . Klink bought it forty-five years ago from a party name of Blaylock. No record of any Koops ever having lived there."

"Nothing in the archives?"

"Nothing at all."

"Could be his family rented the place from the former owners."

"I asked about that."

"What'd he say?"

"Nothin'. Just smiled at me, funny like."

"Smiles a lot, this Koops."

"And nods his head," Pickering added dryly. "He likes to nod his head."

"A flake."

"Right off the wall, Frank. Believe me."

Both men nodded sagely. It was early morning at Manhattan South. The squad room, full of smoke and noise, clattered with the motion of the first shift muster. Names fired back and forth in the morning roll call. Chairs scraped across the floors. Shoes scuffled. Lockers clanked open and shut in the noisy corridors where men shed uniforms for street clothes and indulged in sophomoric joshing peppered with epithets, prior to going home.

Under the watchful, slightly anxious gaze of Rollo Pickering, Mooney affixed his signature to a sheaf of dusty reports with the busy, distracted air of a man who'd already forgotten what had just been said. "And no prior police record?" Mooney suddenly asked; all the while his pen continued to scratch fitfully across the reports.

"None."

"How long he say he lived up on Eighty-first Street?"

"Two years in January. Landlord confirms it. Says he's an ideal tenant."

"That just means he pays the rent on time. Sits still for all the increases."

"That's about it," Pickering assented. He had no heart left for disputation. "Frank, this kid ain't the Dancer."

"Who said he was?" Mooney's hand rose mechanically to accept a mug of coffee from a rookie patrolman. "The point is, what the hell was he doing out there on Bridge Street, three nights in a row?"

Mooney drank coffee and returned to his reports, while Pickering mulled the question over in his head.

"Drifting. Wandering. Who knows? His lawyer says he's a bit simple."

"What's the lawyer's name again?"

"Drummond."

"Drummond?" Mooney glanced up. "Haven't I heard that name somewhere before?"

"Probably. He's one of the top piranhas for Wells, Gray."

Mooney whistled. "Wells, Gray, eh? That's pretty big league for a flake. Where does this kid get the bread to retain a gilt-edge shyster outfit like Wells, Gray?"

Pickering suppressed an urge to scream. "I already told you, Frank. They're trustees of Koops's annuity. Apparently, old man Koops was pretty well-heeled. Lost a fortune in real estate at the end of his life and died of a broken heart. He left the kid pretty well off. No fortune, mind you, but enough to take care of himself for the rest of his life."

"What does Drummond say?"

"Drummond was in here last night, spouting the Constitution and the New York State Penal Code."

"What's he think about our holding him? You didn't say he was a suspect in this Dancer thing?" Mooney glared up at him sharply.

"All I told him was he was picked up for loitering and acting in an irrational manner in the streets."

Mooney made a face of despair.

"Drummond wants him out. Says we've got no reason to be holding him."

"He's right. We don't." Mooney scratched off his signature on the final report and shoved the whole stack of them aside with a grunt of disgust. "What about prints?"

"We took a set when we booked him. Drummond nearly hit the ceiling when he heard that."

"Let him scream. It's routine." Mooney was up and moving. "How soon can you throw together a lineup?"

Pickering's eyes traveled to the ceiling. "Gimme an hour or so."

"You got it. In the meantime, send a car up to Washington Heights. Pick up Berrida and bring him down here."

"What about the Pell dame?"

"No go. I've been on that for a week. The doctors still won't permit it. Have the photographers get me a couple of mug shots before we release him. I'll take them out to Rockaway myself."

Galvanized by the older man's sudden momentum, Pickering started out the door at a dash.

"Hey, Rollo," Mooney called after him. "What about the teeth?"

"Whose teeth?"

"Koops's, dummo." Mooney glowered. "The incisors? The front teeth. Remember?"

"Oh." Comprehension flooded the detective's face. "Straight as an arrow, Frank. Pretty as pearls." Pickering shrugged gloomily. "Sorry."

"Look close. You gotta be sure now."

"I'm lookin'. I'm lookin'."

Though the temperature in the street was in the thirties, and not much higher indoors, Hector Berrida was in a sweat. Unaccustomed as he was to the presence of uniformed police all around him, he felt a certain pressure to oblige.

"What d'ya see?" Pickering asked.

Hector Berrida glared hard through the big one-way picture window, his neck thrust a good way forward from the rest of his body. The object of his attention was a lineup of ten men standing before a blank wall, with nothing but a series of black horizontal lines spaced at intervals up the wall's length to indicate the height of each subject. From where he stood they gave the impression of ten cardboard silhouettes in a shooting gallery.

"Well?" Pickering persisted.

"I'm lookin'. I'm lookin'."

"Take your time, Hector. We can't afford mistakes." Mooney spoke with reassuring calm.

"One guy says hurry. The other guy says take your time. I'm tryin', man. I'm doin' my best."

"Is there any one of them at least looks familiar?"

A vein throbbed visibly at Berrida's throat. "I don't know." His voice quavered with fretfulness and doubt. In his mind he thought he knew what they wanted, and he feared what they might do if he failed to comply. Experience had informed him that that was the way it was with cops.

"That night you bought that amplifier," Mooney prodded delicately. "You said you got a good look at the guy."

"Sure, sure," Berrida agreed eagerly. "I was lookin' at him face to face. Close as you're to me, right now. Close as that."

"What time of the evening was it, Hector?" Mooney asked.

"Right after supper. Seven o'clock, or so."

"How much light was there in the street?" Pickering asked.

"It was summer," Mooney reminded him. "Early June. At that hour there must've still been light."

The nodding of Berrida's head was in direct ratio to his degree of agitation. "Sure — there was plenty of light. I could see him. No trouble, man. No sweat."

"Clear?"

"Clear. Like you and me, now."

"Okay." Mooney patted the young man's shoulder reassuringly. "Don't look at me. Look at those guys out there." Mooney flung an arm out at the window.

Berrida's frightened eyes returned to the glass, swarming across it right to left and back again. Painfully conscious of all the uniformed personnel about him, the stenographer taking down his every word, he felt a pressing need to come up with some kind of a response. "That guy. Over there on the right. Maybe . . . "

"Which one? The far right?"

"No. Not him. Next to him."

"The dude in the chino vest?" Pickering asked.

"Yeah. That could be something like him."

"Something like him." Pickering bristled with scorn. Ferris Koops was positioned about seven men down, a good way over on the other side.

Mooney was aware of time running out, as well as of the costly talent of expensive law firms at that very moment drafting scorching depositions against the city. He sighed. "Look again. Once more, Hector. Just to be sure."

Berrida could see something in the detective's eyes that told him he'd failed. Beneath the beehive Afro cut, sweat glistened on his brow. Sitting cross-legged, his sharply pointed patent-leather shoe elevated as the toe pumped up and down like a piston. The hurt, anxious gaze still swept back and forth across the glass at the lineup of faces — all different but somehow exasperatingly alike. The context in which they appeared made them all very similar. The framing of the picture provided by the window gave it the posed, static look of a class graduation photograph.

"Maybe that other guy." Berrida's gaze seized on a darkish, Hispanic-looking young man whose features wore the expression of sullen boredom typical of the street-hardened, socially disenfranchised.

"Which other guy, Hector?"

"The Spanish guy," Berrida said, with a note of regret. He felt like a traitor, but he was certain that particular response would get him out of there faster.

Mooney sighed and snapped his file folder shut. "Okay, Hector. You can go now."

Berrida looked wary. "That's it?"

"That's it, Hector. We'll be in touch if we need you again."

The young man looked back and forth at each of them distrustfully. He was certain there was more to come. He sat there for a moment, waiting for it. When nothing happened, he rose, or rather bounced, to his feet, shifting there hesitantly. "Okay?"

"Okay, Hector." Mooney nodded slowly. "Right through that door there at the rear. The sergeant'll show you out."

When the young man had gone, Pickering flicked a switch and spoke into a microphone with speakers on the other side of the glass. "Okay. That's it. Sweep 'em out."

In the next moment, a burly sergeant appeared. They could hear the loud clap of his hands on the other side of the glass and watched the line face left and straggle off.

Mooney and Pickering sat unspeaking in the darkened little room, their feet propped up on the ledge projecting out from beneath the glass.

Pickering cleared his throat uneasily. "Well, what now?"

"You got me those mug shots?"

"Out there on your desk. Looks like Koops is in the clear."

"Who says?"

Pickering's troubled gaze searched the older man's face. "What's that supposed to mean?"

"Means that Koops is not the dark, romantic-looking one. But he sure as hell could be the pale blond wispy one the Bailey kid described, as well as the guy the doorman up at Eight Sixty Fifth Avenue described in the Bender job." Mooney stared gloomily out at the vacant lineup room where the indirect fluorescent lighting cast a harsh, ghostly blue sheen over the emptiness. "I haven't given up on Koops yet. I still can't figure what the hell he was doing out in front of fourteen Bridge Street three nights in a row — the same address as the one on the registration for our missing Mercedes. Too much of a coincidence."

The door behind them opened suddenly, spotlighting them in a shaft of mote-filled light from the outer room. "Phone call out here for you, lieutenant," a desk sergeant barked at them.

"Who is it?" Mooney barked back.

"Guy called Drummond."

"Jesus," Mooney moaned. "The Wells, Gray piranha. Tell him I'm out."

"Where are you?" the sergeant inquired.

"I'm in Rockaway. On a job. Not expected back for the rest of the day."

The door closed with an emphatic click and once again the two detectives were alone in the gray darkness behind the glass.

"You going out to see the Pell dame?" Pickering asked.

"You betcha."

"What about that snotty doctor?"

"What about him?"

"Hasn't he put the kibosh on all interviews?"

"I don't recall his saying that." Mooney's smile was slightly askew as he started out.

"Want some company?" Pickering called after him.

"This one I think I better do myself."

"What about Drummond?"

"Tell him there's a hitch in the paperwork. It's just a formality. Don't release Koops till you hear from me."

TWENTY-FOUR

YES, SHE WAS LOOKING SO MUCH BETTER, HE heard himself say. A vast improvement since the last time. And the new apartment was a fine idea. Spectacular view out over Jamaica Bay on one side to the spangled waters of the Rockaway inlet on the other.

His mind obsessed with Koops and his ferocious attorneys, Mooney fidgeted in his chair, desperate to get beyond the chatty amenities.

Claire Pell, on the other hand, was not. She knew the purpose of his visit, and, firmly but graciously, she dug herself in to forestall anything substantive in the way of talk. She had made progress toward a modest recovery over the past several months since the "incident," as it was now referred to. Her move to the bright new highrise condominium, not far from the old house, but seemingly universes away, had been felicitous. Once again she was sleeping through the night and could hold down food. Her physicians were not yet ready to risk a relapse by exposing her to interrogation by the police.

Mooney knew he was there against the wishes of her doctor and without authorization from the department. The breach of regulations in this instance seemed justified. If Ferris Koops was in any way implicated in the Dancer killings, Mooney was not yet ready to set him free. True, he had no trump cards in his hand with which to make a strong case for holding him. But the outcome of his meeting with Claire Pell could very well change all that.

"How do you spend your time?" he asked, full of bogus concern while watching for the propitious moment in which to spring.

She smiled wearily, miles ahead of him, knowing precisely where he was attempting to lead her.

"I read a lot. Do crossword puzzles. The television. I keep busy."

"Beautiful place you've got here," Mooney went on with desperate cheer. "I like the way you've fixed it up."

"My daughter helped. She's a designer, you know. Actually, she's a housewife, but she does a bit of designing on the side. She's got a real flair."

"Great to have a talent like that," Mooney replied with feeble enthusiasm.

They lapsed into another silence. Mooney ransacked his brain for some conversational key with which to adroitly unlock the gates barring the way to discussion. Curiously enough, it was she who finally gave it to him.

"I couldn't very well go back to the old house."

"Of course not," he agreed.

"To have to sleep in that room again."

"You did the right thing."

Mooney watched her rise and stroll toward the large picture windows fronting the bay. He rose and followed her. Together they stood staring out over the flat brown swampland that crept out in tufts and hummocks toward the choppy waters of the inlet. "Beautiful view," he rattled on breezily. "You'll enjoy that terrace in the summer."

It was then she turned and gazed at him ruefully. "You know, lieutenant, I'm not supposed to talk with you. My doctor said . . ."

"Yes," he murmured. "I know what he said. If I were him, I'd say the same. He's doing his job. He's looking out for you."

"And you?" She stared at him pointedly. "Who are you looking out for?"

With all of the evasions and circumlocutions that had

preceded the moment, the directness of her question took his breath away. Before he could reply, she'd answered it for him. "For yourself, of course."

His smile grew a bit more strained. "I have my job to do, too."

"Of course," she replied and turned back to the vast prospect of sky and water beyond the glass. They both grew quiet again, absorbed in the stubborn progress of a small trawler bouncing its way over the choppy waters heading out to sea.

"What exactly is it you want of me?" she asked. There was nothing of ill will in her tone, but it did suggest she wished to terminate their meeting as quickly as possible. She turned and moved a trifle unsteadily back to her chair.

He followed her there and sank into a soft, infinitely yielding divan beside her. "I'd like to show you a picture."

Her back stiffened and her eyes shifted sidewards, as if she were regarding him from beneath her lashes. "What sort of picture?"

"It's a photograph. A young man. All I want you to do is tell me whether or not you've ever seen him before."

He watched her, her gaze riveted to the floor, deeply aware of some sort of struggle going on behind the pale, waxen oval of her face. An audible acceleration in her breathing was the prologue to her reply. "I don't want to see any pictures, lieutenant."

"I can appreciate that. All the same — "

"My doctors have said — "

"I understand. Believe me, I wouldn't have bothered you today if I didn't feel this was absolutely crucial."

"And is this picture . . . this man . . . is he supposed to be the one . . ."

"Possibly."

"I don't want to see that man again." Her voice suddenly rose. "I never want to ever — "

"I understand," he said softly, using his voice to assuage

her. "I have this man in custody now. Based on what you might possibly tell me here today, I must either release him or hold him, pending further investigation. So this is quite important."

"Why do you believe this is the man?" Her manner had grown a trifle waspish and peremptory.

"For a variety of reasons that may sound vague to you and possibly just coincidental. I've been close to this case for over a year now, and, quite honestly, I still can't answer these questions to my own satisfaction."

In the next moment, he withdrew an envelope from his inside jacket pocket. He watched her eyes follow his hand to the point where it stopped and held the envelope dangling between two fingers.

She stared at it, slowly shaking her head back and forth. "I can't."

"It would make all the difference."

"I'm sorry." She suddenly rose. "I really can't."

He watched her move off again, aware of some quiet struggle raging within the taut, narrow frame.

"My husband's been gone four months now," she suddenly announced. "There isn't a day goes by I don't think of him."

"I can appreciate that," Mooney replied. He couldn't think of much more to say.

"I want to go away from here," she chattered on, almost irrelevantly, struggling to regain equanimity through her voice alone. "I don't care for this apartment. I hate this apartment. I want to go away. Someplace warm. Maybe South Carolina. I have family there. Would you like some coffee?" she asked suddenly, bolting for the kitchen. "I have some fresh."

"No, thank you."

She looked distraught. "Neither do I. I drink too much coffee."

"I can't handle the caffeine," Mooney offered sympathetically.

"It's not the caffeine with me. It's the acid." She

patted the area just below her breastbone. Her eyes strayed back warily to the envelope dangling from Mooney's hand.

"My husband was a very fine man," Claire Pell went on, visibly subduing the demons leaping inside her. "A gentleman of the old school. People adored him. He built up a very successful printing business before he retired. He was also quite an accomplished musician. A violinist. I don't suppose you knew that?"

"No, I didn't," Mooney murmured, at a loss.

Her eyes glistened vividly out of the chalky pallor of her face, her gaze transfixed on the small white paper rectangle. "I suppose I owe this to Martin." Her searching, frantic eyes looked up at him for confirmation.

"And to eighteen others as well," Mooney wanted to add, but resisted the impulse. He held his breath, watching her with the same morbid fixity with which one watches a high-wire act that's about to get into trouble. From the appearance of self-possession he encountered on first entering the room, what confronted him now appeared unstable and unpredictable. Oh, God, he thought to himself, don't let her pop now. Not now.

"If it were the other way around, I'm sure Martin would never have expected this of me," she continued, while backing away from him. "He would not have wanted to put me through this."

"Probably not," Mooney readily conceded. Inside, he was crumbling, the specter of Sylvestri panting down his back.

"I don't think so, either, lieutenant." Her back stiffened. "I'm sorry. I just can't, and let's leave it at that."

She wheeled off again toward the windows, then just as abruptly turned back. "If I were to look at that face again . . ." Something caught in her throat.

"It's okay. I understand."

He had the impression she'd been disappointed by his patience and sympathy. It was as though she'd wanted him to quarrel more about it, to press the point. To get

away from him, she started for the front door. He shuffled after her like a large, docile bear.

"Well, wherever you go," Mooney said as they stood
in embarrassment at the open door, "I wish you the best
of luck."

"Thank you," she said. "That's very kind of you."

Her hand rose to take his. It was his right hand, the
one still holding the envelope. He made to shift it to his
left but before he could, she snatched it, tore the envelope open, turned half away, and plucked the mug shot
out. Mooney lurched for the empty envelope fluttering
downward to the carpet. From a point beneath her waist,
he had a sharp prospect of Claire Pell glaring down at the
photo. There was something hard and unrelenting in her
eyes. For what seemed an agonizingly long time, he held
his breath. In the next moment, she laughed aloud,
relief and color suffusing her features. "I've never seen
this man before in my life."

He called the office from a public phone booth in a small
stationery store downstairs. Pickering's voice snarled
with exasperation. "That prick Drummond's been on the
phone every half hour since you left. They're pressing
charges of illegal detention."

"Tell Drummond to hold his water. We're releasing
Koops. We don't have a thing we can hold him on, but
let's keep a tail on him all the same."

Driving up West Side Drive that evening, Warren had
become increasingly uneasy. He was certain he was being followed. The garage attendant had been too
friendly. Why had he told him so much? The panic he
felt in his haste to get away from the city had unnerved
him. The thought of the police coming to Bridge Street,
the awful certainty that they'd traced him there through
his car, and, most unsettling of all, this Koops person
who went about imitating him represented something
potentially disastrous. Though he'd steered clear of

Bridge Street for several days, sleeping in a succession of seedy transient hotels, the knowledge that he should have been far from the city by this time wore heavily on him. To delay any longer was reckless.

Though it was cool, even cold, in the car, Warren could feel sweat trickling beneath his clothing. He switched on the radio, playing it very loud to drive the demon thoughts out of his head. But then Suki came crowding in, muscling aside the shattering decibels. It was she, he was suddenly convinced, not the auto body shop, who had betrayed him to the police.

The flat, dark sheet of river, sliding past on his left, flashed and shimmered with lights from large housing complexes across the water on the Jersey shore. Farther north, up around the Cloisters, a sky bathed orange in the haze of incinerator smoke and neon lights heightened his sense of flight from some approaching cataclysm.

All the way up from lower Manhattan a part of his mind — that part not preoccupied with his own swirling terrors — had been watching license plates, tallying up their numbers, studying the frequency of their patterns for some hint of what augured for his future. At the beginning of his flight, when he'd first rolled up the ramp at 49th Street onto the West Side Drive, the pattern that had asserted itself was distinctly bad. By and large there was a preponderance of three-digit numbers all adding up to the inauspicious twelves or sevens, or, worse yet, the doomed sixteens that he feared so much. Between 49th Street and Riverdale he had added up so many license plates that the act itself had become compulsive to the point of involuntary reflex. He could no longer stop himself. Numbers racketed about in his head at a fearful speed. At a certain point, as he struggled to add every set of figures that came within his gaze, he had the sensation that he was watching a Ping-Pong ball bouncing back and forth over a net at ever-increasing speeds. At last the ball had become a white blur. It was an image from which he could no longer avert his gaze.

In time, the need to compute every series of numbers he saw induced in him a mental numbness behind the eyes and a drowsiness, as if he'd been hypnotized. At last he had to roll down the windows and open the dash vents and gulp air to keep himself awake.

Weary as he was, still he couldn't stop himself from counting. After a while he made a concerted effort to avoid seeing numbers, raising his gaze above the level of the car plates ahead. For a time this worked, but if he relaxed his concentration for even a moment, his head would droop to a more normal, less unnatural, position and there would be the numbers again, flashing at him like some remorseless taskmaster: 286 WCD . . . 322 FLV . . . 606 WDH . . . 421 DOV.

At Hawthorne, where he turned onto the Taconic, his hands cramped from grasping the wheel so hard. The air rushing through the open vents and windows was nearly frigid, but he was in a sick sweat. Near Peekskill, he was overcome with an uncontrollable desire to sleep. The effect of adding numbers, endless numbers rapidly, shouting them out loud as if in defiance of someone or something only he could see, had increased the speed of the small white dot jumping back and forth behind his eyes. It made his head swim and his temples throb.

He thought of pulling off onto one of the grass shoulders beneath a tree and then sleeping. But if he did, he knew he risked attracting the attention of the troopers, who plied regularly up and down the parkways at night, looking for just that sort of thing.

North of Claverack he pulled off the parkway onto a service road where he found a diner. There, he drank three cups of coffee and ate a stalish sticky doughnut that tasted of lard and left a queasy-making taste on his tongue.

He still wasn't at all sure where he was going. He had a direction. Suki had said north, but as of yet he had no specific destination. Possibly Canada, as the old lady had suggested, crossing over at Niagara. He wasn't convinced that was wise. True, the customs people were lax at the border crossings. Very seldom did the Canadian customs ask for identification when you entered, nor did U.S. customs when you came back in. But, occasionally, they could surprise you, if they didn't like your looks. It was precisely the kind of surprise he wished to avoid. He didn't have the sort of papers that could stand up to close scrutiny.

At Chatham he headed briefly west on the Massachusetts Turnpike, then north on the New York State Thruway. The large infusion of caffeine kept him going until Albany, where at last he turned off the Thruway at a Ramada Inn, rented a room, and fell into bed with his clothing on.

Six hours later he awoke with a shaft of sunlight poking its way through a frost-rimmed window. He rose and moved toward it. Standing there in his rumpled clothing, peering out beyond a cloverleaf to the parkway already teeming with traffic, he etched the word *chaos* with his fingernail on the frozen pane.

The small patch of neatly barbered grass outside his window was laced with frost. A flock of sparrows foraged across it, pecking at the hard, unyielding earth. For the first time in nearly seventy-two hours he stripped off his clothing and bathed. Next he shaved, lingering long before the fogged mirror, savoring the good feeling of hot water, soap, and cologne. He dressed in a fresh shirt and trousers and shined his shoes from a complimentary kit provided by the management.

Cleanliness and creature comforts meant a great deal to Warren Mars. He had an abhorrence of personal filth that amounted to a phobia. The fact that he called home a place as notable for squalor as 14 Bridge Street was simply one more irony in a life charged with ironies.

Downstairs in the coffee shop he devoured an enormous breakfast: fruit, cereal, pancakes and sausage, all washed down with sizable drafts of sweet coffee. Then he went out, chatted amiably with the cashier for a while, and settled his bill.

When he stepped back out into the parking lot, carrying his suitcase, a toothpick drooping from the corner of his mouth, the sun, moving out from behind a low scudding cloud, suddenly blazed resplendently upon him. He took it as an augury of good tidings and started to whistle.

The Mercedes coupe, so recently green, wore its fresh coat of pearl gray with such natural ease that it would have been hard to imagine that it ever was another color. Its big lacy chrome grille flashed like a million bits of broken glass in the morning sunlight. In addition, the car sported four new tires and had recently been tuned up at the garage.

It stood there, glistening in the early-morning sunlight as though it had been champing at the bit waiting for him. Sitting behind the wheel, he turned the key. The ignition roared instantly to life. The red indicator dials on the dashboard sprang hard right and quivered at the top digits. He switched on the defroster and the fan, then watched the wipers carve large graceful half-circles onto the befogged glass.

Waiting for the engine to warm, he gunned it several times, enjoying its roar, feeling its enormous power so instantly receptive to the slightest pressure of his foot.

Rolling out of the parking lot, it occurred to him that all of the dark demons of the night before had fled before the warm, purging sunlight of the new day. Gone were the evil humors, the dark premonitions, the bad auguries that had foretold doom in a whirlpool of numbers.

Bridge Street and all of its attendant cares — Suki; the police; his pursuing fury, Ferris Koops — all seemed very far away. He thought momentarily of Janine with a shrug of regret. Well, he would even that score too. There were many scores to be evened. But not just yet. In time, he told himself. For now, he must withdraw from the field and wait.

Now, it was just him and Mother, as it had been for so many years. He placed his right hand down on the console of the Mercedes and stroked it almost sensuously, as if it were warm, living flesh. That, too, was an additional unpleasantness that would have to be faced. Suki had said he must get rid of the car. With the police having now traced it to Bridge Street, he knew she was right. Still, he couldn't quite bring himself to entertain the notion. It was like abandoning a child you'd cosseted and cared for and nurtured into maturity over the course of years, through good and bad times, and then been told the child had a fatal illness and must surely die.

A twinge of sadness like a lowering cloud put a chill to his morning elation. He pushed it aside as if waving off a puff of bad air. There were problems ahead, to be sure, but for today at least, he wouldn't worry. Up ahead, through the circular three-pointed hood insignia of the car, the north country loomed. Like a compass, it pointed the way to lakes and mountains, to immense pine forests that rolled on endlessly for miles, vast distances in which one could lose oneself for just as long as one chose.

At the Rensselaer intersection of the New York State Thruway, he had a scare. Automobiles were lined up to approach the tollhouse, where dozens of troopers had circled the area with their cars. He felt a fist close over his heart. They appeared to be checking everyone going through the toll. He was certain that it was a roadblock and that they were looking for him. Those cops had undoubtedly gone back to Bridge Street and questioned Suki. She'd broken, told them everything, given them a full description of him and the car and where he was heading. There was already a line of cars behind him and there was no turning around at that point. If he had, it would have drawn immediate attention and they would have assuredly come after him.

As the car inched forward to the tollbooth, he fell into a cold sweat. His hands, gripping the wheel, were ringing wet. For a moment he thought of getting out of the car and making a dash for it. But where? There was nothing but wide open space around him, and on foot they would run him down in a minute.

There were only four or five cars ahead of him now. From where he sat, it appeared they were checking registrations and, in some cases, going around the back to check license plates. With only two cars ahead of him, his heart banged fitfully away in his chest. Dark spots jumped before his eyes. Breathing deeply, he counted numbers to himself in an effort to regain his composure. As a tall trooper under a big felt Stetson sauntered his way, Warren smiled jauntily.

"What's up?"

The trooper stooped slightly, looking at his front plates, then came around the side and glanced at his windshield. "Just checking your inspection sticker. Have a good day." The trooper flicked a finger to the wide brim of his hat and waved him on.

"You, too," Warren returned heartily, picked up a mileage card at the booth, and rolled through. His heart was still thumping and his hands were ringing wet where they'd gripped the wheel.

Ahead of him was a tangle of route signs. He had still made no choice as to a destination. He could take the Thruway west, farther into New York State, toward Schenectady, Syracuse, Buffalo, Niagara, Canada, or Route 7 east, out of Troy toward Bennington and over the Green Mountains into New Hampshire, heading north on into the rugged peaks and notches of the White Mountains.

There was traffic coming up fast behind him and still more troopers pulled up on the other side of the toll. Trying to decide, his feverish gaze swarmed over the woozy letters of the road signs before him. As he had done so often before under similar circumstances, he finally sat back at peace and decided to let Mother make the decision for him. By means of some vague pressure, some subtle pulse passing between his hand and the wheel, a message was conveyed to the automobile. The machine responded instantly by veering east. In the next moment, he was roaring into the blinding glare of sun. It was still rising above the distant peaks, like some huge hot-air balloon cut loose from its moorings. He was hooting and laughing at the top of his lungs.

PART V

TWENTY-FIVE

IT HAD BEEN QUIET FOR THE BETTER PART OF ten weeks — the sort of quiet that makes an old cop edgy, knowing that for each day of quiet savored, a tithe would be exacted in the currency of havoc.

Mooney went about his appointed rounds, tracking down old leads on the Shadow Dancer and following up new ones. Keenly aware of time running out on him, he prayed for the Dancer to resurface and the carnage to start anew. All to no avail. The raging fever of Dancer-mania appeared to have finally abated.

Still, it hadn't abated in Mooney's mind and wouldn't. Some two weeks later, on the day before Sylvestri's accession was to occur, Mooney, attired in his best Sunday suit, appeared in Mulvaney's office to plea for a stay of execution.

"I know what you're here for, Frank." The chief of detectives shot a scathing look at Mooney's Sunday finery. "The answer is no."

"I'm close to this thing now, Clare. Just a little more time."

"*No.*" The *o* sound of the word came long and resonated through the bare, dusty room.

"Sixty days, Clare. Two months. Two months more."

Mulvaney's lips curled in a scornful smile. "I will say one thing for you, Frank. You got a lot of brass."

"I can wrap this whole thing up in that time."

"No way, my friend. No way." Mulvaney busied himself with paperwork.

Standing there, fuming above him, Mooney chewed the inside of his lip. "Six weeks," he heard himself plead pitifully.

Not speaking, Mulvaney rose, returning several folders to his file. When he returned to his desk and resumed his seat, Mooney was still waiting there for an answer. None came. Mulvaney busied himself with more paperwork.

"What would you like me to do, Clare, get down on my knees and beg?"

"I'd like to see you clear out of here so I can get some work done." Mulvaney never looked up from his papers.

A look very much like desperation crossed Mooney's features. "What if I offered to quit?"

That did succeed in bringing the chief of detectives' head up. "Quit?"

"To go now instead of waiting out my ten or eleven months. Wouldn't that be a great pleasure for you, Clare? Not to have old crabby nutcase Frank around here anymore?"

A look of mild interest flared momentarily in the chief of detectives' eyes. He stirred slowly, shifting his weight in the chair. "What's the deal?"

His barely concealed enthusiasm hurt Mooney, but he couldn't afford to grieve about that now. "You give me an extension of six weeks. If I haven't delivered the Dancer by then, I'm walking."

Mulvaney nibbled the rubber nub at the tip of his pencil. "You'd be losing a wad of pension money."

"That's my loss."

Mulvaney pondered that a moment. "One month."

"Come on, Clare. Have a heart."

"One month. Thirty days," Mulvaney snapped with cold finality. "You got nothing by then, you walk. That's final."

Early in December, Mooney had a birthday. It was the occasion of a small celebration at the Balloon. Fritzi, in her quiet, methodical way, had gone about the business of digging up names — Mooney's cronies from the bad old 19th Precinct days, most of them now retired.

It was a loud and vinous evening. Mooney's sidekicks, while considerably unloosened, still felt a certain constraint in the posh setting of the Balloon, with its tony uptown clientele and its striking owner.

Did Frank Mooney, the chronic misogynist, actually snare this imposingly handsome lady? They'd all heard about Fritzi and were fully prepared to dislike her. Frank, they'd heard, had lost weight and put on airs. He used *doesn't* for *don't, not* for *ain't,* and placed his knife down on the plate each time he raised a forkful of food to his mouth. Worse even, he no longer drank beer.

"Well, Jesus Christ. Ain't he piss elegant? Ain't she some piece of business, though?" — there was none of that sort of talk that evening. It was fun and old times and letting hair down. They sang a few beery saloon songs. There were several hilariously wicked imitations of old precinct chiefs, and a few brief awkward moments of dry-eyed memorials to old buddies long since gone.

Fritzi was the unqualified hit of the evening. Far from being aloof and standoffish, as they half expected, she spent a good part of the night at the table with them, singing a chorus or two of "My Wild Irish Rose," talking horses and swapping salty stories, trading them one for one. Fritzi's were salty but never vulgar. By the time brandy and cigars came around, she had them eating out of the palm of her hand.

Mooney, attempting to look his most irascible, merely glowed — more the proprietor of the famous old steakhouse than the owner herself. He kept waving expansively at people, ordering rounds of drinks, and sending back food he thought improperly prepared. He'd learned it all from her but, of course, assumed that he'd been a connoisseur from birth.

It was a show and they all knew it. What of it? Mooney

had waited a lifetime to make his move. Now that it was made, he could gaze on his work and wonder at his good fortune. No one knew about his desperate deal with Mulvaney.

Christmas was rapidly approaching. The tree was already up in Rockefeller Center. Salvation Army Santas clanged bells at every corner. People were jammed five-deep in front of the windows of Saks Fifth Avenue, Lord & Taylor, Bonwit's and Macy's to see the animated fairy tales, the magic shows, the street corner buskers and the Neopolitan crèches depicting the ancient story of the Magi and the coming of the Prince of Peace.

TWENTY-SIX

THE ROADS AT THAT HOUR WERE EMPTY. DE-spite the ice and bitter temperatures, they were reasonably passable. Twelve miles farther south, he'd begun his climb over Pinkham Notch. The fearsome gorge on his right was ringed with the dark, jagged silhouettes of peaks. Awesome vistas of pine forests slumbered beneath thirty inches of snow at an altitude of two thousand feet.

The road descending into the notch was narrow, recently sanded, and plowed, with the banked snow at the edge of the road serving as a sort of road guard. Above the notch the phantom moon rode pale and remote through the scudding clouds.

Somewhere just below the top, where the state road starts to make its dizzy descent into the craggy gorge, Warren pulled the car over toward the edge, turned off the headlights, and sat there for a time, looking out at the frozen lunar landscape. With the engine idling and the heater blowing warm air up around his trousers, he made his goodbyes. There was an attitude of communion and bereavement about it, as if he were saying farewell to a dying friend.

In ten minutes' time he turned the headlights back on, opened the door of the car, and stepped out into the howling winds. Moving quickly now, he went around to the back of the car and removed his small suitcase from the trunk. In the trunk there was also a five-gallon can of gasoline, half full.

His jaw set grimly to the task, he proceeded to sluice the contents of the gas can over the interior of the Mercedes. When he'd done that, he returned the can to the trunk of the car and locked it. Next, he released the emergency brake and put the car in gear.

While it hovered there at the edge of the road, somewhat impeded by the bank of plowed snow, Warren pulled out a Zippo lighter from his pocket, cupped a hand over it, and flicked it. Standing back beside the open door, he held it in contact for a moment with the fuel-drenched upholstery of the back seat.

There was a sudden audible *whoosh*, as of air sucked inward, violently imploded. A large flash followed closely on its tail. In the next moment, the interior of the car was ablaze. He went around the back again, and putting his shoulder to the trunk, he pushed, even as the front tires, slipping and sliding, began to creep laboriously upward over the banked snow.

A wall of heat rushed outward from the open door with almost palpable force. Arms raised before him, Warren fell back from the car, fearing that the gas tank might explode at any moment. He watched with fascination and a terrible sadness the awful death struggle of the torched car as it slipped and climbed the snowy embankment like an injured insect. Torn between a desire to extinguish the flames and save the car and an urgent, almost panicky need to flee, he chose the latter. But even then he gazed sadly at the stricken car, full of a sense of his own treachery, his lack of gratitude, watching the flames behind the cracking glass glow almost festively. The front tires by then had breached the top of the bank and straddled it, hanging free in space while its rear wheels spun and whined, pushing puffs of powder out behind them.

It seemed to him he could hear the noble thing groan, as if suffering its awful death throes. Without considering his own safety, he darted to the rear of the car, his bare hands splayed across the blistering paint of the trunk, his feet slipping and kicking behind him on the icy road, and with a superhuman effort, heaved.

Nothing seemed to happen, but in the next moment, the car appeared to sigh and shudder forward. His weight bearing down on the trunk had given the spinning rear wheels just enough traction for the blazing vehicle to renew its ascent.

Watching it creep forward, its nose dizzily elevated, he fell back from it, gasping and winded, watching open-mouthed as the hood of the car with its proud three-pointed star symbol rose into starry space, then dipped. The rear end followed.

There was an enormous explosion, followed almost instantly by a ball of flame swirling up above it. Warren dashed back to the edge of the road, standing atop the shattered bank, with the black skid marks of the tire treads imprinted clearly in the snow.

From where he stood, he was able to stoop and peer down into the gorge, watching the ball of flame bounce and spin and turn head-over-tail in its fiery descent into the ravine.

He hovered there atop the bank for some time after, peering down into the gorge. Having followed the progress of that giddy slide, he watched it subside and gradually rumble to a halt several thousand feet below, the car buried nose first in a tomb of snow. Standing poised like a sentinel above the gorge, he could see the flames lick and crack and consume themselves. There was the acrid smell of fuel and burned rubber carried upward on the frozen air, and the sharp crack of sparks shooting skyward. A number of small brush fires broke out in the vicinity of the wreck, burned briefly like flambeaux, then sputtered and went out.

It occurred to him that people in homes nearby might have seen the flames and heard the explosion and that he'd best be off before the police came round to investigate. Buttoning his coat, he hauled his collar up about his ears, grabbed his suitcase, and, with the keen agility of an animal, vanished instantly into the fringe of forest bordering the road.

For some time, he moved along the roadside, but well within the covering of the forest paralleling it. He was terrified of losing his way in the woods. Moreover, the snow there was deep and his feet had begun to sting from the cold. Icy blasts moaned through the trees, sending clots of fresh-fallen powder down into the collar of his coat. His ears had begun to burn and he swiped irritably at his tearing eyes. He didn't even know that he was crying.

TWENTY-SEVEN

IT HAD STARTED TO RAIN ON MASS. STATE 113 at a point just south of the New Hampshire border. Slightly past five A.M., it was still dark, but a darkness just beginning to yield to the first tentative gray patches of dawn. A combination of rain and sleet pelted down obliquely on the hushed frozen countryside, making a faint hissing sound.

Spotting the car drawn up on the inclined shoulder of the road, the Massachusetts State trooper pulled off the road and nosed his car carefully up the icy grade behind the late model Chevrolet.

In most instances, with cars pulled up in that fashion, off the road at that hour of the morning, the trooper expected to find someone shivering behind the wheel, waiting for a mechanic to arrive; or, more commonly even, someone heavy in drink, three sheets to the wind, and sleeping it off.

Removing his flashlight and ticket book from the glove compartment, he buttoned his rubber poncho and prepared to leave the cozy warmth of his front seat to bear the icy blasts of night air battering the hood of his car. Stepping out into the cold, dripping dark, he approached the Chevrolet, his feet crunching over the thin crust of slushy ice mantling the earth.

A hump of drier snow had mounded up over the roof of the car, suggesting that it had come down from someplace further north where the snowfall had been far heavier than here in northern Massachusetts. Approaching, the trooper noted that, somewhat oddly, the two front doors on either side of the vehicle hung open, swinging slightly in the buffeting wind. The beam from his flashlight, filled with sleet, widening slowly from its source, picked out the license plates on the back. They were New Hampshire plates.

Something about the way the doors hung open, the pale orange of the dome light inside glowing dimly, the general desolation of the place, made the trooper reach down, almost involuntarily, and check the holster under his poncho.

He approached from behind on the driver's side. Stooping down, he flashed his light inside. The car was unoccupied, yet the radio played softly, dance music from an all-night disc jockey. Glancing over the roof of the car, he peered into the fringe of trees beyond, half-expecting to see someone emerge from there. He glanced down again, shining his light back inside the car. This time his eye caught the vivid splash of red on the floor beneath the front right-hand seat. He moved around to the other side of the car to check that. He almost didn't have to. He knew it was blood. Sticky and quite fresh. His action had served only to confirm it.

Inside, the car smelled faintly of cigarettes. Otherwise, there were no signs of the occupants. Over on the passenger side where the trooper now stood, marked clearly in the freshly fallen snow, were footprints. Two pairs, the trooper quickly determined when he'd played his beam on them, following it with his eye to where the prints trailed off into the little copse running parallel to the road.

He followed the prints up toward the trees, pausing here and there occasionally to study some aspect of them more closely, as though they were a Morse code that only he could decipher. He followed the prints up to where they disappeared in the tangle of brush. Fumbling beneath the dripping rubber of his poncho, he withdrew the .45-caliber police special from its holster and started into the trees.

It didn't take him long to find what he was seeking. It was no more than twenty feet or so into the trees, where the bare branches laced with ice rattled and clicked against each other as he brushed against them in passing.

The body — his beam picked it out easily — had scarcely been concealed. It lay on its side, facedown in the slushy snow. Approaching it warily, he wondered if the owner of the second pair of prints was still somewhere about. When he stooped down and put his beam directly on the body, he could see a fanlike shape of pale rose leeching out from just beneath the face, half-buried in the snow.

Before turning the body over, he looked around once again over his shoulder, playing his beam of light out in front of him. It had the effect of transforming the short, stumpy, leafless second-growth trees into crouching, twisted shapes. The noise of the sleet dropping steadily through the trees made a low hissing sound.

With his pistol in one hand, he turned the body over with his foot so as not to have to bend or stoop or become vulnerable for an unguarded moment.

The sight he saw there was one he would not soon forget. The body was that of a man. The throat had been slashed so deep that the head was barely attached to the shoulders and hung from a thin, stringy tendon of muscle in the neck. The cartilage of the throat protruded in the gap. Crystals of ice, like broken glass, adhered to it.

It had been a man, a rather youngish man, the trooper guessed from the build and the smooth, unblemished skin of the bare hands. But he had no way of knowing for certain.

There were no features left where the face had been. They'd been erased by a series of long, unbroken knife slashes that traveled from just beneath the hairline to below the chin. Each was a thin, perfectly drawn line, executed by a strong, steady hand. Each no more than an inch apart, they looked like the dirt ridges carved out by a tractor in a freshly plowed field. The precision of the markings gave the impression that someone had gone to great pains to produce such a careful design. About it, there was something mysterious and ritualistic, the deliberate scarifying still practiced by some primitive races as initiation into manhood. It was as if each stroke of the blade had been intended to convey some special significance, a kind of wall graffiti, transferred to human skin.

PART VI

TWENTY-EIGHT

"HOW FAR?"

" 'Bout six miles down. Just south of the New Hampshire border."

"When was it?"

" 'Bout five A.M. yesterday morning." The chief, a man by the name of Sanderson, at the state police barracks in Concord paused. For a moment Mooney could hear him going over some report that had just been put down before him.

"Lieutenant — you still there?"

"Still here," Mooney snapped when the chief came back on. "You get any prints off that car?" Mooney asked.

"Millions of 'em. That's the trouble."

"I get your drift," Mooney replied glumly. "What makes you so sure this is our guy?"

"We get all of your 'all-points' up here. Been reading about it in the papers. Seeing it on TV. If you'd seen the body I saw at the morgue . . . "

"That much damage?"

"Damage is hardly the word."

"You didn't happen to find the weapon."

"No, but our forensic people say it was a knife. Six inches at least, with a serrated blade."

"Sounds like our guy, all right."

"To me too. What's more, this Murchison chap . . . that's the victim's name . . . turns out he lived right up around that notch where your boy's car went into the ravine. That was a 'sixty-eight Mercedes he was s'posed to be driving?"

"Right," Mooney confirmed. "A two twenty. This Murchison: probably picked him up on the road that night. Offered him a ride."

"Looks that way," the chief huffed. "Last ride that poor sod'll offer anyone. I figure your boy's probably traveling your way right now."

"What makes you say?"

"The New Hampshire troopers found no trace of a body in or around the Mercedes up in the notch, and there wasn't a sign of him around the Chevy down here. . . . Ever see a New Hampshire license plate?"

"Not so's I can recall details."

"It's a white plate with green letters and numbers." Mooney waited, perplexed. "What about it?"

"The state motto is printed right above the plate number. Know what it is?"

"Don't have the foggiest."

" 'Live free or die,' " Sanderson proclaimed, then grew silent as though he'd delivered some earth-shattering revelation.

Mooney's perplexity deepened. "I don't get it."

"It's not so much the motto," Sanborn chuckled. "It's the way we found it on those plates."

"How?" Mooney asked with mounting exasperation.

The chief waited, letting him simmer a bit longer. He suddenly resumed. "On both of them plates, both front and back, all around the motto, someone had drawn a big circle in pink crayon. Now from what I read of your boy, he's given to crayon drawing. Our people tell us the crayon on the plates was applied in the last twenty-four hours."

"Okay — I don't doubt this is our guy. That I.D. plate you took off the car in the gorge . . . "

"What about it?"

"It's the same V.I.N. as the one on the registration we

located here. It's him, all right," Mooney finally conceded.

"No doubt," the chief remarked laconically. "And he's all yours. Massachusetts is overjoyed to be rid of him. Merry Christmas to you all down there."

Mooney's desk was stacked with bulletins and reports. There were nearly a dozen message slips with telephone numbers to call back. The call from Concord had been his first of the morning. From there on, the phone started to ring with a vengeance. The gist of the Concord message was not unexpected. Mooney had more or less projected the same scenario himself: the car commandeered, driven across state lines, the owner murdered, and both abandoned at the side of the road. The trip from there, no doubt, continued via ground transport — a train or, more probably, a bus. Then a discreetly unobtrusive reentry into the city, back to the old hunting grounds. It was precisely the way Mooney would have imagined it to have happened. What he'd not foreseen, however, was the uncommon swiftness, the gathering momentum of events culminating in the Shadow Dancer's return.

While the thought that the Dancer was probably back prowling his old haunts around the city was disquieting, Mooney felt a curious excitement at the idea of his sudden proximity. There was a sense of things rushing to a head.

Moments after he'd hung up the phone, he was back on with Mulvaney, apprising him of developments, as well as giving him the bad news that their old friend had probably returned and that, if he had, undoubtedly they'd be hearing from him soon.

"Anybody watching Koops?" Mooney inquired, after they'd conferred.

"Who?"

"Koops. You remember. The kid we picked up on Bridge Street. The lineup?"

"Oh, sure." Mulvaney sounded puzzled. "What about him?"

"What's he been up to?"

"How the hell should I know? We pulled our tail off him the day we released him."

"But I asked expressly — "

"To put a stake on him. I know. And I told you, I checked with our lawyers. They said absolutely not."

Mooney had to restrain himself from shouting. "I don't see that at all."

"You don't? Was there any positive witness identification of Koops?"

"No."

"Was there a prior arrest record?"

"No."

"Did Washington show fingerprints or a possible alias on this kid?"

"No."

"Then there was no legal basis to hold him. Right?"

"Right, but — "

"No buts, Frank. Our own counsel is scared stiff of this fancy-pants law firm that represents Koops. This Drummond has a reputation as a real flamethrower. Add to that, one day after we released Koops, the ACLU got on his case. All I need now is that crowd breathing down my neck. I can just see the headlines: POLICE CHARGE RETARDED YOUTH AS DANCER SUSPECT, THOUGH ADMIT NO EVIDENCE." Mulvaney's snarl trailed off into bitter laughter.

"I've got a feeling about this Koops kid. Something about him . . . "

"You keep saying that, but you can't tell me what."

"I don't know. I can't put my finger on it. But there's something there." Even as he spoke he could hear how lame it must sound. "Why the hell would Koops wind up down on Bridge Street, watching that house night after night? You know where we got the address of that house?"

"Sure. Off the registration you got in the auto body shop from the alleged car of this alleged Dancer, who allegedly resided there at one time, but of whom you could find no real trace when you searched the alleged premises. Am I right, Frank, when I say this Bridge Street connection is pretty thin?"

"Okay," Mooney conceded feebly. "But doesn't it strike you just a bit odd this kid would be watching that particular house?"

"What's odd about it? Nothing odd. That house is in the heart of the financial district. Thousands of people pass it every day. Why not Koops?"

"First of all, it wasn't in the day. It was at night. Second, he didn't just walk past it. He stood out in front of the place three nights in a row before they picked him up. That doesn't sound like no coincidence to me."

"Look, Frank."

Mooney could sense the impatience in the chief of detectives' voice.

"I'm telling you, we've got nothing on this kid. No justifiable basis for placing him under twenty-four-hour-a-day surveillance."

"I grant you that."

"But still you've got this bee in your bonnet about Koops being the copycat of the Dancer."

"Or the Dancer himself. Why couldn't he be?"

"Are you suggesting Koops and the Dancer know each other? A couple of old buddies trying to outdo each other on the just-for-kicks scale?"

"I didn't say they know each other, but it sure looks like they're watching each other pretty closely."

"Why?" Mulvaney's jaw jutted forward. "Just 'cause we find this flake Koops down on Bridge Street watching some old fleabag house?"

Mooney's face flamed with exasperation. "All I'm saying is if we'd kept a tail on Koops, like I asked, we'd have had an answer — the classic laboratory control situation. There's a copycat factor operating here. That's clear as day. And just on the outside chance that Koops is the copycat and had tried something while the Dancer was temporarily off stage up in New England, we could've learned a great deal. Now that opportunity is lost."

There was another pause while each of them waited for the other to speak. It was Mulvaney who finally broke the silence. His voice was quiet and carried with it a note of weariness. "Look, Frank, I appreciate what you're saying. But I'm not particularly impressed by it. I had no objection to keeping a tail on Koops. But I had no choice other than to act on the advice of our counsel. I was told expressly and in no uncertain terms to cool it. From our point of view and the D.A.'s point of view, Koops is clear. Now forget it."

The cast-iron lid with the portrait of the bearded man imprinted on its center rotated left, then right. It made a scraping, grinding sound as the rotation continued.

At last the lid rose, coming from a corner as if it were on a hinge. Bits of dirt and gravel rained downward along the edges. From beneath the partially elevated corner, a pair of hands appeared, raising the lid above the head that followed. Grunts and gasps whispered through the darkened cellar. A sharp clank resonated loudly as the lid, falling backward, struck the iron crowbar leaning against the wall behind it.

An oath, half whisper, half snarl, ripped through the rank shadows. This was followed by the emergence of a stooped figure rising out of the earth, beating dust and dirt from its arms. Warren Mars was home.

Recalling his hasty departure from Bridge Street with police searching the house, he thought it prudent to arrive the way he had departed that night nearly three months before. Through the tunnel. Taking no chances that the house might still be under surveillance.

Though it was early afternoon, the cellar was almost pitch-dark. Groping and fumbling his way up the stairway, the only light he had by which to orient himself was from the narrow little rectangular windows set into the foundation at ground level. The accumulated mud and

grit of years had spattered the panes with a brown scurf
and rendered them nearly opaque. All that penetrated
them now was a pale gray diffusion of light.

Warren groped and fumbled across the cluttered dirt
floor, winding his way through a precarious tangle of
crates and barrels. Furiously, he swiped the filaments of
broken cobwebs from his hair and pushed forward to the
stone stairs leading up into the house.

At the top of the stairs he pushed the door open a
crack and peered out, uncertain what he might encounter there. Since it was barely two P.M., he expected Suki
to be home, puttering in her kitchen or, possibly, even
still asleep upstairs. The house, however, was strangely
still. The solitary mewling of a cat somewhere in the
upper reaches only served to emphasize the silence.

Then there was the smell. When he poked his head
through the door, it struck him with almost palpable
force. Like walking into a wall. There were times when he
imagined that the smell was inside him, in his head, so
sharp and pervasive that it permeated his skin and clothing. No amount of soap or scrubbing could cleanse him of
it. It was a smell he had committed to memory. Thousands
of miles away from it, he could summon it up and replicate
it in his head, dismantle it into its component parts:
mildew and rot, old threadbare fabric, clogged drains and
broken plumbing, food decomposing on unwashed
dishes, cat urine, and the sweetish fetor of uncollected
trash. A vast medley of putrescence and mold.

She was not in the kitchen when he walked in there.
Nor was she upstairs in her bedroom still asleep. She was
nowhere in evidence, and, when he called out to her
several times, the sound of his voice, tremulous and childlike, echoed back to him through the dusty vacancies.
Something about it made him strangely uneasy. It was not
her style to be out in the daytime, in broad daylight. She
was a nocturnal creature. She shunned the sun, only
feeling comfortable beneath streetlights and the moon.

It irritated him that she was not there to greet him after

his long absence, particularly since his trip home had scarcely been pleasant. It had been fraught with peril and risk and there'd been a few close calls. Worst of all was the loss of his beloved Mother, and then he'd had to come home on a deliberately circuitous route that had taken him on dirty uncomfortable buses as far west as Schenectady and as far south as Atlantic City. All to evade what he felt certain was a police tail just behind him.

In addition to which, he had a deep, unsightly scratch on his face that had begun to fester beneath the Band-Aids he'd hastily applied after his brief scuffle with the hapless young man who'd been imprudent enough to offer him a ride. Now to return home after twelve weeks only to find there was no one to greet him was just about the last straw.

Warren started to prowl through the house, all the while growing increasingly infuriated with Suki's absence. What right had she to be out at this time? Immediately, he suspected treachery. Perhaps she'd spoken to the police, had told them all she knew, then went off with them to some undisclosed "safe house" where she'd reside in perfect safety until they'd have him in custody. By the time he'd climbed up to the little attic room beneath the cupola, he was seething.

Eyes blazing, he banged into the room, half expecting to find her there. When he didn't, it pleased him in that it served to heighten his sense of betrayal. He could imagine the most elaborate forms of treachery going on behind his back just then.

When he'd entered, he came fast through the door, as if intending to surprise a thief. But there was nothing there — nothing but the old familiar symmetry of light, shape, and shadow.

Sun streamed through the cupola glass overhead and the room was beastly hot. He stood there for a time, fists clenched, breathing hard and feeling a bit at a loss. The moment, with its anger and disappointment, cried out for some sort of action. What form exactly, he didn't know.

When at last he could accept the fact that he was alone, he started to move quickly about the room. First in short, fierce thrusts, snarling half-turns, as if still challenging the disagreeable state of things presented him there at that moment. His eyes ranged avidly over the place. Something about the appearance of things, something vague and intangible, felt altered. It was not alteration in some minor way, either, but in some large, irrevocable way that he found threatening.

The more he spun and thrust and jerked about, like a child blindfolded in a pin-the-tail-on-the-donkey game, the more he was gripped with the growing conviction that something significant had occurred in his absence. And yet, for all of its significance, whatever it was, it remained to him stubbornly elusive.

He recalled having fled the room that day several months ago. Suki had awakened him, informed him there were police on the street out in front of the house. He had gone in haste, he recalled. The room that he left was in a state of great disorder. The room as it appeared now was a model of decorum. The bed had been made. The various odds and ends of his clothing — socks and underwear, discarded sneakers — generally strewn about, were nowhere to be seen. Left in their place was an order he was not accustomed to. More than anything, it was this that filled him with a growing sense of estrangement.

In the next moment his eye glimpsed a corner of the closet. It was the single closet in the room and the door of it stood slightly ajar. The quick glimpse he had of the interior was just a narrow wedge of it, the part just visible where the door hung open. Gazing at it, he knew at once there was something awry.

He stood there baffled by the peculiar unfamiliarity of the image, his head tilted sideways as if to see it from another perspective. It was then that it occurred to him that the closet was empty.

Something inside him seemed to snap. In the next moment, he lunged at the door, yanking it open. He'd not been mistaken. The closet, nearly full to capacity when he'd left, now stood cold and bare. All of his clothing was gone. The plain pine bar from which shirts and trousers had hung was stripped, the wire hangers on it clanging lightly against each other.

A rickety wicker chair stood within arm's length. Warren grabbed it, dragging it across the uncarpeted floor and banging it down beneath the ceiling light fixture. Scrambling up onto it, his hands tore at the frosted globe of the fixture as he struggled to unscrew it from its cheap brass housing.

Then, suddenly, the globe was off in his hands, dust rising slowly from inside it. He turned it upside down and shook it. From within it, the desiccated husks of moths and flies drifted languidly down onto the floor beneath the chair. Other than that, the globe was empty. But there was no need for him to dismantle the fixture to know that. He'd known it the moment he'd scrambled up on the chair, or, possibly, before that when he'd had his first glimpse of the empty closet. He knew what he'd sought there was gone. And he knew who took it. In point of fact, he'd been evicted and all of his belongings confiscated.

A rosy flush flamed across his throat and cheeks. There was a sense of uncomfortable congestion in his chest, as if he had to cough badly. When he tried to cough, it was more like a scream that emerged, a kind of strangled yawp that finally broke from his mouth.

When he leaped from the chair, he gave the peculiar impression of being in flight. The recoil of the leap sent the chair hurtling backward, crashing against the wall. Clattering down the stairs, muttering obscenities, he could still hear it echoing through the empty house.

Suki Klink toddled up the walk to her house on Bridge Street. She hummed an old Irish jig as she went. The wind blustering at her back propelled her along, billowing her multifold skirts about her. The night's pickings had been exceedingly good. The rusty old shopping cart with its wobbly wheels that she pushed before her was filled to overflowing with the assorted treasures gleaned from her rummagings. Aside from the usual complement of old magazines and plastic deposit bottles, she'd also managed to salvage from dozens of trashcans about the terminal several pairs of discarded shoes; a macramé holder for hanging plants; a beaded cushion, punctured and nearly eviscerated of its soiled stuffings; a vase of plastic poppies; a tire iron; and a red rubber enema bag. In the days ahead, she would manage in her canny way to convert it all to cash.

Through the bitter, blustery early morning, she could hear the wind soughing out of the west over the choppy waters of the Verrazano inlet. She watched it lean heavily on the old azaleas and frozen rhododendrons around the porch, cuffing them harshly and rattling their dry branches against the house.

On the little entryway beneath the copper overhang, she paused to fish the keys out of her rope bag, still humming in tune with some lively air she heard through the earphones of her Walkman. Plucking the key out between two bony fingers, she squinted an eye, then stooped to find the keyhole. Going through her head just then was an enticing vision of the pot of coffee she intended to put up the moment she got in.

In her bag, along with the assorted siftings and debris of the night's forage, were a couple of rolls and some crusts of bread she'd scavenged from Zaro's inside the terminal. She knew a woman there, an old black lady, who always saved her some leftovers.

Just as the door squealed open on its hinges, a blast of wind at her back shoved her forward into the dark and a pair of hands closed round her throat. She felt herself being dragged headlong into the house, the tips of her shoes scuffing over the bare floors, the wires from her Walkman tangled around her neck and head. The wheels of the shopping cart squealed madly as it broke from her grip and caromed across the floor, banging into something just ahead and overturning its contents.

As she struggled for air, her arms flailed wildly against the black, heaving shape that dragged and kicked her and sprawled all over her as she tried to fight back. The darkness had gotten darker. Nearly strangled by the viselike grip round her throat, the inside of her head felt inflated, as though engorged with trapped blood and about to explode.

Just as she thought she would lose consciousness, a blow to the pit of her stomach emptied her lungs. A bolus of half-digested food shot into her mouth and geysered out between her lips, spreading over her chin and clothes as she crumpled into a heap on the floor.

A shaft of light suddenly flooded the room.

"Bitch!" Warren stood above her, straddling her, kicking her arms and legs. "Bitch, Bitch!"

She tried to protect her head from the hard tip of his boot. "Lay off! Lay off!" she screamed, flailing her arms feebly in the air before her.

He stooped down and wound the wire of the Walkman tight around her throat. "Bitch. I oughta squash you."

"Lay off. I can't breathe."

"Where the hell is it? What the hell did you do with it?"

"With what?" A bubble of saliva swelled at her lip.

"Don't give me that shit. You know what." With one hand he lifted her head by the neck and kept banging it up and down on the floor. "Come on! Give! You're lucky I don't cut your fucking head off."

She tried to answer but he'd put his foot down on her windpipe and in that fashion had pinned her squirming to the floor. "Where's what?" she gasped.

"My stash. My fucking goods upstairs. You know what I mean." He clenched his fist and thrust it in her face. "If you sold that stuff . . ."

By then her face had purpled and she was gagging.

When she could no longer talk, she gestured with her hands. The message got through and he lifted his boot, holding it an inch or so above her throat.

"Downstairs," she gasped, wiping vomit from her lips with the back of her hand. "The tunnel."

"Where in the tunnel?"

"The barrel. The barrel."

"Which barrel, for Chrissake?"

"The small one."

He gripped her by the throat again and shook her hard. "It better be there." His eyes flashed at her, questions fluttering in and out of them. "What the hell you think you're doing, taking my stuff? Goddamn you — don't you ever . . ." The fist rose again, threatening to come down.

She rolled frantically away from him across the floor. He followed quickly, still kicking her as she went.

"Had to hide it." Her eyes, watching his boot tips, rolled in her head. "Had to hide it. Police all over the place. Had to hide it. Hide your clothes."

"Police were up there?" His fist went limp in the air. "In my room?"

"Searched the place," Suki panted. She watched fear creep back into his eyes and seized the offensive. "Had to hide all your stuff. Lucky I was here. If they'd found it . . ."

She could see fright and suspicion in his eyes and it pleased her. She wiped her befouled chin with the back of her sleeve. "Crazy fool. You nearly killed me."

For a moment he appeared contrite and she thought she had him back under her thumb. But in the next moment, he was swaggering again, brandishing the fist beneath her nose. "From now on, there'll be some changes here."

"Changes?"

"I'm in charge now. I run things in this house."

"Sure." Suki's eyes narrowed. "Sure, sonny. Sure."

"I don't care about no fucking police. Don't you ever

touch my stuff again. I don't even want you in that room
again. You stay outta that room now. Hear? Stinking old
bitch."

He turned and slouched off toward the basement.

After he'd left, she lay there for a time on the floor,
recovering her breath. Her mind was whirling. She
could hear him moving through the cellar below her,
kicking crates and boxes aside. The noise echoed hollowly in the space beneath the floor. Though she was not
cold, she started to shake. Shortly, the shaking grew
violent and uncontrollable until she was virtually convulsed with it. When at last she tried to rise from the
floor, her legs buckled like wax beneath her

It was several hours later on upper Fifth Avenue. In the
cold winter light of dying afternoon, the sun still hung
fiery in the west, while the pale white disc of the moon
was already visible in the east. The frozen air had the
quality of clarity so typical of winter light.

Across the way from 860 Fifth, Ferris Koops stood,
hunched up in his trenchcoat and shivering, but scarcely
aware that he was cold. The sunlight slanting sharply west
had set the facade of the building ablaze with reflected
light. The young man's eyes were riveted to a line of
windows on the fourteenth floor. He watched them,
transfixed with an odd, rather vacant, smile. At that moment in the corner window of 860 he imagined he saw the
face of a small boy peering out toward the park.

It brought him back nearly sixteen years and filled him
with some vague, half-forgotten sorrow. He was there
himself in the window now, gazing out at the encroaching twilight.

Ferris had not been to 860 for weeks. The need, the
strong craving had not been upon him until sometime
late that afternoon, when he felt suddenly impelled to go
back there. This need came to him in the form of a
terrible certainty that whatever he'd had there, whatever had been precious to him for so long, had all been

suddenly withdrawn. The idea of such a loss filled him with panic.

When at last he reached there, late in the afternoon, running, half-stumbling most of the way, anticipating the worst, what a relief to find that everything was all still there, just as he'd left it weeks before. Nothing had changed — the building, its proud facade, the line of windows on the fourteenth floor, and especially the little corner window. It was all still there.

He felt better at once. He almost laughed aloud. He felt his old self again. But hadn't things always been that way? Whenever he'd had this feeling before, this sensation of impending loss, estrangement, dissociation from himself, there would be the panic until he could struggle and battle his way back to himself. One moment he was Ferris, and the next he was not anyone. He was a void. He was air drifting on a current, whatever grip he'd had on reality grown even more tenuous.

Then, when he'd return there and stand outside, across the way from 860, it would all come back to him again with that reassuring rush of warmth. He'd gaze up at the corner window and see the face, his own haunted elfin face peering down at him, and everything would be all right.

And so it was that afternoon. Nothing had changed. Everything was still the same. Everything in its own cozy, familiar groove. Everything, that is, except one small detail. Ferris had noticed it at once. The old doorman (he didn't know his name, but they'd always seemed to acknowledge each other's presence) was gone. Ferris didn't know the man but felt some strange, unaccountable affinity with him. There'd been something jolly about the corpulent figure brightly clad, swelling importantly in green and scarlet at the front doors. For Ferris, it brought back sad, sweet memories of Christmases past. He had no way of knowing that the old doorman had recently retired. Now with the fellow gone, Ferris experienced a keen sense of personal loss.

Ferris was upset. But long before he'd come there that day, he'd been upset. He'd read in the newspapers that the police had reason to believe that the man, the one they called the Shadow Dancer, was back again in New York.

Ferris had read about this early in the day, with a sinking sense of impending doom. Ever since this man had made his way to Ferris's front door, Ferris had felt a deepening sense of communion with him. For each individual the Dancer had slain, Ferris felt guilt and shame, as if in some way he might have been able to prevent it. As vile and repugnant as the man and all of his activities were to Ferris, still he couldn't deny the inescapable attraction this monster held for him.

In his mind, Ferris was convinced that he was the only person who knew the true identity of the Dancer. Certainly he'd been the only one canny enough to have tracked the fellow to his lair. Not only that, but hadn't he stood guard over the place at the lower tip of Manhattan in an attempt to prevent further senseless slaying? And what was the reward for all of his good work? The police had picked him up and attempted to charge him as a suspect in these ghastly murders. He, Ferris, who would never knowingly hurt a fly. What a god-awful mess he'd made of things.

And now, the terrible irony of it was that he couldn't even tell the police all that he knew about the man who lived in the funny old house on Bridge Street. For one thing, his lawyers forbade him to speak with the police under any circumstances. More damaging, he had no actual proof, other than his own deep convictions, that the man who lived on Bridge Street and the man they called the Dancer were one and the same. And of that, he could say nothing.

Silence then, at least for the time being. Silence, but not inaction. He had knowledge in his hands. Knowledge available to no one else. In that sense, he had power. Power and responsibility. If this man was truly back in New York, by merely keeping him under surveillance, without attracting attention to himself this time, Ferris might once again prevent further bloodshed.

Ferris's heart beat faster. There was a kind of exhilaration, as if he'd been summoned to some exalted mission. As the shadows gathered about 860 Fifth and dusk descended, the lights from the building began to glow on the street. With a final nod to the small, haunted face in the fourteenth-story window, Ferris turned on his heel and, with a quick, urgent stride, started home.

TWENTY-NINE

FROM THE SEVENTIETH FLOOR OF THE NEW United Mercantile Building, Manhattan looked serene in the cold December light. Half completed, it occupied the entire southeast corner of 61st and Madison.

At that elevation there was no sound of traffic, no suggestion of the teeming, turbulent waves of life below. If you looked down (that is, if it didn't bother you), what you saw was a kind of grid over which innumerable tiny specks swarmed like some primitive, unicellular life in a miscroscopic field.

In the dazzling clarity of winter light the skies were a cloudless, nearly electric blue, the visibility perfect. Off to the west lay Passaic, and to the north the Yonkers skyline seemed but a stone's throw away.

Down on the street the temperatures hovered just above the freezing mark. But high up on the beams and girders of the United Mercantile, the wind chill produced by gusts of up to twenty miles per hour buffeting through the skeletal substructure made it feel close to zero.

The men working up at that elevation — welders, masons, pipefitters, plasterers, electricians — were accustomed to those conditions. Wrapped in thermal underwear, innumerable sweaters, hooded parkas, and gloves, they moved about, ponderous in their wrappings, like some ancient druidic sect celebrating mysterious rites. Silent, they scarcely acknowledged each other. The howling wind made all but the most primitive communication virtually impossible.

It was one hour to quitting time. Aside from the punishing conditions up at that elevation, the men laboring on the site worked particularly hard and fast. At five o'clock there would be a topping-out party to celebrate their passing the three-quarter mark.

All that afternoon they'd watched deliveries of cases of scotch and imported beer, pots of steaming meatballs and sausages, and platters of cold cuts arriving by the truckload. Below, at that moment, on the sixtieth-floor level, they were setting it all out on trestle tables in an area protected by a large tarpaulin that wrapped around two sides of the building and hung down nearly ten stories.

Kneeling down, Michael Mancuso leaned out over a huge corner beam and sent a shower of sparks spraying skyward from his welding gun, neatly sealing the seam between two girders together. More than the topping-out party, he had an even more pressing reason to work fast. Janine had gone to the doctor that afternoon. Her period was nearly five weeks overdue. She'd been on the pill, of course, but that was not entirely foolproof. She'd gone to the doctor that day for a more final determination.

They were still not married. That was scheduled for the week of Christmas. But if, as they suspected, she was pregnant, they would want to move their date up. That was for Mickey's parents and appearance' sake. Janine had no parents to mollify.

Working mostly by himself (his partner had been out with the flu for the past week), he'd accomplished a great deal that day. Several rapid bursts from his gun sent a shower of sparks like a huge orange peony blooming gaily all about him. Detecting a seam between two girders he'd missed, he leaned out somewhat farther, splayed nearly flat on several planks that served as a platform between beams.

Working intently to close the seam, the upper half of his torso almost inverted from the edge of the platform, he scarcely noticed the heavy, clunky pair of workman's boots that had planted themselves firmly on the platform in the vicinity of his elbow. Imagining it to be someone attending to some other task nearby, he went on with his work. It had not occurred to him that the boots, which he saw from the curious perspective beneath his arms, never moved. They simply remained there with an odd stolidity, covered with plaster dust.

Hanging over the edge of the platform, Michael Mancuso sent his great orange blooms wafting skyward. Still the boots didn't move. They merely waited, patient, unquestioning, detached from any living thing. An entity unto themselves. It then occurred to him that the boots had something to do with him — with his being there. Someone had come out to where he was working and was waiting for him with instructions or, possibly, a message.

Rising slightly from the planks, he half-turned his back and glanced up. A figure was standing there. The sun streaming directly over his shoulders made of him mostly a blur. But from what he could see, it was a man in a blue hardhat staring down at him from behind a welder's mask. The sun streaming into Michael's eyes gave the masked, helmeted figure an unearthly look, rather like a comic strip sci-fi conception of a humanoid from a distant planet.

Certain this person was waiting there to tell him something, Michael started to rise. It was at that moment the boot rose too, coming down hard on his chest, knocking the air from him and pinning his back and shoulders to the platform. As alarming as that gesture was, he still couldn't imagine what this individual behind the green plastic visor had in mind.

Michael started to squirm beneath the boot. That only caused the boot to bear down harder. He felt the air suck from his lungs. Panicking, he struggled to rise.

Why did no one come and help him? Couldn't they see? Then he realized that he'd been working on a side of the building that was mostly complete. Only a few stray workers were still about the area, putting the finishing touches on their work. Most of the other activity was going on around the corner on the northeast side of the building.

Recognizing his peril, Michael started to shout. He thought for a moment that the noise alone would frighten the man. But instead of turning and fleeing, his boot retracted slowly, then came back with a mighty force, crashing into his ribs. The impact of the blow spun him around, propelling him somewhat closer to the edge. When he raised his arms to protect himself, the welding gun flew out of his hand and shot out over the edge. He made a lunge as if to grab it, but missed. The boot came again. This time it landed squarely in the groin, doubling him up in exquisite pain.

Both of his legs now dangled over the edge. In trying to protect himself, the glove of his right hand had slipped off and he held precariously to the platform with his bare hands, clinging to a rickety brass guardrail.

By then he was fully panicked and shouting at the top of his lungs. But the wind howled well above the volume of his cries. The boot rose again and came down with crushing weight on his face. The *coup de grace* was the descent of the boot with its studded sole, grinding his frozen hand against the rail.

Letting go was easy, he thought. Scarcely aware that he was airborne, that he had started his long tumbling, descent, the last thing he saw and heard before his eyes went black was the gay, red and white stripes of the kangaroo cranes on the roof and the sound the wind made whistling through them.

The phone had started to ring shortly after she'd gotten home that evening. The first call was from the job when they'd told her there'd been an accident. Right after that the police called and asked her to come down to an address on First Avenue in the Thirties. They said it was

Bellevue. They wouldn't give her any details, only repeated what the foreman at the site had said. Simply that there'd been an accident.

By that time her heart was beating wildly in her chest. But since they'd described it as an accident, she still didn't believe that it was anything dire. The doctor that afternoon had told her she was pregnant, probably within the seventh week of her first trimester.

When she reached First Avenue and 31st Street, she discovered that the address the police had asked her to come to was not the hospital, but the medical examiner's office. At that point, she still didn't realize that it was the morgue.

She was met there by a kindly, solicitous plainclothesman who spoke to her in a low voice. He interviewed her in a large room at a desk surrounded by a half-dozen other desks. People were moving all about. Phones rang constantly. There were several men there, too, from the construction site, also answering questions.

In a voice that seldom rose above a whisper, the detective informed her that indeed there had been an accident. Mickey Mancuso had fallen to his death from a girder seventy floors above the street. The papers sent over to the morgue from the union local had designated her, as his fiancée, sole beneficiary. There were papers to sign: payroll slips, insurance forms, whatnot. She would, of course, have to identify the body.

She sat there, mute, stunned, hands folded in her lap, comprehending very little. She thought she should be crying, but instead, she sat blank and nodding, watching the lips of the detective move as he rattled off in hushed tones a multitude of things that would have to be attended to.

"*Seven weeks, I should judge,*" the doctor's jovial voice rang inside her head. "*Possibly eight. Now I'd like you to . . .*"

"It's a damned shame to have to put you through this," the detective murmured apologetically. They stood in a

bare green room that smelled of fresh paint. There was
nothing in it but a long pane of horizontal glass beyond
which could be seen the inside of an elevator shaft, steel
cables swaying lightly on their anchors.

He pressed a small red button beside the window.
Instantly, she heard the high whirr of a motor and
watched the cables rise up through the shaft. Her knees
started to buckle beneath her.

In the next moment, a steel table rose up to the level
of the window and halted there. It was only the head she
saw. The rest of it lay beneath a white sheet.

It was not his face, she thought. The awful rictus of
death had transformed it into something else. The thing
lying there under the sheet had nothing to do with him.
She didn't know this person. But it was clearly Mickey.
The sheet that so carelessly draped him was spattered
with blood. She could tell from the way he lay there that
the wreckage beneath was considerable.

She'd taken all of that in within a glance. In the next
moment, she whirled sharply away from the glass, as if to
erase the image forever from her mind.

She felt the detective's hand graze her shoulder
lightly. "Is it him?"

She nodded and stumbled blindly toward the door and
out of the room. There were more people there now.
More talk of the accident. Mickey's friends from the site,
saying what a "damned shame," and what a "damned
good guy" he was.

A representative of the union was there. He took her
aside and told her that the funeral would be paid for.
They would see to all the details. His voice dropped
respectfully when he told her that there was life insurance and that she would be entitled to some pension
benefits as well. Nothing grand, of course, but good old
Mick had wanted to be certain that all was taken care of
when they'd gotten engaged.

It was nearly ten P.M. when she got back home. Letting herself into the tiny apartment, she half-expected to

find him there, sitting in a sleeveless undershirt on the seedy old Morris chair with a beer in his fist, watching the hockey game.

Still, she couldn't quite grasp what had happened. She was never one to drink. Possibly a glass of wine on the rare occasion. But that night she poured herself a stiff scotch and drained it off neat in a single gulp. Then she poured another.

She turned off the light and sat for a while in his chair, big and floppy and reassuring, sipping her scotch, hearing his voice all about the apartment. "Hey, Janine. Where are the Band-Aids?" Smelling his smells — the good musk of sweat raised at honest endeavors, the scent of talcum, freshly laundered undershirts, and cheap colognes.

Figures drifted all about her. Voices from earlier that day — the doctor, the detective, the foreman from the site — whispering all about her.

Still huddled in the dark, she sipped her drink, then rose to put on the television. It was right there on the eleven o'clock news. Right at the top. Construction worker falls to his death on 61st Street, and the mayhem it caused during rush hour. There were clips showing police cars, ambulances, spectators milling about a humped, formless shape beneath a tarpaulin hastily drawn across it.

It was all a blur to her. She couldn't connect any of it with Mickey. Then, suddenly, the reporter's voice, which up until that moment had been no more than a dim, distant hum, rose, penetrating her consciousness. ". . . Police had formerly been characterizing the death as an accident, but only moments ago, Channel Two has learned that a worker on the site, after hesitating several hours, had come forward to disclose that he'd witnessed the incident, and that it wasn't an accident. The victim had been pushed."

She listened, horrified, unbelieving, as the reporter described how the witness had seen a man in a blue hardhat and welder's mask go out on the plank where Mickey had been working and kick him two or three times until he'd fallen over the edge. The man who'd witnessed the incident had been standing on another platform a hundred or so feet off, separated by a yawning gulf of freezing air. He watched, horrified in disbelief, as the body tumbled headfirst into the yawning chasm below.

He shouted at the man in the welder's mask, who'd turned the moment the body had pitched over the side and dashed into one of the freight elevators. He followed, but by the time he'd gotten down to the ground floor, the man had already disappeared.

The witness, who wished to remain nameless, claimed that he'd not immediately reported what he'd seen out of fear. Working on construction sites all of his life, he knew that such jobs were full of rivalries and vendettas, competition between unions, kickback squabbles. Lots of hotheads worked around these places. Men came and went all the time, and, most of all, they had a way of settling scores among themselves without outside interference.

The man had known Mickey Mancuso for a few years and knew him to be clean. They used to eat lunch together periodically, and it was not until he'd gotten home that night and blurted out to his wife what he'd witnessed that he decided to inform the police. He did so, but, unfortunately, he was unable to provide them with any clues to the murderer's identity.

Janine listened, numb and stunned, to the report. At first, when the detective at the morgue told her what had happened on the site that afternoon, she had no trouble accepting the fact that it was an accident. Mickey, she knew, was an exceptionally careful person. But accidents on construction sites do happen, even to the most circumspect. This new disclosure, however, made far more sense. And while the police remained in the dark as to the murderer's identity, she unfortunately did not. She knew only too well the masked figure's identity. She knew the old Warren Mars style. Hadn't he even told her what would happen if she failed to comply with his wishes?

She sat mute and crumpled in her chair for an hour more before the television, watching phantom figures drift across her screen. At a certain point, she rose unsteadily, threaded her way through the darkened room to the kitchen, and poured herself another scotch. She carried it back out to the living room, where once again she resumed her place in Mickey's chair.

Bringing the drink to her lips, her hand shook to the point where she had to put the glass down. In the next moment, her whole body was convulsed in waves of tremors. She had the feeling that she'd lost physical control of her body.

Then it seemed to her that she'd fallen asleep. When she awoke it was several hours later. She was still in the chair. The glass had fallen to the floor. The TV was still on, but there was no longer any picture and no sound, only the blank lighted screen with a grainy, pin-striped pattern wiggling through it.

She had a headache and her mind was muddled from the effect of three scotches. She'd been dreaming. She couldn't recall the details of the dream; only the tag end of it was she able to retrieve. The final image was that of birds diving through soft, fleecy clouds.

Curiously, she was not thinking of Mickey at all. It was slightly past two A.M., and she couldn't quite recall why she was sitting in the chair at that late hour and not in bed. There was work in the morning. She'd better get to bed.

She started to her feet. Then, coincident with that motion, she heard a sound. It was a soft, barely audible noise, at the front door, the sort of thing one barely notices unless it's pointed out. Yet, there was something singular about this sound. It consisted of light, metallic clicks occurring in rapid succession — rather like the sound of blinds through which a breeze is blowing, only more rapid, and the rhythm far more regular.

It went on like that for nearly twenty minutes, the tapper content merely to stand out there in the hallway, taunting her. For that's what it most assuredly was, taunting. If there'd been any urgency about it, any genuine purpose, whoever it was would have rung the bell, or called her up on the phone. No, this was taunting, of the most perverse sort. Adolescent mischief with an edge of genuine horror. And she knew very well who it was.

Then, abruptly, the sounds stopped. She covered the space between herself and the door in three swift steps and put her ear to it just in time to hear footsteps retreating down the carpeted hallway to the elevator. She waited there, breathless, until she heard the whirr of the elevator through the wallboard, the door sliding open, then closing, and once again the high whirring sound.

She sank to her knees and slumped against the door, where she sat for some time, the chill metal of the door seeping through the thin material of her blouse. Her limbs shook so badly that she thought she would blow apart.

The next day she disconnected her phone and turned off the refrigerator. She called her employers and resigned over the phone, giving no specific reason for her action. Finally, she threw some articles of clothing into a bag and paid her rent for the next three months.

Janine McConkey had few close friends, but the closest she ever had to a real friend lived in a suburb of Philadelphia and that was where she was heading now. Not at a leisurely pace. Not by an orderly route. But in headlong retreat with all due dispatch.

THIRTY

"BELIEVE ME. TURF IS AN ENTIRELY DIFFER-
ent ball game from dirt. An old claiming nag who couldn't
even zero on the main track can be gangbusters on turf.
I've seen it happen. A horse who dies in sprints on the
main track may be a knockout distance runner on grass.
Take Dauntless . . ."

Mooney was holding forth at the bar to a handful of
anointed cronies. Shortly after noon, it had started to
snow in earnest. Blizzard snows had been predicted
throughout the night and early into the next morning.
Companies had sent their personnel home early and
accordingly there'd been a barrage of dinner cancella-
tions at the Balloon that evening. Business was way off.

Most of the waiters were sitting around in the back,
drinking 7-Up. Arms folded, they leaned against the
walls near their stations, gazing hopefully at the entrance
for prospective clients. Though it was bad news for
Fritzi, it was just the sort of thing Mooney relished. He
had the place to himself, or nearly to himself. Those that
were there were the old crowd, the regulars, there because, like him, they loved it.

"If you're lookin' to pick winners on the turf," Mooney
went on expansively, warming to his subject, "look for a
horse with a track record on turf and ignore their dirt
form. I mean, forget it entirely. . . ."

Nodding and murmurs of approval followed this pro-
nouncement, as if a sage had spoken.

"Hey, Mooney, wanna take a call over here?" Patsy called from across the bar.

"No!" Mooney shouted back and resumed his talk.

"Hey, Mooney!" Patsy shouted again, this time waving the receiver in the air above him.

"Who is it, for cryin' out loud?"

"Pickering."

"I'm not here."

"He hears me talkin' to you, for Chrissake."

Mooney muttered something, drained his drink, and lumbered across the bar to where the phone awaited him. "This better be good, Rollo," he snarled into the receiver.

"Trust me. You'll like it."

"If I don't, you're in a lot of trouble."

"Looks like we got another Dancer job."

Mooney paused, peering into the speaker. His mind had not yet disengaged from the esthetics of turf running.

"Frank? You there?"

"Of course I'm here," he fumed at the question. "Who says we got another Dancer job?"

"The Hundred and Twelfth, up in the North Bronx. They called a half-hour ago to say they're pretty sure they got one."

"How would they know?"

"They know. They read the papers. It's got all the earmarks. Married lady. 'Bout forty-four years old. Semi-detached residence. Split-level. Right off the Thruway on the east side approach to the Throgs Neck Bridge. It's a mess. Wanna go see?"

Mooney looked outside. "There's six inches of snow and another eight coming."

"Nine days," Pickering snapped, alluding to the swiftly approaching coronation of Sylvestri. "Nine days is all you got left, Frank."

Mooney could feel the heat rising from beneath his collar. "Hang on. I'm calling for a car."

"Don't bother. I've already got one. Be out front. I'll be by for you in twenty minutes."

HOMICIDE IN BRONX SUGGESTS
RENEWED DANCER ACTIVITY
AFTER LULL OF THREE MONTHS

Mrs. Ada Billeto of 1340 Bell Street appears to be the nineteenth victim of the so-called Shadow Dancer. Known for a series of particularly grisly homicides commencing twenty months ago with the brutal slaying of a woman in her home in the Richmond Hills section of Queens . . .

According to police, this latest outrage occurred late yesterday when the Shadow Dancer gained access to Mrs. Billeto's bedroom on the ground floor of her semi-detached tract house in the Throgs Neck district of the Bronx.

The body was discovered by Mr. Billeto when he returned from work. Police described the scene as "grim," adding that details of the slaying had all the special earmarks of the Shadow Dancer, including ritual mutilation and macabre crayon drawings of mostly sexual content scrawled on the walls.

Forensic units of the medical examiner's office have been combing the site all day in an effort to . . .

The jangle of the phone on Mooney's desk brought his bleary eyes up from the newsprint he'd been poring over.

"Detectives. Manhattan South. Mooney speaking."

"Did you read it?" Mulvaney snapped. It was not quite eight A.M. and already he was skirting dangerously close to apoplexy.

"I'm reading it now."

"What d'ya think?"

"It's him, all right."

"You're sure?"

"Ninety percent."

"Witnesses?"

"Nobody saw anything. Nobody heard anything."

"Naturally," Mulvaney muttered bitterly. "What did it look like to you?"

"The typical stuff."

"A mess."

"A little worse than the usual, I'd say."

"Worse?"

"This poor lady looked like she backed into a buzz saw. Blood and hair all over the walls."

Mulvaney made a sound of disgust. "Spare me the details. So we've got him back again, eh?"

"Looks that way. But who knows? Could be the other guy. The pretender to the throne."

"You think this might be the copycat guy?"

Mooney wanted to say, "We'd know possibly, if we'd kept a tail on Koops," but what he settled for was, "We'll know more after we've had the M.E.'s report. Offhand, though, I'd say no. This one's in the classic mode. The hand of the master is everywhere present."

Mooney proceeded to enumerate for the chief of detectives the diagnostic characteristics they'd come to associate with the work of the Dancer. At the conclusion of their talk they agreed that the similarities in the most recent slaying far outweighed whatever small deviations in style they'd noted from the Dancer's typical M.O. It was more than enough for them to discount the possibility that they might be dealing with the counterfeit rather than the authentic. "I still have eight days," Mooney said at the end of their talk. Mulvaney didn't reply. He simply hung up.

After that, the phone started to ring in earnest. Mostly, it was newspapers and television news shows asking for interviews. The mayor's public relations flak absorbed a full half-hour of his time, pleading for any positive development the mayor could report to a nervous city at his press conference that afternoon. Several neighborhood associations called, demanding additional police patrols, and a handful of the usual anonymous callers denounced Mooney viciously in language unfit for print. On these he slammed the phone down with a whoop of malevolent joy.

The next call, however, was a significant one. It was Paul Konig at the medical examiner's office, asking him to come down immediately.

". . . And the tooth marks around the breasts and inner thighs match perfectly."

"What about the blood type?"

"The serology reports are incomplete. But, so far, from the semen samples we managed to get, it looks like an AB pos. Also, this specimen had normal sperm," the young woman in the blood-spattered surgical smock added pointedly. She watched the information register on Mooney's face.

They were gathered in the large autopsy suite in the basement of 334 First Avenue, the medical examiner's office: Mooney and Pickering, Konig and Dr. Joan Winger. Barely nine A.M., the place was already a hive of activity. Thirteen steel trestle tables stood in a line, each bearing a flayed, naked cadaver, the accumulated carnage of the night before. Each body lay open on the table, each with a long Y-shaped incision commencing at the tip of the scapulae, plunging through the breastbone, and terminating at the pubic symphysis.

There was a low, remorseless din as police surgeons, medical students, and dieners milled about the tables, sectioning organs, plumbing the entrails and orifices of the remains in the quest for clues to the mystery of death, sewing up the cadavers when they'd finished, then carting them off.

Mooney stared down at the gutted, battered remains of what only twenty-four hours before had been a happy, healthy forty-four-year-old wife and mother of three. She now lay on a steel table, viscera exposed, the sparse, pale furze of pubic hair beneath the abdomen looking strangely childlike. People barged back and forth past

her, impersonal and businesslike — the awful indignity
of bureaucratized death.

"Sure messed her up pretty good." Pickering stared
down at the remains, wonder and fear mingling on his
face. The eyes were half open, the irides glinting out
from beneath. A portion of the tongue had slipped out
through the gap, settling at the corner of the mouth.

Konig was talking now, pointing out a number of
similarities between the injuries present here and
those found on other Dancer victims. Mooney made a
show of attentiveness, trying hard not to see the electric band saw at the next table, slicing through the
skull of a young black man of princely dimensions.

"It adds up," Mooney nodded, anxious to be gone
from there. "The M.O., the method of entry, the type
and location of the house . . ." His eye had fastened on
something several minutes before while Konig was in
the midst of a lengthy disquisition on the nature of the
injuries. "What are those marks on her face, anyway?"

Konig's eyes twinkled. "I thought you'd never ask.
Perhaps Dr. Winger would care to explain. She's come
up with something rather interesting."

They all turned to her in a single motion.

"Boot marks," she replied curtly. "Someone stepped
all over her face."

"That's what I figured," Mooney said.

"Just like Bailey, Torrelson, and some of the others,"
Pickering added. "We found the same markings stamped
on the faces there, too."

All eyes switched back to the young woman. This time
she appeared flustered by the sudden attention.

"Would you step down this way, please." She
pointed with her head to the right, then led them to
another dissection table about five places down. A
group of medical students, working under the supervision of an Oriental pathologist, stood away from the
table as Konig and his party approached.

As they parted from around the table, Mooney had a

sudden view of what they'd been working on. It was the body of a young man, roughly in his mid-twenties. The limbs and appendages all showed the sickish purple of lividity. Moving in closer with the others, he could see the broken, shattered ends of bones where they had burst through the outer skin at nearly every point of the body. Like the other cadavers in the room, this body had been flayed open. The organs showing from within swam in pools of blood.

"What the hell happened here?" Mooney asked.

"Construction worker. He took a nasty fall on Sixty-first Street," Konig explained, with mirthless glee. "From the seventieth story of a building site. They now say he was probably pushed."

"Broke every bone in his body," Dr. Winger added. "Ruptured most of the organs. He literally exploded on impact. From inside out."

Pickering gaped down at the remains, that expression of wonder and awe making him look foolish. "I heard about this one the other day. Came over the wire at headquarters."

Konig grinned. "One of the workers on the site saw it happen. Some guy just came out on the beam where this kid was working and kicked the poor bastard over."

"They get the guy?" Mooney asked, mildly curious. "Any identification?"

"Nope. Number one, the guy who did it was wearing a welder's mask, and number two, he got away before anyone up there could grab him."

Mooney grew thoughtful for a moment, then shrugged. "Okay. Very interesting. What does all this have to do with me? This is Midtown North's problem."

"Maybe," Konig said, his eyes dancing merrily in his head. "Maybe not."

"Look at his right hand, lieutenant," Dr. Winger said. She pointed to the back of the dead man's hand with her pencil.

Glancing down, Mooney at first saw nothing. Then

suddenly he saw the abrasions and the strange purple grid patterns he'd observed moments before on the twisted death mask of Mrs. Ada Billeto. His eyes rose to meet those of the young woman pathologist, who was smiling. "Boot marks?"

Mooney and Pickering exchanged looks. Both appeared to be bewildered. Mooney held both hands up defensively, as though he were trying to hold back an onrushing locomotive. "Now, wait a minute. You're not suggesting . . ."

"Why not?" Konig smiled irritatingly.

"This is different," Mooney protested. "I mean, the M.O. is completely different."

"The boots, Mooney. The boots," Konig pressed him.

"What about them? Millions of guys in this city working on construction sites . . ."

"Even guys not working on construction sites," Pickering chimed in.

". . . wear boots like that," Mooney sputtered on. By that time he was red in the face. "You're not seriously telling me that this masked nut who kicked this poor bastard off a beam on Sixty-first Street is —"

"The Shadow Dancer." Konig's grin never faltered. "Before you have a stroke, would you step upstairs a moment. We've got something to show you."

Moments later, they were in the cool shadowy silence of Dr. Winger's office, gathered round a viewing screen. Three slides were already up on the screen. She flicked a switch and the blue-white glow of fluorescent illumination suffused the room. The three slides projected before them had been magnified many times. On first glance they gave the appearance of an eerie lunar landscape: bumps and crevasses, deep fissures and jagged excrescences. All of it was laid out in what was clearly a circular pattern.

"Do you know what these three slides represent?" the young woman asked.

"Let me guess." Mooney dripped sarcasm. "They're photo enlargements of the sole prints taken off of Torrelson, the Bailey kid, and our latest entry to the charmed circle, Mrs. Billeto."

Konig applauded. "Very good, lieutenant."

"Would you please take note," Dr. Winger continued, "of the areas I've circled in red crayon on all these enlargements."

Mooney, still smoldering, leaned forward and studied the circled markings.

"You observe anything unusual, lieutenant, about the nature of these markings?" Konig taunted.

"Certainly," Mooney rose to the challenge. "The markings on all three of these enlargements are in precisely the same location on the boot sole."

"Remarkable." Konig winked at his young assistant. "Isn't that remarkable, Dr. Winger?" He turned back to Mooney.

"Would you care to point out for us now, lieutenant, what characteristics are common to all three views?"

Mooney glowered. He appeared to be swelling when he stooped once more to the viewing box and squinted at the illuminated images floating there.

He studied the slides for a moment, twisting his lips from side to side as he did so. Then, standing erect once more and straightening his shoulders, he spoke: "On the outside I see four consecutive studs worn flat on all three sides. On the inside shank, separated by a channel in the vicinity of the vamp, I see two more worn studs, separated by one that appears not at all worn."

Konig and Dr. Winger stood silently by, their arms folded, appearing mildly amused.

"Splendid," the M.E. enthused. "In that case, Dr. Winger, would you kindly produce the fourth specimen?"

The young woman withdrew another slide from her desk drawer and mounted it in a conspicuous position amid the other slides on the light box. "This one is a photo of the boot sole markings we found on Michael Mancuso's right hand."

"Michael who?"

"Mancuso." She smiled at Mooney. "The gentleman you saw laid out there a few minutes ago. Would you care to examine the red circled markings I've indicated here?"

Mooney and Pickering exchanged quick glances. It was the first time during the course of their interview that Mooney betrayed confusion.

"Take it from me, lieutenant, he was a prince. Everyone here was crazy about him. He was a sweetheart."

"No enemies? No grudges? No gambling debts?"

"Clean. Mickey was clean. Absolutely spotless. If I ever find the son of a bitch . . ."

The wind up on the seventieth floor of the partially completed United Mercantile Building whistled through the naked beams and girders. They were standing in the protective lee of a canvas tarpaulin wrapped three quarters of the way around the structure. The winds pummeling it from outside caused it to billow and flap, periodically producing a loud, concussive sound not unlike a cannon shot.

"Believe me," Mr. Gus DeAngeles, the construction foreman, went on, "I never had this kind of thing happen to me on any kind of job I ever ran before. We don't tolerate that kind of thing up here. Ask anyone. Troublemakers, I don't tolerate. I see a troublemaker, I throw him the hell out. He can't work for me."

"Then you're pretty sure this guy up on the platform with Mancuso was not one of your people?" Pickering asked.

"Never. Could never be. Like I say, how this *strónzo* ever got up here on the site without a pass, I don't know. But I'm sure as hell gonna find out, and there's gonna be hell to pay for some poor son of a bitch. You better believe it. And I still haven't forgotten that puss-head who stood around up here with his fingers up his ass and watched."

Suddenly caught up in a swirl of emotions, Mr.

DeAngeles looked away. "You already talked to Pendowski, I s'pose."

"You mean the electrician who witnessed it?"

"That's right."

"We spoke to him." Mooney nodded. "He told us essentially the same story he told the guys from Midtown North. It checks out all right." Mooney stared off at the Jersey skyline so as not to see the teary red eyes of Mr. DeAngeles.

"That kid was just like my own." The foreman sniffled noisily. "I treated him like he was one of my own kids. I knew his dad, Vinnie. Was a welder, too. Used to work with me over the Brooklyn Navy Yard. Sweetheart of a guy. A real gent. And you know, the kid was just about to get married."

"That's rough," Pickering commiserated, putting on his best long face.

"Planning a Christmas wedding, they were." The foreman flapped open a crumpled red handkerchief and honked loudly into it.

"Weren't having no troubles, were they?" Mooney inquired. "No little lovers' spats?"

"Nothing. Nothing like that." Mr. DeAngeles banished the notion with an abrupt chopping motion in the frigid air. "These kids were crazy about each other."

"What's her name?"

The foreman's mouth dropped open in puzzlement. "Who?"

"The girl. Mancuso's girl."

"Oh." There was a pause as Mr. DeAngeles resonated into his handkerchief again.

The two detectives watched while he attempted to dredge the name up from the past. "Ain't that funny? It's right on the tip on my tongue. Jean. Jane, something. How do you like that? I just saw her yesterday. We was all over to the morgue together. Identifying the remains . . ."

The mere mention of the word was too much for the

man. His eyes filled again. "Oh shit. *Man naggia mia.*
Ain't this somethin'? You gotta forgive me, goin' on this
way. Thirty years I'm doin' this work, I never seen
nothin' like this."

Mooney waited patiently for him to regain his composure. "You were about to tell me the girl's name."

"The girl? Oh, sure, the girl. I got it right over here in
some papers. What's she got to do with it?"

"Probably nothing." They started toward a little cubicle, hastily erected and comprised of a desk, a chair, files,
and a telephone. "But it wouldn't hurt to talk with her."

They crowded into the breezy little area, with its
desktop littered with ashtrays and paper coffee cups.
Mr. DeAngeles, too big for his chair, took his place
behind the desk with sudden pomposity. "Couple of
weeks ago he asked me to switch the beneficiary on his
union life insurance policy."

Mooney's ears perked. "He did?"

"From who to who?" Pickering followed up quickly.

"To this girl I was telling you about. The one he was
marrying. He switched it from his mother."

The foreman hunched above his file drawers, riffled
through them quickly. "Yeah, sure. Here it is. Michael
Mancuso, as policy owner, to Janine McConkey, as sole
beneficiary. That's capital *M*, small *c*." The foreman
spelled it out with agonizing deliberation.

"Got an address on that, too?" Mooney asked. He was
shivering in the blustery, frozen air and anxious to be
gone.

"Sure. That's one twelve East One Hundred and Third
Street. But take my word for it: these kids are clean.
Both of them."

"Sure," Mooney said, extending his hand. "Thanks for
your time."

"Very nice people. Very quiet. Never had no problems
with them. Respectable. Polite. Always paid their rent
on time."

The building manager at 103rd Street and Madison Avenue on the fringes of Carnegie Hill was a dignified black gentleman by the name of Mr. Tudor. They sat in the tidy coziness of his ground-floor office, drinking coffee as an electric floor heater hissing away warmed their frozen feet.

"It's a coincidence your coming in here just now," Mr. Tudor continued. "I just found this on my desk this morning."

He slid a small white envelope across the desktop toward Mooney. The detective picked it up, holding it tentatively between two fingers. "Is it okay if I read it?"

"If it weren't, I wouldn't have offered it." Mr. Tudor's toothy smile glowed warmly.

Inside, Mooney found the check with three months' rent and a letter of sketchy explanation. When he finished, he stared up at the building manager. "She left in an awful big hurry, didn't she? She give any reason? She leave a forwarding address? Anything?"

"All I know is what you got right there in your hand."

"From the letter it sounds like she plans to be back in, maybe, three months."

"Sounds that way. Awful business the way that boy died like that. I guess it shook her up pretty bad."

"I guess so." Mooney nodded and there was a somber moment of obligatory silence to acknowledge the awfulness of things in general. "Still," Mooney persisted, getting back to the nitty gritty of business, "she was sole beneficiary of his life insurance policy, a hundred thousand bucks, face value. And she did pull out of here awful fast."

"Could be she just went off to stay with relatives awhile." Mr. Tudor preferred a more charitable explanation.

"Or could be she was scared of something and had to get out quick," Pickering suggested.

They were silent for a moment, all of them regarding each other warily.

"I don't suppose we could have a look at the apartment?" Mooney asked.

"I'm not supposed to let anyone into any apartment without authorization from the tenant direct."

"Or a warrant from the district attorney's office," Mooney added pointedly.

Mr. Tudor caught the implied threat in the detective's voice.

"I could have one in twenty-four hours," Mooney went on solicitously, full of sympathy for Mr. Tudor's predicament. "But it's a shame to lose time while the trail's hot."

The building manager frowned his disapproval. "That girl's done nothing wrong. You're wasting your time, lieutenant."

"Maybe," Mooney conceded. "But I'm still gonna have a look at that apartment to put my own mind at rest. Either now or twenty-four hours from now."

"She's not a suspect, is she?"

"Not in this Mancuso business, which isn't in my jurisdiction anyway. But she may very well be in something else I'm working on at the moment, and which I'm not at liberty to disclose. So, as of now, I'm treating Miss McConkey as a suspect."

Mr. Tudor looked back and forth from Mooney to Pickering, his face marked clearly with the conflict he was trying to resolve. At last he spoke: "Let me make a call, will you?"

While they sat there across from him, he called the landlord's office, explained the situation, and was granted permission to open the apartment.

Several minutes later they had ascended in a rickety coffinlike elevator to the sixth floor and were rummaging about in the cramped confines of the little studio dwelling.

It consisted of a single room and a kitchenette. It took them barely any time to go through it. As they went about their work, Mr. Tudor hovered in the background, clearly uneasy with the part he was playing there.

She had undoubtedly left in a great hurry. The drawers were still full. Food had been left in the refrigerator, which was still cool, even though it had been disconnected.

Mooney had started with the closets, Pickering with the drawers. There was one large, battered old chifforobe. The upper two drawers contained male clothing: socks, handkerchiefs, underwear, etc.; the lower two were female.

Pickering discovered nothing there and moved on to a desk. The top drawers contained bills, check stubs, and a stack of American Express receipts bound with a thick rubber band. There were, in addition, pens and pencils and paper clips.

The drawers on either side of the well were filled with manila folders upon the front of which a variety of categories had been entered in large bold capital letters: HOUSE PAPERS, PERSONAL PAPERS, INCOME TAX. One had been designated WEDDING PAPERS and contained contracts executed with a catering hall in Brooklyn, two airline tickets to Bermuda, blood tests from the Board of Health, and various related documents. Sifting through it all, Pickering had found nothing.

Meanwhile, Mooney had moved on into the kitchen where Pickering joined him, followed by Mr. Tudor, looking quite glum by then.

Mooney at that moment was going through the upper cabinets. Pickering turned his attention to the lower ones. For the most part, they contained no more than the most prosaic of cooking utensils: pots and pans, cookie sheets, Pyrex plates, several Mason jars. As he went about his work, Pickering had been kneeling, his knees feeling the effect of cramp. Mooney had quit the upper cabinets and was back in the living room running his big, meaty hands beneath upholstery cushions and drapery cornices.

Just on the verge of quitting, Pickering's wrist happened to dislodge a copper omelet pan from its place, revealing beneath it a small square of crumpled white paper that had been folded neatly into eighths. He unfolded it and proceeded to read the writing that appeared there. A minute or two later he was back out in the living room, flagging it excitedly at Mooney.

"Dear Janine," Mooney started to mumble half beneath his breath. "I still think of you. Don't be scared. Not in the bad old way, but the way it was . . ."

When he finished reading he looked up, the crumpled square of paper trembling in his hand.

Pickering was grinning broadly. "Did you get a load of the handwriting?"

Mooney gazed back at him blankly, not answering the question. Instead, he shot back, "Let's get an all-points out on this McConkey kid right away."

THIRTY-ONE

ARLETTE COLES MOVED SMARTLY DOWN Smith Street in the Marble Hill section of Brooklyn. Despite the fact that it was two in the morning and the streets were deserted, she was not uneasy. It wasn't her custom to be uneasy. In her time, she'd been in a lot more questionable situations and always managed to come out on both feet.

A striking, statuesque black woman, she'd never married and did not regret the fact. For a girl who'd barely finished high school, at thirty-six she'd come a considerable way. Having served two years in Panama with the U.S. Army, she'd parlayed her mustering-out pay into a prosperous little beauty salon in this rapidly gentrifying area and was looking for another location to open up a second.

If she had one great passion in life, it was ballroom dancing, which was frequently the cause for her arriving home at such late hours. She was an assiduous participant in dance competitions all about the city.

That morning the sound of her heels with the metal taps on the toes rang through the vacant streets. Her shoes made rapid, vibrant clicks on the concrete, almost as though they were still joyously battering the dance floor. If she was feeling particularly good that evening, she had reason to. She'd come off with the second prize trophy (a twelve-inch dipped bronze figurine of a fandango dancer) in a hotly contested tango competition.

The trim little brownstone, enclosed by its freshly

painted white wrought-iron fence, that served as her home glowed its welcome to her at the top of the hill. She'd just purchased it the year before from its former owner with a 40 percent down payment to the bank and a twenty-year mortgage.

For a child who'd grown up in hard times with no advantages other than loving parents who'd been able to bequeath her only a strong sense of her own personal worth, Arlette had done herself proud.

She'd left lights on in the front parlor, as she always did on these late evenings. Glowing there in the chill of early morning, they imparted to the little brick three-story brownstone a kind of dollhouse miniature grandeur.

Fumbling for the key in her purse, she found it and inserted it into the lock. Simultaneous with that action, even as her wrist turned, she felt a pair of palms flat on her back and then a fierce shove. The door swung open, and before she could cry out, a pair of powerful hands, smelling faintly of rubber, gripped her around the throat and pushed her in. It was as though she'd been sucked down a black hole by the sudden creation of a vacuum. The door slammed behind her, and, in the next instant, something dark and faceless was swarming all over her.

A stream of words, mostly vile and abusive, hissed hotly into her ear. From that point on, a fierce struggle ensued as she grappled with the dark, shapeless thing that clawed at her, tearing at her clothing.

Before she knew what was happening, she was flat on her back, the figure sitting astride her chest, the rubbered fingers closing inexorably around her throat, slowly cutting off her air.

"Shut up and you won't get hurt."

Until the words had come, she hadn't connected her assailant with anything human. Now for the first time she opened her eyes and found herself staring into a pair of large dark eyes that smiled down upon her. She was struck by how kind the eyes were, making what the hands were doing at the same time seem a cruel paradox.

She felt the grip on her throat loosen and air rush back into her lungs. Then the hands were gone, but only for an instant. When they reappeared, one of them, the right, held a shaft of long, glinting steel she immediately recognized as a steak knife, feeling its razor-sharp point piercing the skin of her throat.

In the initial melee (it had seemed to her it had gone on forever, but its actual duration was little more than a minute), she managed to hold on to her trophy (not out of fear that it was going to be taken, but that it might get broken). All the while she was being assaulted, she continued to hold the trophy, swathed in silver wrappings above her head, out of harm's way.

In the cozy orange glow of the parlor lights, the features of her assailant came gradually into focus. The face was a soft oval. It was an attractive face, she thought, except for the row of broken teeth that imparted to the lower portion of the face a wild, rather feral appearance. They looked as though they could rip one open.

"You just do what I tell you," he said, leaning forward and putting his warm face up close to her cheek, while one hand held the knife at her throat and the other proceeded to grope beneath her skirt.

That evening she'd chanced to wear a rather spectacular black sequined gown for which she'd paid $700. Purchased from a highly regarded designer collection, it was her pride and joy. All she could feel now was the rude thrusting hand clawing at the lining beneath the skirt, his intention clearly to pull it over her head like a sack, thus pinning her arms inside. The skirt was well above her thighs by then and the bodice had ripped, sending a blizzard of sequins spilling into her armpits and onto the floor. As the man with his wild plunging motion continued to hoist the material up around her, the sequins cut and scratched her legs.

In matters of sex Arlette was not prudish. She could bear the rough hands and the steady stream of vile filth that poured from her assailant's mouth. But this sheer, wanton destruction of her beautiful dress was a bit much for her.

In the next moment the arm carrying the tango trophy rose and swung sharply downward, clipping her assailant solidly on the jaw. The weight on her chest instantly shifted to one side, then just as quickly righted itself. Suddenly, she found herself looking into a pair of stunned, rather hurt eyes, as if she had done her attacker a tremendous injustice.

Dazed, he sat there unsteadily atop her, rubbing his jaw. She took advantage of the unguarded moment to squirm out from beneath him and scramble to her feet. Still holding the tango trophy, she brandished it above her head. He stood there in a half-crouch, watching her warily, waving the long kitchen knife in wide, slow loops before him.

At first, when she'd been shoved unceremoniously through the front door and had no idea what manner of thing was swarming all over her, she was frightened. But seeing finally the instrument of her fear to be no more than a mere mortal man, not all that big at that, the paralyzing terror of her imagination fell from her like something weightless and inconsequential. Suddenly, she was calm.

"Okay, you got yourself in here, slime; now you better turn your ass around and slither right back out."

The smile, once so benign, had turned to an impudent grin. He continued to wave the knife in the air and started to move slowly toward her.

Her voice was calm and quiet as she spoke: "I'm gonna count to three. If you ain't outta here by then, you gonna hear some real shoutin'. Shoutin' to wake the dead. I read all about you, motherfucker. I know what you are. You don't scare me none."

He came on smiling, almost hypnotically, cutting long, graceful loops through the air with his glittering blade.

"Come on, you fucker." She beckoned him with her

free hand, while the other hefted the trophy more securely above her head. "You may get me, but you gonna pay dear for it."

Even before she'd gotten the last words out, he hit her broadside across her middle. A flying tackle, lightning swift. They went down together in a loud crash, a tumbling, windmilling, thrashing scuffle that ranged over the parlor floor. The trophy toppled from her hand. He tried to pin her to the floor with his knee, but she wriggled out again, swatted at him with her hands. She caught hold of a clump of hair and yanked hard. He shrieked and slammed his fist hard up against her temple. She felt her eyes rattle.

A floor lamp went down behind them with a loud crash, projecting huge shadows, humped and whirling large against the spinning ceiling.

The whole front of her bodice had been torn and hung down in shreds against the bare skin beneath. Once again the hand was pawing her, trying to caress her, while the other held the knife point against her throat, just below the chin.

Straining beneath that heaving weight, as though she were caught in the gears and sprockets of some demonic machine, she looked around the room, searching for an object, a weapon with which to fend off her attacker.

In that moment, the full horror of the situation became crystal clear. This man, this flailing thing on her chest, intended to kill her. Why? For what earthly reason? What harm had she done him? Well, let him try. She had no intention of making things easy for him.

Suddenly, she was screaming. But not merely screaming. It rose from someplace far down inside her, some dark place she scarcely knew existed. No mere human sound, it was more like the wailing cry of banshees rising from the netherworld.

Her shouts were now answered by the sound of voices hollering from windows in the adjoining houses and, shortly, footsteps pounding on the pavement outside in the street.

The stream of vileness continued from her assailant's mouth, borne on a breath that smelled meaty and putrid, as if he'd recently fed on something not quite, but nearly, spoiled.

She felt the cold tip of the knife pierce the skin of her throat, then sink beneath it. There was a spurt, then the flow of something wet and warm.

Someone had started to bang on the front door. She could hear the whooping of a police siren not far off. Barely conscious, she felt the weight lift from her chest and, out of the corner of her eye, saw a figure flee toward the rear of the house.

In the next moment, she was half up, holding her hand pressed over her throat where blood seeped between her fingers. The wound didn't keep her down for long. Instead, scrambling to her feet, she pursued the fleeing figure through the dining room out into the kitchen where the back door now stood open, and through which her assailant had fled.

"Motherfucker! Motherfucker!" she bellowed into the huddled dark. The icy air had revived her and she kept shouting. "Get outta here! Get outta here! You pig! You scumbag!"

Neighboring voices shouted back at her across the courtyard, assuring her that help was coming.

There was a rending sound from out front. The front door burst open. Dozens of people in pajamas and robes poured in: old, toothless black women with nylon stocking nightcaps on their heads, middle-aged men in outlandish pajamas with frightened eyes, carrying baseball bats in their hands; the police followed, pushing through the crowd, streaming into the kitchen, where Arlette Coles stood in a pool of sequins, shivering in her shredded dress, the bodice down around her front, a hand held to her bleeding throat. The other hand pointed out the door like a road sign in the direction of the fleeing figure. She was still shouting obscenities after him at the top of her lungs.

**SHADOW DANCER ON NEW RAMPAGE
CITY IN PANIC**

**MAYOR DECLARES STATE OF EMERGENCY
VOWS INTENSIFIED HUNT**

**SECOND ATTACK IN THREE DAYS INDICATES
QUICKENING OF SLAYER'S ACTIVITY
$25,000 REWARD OFFERED FOR INFORMATION
LEADING TO KILLER'S APPREHENSION**

**CITIZENS GROUPS AND NEIGHBORHOOD
VIGILANTES PROWL CITY STREETS. SOME
NEIGHBORHOODS DESCRIBED AS
ARMED CAMPS**

**RUN ON ALARM SYSTEMS AND ILLICIT STREET
GUN TRADE UP 100%. POLICE OFFICIALS
CONCERNED AT TURN OF EVENTS**

**SHADOW DANCER FLEES ATTACK SITE
CHASED BY ANGRY MOB WIELDING
BATS, TIRE IRONS, AND FRYPANS**

The phone rang. Mooney looked up from the stack of clippings on his desk and gazed morosely at it. He knew who it was before he'd even lifted the receiver.

"It's all here on my desk," he said, without bothering to say hello or good morning.

"Well, read it and weep," Mulvaney's voice rasped into the phone. "His Honor's been on the phone two hours this morning with McClenahan. From what I hear, they're still at it."

"What d'ya s'pose they're talking about?" Mooney's voice croaked wearily.

"Not about the weather, I can assure you. More probably, something about your job performance."

"A bit about yours, too, no doubt."

Mulvaney's long, tired sigh drifted across the wire. "Heard anything on McConkey?"

"Not a word. Her name's out all over the AP wire and the networks. Her face is plastered on every rag in the country. If she's out there, anywheres, and still alive, she's gotta have seen something by now."

Mooney waited for some response. When none came, he spoke again. "Now that's the bad news. Would you like to hear some good news?"

"I'm all ears," Mulvaney said with a conspicuous lack of enthusiasm.

"The Coles dame."

"Who?"

"The lady who was hit last night. Arlette Coles."

"What about her?"

"I spoke to her on the phone this morning," Mooney went on, trying to suppress the excitement in his own voice. "She's over at Kings County now. Got a nasty puncture wound in her throat, but the doctors say she's gonna be fine."

"She willing to talk?"

"Talk? Sing. Shout at the top of her lungs is more like it. I could barely stop her. This is the first solid description we've had."

"And it's our boy?"

"No chance it could be anyone else. Dark, straight hair. Broken front teeth. Caucasian, or possibly light Hispanic, or mix. And get a load of this: they picked up a broken pink crayon on the floor where they were scuffling. Fell out of his pocket."

"Any prints?"

"She says he was wearing rubber surgical gloves,

which fits with everything else we've heard about him. That accounts for the fact we never come up with any prints. But this time the forensic guys think they may lift something off the Crayola."

"When you seeing her?" Mulvaney asked grimly.

"I'm going over this morning with Rollo. Soon as I finish up here."

Now that it was all out, Mooney felt breathless and a little lightheaded. If he was waiting to hear some expression of approval, he didn't get it.

"Frank." Mulvaney's voice dropped several decibels lower and, suddenly, sounded portentous. "This case has now been transferred to Sylvestri."

There was a pause. A long, embarrassed silence. "Sylvestri?"

"That's right. It's what we've been talking about the last few months. Eddie Sylvestri is in charge now."

"Sylvestri." He whispered the name again, as though he'd never heard it before.

"Don't say you weren't warned, Frank. It wasn't my decision. McClenahan tossed this at me six o'clock this morning. I guess that's part of what came out of the talks with the mayor."

Mooney had recovered sufficiently to sputter, "What about my extension? I've still got about six days to go on our deal."

"The mayor doesn't care about our deal. He just wants this thing resolved, and for nearly two years you haven't been able to do that."

"First of all . . ."

"Let me finish, Frank. Then you can talk. If you want it straight, here it is. Eddie Sylvestri's marked for a captaincy and, possibly, a divisional job. He's considered by management to be the coming thing."

Mooney's face was hot and a pulse throbbed at his temples. "All I need is a few days more on this thing and I can — "

"Sorry."

Though he'd been expecting it for some time, it still felt as if he'd been kicked in the stomach. "Gimme five days. Just five days more." Mooney could hear himself pleading. "Four . . . give me four."

"Sorry, Frank."

"Three."

While the voice was sympathetic, it was uncommonly firm. Mooney recognized the tone. "So this means you're throwing me off the goddamn case now?"

"Worse," Mulvaney said. "It means you're still on it. Working for your old pal, Eddie Sylvestri."

THIRTY-TWO

IN A BATHROBE AND SLIPPERS, SPRAWLED ON a day couch that converted to a sleeper at night, Janine McConkey watched the gray phantom figures drift across the television screen. She lay in a darkened parlor, in a small suburb of Philadelphia, while her oldest and dearest friend, Bobbie Murdoch, slept heavily in an adjoining room.

The figures moving back and forth across the screen were mostly black people. They wore robes and pajamas with overcoats thrown over their shoulders. They brandished sticks and other objects. Police were getting in and out of patrol cars. Neighborhood merchants discussed the awful scourge of the Dancer and the heavy toll exacted on small businesses that remained open all night.

A tall, attractive black woman appeared on the screen, her throat swaddled in bandages. In a rasping, rapid-fire delivery, peppered with expletives, she related her experience to reporters. She was shortly followed by a tall, rumpled detective with a thatch of white hair and staring eyes that gave him the fierce look of a totem god. He stood in a hospital corridor growling curt replies at clamorous reporters and seemed anxious to go.

As he quickly summarized all that was known by the police up until that time, Janine McConkey attempted to follow developments, but the thought of Warren Mars obsessed her, crowding everything else from her mind. Where was he at that moment and, more critically, had he any idea where she was? The thought that he might almost suffocated her with panic.

She knew Warren well enough to know that eventually he would come after her. Once his mind was set on something, nothing could deflect him. He would not stop until the business was accomplished. Indeed, hadn't that been precisely the case with poor Mickey?

It was unlikely that Warren knew where she was at that moment. She told no one where she was going. She'd left no forwarding address. No one had seen her leave the apartment. No one, to the best of her knowledge, had followed her to the Port Authority building and watched her purchase a ticket or board the bus to Philadelphia — at least, no one she was aware of. However, with Warren, you could never be certain. His powers of tracking were uncanny, and, while he'd never met her old friend, Bobbie Murdoch, whom she'd known since they met in a foundling home when they were both five years old, she had often spoken to him of Bobbie. She couldn't be certain, however, if she'd ever mentioned to him the fact that she lived in Philadelphia.

". . . Janine McConkey, aged twenty-three . . . " The sound of her name droning quietly over the television speakers sounded curiously alien to her, like the name of someone else. Some perfect stranger. It was only when the snapshot of her, a fairly recent one taken at an outing the year before at Coney Island, flashed on the screen and the name and face came suddenly together that she recognized herself.

". . . believed to be a vital link to the Dancer. . . . " The voice droned on through the darkened room, even as the image of her face smiled pleasantly out at her over the airwaves.

. . . police are searching desperately for this young woman who it is said may hold the key to the identity and whereabouts of the Shadow Dancer. Police characterize her sudden disappearance from both her home and job as

ominous. Sources fear she may have been abducted by the
Dancer and her life may be in danger. . . . Any person
having information leading to the whereabouts of Miss
McConkey is urged to call the following toll-free number:
one eight hundred, six two four, five three hundred. All
calls will be kept strictly confidential.

Her image faded from the screen, leaving in its place
a scene of a soccer game in a teeming stadium in São
Paulo, where thousands of fans had proceeded to riot.
Long after her image had faded, she continued to sit
there on the futon, her head swimming, her knees drawn
up tight to her chest while she hugged them for dear life.
She had the feeling that if she dared let go, she'd be
swept off by some swift, engulfing tide.

She started up to wake Bobbie and tell her. Then, she
thought better of it. If she told Bobbie that the police
were searching high and low for her and, possibly, Warren too, friend or no friend, Bobbie might very well ask
her to leave. She had no place to go. For her part, Janine
never wanted to go out into the world again. She wanted
instead to huddle there in the dark, curled up in a little
ball on that lumpy futon that smelled of mold and tired
bodies. Safe and warm in the dark forever.

She racked her brain, trying to figure how the police
had established this "vital link" between her and Warren. She knew where they'd found the photograph. That
was easy. It had been on a shelf in the kitchen. So,
they'd been to the apartment and had, no doubt,
searched it. But what had they found there to make the
connection? There was nothing. Nothing incriminating
that she could think of. A surge of elation went through
her, only to be dashed the next minute when she recalled the crumpled letter, smoothed out and pressed
flat beneath a stack of pots and pans in a kitchen cabinet.

Could they possibly have found it? Obviously, they
had. If someone were searching, seriously searching,
common sense told her that in such a tiny apartment it
wouldn't have been too difficult.

But still, how had they known enough to go to the apartment in the first place? Then she thought of Mickey and what had happened, and then it was clear. She knew at last how the connection between her and Mickey and Warren had been made. And that's why the police now wanted her so badly. Well, they could forget about it. She had no intention of turning herself over to the police, not with Warren Mars out on the loose. Not even with Warren Mars in captivity. She knew quite well how that all worked. If information she provided resulted in Warren's capture and conviction and they put him away for life, okay. But it seldom worked like that. More likely, the scenario ran to appeals, with the possibility that Warren would be out on bail or, if he was convicted, out on parole after serving only a few years, then declared "rehabilitated" by the penal system. Since he'd know that his conviction had stemmed largely from her testimony, it wouldn't take Warren long after he'd been released to be around again, looking for her the first opportunity he had. Warren never forgave and never forgot.

No, there was no way in the world she was going to surrender herself to the police. Better stick your head in the oven or jump off a bridge, she thought. Instead, she was going to stay put right there, if Bobbie would let her. If not, she'd make a run for it. There was a whole country out there in which to lose oneself. She was frightened to go it alone, but anything was better than the alternative offered by the police.

Now, for the time being, for the few hours remaining until dawn, she would sit right where she was. Pull the blankets up over her head, hide in the stuffy, comforting warmth of the dark, and pray not to hear a tap or a sudden nervous scratching at the front door.

On Sunday morning Mooney slept late. It was his custom to do so, then to rise about ten, shower and shave, and while still in his robe, enjoy a long, unhurried breakfast, lingering over coffee and the racing forms. It was ritual, hence inviolate. Nothing was ever permitted to intrude.

On this particular Sunday morning, however, Mooney remained in bed. He had not slept all night. He had no particular appetite for breakfast and no great zest for news of any sort. His mood was one of anger and despair — anger that he'd been replaced by his arch-rival, Eddie Sylvestri, fifteen years his junior, who had already amassed a notable record for himself on the force and who was destined, so they said, for greatness; and despair that after nearly two years of hard, thankless rooting about, he'd at last picked up a strong scent of the Dancer. It was now sharper than ever before and, keenly, he felt the distance between himself and his quarry closing. But he no longer headed the case.

A bright wintery sun came streaming through the windows over 83rd Street. He could hear Fritzi out in the kitchen, puttering about. There was the smell of coffee and the doughy, slightly burned smell of pancakes frying on the griddle.

Still, he had little inclination to rise, even to the temptation of those enticements. His pride bristled far too much for him to derive any solace from the gratifications of the stomach. The prospect of now taking orders from a brash *Wunderkind* like Sylvestri, whose nose was never too far from the commissioner's ample fundament, literally sickened him. What had kept him sleepless and tossing all night was the growing certainty he felt, that Sylvestri, capitalizing on Mooney's hard work, would march right in now, nab the Dancer, and take all the credit for himself.

"Breakfast's on," Fritzi trilled from the kitchen. That was followed by a stream of coarse invectives out of the throat of Sanchez.

Mooney's response was merely to lie there, fuming in his rumpled bedding, feeding on his own intestinal lining.

Shortly, Fritzi herself appeared in the doorway, looking cross. With an apron wrapped around her still-girlish waist, her thick reddish hair barely brushed, she made a pretty picture.

"You're waiting for me to carry you piggyback to the table?"

"I'm not coming to the table."

"I've got a stack of flapjacks out there, and you're coming to the table."

"I'm not hungry."

A look of perturbation crossed her face. In the next moment, she smiled with mock commiseration. "Ah, I see we're feeling sorry for ourselves this morning."

"Look, Fritz, I'm really not in the mood." He rolled over on his side and faced the wall.

"I'd think you'd be relieved. I'd think you'd be ecstatic. It's not your headache anymore. It's that twit Sylvestri's. He's welcome to it, I say."

At the mere mention of the name, Mooney's hands flew to his ears as if to block out the hated sound.

"Now, you listen to me, Mooney. You get out of that bed and march right out there to breakfast." She hauled down the blankets and proceeded to yank him up forcibly.

He tried several times to pull the blankets back up around him, but each time she yanked them back down. He groaned and bayed and flailed the air with his hammy fists until at last he capitulated. Robed like the priest of some esoteric cult, he permitted himself to be steered across the long living room to the pretty little breakfast nook adjoining the kitchen.

The marble refectory table was set with stoneware mugs and bright Quimper crockery. A tall tumbler of freshly squeezed orange juice stood beaded and chilled at his place and coffee gurgled fragrantly from the percolator. Even the surly, sardonic Sanchez seemed more solicitous of his feelings that morning.

"Morning, Mooney. Morning, Mooney."

Mooney sneered at the bird and took his place grumblingly at the table. In a burst of lively chatter intended to distract him from his woes, Fritzi poured coffee and set a stack of flapjacks before him.

She kept the chatter up. Mostly it was about horses, primarily their own. The talk was almost entirely one-sided, intended to divert Mooney from his morbid thoughts. He scarcely replied, only sat there picking morosely at his pancakes and occasionally nodding at some remark.

She didn't expect much more. She knew the depth of his disappointment and hurt, but she refused to acknowledge any of that to him. "You've got nothing to be ashamed of, Mooney. You've done a great job."

He gazed up at her sourly. "I've never been bounced from a case before."

"That's their tough luck." She poured him fresh coffee. "And their bad judgment."

"My luck, Sylvestri'll wrap the whole thing up in the next forty-eight hours. After I've done all the dirty work."

"Let him. You don't need that. It's his headache now. Just think, Frankie, my young buck: in another nine months or so you're going to be free as the wind. I've been giving it some thought. Don't think I haven't. You and I are going to take six months off and do the world. Go to the race tracks everywhere. Deauville. Longchamp. Aberdeen. Baden Baden. Ascot. Chantilly. Down Royal. Del Mar. Disconnect the phone. Sleep late every morning. Do nothing. Answer to no one."

Glowing with enthusiasm, she brought her chair up beside him and threw an arm round his burly shoulders. "How does that strike you?"

"Wonderful," he grumbled.

"Wonderful," Sanchez assented.

"My heart's all a-twitter," Mooney sneered.

Sanchez nodded. "Twitter. Twitter."

Fritzi flung her hands up in despair. "Now, look, if you're going to sit around here sighing and moaning . . . "

"I like to sigh and moan."

"Well, if it makes you feel good."

"It does," he snapped with finality and rose.

"Do you hate your job?" she asked suddenly.

"I despise it. Everyone there's a lackey and a twit."
Swelling dangerously in his rage, he glared at her.
"Why the hell should that turd Sylvestri get all the glory?"

"Ah, so it's glory we're after? You never told me that.
You always scoffed at glory."

"What's wrong with glory? I did all the damned work.
Now he just walks in and — "

"You're still on the case, aren't you?"

"Sure. But under him. That's as good as being off it.
He's not there to give me opportunities."

Fritzi rose and started to clear the dishes. "Why
should he give you opportunities? Would you give him
any if the tables were turned? The answer to your problem, my friend, is quite simple."

"Oh, yeah? What is it?"

"Make your own damned opportunities."

He looked at her quizzically.

"Or just go out and take them," she continued hotly.
"Just don't sit around waiting for Sylvestri to hand you
something. He won't. You're still on the case, aren't
you? What does it matter if he's the big honcho, or you?
Honestly" — she started to load the dishwasher — "men
are such babies. Go out, for Chrissake, and get that
goddamn Dancer and stop worrying about fancy titles."

"Fancy titles." Sanchez's voice echoed hollowly
through the bright Sabbath sunlight.

Later that morning Fritzi went out to Mass. While proclaiming to the world her unyielding agnosticism, one of
her secret pleasures in life was regular attendance at late
Sunday morning Mass at St. Patrick's. She'd long since
given up trying to get Mooney to attend with her. His
reaction to the business of institutional religion was
mostly to scoff.

Left to himself that Sunday morning, his ego badly bruised, his funk deepened. Slumped in the battered old Morris chair, morose and fretful, he wondered why this struggle with Mulvaney and Sylvestri over the conduct of a police investigation that he'd failed to conclude successfully should so mingle itself with bitter memories of other, past failures, and why he should now reprove himself for the way things had turned out.

Mulvaney, Sylvestri, Fritzi, and the faceless Shadow Dancer all rose now like troubled specters in Mooney's roiled brain, all somehow bound together in the hapless, drifting investigation of eighteen brutal slayings that had dragged on for two long years. Circumstances and plain bad luck had conspired to defeat him, Mooney told himself, while at the back of his mind he wondered what part dumb pride and lack of resolve had played in his failure. Whatever it was, the sense of defeat was immense.

Such were the gloomy thoughts that whirled about him that Sabbath morning like a plague of gnats. When Fritzi returned shortly after Mass, she found him unshaven, still in his pajamas and robe, seated in the old Morris chair where she'd left him, and glaring straight ahead at the phantoms still lingering in the sun-flooded room.

By six that evening, she'd convinced him to shave and dress, tempting him with an early supper at Pearl Wong's, a favorite haunt of theirs, prior to reporting to the Balloon for the Sunday evening rush.

Pearl herself met them at the door and personally supervised their dinner. They supped on hacked chicken, velvet shrimp, lobster in its shell, followed by Pearl's own crispy orange beef.

But not even all of that largess could rouse Mooney from his despair. The specters of the afternoon still plagued him. Fritzi watched him pick disconsolately at his food.

"I said a little prayer for you at Mass this morning," she remarked.

"Who'd you pray to? Mulvaney? The commissioner?"

"To Baumholz," she beamed brightly. "I thanked him for being savvy enough to make all that money in the market."

"And for leaving it to you. No strings attached."

"No strings attached." She nodded with great contentment.

Mooney's chopsticks speared glistening slivers of beef. "So?"

"So, that means we've got all this, if you'll pardon the expression" — her voice dropped and she gazed quickly around — " 'fuck-you' money. Anytime you want to leave the force, Mooney. When you feel you've had a bellyful . . ."

Mooney lowered his eyes and pried intently at a lobster claw.

Her head tilted and she smiled across at him archly. "Baumholz told me to tell you not to worry. He'll take care of everything."

"I feel better already," Mooney said, spooning black bean sauce over his rice.

"In a tight spot, Baumholz was always a good one to have in your corner."

"Next time you talk to him, please convey my warmest regards."

"Baumholz is very fond of you, Frank."

"And I of him," Mooney assured her with great solemnity. If she could handle this with a straight face, he was determined he could too. "Didn't I marry his old lady, and luck into a warm, cozy spot beside her in bed? I sure hope Baumholz doesn't resent me."

"Resentment," Fritzi assured him grandly, "was not in the man's makeup."

Mooney laid his knife and fork down very deliberately beside his plate. Then, clasping his hands before him, he fixed her icily. "Can we quit all this cute stuff now?"

"Sure. But wouldn't you like to hear what Baumholz advised?"

Mooney pulled a long, suffering face. "Okay. Tell me. I'm all ears."

"I can't. He told me not to tell you. He wants it to come as a surprise." She was deadly serious as she informed him of this.

Mooney started to puff and swell ominously. Then, catching the glint in her eye, he laughed in spite of himself.

She'd broken his gloom for the moment.

"Sweet revenge, old pal," she said.

He raised his glass and touched it to hers. "Sweet revenge."

That evening before bed he went up on the roof of their building. Hunched above the shallow parapet in his fleece-lined jacket, he watched the stars wheel overhead in the bright December sky. Off to the west, Orion hung above the Jersey Palisades and in the east he saw the rising Pleiades.

Nothing much had really happened to dispel his gloom, yet, inexplicably, in that moment, he felt a weight lift from his heart. With the rising of the Pleiades he sensed some coming shift in his fortunes for the better.

Fritzi was still off at the Balloon and wouldn't be home for several hours. Feeling curiously at peace and looking forward to the morning, he went to bed. No sooner had Mooney laid his head on the pillow than it was morning and the phone was ringing by his head.

"Where are you?" Pickering asked.

"In bed. Where the hell would I be at this hour? Where are you?"

"In the office. Throw some clothes on and get down here. Everything's popping."

Still drowsy, Mooney stared mystified into the receiver. "What the hell are you talking about?"

"We got McConkey. But I'm sorry to have disturbed you. I'll just turn the matter over to Sylvestri."

"You got who?"

"McConkey. You heard me. She just breezed in here on a bus from Philly."

"You've gotta be kidding."

"Listen, Frank." Pickering's voice dropped sharply. "I can't hold her here too long without notifying Sylvestri. But we've got an out. She came in here asking specifically for you."

Mooney waited, his mind alert and speeding. Pickering rushed on.

"Seems she saw you on the TV down in Philly. Asked for you by name. She'll talk only to you."

Mooney was still frowning into the receiver.

"Frank," Pickering whispered once more. "You still there?"

"I'm here," Mooney said, throwing his bulky calves from beneath the blankets. "Listen, if Sylvestri calls, tell him nothing. Hold on to her. I'll be right down."

Mooney bounced out of bed with a shriek of joy. "Praise be, Mr. Baumholz. You're my man."

She looked small and tired and very frightened. She was pretty, Mooney thought, but not in any obvious way. Her clothing was rumpled and her hair straggly. She looked haggard and gray the way people look when they've sat up in a bus all night. They feel dirty and their mouths taste awful.

She was drinking coffee from a paper container when Mooney came in. Holding a sugar doughnut in her hand, she sat there as if it were some encumbrance she couldn't quite figure out what to do with.

Pickering was there with several others moving around her in the office. "I'll take it from here," Mooney said. "Everyone clear out. Rollo, you stay."

When the others had all shuffled out, he closed the door behind them, then crossed back to where the girl sat miserably in her raincoat with the doughnut in her lap.

"I'm Lieutenant Mooney," he said.

"I know," she replied, and he thought she was about to cry. He reached for the doughnut.

"Would you like me to take that?"

She smiled crookedly and surrendered the doughnut to him like a docile child. He put it down on the table beside her.

"I'm glad you came in by yourself, Janine. You had us all a bit worried."

No sooner had he said the words than she dissolved in tears. They watched her quietly, not speaking, waiting for the racking sobs to end.

"Let it out," Mooney said. "Let it out." His hand rose to pat her quaking shoulders, but shrank somewhere just short of contact. "Let it all out."

It took several minutes and then it was over. She looked up at him, her tear-washed cheeks glistening in the dirty gray morning sunlight.

"You think you can tell us about it now?" Mooney asked, his voice unnaturally soft.

She gaped at him for a querulous moment, then in a small, tired voice she proceeded to speak. "His name is Warren Mars . . . ," she started hesitantly, and, as she did, Pickering's pen began to scribble into his pad.

She told a story of two children — waifs, runaways, one five, the other seven — and how they'd found each other in an abandoned tenement building in the heart of Hell's Kitchen.

At first, she said, they came together out of a mutual need for survival. Later, it became something else — a strong emotional tie, possibly romantic . . . at least she thought so when they were young. She couldn't be certain now.

She told them about Martinez, the crazed janitor who'd refused to leave the building after both the landlord and the city had condemned it. A fiery little Chilean, he had an incendiary temper and had gathered about himself a band of waifs and castoffs, keeping them imprisoned in the basement of the tenement, letting them out early each day to steal, to hustle, to sell themselves in the West Side tenderloin. At night, when they returned and brought him money, he fed them. When they came back with nothing he menaced them with razors and locked them in a dark basement coal bin for hours. His name was Martinez, and all of his foundlings were somehow christened "Mars" by the other kids in the neighborhood, she explained.

"You don't happen to know what Warren's real name is," Mooney asked.

She looked at him blankly and shrugged. "To me, it's always been Mars."

In her tired, expressionless voice, she related a chronicle of adolescent crime — muggings, break-ins, addiction to cocaine at fourteen.

"It was when Warren started the really bad stuff that I got out," she said, gazing red-eyed up at Mooney.

"You left him?"

Her eyes opened wide. "You don't leave Warren. You run away and hope he doesn't notice it."

"He came after you the other night though?" Mooney asked.

She nodded blankly. Then she told them how, after she'd run away from Warren, she hadn't seen him for years, but that she continued to get letters from him. As often as she moved, changed addresses and jobs, somehow he always found out where she was. She told them how she'd earned a diploma in a high school equivalency program at night. How she got off drugs in a rehabilitation program and got a job. How she'd met Mickey Mancuso.

"He's the guy fell off of the construction site up on Sixty-first?" Mooney asked.

Again she nodded in that childish way and told them how she felt responsible for Mancuso's death, since Warren had more or less told her that he intended to kill him if she didn't break it off herself.

"I never loved Mickey, you know. I never loved him." She said it over and over again, flailing herself with the words. "I guess I liked him. He liked me a whole lot more. I didn't ask for that. It was Warren that really got to me. But scared the hell out of me, too. Maybe that was the big turn-on for me."

Her eyes glistened. A narrow band of white, the reflection of an overhead fluorescent, shimmered on the surface of her pupils. "I guess that's maybe why I feel so lousy now. I mean, about Mickey and all. He was too good to me. Too kind. I could've never given it back to him the same way. Why did he have to go and die? For some dumb bimbo who really didn't care that much? I guess with Mickey I was just looking for a quick fix."

She started to cry again. Hot, stinging tears washed her cheeks and eased the fear and grief she'd bottled up inside for so long. Then she broke off suddenly and looked up at them. "How did you put all this together?"

"There were things the medical examiner found on your friend's body that he also found on the bodies of several of Warren's other victims."

"So you went up to my apartment?"

"Mr. Mancuso's boss gave us the address."

"I figured that," she said listlessly. "And you searched it?"

Mooney's eyes studied her face for the intent behind the question. "You're not angry that we did?"

She shrugged with indifference. "It doesn't matter anymore. You found the letter, I s'pose?"

"In the kitchen cabinet," Mooney said, pulling it out of his desk drawer. He pushed it across the desk toward her.

She glanced down at it with the same tired indifference.

"Are you sorry you came in?" Mooney inquired.

She looked at him blankly, then shook her head slowly back and forth. "Now that it's all over, I'm glad."

She picked up the doughnut and started to nibble at

it. Pickering poured her fresh coffee. When she attempted to swallow some, she started to choke and cough. In the next moment, she was crying again, wiping crumbs of sugar from her lips. "This time, he'll kill me," she said. "He'll know I've been here and he'll kill me for sure."

"No, he won't," Mooney said. "He won't be able to get near you. As of now, you're in protective custody until we get him. But we'll need your help."

She gazed back and forth at them questioningly.

"Where can we find him?" Pickering asked.

She shook her head. "I don't know. All I know was the old place."

Mooney leaped at it. "What old place?"

She appeared confused. "Way downtown. You know, the financial district."

Mooney's eyes narrowed and he glanced at Pickering. "Not Bridge Street?"

"That's it," she said, a momentary spark animating her. "Bridge Street. That's it."

"Briggs." Both Mooney and Pickering blurted the name out at once, as if in a race to proclaim it to the world.

Mooney thumped his forehead. "Briggs *is* Warren Mars."

"That ditsy old broad."

"Suki," he snapped at Pickering. "The old bag lady. That was her name."

"How'd you find her?" Janine asked.

"It's a long story," Mooney said. "Something to do with car registrations."

"Then we picked up a guy who looked like he was casing the place." Pickering continued the thread of events. "For a time, he looked like a suspect. Turned out to be nothing."

Mooney pulled out the mug shot of Koops from his desk drawer. "He'd been hanging around out in front of that Bridge Street house three nights in a row. We thought it was funny. So we picked him up. Brought him in. Name's Ferris Koops."

He pushed the mug shot toward her. She lifted it from the desktop with the faintest curiosity, looked at it a moment, then frowned. "What'd you say his name was?"

"Ferris Koops," Mooney repeated.

"I don't know nothing about no Ferris Koops. But this guy you got here is Warren Mars."

THIRTY-THREE

"OH, MY GOD."

"I don't understand. Explain it to me."

"Oh, my God . . . my God."

"You keep saying that. It don't help me. Explain it, for Chrissake."

"I can't. I mean, I understand it. Not all of it. Just part of it."

"But I don't understand. It blew right past me. What happened? What's going on?"

"Oh, my God. My God." Mooney pounded his forehead with his palm and continued to invoke the Almighty while they roared up First Avenue in a patrol car.

"They're the same guy," Mooney boomed so loud the driver flinched and the car swerved. "Don't you see? It's the same guy. All the copycat crapola. All that doo-da. It was always just one guy."

"I know. I know. That's what you said. But I still don't understand. I mean, I heard the girl. I saw the picture, too. But it still don't make no sense."

The siren screamed above their heads. Faces whirling past on the street were a gray blur.

"Don't you see? He's one of those multiple whatchamacallits — personalities. When he's in one place, like Bridge Street, he's Warren. When he's up on Eighty-first Street, he's Ferris Koops. Wait till Mulvaney hears," Mooney groaned. "We had the son of a bitch in custody. In our hands, goddammit, and we let him go. We let him walk right out the front door."

Mooney suddenly began to giggle.

Pickering scowled, understanding very little of his partner's glee. "What the hell's so funny?"

"I love it. I absolutely love it." Mooney's giggles swelled to hooting laughter. "Well, he can't hang this one on me. I'm the one who said hold him. He's the one who said let him go. Didn't he say that, Rollo? Didn't he?"

"Yeah, sure."

"And wasn't I the one who said put a tail on him? Wasn't I?"

"Sure. That's right."

"But, oh no. Not them. They're too smart. Too wise. The corporation counsel says . . . " Mooney pressed his jaws between his palms. "Bullshit the corporation counsel."

"You said it. You said all that," Pickering conceded. "But I still don't understand. I don't see. So he was a blond guy who rinsed his hair black from time to time. What about the broken teeth?"

"Broken teeth just when he was dark. Nice, straight teeth when he was fair. Bridgework, dummy. Didn't you ever hear of bridgework? The temporary kind. You put it in, you take it out. Talk to Konig. He'll tell you."

"And the blood type?"

"Very easy. Both of them were AB pos. Naturally." Mooney slammed his forehead again and laughed out loud. "I keep saying both of them . . . "

"That isn't what I meant," Pickering fretted. "I mean, the two sperms. That don't explain the two sperms. The azo-whatever you call it."

"The sperms?" The mirth faded from Mooney's face. "That's right. How the hell can one guy alternate between fertility and infertility? That doesn't make sense." He took his pad out and scribbled something onto the page.

Pickering's frown deepened. "And how come the Pell dame didn't recognize him when you showed her the mug shot?"

"That's easy. She was looking for a dark-haired guy

vith broken teeth. I showed her a blond pretty boy with
traight teeth. Naturally, she didn't recognize him. But,
he sperms. I don't get that . . . ," Mooney fretted.

"And what about Berrida — Berrida saw him face-
o-face in the street and then he saw him in a lineup."

"Same thing. Berrida said he was looking for a Latin
ype. 'Cause that's what he saw in the street that night.
Ve showed him a preppy Wasp kid. Remember. The
nly time Berrida saw Koops, or Mars, or whatever the
ell, it was at dusk and then he saw him for maybe only
minute or two. Same thing with that Coles babe. She
aw a dark guy with busted teeth who smelled bad."

"The only one who saw a blond . . . "

"Was the Bailey girl. And then that old doorman,
vhat's-his-face?"

"Carlucci."

"Right. Carlucci. Up on Fifth Avenue. Where the
3ender kid lived." Mooney flipped rapidly through his
oad, flipping back and forth until he found the entry.
'Carlucci. Here it is. 'Anthony Carlucci. Doorman.
Eight-sixty Fifth Avenue. Claims to have seen young
olond man. Five eight or five nine. Approximately
wenty-two, twenty-three years old, watching apartment
nouse from across Fifth Avenue. Followed Carolyn
3ender into the park the night of August third.' "

"We never called Carlucci in to make an identification."

"After we struck out with Berrida and Pell, it made no
.ense to." Mooney glanced up and out the window.
'Where the hell are we?"

"Ninetieth and First," the driver replied.

"Hang a right," Mooney boomed. "Five'll get you ten,
Koops has blown the place."

"Koops?"

"Koops. Mars. Whatever. I'll lay odds he's skipped."
Mooney thumped his head again. "My God. My God.
We had him right there in our hands. How could I have
missed this so . . . "

Up ahead they could hear sirens and see blinding

lights. A half dozen patrol cars had all nosed into the curb in front of 420 East 81st. Dozens of uniformed men were already out cordoning off the block.

When they pulled up in front of the small, six-story residential building hard by the East River, the street in front of the building was overrun with SWAT personnel in navy windbreakers toting shotguns. Pedestrians on the street were being herded off to safe spots behind the blockades. The windows in the buildings overhead were full of people staring down into the street.

Mooney grabbed one of the special forces men moving past just then. "Anyone been up there yet?"

"We been up already. Looks like no one's there."

"The place locked?" Pickering asked. "Can we get in?"

"They're tryin' to locate the super now. Why don't you just go right on in, lieutenant. They're all inside in the hallway."

Inside, there was more confusion than out on the street. The hallway was teeming with police and nervous neighbors poking their heads out of the doors. A steady stream of special forces men kept clattering up and down the steps. You could hear them bellowing instructions to each other from floor to floor.

"Hey, Mooney," someone shouted down the hall from behind them. "Over this way. I got the super."

Mooney and Pickering threaded their way through a maze of teeming activity. At the end of the corridor, in a reeking little cul-de-sac, Jimmy DeFranciscus, an old buddy from the 82nd, stood talking with a short, barrel chested man with a helmet of short cropped blond hair full of tight, knotty little curls.

"This is Mr. Schuttle." DeFranciscus made the introductions. "He's the superintendent. He says the Koops kid ain't around."

"How long since you seen him?" Mooney inquired.

What followed was a stream of heavily inflected, barely comprehensible English. DeFranciscus observed the consternation on Mooney's face.

"He says he ain't seen him in a couple of weeks. But that's not unusual. Guy's in and outta here a lot."

Mr. Schuttle nodded stolidly. "Yah. In and out a lot. Sometimes we don't see for weeks."

"Can we get into the apartment?" Mooney asked him, almost shouting, as if he were talking to a deaf man.

"That's what we're working on now," DeFranciscus explained. "He just sent his wife downstairs to see if they have a spare key. He says Koops was a nice, quiet fellow."

"Yah. Nice. Quiet."

"A pussycat," Mooney muttered.

There were three sharp claps followed by a stir at the head of the hall. Crowds parted as a small, dark, energetic man with darting eyes bustled into the area. He clapped his hands hard. "All right. Can we get some of these people outta here. Anyone without official business, back out on the street." He wheeled about on his heels and barked at anxious residents hovering in their doorways. "Okay, folks. Nothing going on now. Everyone back in their apartments. Have a cup of coffee. Let the officers do their jobs here."

Edward Sylvestri clapped his hands again, his eyes flashing up and down the hallway. Spotting Mooney and Pickering with DeFranciscus and the superintendent, he bustled over, pumping his shortish arms importantly. "Hey, Mooney, what's the big idea? Who authorized all this?" Sylvestri looked around at all the SWAT personnel crawling over the site.

"I did. You were on a job up in the Bronx and there's a chance right now we maybe nab this guy."

Sylvestri's eyes narrowed skeptically. "Who told you to interrogate the McConkey girl? Why wasn't I called immediately? I wanna know the name of the man who notified you before me." He stared hard at Pickering.

"I called you." Pickering's voice squawked unconvincingly. "You were out. I left a message on your wire."

"That message was left on my wire around ten A.M.

That's about an hour and a half after you had the goddamn girl in custody."

Pickering's jaw dropped. He was stymied. "I
figured — "

"From now on, Rollo, you figure nothing. Okay?"

"It wasn't Rollo's fault," Mooney intervened. "The girl
saw me on TV and asked to talk with me."

Sylvestri's chest thrust forward pugnaciously. "Oh,
she saw you on the TV, did she? And would only talk to
you?" The small, dark man swelled dangerously. "Now,
listen up, my friend. Just so's we have no more fuck-ups.
In future if there's any opinions to be expressed to the
media regarding this matter, it's yours truly who'll do
the expressing. Okay? We understand each other?"

Just as Mooney was about to reply, an immensely fat
woman with a red splotched face waddled up. The strong
ammoniacal odor of perspiration reeked from her clothing.

Mr. Schuttle proceeded to rattle off something in Ger-
man to her. Puffing heavily she held a key up in her
pudgy fist.

"Okay. We got a key," DeFranciscus said, uneasy to
find himself between two warring factions. "I guess we
can go on in now."

There was an awkward pause while the two men stood
glaring at each other.

It was a peculiar little place, diminutive and spotless.
Everything was immaculate and in precise order, almost
obsessively so. It was hardly what one might expect from
the "Monster of Chaos." It gave, instead, the impression
of being a little place for little people, excessively fussy
but well kept, like a dollhouse. It was as if a little old lady
had lived there, rather than the notorious Shadow
Dancer.

Moving about inside, Mooney stooped as though
afraid to graze his head on the ceiling. Most curious of
all, as they moved about through the neat little rooms,

no one spoke, and when they did it was in a whisper. It all had an air of reverence about it, a sense of awe, more appropriate for churches and funeral parlors than for the lair of a murderer.

Mooney had left the others and was circling about the apartment, moving from one tiny room to the next. Mr. Schuttle followed doggedly at his heels. He shook his head and muttered to himself while Mooney went through the little Pullman kitchen, opening drawers and cabinets and poking about.

From behind he could hear Sylvestri's high, nasal voice issuing a rapid-fire stream of orders, full of scorn for what he kept referring to as "shoddy police work." He went about strutting and fretting, glancing sharply at people to see what sort of an effect he was having. Less than convincing, he gave the impression of a person who'd recently completed a mail order, self-assertiveness course.

Trying not to hear him, Mooney continued his own perusal, full of regret and misgivings, plagued by a host of deep, unsettling thoughts. His wanderings took him from the kitchen into the tiny bathroom just behind it.

It was an innocuous little place with a toilet, a shower, and a tub. The floor showed a good deal of chipped black-and-white tile with large unsightly patches of grouting looming up from beneath.

A pink shower curtain upon which astrological signs floated drooped from a chrome bar above the tub. Sliding his fingertips lightly across it, he noted that it was rusty in places and slightly damp.

Mooney stood for a while at the sink, aware of his image floating in the mirror before him. Gazing down at the cracked porcelain, he noted a dark stain that rose from the bottom of the bowl to a point roughly up to the sinktop.

He stared at it for a time, then opened the door of the medicine cabinet behind the mirror. On first glance it contained nothing unusual: aspirin, mouthwash, a plastic bottle of baby oil, a half-used tube of lather shaving cream, a tatty beaver brush with which to apply it, a plastic injector razor, and some prescription drugs with the name Koops on their labels.

He started from the bottom shelf and began working his way up. On the top shelf he had his payoff. It came in the form of ten paper packets of black Clairol hair rinse, which explained not only the discoloration of the sink, but also the discrepancy between the two descriptions of a man who, for nearly two years, was believed to be two entirely separate and distinct individuals.

Pickering's big, red face poked itself in through the open door. "Looks like he's blown." His eyes followed Mooney's gaze to the upper shelf of the medicine cabinet and the Clairol packets. He moved into the room and stood just behind Mooney.

"Jesus."

"Yeah," Mooney muttered and they stepped back out into the living room. Two or three forensic people had come in during the interim and were already on their knees, working with tweezers and plastic envelopes and dusting for prints.

Sylvestri was still out front, staging a tirade, finding dissatisfaction with everything.

Mooney nudged Pickering in the ribs. "Come on. Let's get outta this." They started out.

"Just a minute," Sylvestri called after them. "Where you two going?"

"Back to the office."

"I'm not finished here yet."

Mooney's jaw tautened. "I got a lot of work to do, Eddie."

"It can wait," Sylvestri snapped.

"I'm afraid it can't," Mooney snapped back and kept right on going.

Sylvestri, standing amid a group of his minions, watched him go, stymied and a bit puzzled by the outright disobedience.

"I'm not finished here yet, Frank," he cried after him.

"You keep right at it, Eddie. Don't let me disturb you. You got a lot of people around here to help you." Mooney's great mass lumbered down the hallway in the direction of the stairs.

"No more surprises, Frank," Sylvestri shouted after him. "No more unauthorized alerting special forces. No more funny business. Like with the McConkey kid this morning. All that goes through me. You hear?"

Mooney never turned. He just kept going. Halfway down the stairs he realized that Pickering was right behind him. He turned and glared up at him. "What the hell you think you're doing?"

"I'm going with you."

"That's dumb. I'm nine months from retirement. You've gotta live with this little prick for another fifteen years."

"I'll take my chances."

"Suit yourself. Don't say I didn't warn you."

They barreled out the front door and into the street, Mooney leading, Pickering trailing hard at his heels. Their car and driver were still out front, waiting for them.

"Where we going?" Pickering slid in beside Mooney and winked slyly. "Bridge Street?"

"How much does Sylvestri know about Bridge Street?"

"Not a lot. There's not that much in the file."

"Like what?"

"Most of it deals with reports of the two cops who picked Koops up that night out in front of the house."

"What else?"

"I filed a report the day we went through the place and talked to the old broad."

"Nothing in there about the stolen car, the phony registration, tracing the car to that address, and the guy upstate, what's-his-face, who's been missing from home the past six years?"

"Griggs. Donald Griggs."

"Right. That's the guy. Nothing about any of that?"

"I don't think so. You remember we figured it was too wild a shot at the time. I never filed anything."

"Good," Mooney snapped. "Sylvestri still doesn't know that the two guys we've been looking for the past two years are really just one?"

"Not yet. But he will the minute he starts talkin' to McConkey."

"Then he'll be down on Bridge Street pretty quick," Mooney brooded. "Let him come. He still doesn't know what to look for."

"Do you?"

"I think so."

As they wheeled out of 81st Street Mooney glowered out the windows, his cheeks still flared and smarting from his encounter with Sylvestri.

In the crowds milling behind the police barricades at the end of the street, a slight dark-haired man hovered at the edge of the throng. He watched the squad car sway past and stared at the grim visage glaring out at the street. Long after the car had sped away up First Avenue, he continued to gaze after it as if he could still see it. In his mind he still saw the image of the angry face behind the window.

Shortly, the crowds started to disperse and straggle off. Still, the young man waited there, watching the police going in and out of the building. A crooked, oddly disquieting smile flickered about his mouth.

A short time later, Warren Mars started down First Avenue. He went at a fairly brisk clip. A faint throbbing had started at the back of his head. He had no specific destination in mind, but wherever it was he was going, he was going there speedily.

It was noontime, unnaturally warm in the street for December, with the kind of soft, lemony haze that presages the coming of spring. Lunchtime crowds were out in full force. Waves of office workers, briefly liberated, were promenading the avenue.

The more quickly Warren walked, the more his head throbbed. Over the past few minutes, the throbbing had escalated into a vague sensation of vibration from somewhere inside his skull. Also, he grew uneasily aware of a dimming of his vision.

The dimming and vibrations were not unfamiliar to him. They were the well-known precursors — the aura he always experienced — prior to those moments when he would begin to sense that he was fading away from himself.

Even though he'd had such episodes for as long as he could remember (starting shortly after puberty), they never ceased to terrify him. That sensation of disintegrating, of breaking up inside himself — from the inside out — filled him with dread. Then the Ping-Pong balls would start to bounce back and forth, gradually accelerating to a frightening tempo until they became a single blurred image planted fixedly before his eyes. Then came the numbers — thousands, millions of numbers — banging and ricocheting through his head. Long, interminable series of them that he would struggle to add up but, of course, never could. All of that was beginning to happen now.

He heard a distant wail of sirens and walked faster. The Ping-Pong balls had started to bounce in his head. Suddenly, all of the colors that had drenched the streets and shops and buildings and all the people in the street, all of the vivid shades and tones along the avenue began to fade like dye running from a fabric. Before his eyes the gorgeous palette of street colors bled from his field of vision, leaving behind a flat, dimensionless monochrome of gunmetal gray.

Suddenly, up ahead Warren spied a slight, fair figure, moving down First Avenue. Even though the figure was nearly a full block ahead and his view of him was from the rear, he recognized the person at once. He knew that mincing, wispy gait. How well he knew it! There could be no mistake. It was Ferris Koops. The source of all his troubles. The cause of so much anguish.

Why hadn't he disposed of Ferris when he'd had the chance? There had been so many opportunities to rid himself of that scourge who'd taunted him so over the years, that snotty little wimp who'd always lorded it over him, treating him like some poor cousin. How he'd despised him — that hateful, whiny, ass-licking kid, whose own parents couldn't bear to have him around. That succubus, that leech who clung to him. Try as he might, he could never escape Ferris. That exemplar, that paradigm of goodness and kindness and Christian charity. That priggish snot whom everyone loved . . . everyone, that is, except his own mother. Why hadn't he killed Ferris? Smashed him like some worm when he'd had the chance?

Ferris had always been Warren's problem. Warren was always trying to act like Ferris. Be Ferris. Be something better than he was. Well, now that the jig was up, now that they knew everything, he would snuff out the little turd. Rid himself of the scourge forever.

He ground his teeth and started after the rapidly receding figure. It was disappearing in waves of oncoming people. Periodically he would catch a glimpse of it, patches of it moving behind shoulders and hats. Warren dashed up the street, covering the distance in little time, only to discover that the figure was no longer there.

He spun about several times like a person who's momentarily lost his bearings. But in the next moment there was Ferris again, eating a frankfurter at a standup food counter across the street.

Dodging the horn-blaring, outraged traffic, Warren darted across the avenue. Barging up to the place, he burst through the front door. People gaped at him, pausing from their hot dogs and sausages and fruit drinks. By that time he had a wild, slightly demented look.

But there was no sign of Ferris at the stand. He must

have seen Warren and fled. Back out on the street again, he saw Ferris up the block, flagging a cab. Not only was he flagging a cab, he was also approaching him from the opposite direction. And then he was standing right beside him, a faint smile of greeting playing about his lips.

Warren's terrified eyes swerved from the figure hailing the cab to the one standing beside him. In the next moment, several other Ferrises appeared. Two or three of them came out of a bank at one time, dressed in business suits. Another Ferris working at a vendor's stand held up a fistful of cheap jewelry, waving it at him.

Sunlight glinting off the facets of cheap glass sent shards of harsh glare stabbing at his eyes. A whole army of Ferris Koopses was all about him now, coming at him from everywhere.

The color had by then bled completely from everything in the street. Once again Warren stood alone in a world he knew so well — the drab, relentless gray of a photographic negative with only ghostly white silhouettes to indicate a person, and all of those silhouettes were Ferris. He alone with Ferris.

When he looked up again, Ferris was still standing there beside him, smiling, his arms outstretched. "I'm here, Warren," Ferris said. "It's all right. Don't worry. I'm here."

The moment he spoke, Warren's eyes flooded with tears. A surge of relief swept over him, as soothing as the foaming ocean surf on a blistering hot day.

Warren's arms opened wide to accept him and they embraced like brothers. Hot tears coursed down his cheeks, his whole body racked with sobs.

"It's all right, Warren. Don't worry. Everything's going to be all right now."

People passing the sobbing, demented figure whirling on the street gave him a wide berth as they hurried on.

THIRTY-FOUR

"YOU UP?"

"Of course. We're always awake in this house at two A.M. Isn't everyone? Where the hell are you?"

"Bridge Street."

"Bridge Street?" There was a pause as Pickering's still drowsy head tried to sort out information. "Wait a minute. Lemme go into the other room. Rachel's waking up."

Pickering staggered out of bed, struggled into a robe, and lurched out through darkness to the kitchen phone. "You still there, Frank?"

"Where the hell would I be?" came the annoyed reply. "Have you seen the papers yet?"

"Sure. Koops's puss was plastered all over it. They had him on the six o'clock news, too. Sylvestri was giving interviews all over the place. He's a movie star now."

"He was down here all afternoon with a special squad."

"Then he must've been on to McConkey."

"He was. Right after we left Koops's place."

"She probably told him everything."

"Depends on what he asked her," Mooney snapped. "Anyway, they were down here five hours this afternoon. Tore the place apart."

"They find anything?"

"I don't think so."

"How come?"

"Just the way Sylvestri looked when he came back out. He had a real sour puss on him."

"That's his natural expression."

"When he left, he took the old lady with him."

"Interrogation?"

"That, and I figure they're looking to press charges."

"For what? Accessory?"

"And harboring. I don't think they got a chance on that. Number one, all they got is the girl's word he lived down there with the old dame. Number two, they didn't find a thing of his in the place, and they tore it apart stem to stern."

"Funny." Pickering yawned. "You'd think they'd have found something."

"If you ask me, the old lady probably cleaned the place out days ago."

"They might still get her on fencing goods," Pickering offered hopefully.

"I'm telling you, they found nothing. Mulvaney hinted they might have found some pot."

"I wouldn't doubt that for a minute."

"So what? How long can you hold someone on chicken feed like that? And, living with a nut case is no crime."

"Sure," Pickering conceded sleepily. "Half the people in this town do. How long you figure you're gonna be down there?"

"When they quit yesterday, Sylvestri left a surveillance team behind. There's a camera unit in the warehouse across the way. They'll be watching the joint round the clock."

"And you're watching the watchers." Pickering laughed softly into the phone. "You figure Koops is coming back to the house."

"I don't figure he really ever left it."

There was a pause as Pickering tried to absorb that. "If they been through the place stem to stern, where do you figure he is?"

"I don't know," Mooney sighed wearily. "But he's got no place to go. Not with his puss all over the papers and TV."

Pickering stirred uneasily in his chair. "So I figure

this call means you got something lousy you want me to do."

"What was your first clue, Rollo?"

"I usually don't have the pleasure of phone calls from you at two A.M. What's on your mind?"

"The Bureau of Deeds down at City Hall opens at nine A.M.," Mooney rattled on, breathlessly. "You be there when the doors open. Go directly to the archives. Ask the person in charge if they've got a set of blueprints on the Bridge Street place."

"That house is nearly two hundred years old, Frank. They don't keep anything goes back that far."

"Maybe. Maybe not. Give it a shot, anyway. If they come up with something, make a couple of copies and bring 'em to me."

"Okay." Pickering sighed. "You better go home, get some sleep."

"I can't. I'm on my way to Poughkeepsie."

"Poughkeepsie? What the hell for?"

"Got a call in the office last night about nine P.M. Guy called Armstead. Runs a fancy boarding school somewhere up there."

"Ain't this a little late in life to matriculate?"

Mooney ignored the quip. "He saw Koops's picture on the news last night and called the number they flashed on the screen. Seems our boy was one of his students there around fifteen years ago. He wants to talk to someone about it."

"And you're the one?"

"Sylvestri wasn't around so they switched him to me. I'm going home first and have a shower and a shave. Fritzi's fit to be tied. I haven't been home for two days."

Pickering started to laugh. "Haven't seen you put in overtime in ten years. Sylvestri's had a beneficial effect on you."

"You betcha," Mooney growled. "There is some shit I

will not eat. He asked for this. Now he's got a real horse race on his hands."

New York Route 55 is a narrow, winding ribbon of road that curves its way east and west through the southern Berkshire foothills. The road was pot-holed and puddled from the unseasonal melt-off of snow still visible in broad patches through the trees. At certain points the melted snow on the hills came coursing down in gushing rivulets to the road below and swept across it to the other side. Through the still unleafed trees blanketing the hills, Mooney could see clearly the humped and solemn configuration of the mountains.

Though a sharp bite was in the air and blasts of wind buffeted the hood of the old Buick, there came with that a distinct hint of spring, still three months off. The light in the sky at ten A.M. was a pale yellow, as opposed to the clear icy blue one typically sees on a late December morning, and there was in the general muddy mess of things a sense of the ice breaking up and the earth thawing.

Branley House was a compound of several buildings, grim and gabled Victorian gingerbread, painted in improbable pastels to lighten some of the unrelieved gloom of the architecture.

Mooney turned into a graveled driveway running between two stone stanchions. In the large field behind the main house, packs of young boys streamed up and down a soccer field, kicking a ball and chasing it avidly, their high, shrill cries ringing out across the sunlit countryside.

Mr. Harley Armstead was a spry, elfin figure of some seventy years, with ruddy cheeks and vivid blue eyes that twinkled out at you from behind a pair of rimless spectacles. About him was that air of amiable incompetence, characteristically marked by a great deal of bustling about to no apparent purpose. He fussed with odds and ends on his desk which was covered with unattended papers and bills and all of the sooty paraphernalia of pipe smoking. As he spoke he kept tamping tobacco into the bowl of his pipe with a large, flat thumb, the nail of which had turned a cobalt blue, no doubt from some inadvertent hurt he'd managed to inflict upon it himself.

"I knew it was him the moment I saw him," Mr. Armstead proclaimed when they'd settled into a pair of commodious wing chairs. "That picture flashed on the television and I turned to Mrs. Armstead right then and there and said, 'Martha, that's Ferris.' They kept calling him Warren — Warren something or other . . . "

"Mars," Mooney offered.

"That's right, Mars. But I knew it was Ferris soon as I saw him. And then I knew I just had to talk to someone."

A drab, grayish lady in a white matron's gown tottered in and set down a tray of coffee before them. While she served, Armstead continued to strike matches, intending to light his pipe but invariably failing to do so. Mooney had started a game of watching the match burn down until it reached the old man's thumb, at which point he would blow it out with a quick nervous huff.

"Must be a good sixteen, seventeen years since he was here," Armstead continued when the woman had left. "He was about seven when he matriculated. We didn't learn much from the parents. All we had was a doctor's report that claimed he was in sound health, but hinted at some evidence of mental retardation. I tell you, I never thought much of that report. I didn't think he was retarded. Not one bit. Possibly a bit muddled. A little vacant and remote. In his own little world, you know. Frightened and confused, maybe. But not retarded. I know retarded. I've dealt with it all my professional life. That boy wasn't retarded. Upset, yes. Frightened and confused, yes. And why wouldn't he be?" Armstead waved his pipe at Mooney as though it were a conductor's baton. "He'd lost a father and a mother in the space of a few months. As I understand it, the father was a fairly prominent financier who'd made a series of bad investments and more or less died from the shame of it. The mother . . ." Armstead paused and smiled slyly. "Well, I met her once. A handsome lady. Socialite. Glamorous, you know. Came up here to see me about Ferris and look the place over. Stayed about twenty minutes. She remarried in what folks of my vintage like to call 'indecent haste.' Three months later, I guess it was, to an older man. A widower. Well-off with his own children grown and out of the house, but still young enough for his head to be turned by an attractive, well-connected woman. Too old, though, to want to start raising a child again.

"As I understand it, they argued about it until it became the sticking point of the arrangement. Almost queered the deal for a time. There were no relatives with which to place the child. Either she gave the boy up for adoption or placed it in a foster home, or no deal. The old boy made it abundantly clear. To make a long story short, she capitulated, and, in the end, they settled on Branley. People call us a warehouse for well-to-do kids with families comfortable enough to pay a large annual tuition for the privilege of depositing unwanted, problem kids and forgetting about them with a clear conscience. Well, I suppose there's some truth to that. I don't pretend that we're a first-rate preparatory school. But we are home to these kids. The only home they have. Mrs. Armstead and myself are mother and father to them. We love each and every one of them just as if they were our own. We feel no shame about what we do here. We teach them. Right up to the limits of their ability. You ask them, if you think not."

Armstead sighed and gazed with sudden unaccountable sadness out the window through which was clearly visible the sight of the young boys racing up and down the soccer field. "Anyway, we were talking about Mrs. Koops."

He struck another match and inhaled fiercely, his

veined cheeks inflating and deflating like a bellows until
at last a cloud of blackened smoke straggled listlessly
from the bowl. But no sooner had he lit it than he forgot
about it, distracted by the image of Mrs. Koops drifting
back at him across the span of years. "She sent him toys
and candy for birthdays and Christmas. Never failed.
But she never came to visit him."

"How long was he here?" Mooney asked.

"I'm coming to that." Armstead waved the pipe at him
impatiently. "Ferris was peculiar. I don't deny that.
Kept to himself. Didn't get on with the other kids. They
recognized there was something funny about him and
were perceptive enough to let him be. He couldn't con-
centrate in class. He was hyperactive, but unlike most
hyperactive kids, he wasn't a discipline problem. The
house psychiatrist here at the time diagnosed him as
borderline autistic, with decided aspects of genius. He
had phenomenal powers of memory. He could recall
whole series of numbers made up of a dozen digits,
glance at three, four of them, then after a moment recite
them back to you by heart without a mistake."

Mr. Armstead shook his head, and, for a moment, his
eyes appeared to mist behind the rimless lenses. "A sad,
morose child, I'd say, who preferred to keep to himself.
The only relationships he could handle were with small
animals — pet mice, birds, cats, to which he was invariably kind." Armstead looked up, suddenly recalling
Mooney. "Don't worry. I haven't forgotten your question.
I'm coming to it."

The twinkle had reappeared in his eyes and he chuckled to himself. "After Ferris had been here about three
months, we noticed a change in him. From a child who,
to all outward appearances, was relatively placid, he
suddenly became subject to fits of violence. One moment he'd be working quietly by himself on a jigsaw
puzzle or an airplane model, and the next he'd be up on
his feet, shouting, running, bouncing off the furniture,
flinging everything within reach about the room. Even-

tually, those episodes increased in frequency and intensity. They became destructive. Frighteningly so. And the destruction was always aimed at himself. He'd been abandoned by his parents, and, as he saw it, he was responsible for that abandonment. There was something not quite right with him, he figured, and he believed that it was because of this that his father died and his mother remarried and left him. To his way of thinking, it was all his fault.

"One morning, after he'd been here, roughly, I'd say, five months, he didn't show up at breakfast. I sent someone back to his room to check. All of his belongings were there, but there was no sign of him. We made a search of the campus and the surrounding woods. Not a trace of him about. We notified the mother first, and then the state police."

"Did the mother seem concerned?"

"Yes, I'd say so." Armstead sucked noisily at his pipe stem. "But she didn't offer to come east. She was living out in Chicago at the time, and I guess Poughkeepsie seemed a long way off."

"What about the police?" Mooney asked.

"Nothing. We waited and waited. They combed the entire area and posted notices in town. But they never found a sign of him. The family, of course, was fairly influential, and enough pressure was brought to bear so that federal investigators finally entered the search. Photos were sent out to police departments and missing persons bureaus all round the country. Pretty soon we started to get calls and messages with sightings from just about everywhere. We checked them all. The police never found him and, after a year or so, they pretty much gave up."

"Did they close the case?"

"Not officially, but in point of fact, the investigation was over."

"What happened?"

"Nothing."

"Nothing?"

"Nothing at all. That's if you mean, did they find Ferris."

A long, uneasy silence settled over the room as the two men regarded each other through the slanting rays of morning sunlight. The sharp, exultant shrieks of youthful soccer players drifted in from the rolling fields outside.

Vaguely miffed, Mooney wondered why he'd taken the trouble to drive up at all. For all he'd learned, the whole matter could have been transacted over the phone.

Armstead appeared to sense his disappointment. "That's the truth of it, I'm afraid. We didn't see Ferris again, until years later."

Mooney looked up, still frowning. "So, you did see him again?"

"He came to visit me."

Suddenly animated, Armstead brandished his pipe. "Just walked in on me one afternoon."

"Did he say where he'd been?"

"All over. Just drifting from one place to the next. Looked pretty tatty and down at the heels, but just as cheerful and polite as ever. Said he was broke. Needed work. I gave him some money and asked him if he was aware there was a trust fund in his name. He didn't know what I was talking about. Wasn't exactly sure what a trust fund was, so I told him, and gave him the name of the law firm who'd been appointed trustees of his father's estate. I knew them since all of Ferris's expenses here were paid through them. He went to see them, and I guess he never had any serious money problems after that. Never thought about him again until last night and that news show."

"That law firm didn't happen to be Wells, Gray," Mooney asked dryly.

"That's right. That's the one. How'd you know?"

"We've had occasion to deal with them."

Armstead appeared to be impressed by that. "Well, that's the firm, all right."

"How long ago was it that he came back here, would you say?"

Armstead's eyes closed again and the head tilted. "Let me see now . . . that would be nineteen and eighty-one. June or July, I'd say."

"Roughly six years ago," Mooney suggested. "The name Griggs mean anything to you? Donald Griggs?"

The name appeared to draw a blank, but in the next moment the old man's face lit up. "Oh, sure — local fellow. Some story about him. Disappeared from here about — "

"Six years ago." Mooney flicked back through his pad. "June fourteenth, nineteen eighty-one, is when your local police reported him missing."

"That sounds about right," Armstead nodded earnestly. "Nice family. Didn't know them well. Wife and three kids. Salesman, he was, if memory serves me. Just drove off one day. Never come back. Local papers were full of it. Why do you ask?" Then suddenly the drift of Mooney's thought struck him. "You're not suggesting there's some connection between Ferris and the disappearance of Griggs?"

Mooney nodded wearily. "It's a long story. Has something to do with a car. Someday when this is all over, I'll tell you about it."

Later, Armstead saw him to the door. They stood there for a while chatting. Then Armstead placed a frail trembling hand on Mooney's shoulder. "Could that poor boy really have done all these awful things they say he's done?"

Mooney shrugged and smiled wearily. "We'll know soon enough, won't we?"

THIRTY-FIVE

"THIS IS THE LAST ONE I HAVE."

"Let's give it a shot, anyway."

Rollo Pickering sighed and hunched above the oak refectory table mounded with books and records and papers culled from the archives over the past five hours at the City Bureau of Deeds and Instruments.

"If it's not here . . . ," Mr. Lydecker, the city archivist, said.

"Then it's not here," Pickering grudgingly assented. By that time, he was more than willing to concede the fact. He'd been there since nine A.M., when the doors had opened.

The offices of the New York City Bureau of Deeds and Instruments were located at the bottom of Water Street, a few blocks west of the river. Occupying a full floor of a badly deteriorating old commercial building dating back to the late nineteenth century, the offices and archives were a drab, depressing affair. Pickering had sat in a long succession of such drab municipal offices in his time. Broken furniture, flaking paint, burst upholstery, the air stale with the smell of decades of dust undisturbed. They were all pretty much the same. As a civil servant himself, such offices and the drab phlegmatic people who occupied them filled him with uneasiness. It was as though he could look down the long corridor of years and see a chilling vista of what lay ahead.

The room he sat in was small and stuffy. It smelled of mold and desiccation. Motes of dust drifted like timeless galaxies through the cramped, unventilated space. Behind them was a warehouse of paper. It divided itself into aisles giving onto a shadowy prospect of floor-to-ceiling clutterment: records, deeds of transfer dating well back into the eighteenth century. Thousands upon thousands of crumbling old manila folders tied up with tatty faded ribbon and stacked perilously one atop the other sagged on shelves that threatened imminent collapse. It was a windowless place where sunlight never strayed.

Each time they pulled out a folder, puffs of dust rose like vengeful wraiths. Pickering coughed. By then his throat was parched. Mr. Lydecker, however, seemed impervious to dust. Having occupied that airless space for nearly forty years, he was no longer discernibly old or young. Dust had effaced all of the usual clues to age. Indeed, the vague shape that slouched up and down those sloping aisles in baggy tweeds seemed more an outline of airy ectoplasm than anything comprised of flesh and blood.

In the five hours Pickering had been there, they'd so far managed to locate a copy of the deed to the house on Bridge Street. That had been perfectly simple and straightforward. Mr. Lydecker had put his bony, claw-like hands on that at once. A largish parchment embossed with a city stamp and a notary's seal, it showed the provenance of the house to date from somewhere in the early 1830s, when one Joshua Crane had built it, going right up until the 1940s, when a Mr. Frederick Klink purchased it for the slightly less than lordly sum of $6,000. But it was the architect's blueprint, the official record of construction, that continued to elude them.

"Trouble is," Lydecker went on, tunneling through quaking columns of paper as he spoke, "those days, folks weren't required to file blueprints of new construction. The bureau didn't exist then and what filing and record-keeping they did was of a fairly casual order. Of course, we do have architectural plans dating back to that period, but no one is sure exactly where they are. I'm just one man here," he explained somewhat defensively. "They took my assistant from me last year. Budget cuts, you know. Ah . . . " The high, stridulous voice trilled as he plucked a crumbling parcel from one of the bins and blew the dust from its wrappings. "Hello — what have we here?"

It was a thick bundle, wrapped in tarpaper, swollen large around the middle and bound by what appeared to be old shoelaces. Someone had scrawled the dates 1820–1840 in black crayon across the front.

"This may be something." The archivist's tremulous fingers undid the bindings with a solicitude that was oddly touching. About it was a sense that he felt it to be almost a desecration to rouse such old documents from the sleep of centuries.

"Just exactly what do you hope to find here?" Lydecker asked, his fingers riffling gently through the crumbling, faded papers he'd uncovered.

Pickering made a pained expression. It made him look a trifle distraught. "I don't know. I guess I just need some idea of the layout of the place."

"Such as whether or not there are exits and entrances to the place not visible from the outside?" Lydecker inquired shrewdly. He didn't wait for an answer but plucked a thin sheaf of clipped papers from the stack. It had been part of a bundle of fading, dog-eared parchment bound together by some loosely tied brown twine. The words "CRANE. BRIDGE STREET" had been scrawled across its front.

"Ah — perhaps this is something." Mr. Lydecker carefully separated it from the rest of the papers in the bundle, carrying it forward to the oak refectory table where they'd been working. Pickering shifted papers and cleared a space on the big wood surface while the archivist laid the documents down, spreading them out side by side.

"Well, there's your blueprint," Mr. Lydecker proclaimed. "Not much of a blueprint as contemporary plans go, but that's what the place looked like a hundred and fifty years back."

Not knowing exactly what he was looking for, and feeling Mr. Lydecker's eyes on him, Pickering felt somewhat at a loss. The archivist had devoted five hours to the search. It did seem only fitting that something tangible should come of it.

Pickering bent above the blueprint and tried to appear deeply absorbed. There was, as Lydecker had indicated, nothing much to it. It consisted of four fairly unprepossessing sheets of parchment, raggedy with water stains. Time had turned them the color of weak tea. In the lower right hand corner, the original builder had drawn a rudimentary compass rose consisting of crossed arrows pointing N, S, E, and W, thus orienting the house.

Each sheet showed an elevation from a different side of the structure, plus a rather basic floor plan for each story. The handwriting on it was in ink and executed in an ornate, curly scrawl that looked Gothic and was all but illegible. It was full of figures and degree marks surrounded by innumerable arcane references to "rods," "chains," and "links."

Pickering could make neither head nor tail of it. The tiny runic symbols swam before his eyes. But the single part of it that was intelligible to him made it abundantly clear that other than the front or side entrances, both of which he knew about, there was no other way in or out of the house.

Clipped to that was another document showing a plan for an extension to the house, submitted to the City Architectural Review Board in July 1878 by its then owner, a Mr. Mortimer Tyler, but never executed.

A sixth sheet of parchment was a new plan, drawn up in 1910 during the Taft era. William Gaynor was then mayor of New York. Lydecker explained that it was a plan for revision, submitted to the board for approval. But for the life of them, they couldn't see how it differed from the first in any substantive way to justify filing for a revision.

They put the three plans side by side on the table and

compared them meticulously. To both of them, the plans appeared to be identical. The more they studied them, the deeper was their puzzlement.

"Can you see any difference?" Pickering asked.

Lydecker shook his head, clearly perplexed. "There has to be something different here, otherwise no revision would have been submitted."

Pickering was tired. He'd not eaten all day, and by that time he was discouraged and more than just a little inclined to cash in his chips. "You have a Xerox machine here?" he asked.

"An old cranky one. But it works well enough."

"Can I get a copy of these three plans?"

Lydecker appeared just as discouraged as the detective. "Why not? Wait here. I'll be right back."

Mr. Lydecker was as good as his word. He was back in little more than two minutes, grinning with a strange, sly delight. He was carrying the Xeroxed copies in his hand and flung them down at Pickering with a triumphant clap. "I've got it."

Pickering wasn't exactly certain he knew what it was Mr. Lydecker had.

"It was right there in front of us all the time." His long, bony finger pointed to a broken line shaded by hatchures, indicating the cellar level. "See that?"

"See what?"

"That broken line. Runs under the central elevation."

Pickering gazed up at him in blank bewilderment.

"It's a sewer line. That's why they had to file a revision. They put in a sewer line under the house. Little stairway here runs right into it from the cellar."

Pickering rubbed his chin thoughtfully as his eyes followed the path of the broken line. "Where does it go?"

"See for yourself." Lydecker flared impatiently. "Out to the river. Easiest place for them to discharge the effluents."

Pickering's eyes swarmed over the parchment. "But where on the river? I don't see."

"There's probably a drain someplace there. No doubt not far from the house itself." Moving more swiftly than his wont, Lydecker strode across the room to a wall where a large topographical survey map of lower Manhattan hung. Pickering followed at his heels.

"Could be any of a number of places along the Hudson littoral in that vicinity."

"Along the what?"

"The shoreline," Lydecker snapped.

"Who'd you suppose could tell me where that sewer line comes out?"

"Well, I couldn't. But I know just the fellow who could. Frank Merton. Chief engineer over at the Bureau of Sanitation and Sewer Maintenance."

Pickering's heart leaped hopefully. "Can we call him?"

Lydecker checked his watch, then rose. "It's three-thirty. He may be gone."

It took him several calls, but at last he located the chief engineer. The conversation seemed to go on interminably. Pickering's nervous fingers drummed the table as they chatted and laughed and traded municipal gossip. At last, Lydecker hung up the phone with a flourish and came back to where Pickering waited.

"Battery Park," he proclaimed, like a man who'd solved the riddle of the Sphinx. "Runs right down to the foot of Bridge Street beneath the park and discharges through a drain cap into the river, just north of the Brooklyn Battery Tunnel."

Pickering made a humming sound through his nose. His mind was racing. "You suppose I could get into that sewer?"

"Merton says that line was sealed off and abandoned fifty years ago. It was installed in the early nineteen hundreds. Sewers of that vintage are made of clay. About four to five feet in height. Same in diameter. Merton claims those tunnels were abandoned because they were in poor condition. Too dangerous and costly to maintain."

"I have to get down into that line."

"Be a bit dicey, I'd imagine. Particularly if it hasn't
been maintained in nearly a half century. You might get
in through the trap drain."

"Would I need authorization?"

"Probably. But who's talking? I'm not." The dusty,
baggy figure of the archivist suddenly brightened with
the smug satisfaction of the man who feels he's done his
job for the day.

He found the drain almost immediately. Just as Lydecker had said, it stood hard by the river, nearly directly on a line with the bottom of Bridge Street.

For obvious reasons, Pickering wished to stay well away
from Bridge Street. For one thing, the place was crawling
with Sylvestri's men — some in mufti going up and down
the block; others concealed with cameras in offices and
rooms across the way from the Klink house. For another,
Pickering had no authorization to be out pursuing the case
on his own. But most important, if Koops was still actually
inside the house, he was no doubt watching the street as
intently as Sylvestri's men were watching the house.
Moreover, Koops now knew Pickering by sight from the
several interrogations he'd undergone at police headquarters. He would certainly recognize him if he were to stroll
past.

It was principally that line of reasoning that made
Pickering park his car behind 14 Bridge on Pearl Street,
then walk across Battery Park in the direction of the
river.

The drain itself was not large — a square cast-iron
grating of four feet by four feet that stood upright on
its end, implanted into a small hill that dropped
sharply from the park to the river. The water itself was
no more than a few feet from the grating.

Pickering stepped gingerly downhill, the soles of his
shoes sinking into the muddy earth. The air wasn't cold,
but a brisk wind blew off the river and carried on it a

strong tidal smell. A long, low-slung tug plied northward against a swift current, whitecaps bursting into spray before its stubby prow. Bits of broken timber flowed past and a white condom undulated lazily in the water near the shore.

Pickering stood for a time, his back to the water, trousers ballooned and buffeted by the wind, regarding the drain. On closer inspection he found that the earth about it was damp and soft. It bore the impression of recent shoe prints. Even the claw marks of gulls that had used the strip as a promenade were still discernible in the mud around it.

When he approached the grating, however, he discovered that while the earth in front of it was wet, that which lay directly beneath it was dry and crumbling. The grating itself was heavy, but when he took hold of its bars and jiggled it, he found that it moved in its housing. The earth beneath it spilled freely down onto his shoes, giving the impression that the drain was not fixed permanently in the ground and that it had recently been moved.

Pickering stooped and peered between the rusty interstices. They consisted of small squares, no more than three or four inches on each side. Beyond the grating he could see a dark clay tunnel, roughly the same height and width as the grating out of which the dark, cool smell of mold issued.

Close to the edge on the inside of the grating there was a scattering of old candy wrappers and discarded beer cans. Pickering hovered there awhile above the grating, hands on knees, still stooped and squinting through the interstices as though trying to see around corners. In the next moment, he gripped the iron bars of the grating with each hand and hoisted. A shower of dirt spilled downward. The grating jiggled back and forth in its housing like a loose tooth.

It was heavy, at least a hundred pounds, but, surprisingly, it came off with little struggle. Pickering let it swing down from the top like a drawbridge and then fall freely to the earth, where it rang like a horseshoe on the sharp stones below.

For a brief time he stood panting outside the main drain, as if waiting to catch his breath. Then, hunching over, moving head first, he advanced three or four steps into the tunnel. Almost at once, he felt it start to descend into the earth on a shallow grade. No more than ten or so feet in, daylight fell quickly away. A few steps farther and Pickering could see nothing before him. He retreated back to daylight, trudged over to his car on Pearl Street, got a flashlight from the glove compartment, and started back to the river.

This time when he reached there, he removed his overcoat. Folding it into a tidy square, he laid it in a neat bundle on the slope just above the grating. Over his shoulder he glimpsed the Jersey shore. His gaze swept down toward the graceful arching span of the Verrazano Bridge. Then, with a wistful, rather despairing expression, he flicked on his flashlight and stepped into the hole.

For some thirty yards or so, he could feel from the backward pressure on his heels and calves the tunnel dropping down beneath his feet into the earth. After that, it seemed to level off, and he walked in a half-stoop, making good progress.

The farther in he penetrated, the colder and more dank it became. He regretted for a moment having left his overcoat outside. It occurred to him that the place was very quiet, except for a low, unbroken whooshing sound he took to be that of water, the timeless tidal flow of the river behind him, running out to sea.

A bit farther on, he was startled by a soft, scurrying sound, some tiny subterranean creature perturbed by the unwelcome approach of a stranger. Full of misgivings, Pickering moved ahead, penetrating deeper at a fairly brisk clip, anxious to reach the end, to confront whatever it was he imagined he would confront. He plunged after the beam of his light, which cast yellow swaying rings on the crumbling clay walls. From his position in the tunnel and his vague memory of the ground above, he tried to judge where he was in relation to Bridge Street. It seemed to him that he was somewhere beneath the park. Possibly halfway through. He had no way of knowing for certain.

A short time later, he began to approach an area from which a hollow rumbling sound issued. The closer he came, the more the rumbling increased in volume. He could see thin streams of dirt and sand spilling slowly through seams in the cracked clay ceiling and feel vibrations underfoot. It was the traffic above, of course, and then he knew he was somewhere under Bridge Street.

The deeper in he went, the more disquieting were the signs of rock and sand spills. In some places whole patches of the tunnel ceiling had dropped out, leaving gaping fissures out of which wet, porous earth dripped. All the while, through his mind the cautionary words of Mr. Lydecker whirled: "*dangerous . . . so badly undermined it had to be sealed off and abandoned.*"

With traffic rumbling overhead, the showers of dirt and gravel seemed to increase. Pickering grew increasingly uneasy. Several times his courage nearly failed him. He kept telling himself that if he didn't find anything within the next ten feet, he would turn back. But he didn't. Something drew him on.

Slightly winded, his back aching from the unrelieved stooping, he suddenly picked out a low, squat object just ahead in the round beam of his light. For a moment he thought it was a box or a crate, but as he moved forward a step, it became apparent it was neither. A puff of air issued from his lungs like a gasp. His hand leaped to the gun holster beneath his arm. Quite clearly he could see now the outline of someone sitting there.

THIRTY-SIX

"WHERE THE HELL ARE YOU?"

"In a phone booth in Battery Park."

"Doing what?"

"Sewer sitting. Come on down. It's beautiful. The World Trade Center. The Statue of Liberty. The Verrazano Bridge. The Arthur Kill."

"I just dragged my ass in here from Poughkeepsie. I'm in no mood for jokes, Rollo."

"What would you say to an abandoned sewer line?"

Mooney sighed. "I'd say to go bugger off."

"I'm saying I hit pay dirt at the Bureau of Deeds and Instruments."

Comprehension came drifting slowly back at Mooney. "Oh, yeah? Tell me."

"I'm telling you. We hit pay dirt. Bingo. We've got a tunnel now."

"A tunnel?"

"An old sewer line. Nearly a century old. Runs under the house on Bridge Street. Out to Battery Park. Lets out on the river."

Mooney's thought processes accelerated. "You can get in and out of the house through the tunnel?"

"Piece of cake. Ladder runs right up from the tunnel into the cellar."

"Have you been through it yet?"

"Right to the end."

"Find anything?"

There was a pause. When Pickering spoke again it was

with giddy excitement, as though he were trying to keep
from laughing. "I found our boy."

Mooney took a deep breath and let the air slowly
expire. "Our . . . "

"You heard me, Frank. Our boy. That's right. Came
right up within twenty feet of him. Didn't see him till I
was nearly right on top of him."

Mooney closed his eyes. His mouth felt dry. "What
was he doing?"

"Sitting there right in the beam of my flashlight.
Watching me. Never saw eyes like that in my life."

"What were they like?"

"Crazy." Pickering started to laugh. "Fucking crazy."

For some reason unknown to Mooney, he started to
laugh too, and for a while the two of them laughed
together, great, long peals of healing laughter.

"You didn't try and take him yourself," Mooney suddenly asked.

"You gotta be kidding. This joker is sitting there on a
ledge like a big rat watching me. In his hand, he's holding a six-inch butcher's knife, pointing it right in my
direction."

"You didn't do anything stupid, Rollo, like trying to
take him yourself? He didn't run, did he?"

"He didn't run," Pickering sounded out of breath. "I
did." He started to laugh again. "I got my ass out of there
fast."

"I want that son of a bitch alive."

"I know you do. If it was up to me I'd've shot the
fucker on the spot."

"Where are you now?"

"I'm watching the sewer opening from the phone
booth. About a hundred yards away."

"He can't get out any other way?"

"Only through the house and the front door. And he
won't do that. The streets out front are crawling with
Sylvestri's guys. They been in and out of the house a half
dozen times since I been here."

"They don't know about the tunnel yet?"

"Obviously not, otherwise they'd have been down there hours ago."

"Good. Now you listen to me, Rollo." Mooney's voice was clipped and urgent. "Keep out of the way. Not a word about this tunnel or what you've seen down there to anyone or, if it's my last official act on this force, I'll have your nuts."

"Thanks, Frank," Pickering remarked with weary resignation. "Your expression of gratitude for all of my efforts is truly touching."

"You have no idea how touching I can be when properly motivated. Now keep out of sight and keep your mouth shut. I'll be down there in twenty minutes."

THIRTY-SEVEN

"WHERE IS HE?"

"Just where I told you."

"You haven't left this unguarded?" Mooney glanced down at the drain opening.

"Haven't had my eyes off it since I got here. He's still down there, Frank. Take it from me. Hey, where you going?"

"See if I can pry him out." Mooney already had his coat off and was heading for the drain.

Pickering scurried after him, trying to wedge himself between Mooney and the opening. "Hey, don't go down there, Frank. He's got a pig-sticker there the size of a saber. He'll cut your head off."

Mooney hauled the .38 caliber police special from its leather nest beneath his arm. "Lemme have your flashlight."

"Don't go down there, Frank. This one's a specimen. I'm telling you."

"Step aside," Mooney replied grimly and with the barrel of his pistol gently nudged his partner out of the way.

Pickering appeared distraught. "Please don't do this, Frank. Not unless you're prepared to shoot his fucking head off."

"This one I'm bringing back alive, Rollo."

Pickering watched the big man stoop and enter the drain. He stood there a moment, then shrugged helplessly. "Hey, wait a minute. I'm coming with you."

"You stay right there," Mooney snapped, plowing forward into the tunnel. "If I'm not up out of this hole in fifteen minutes, call the National Guard."

Five feet from the entrance, it was pitch-dark in the tunnel. The flashlight helped, but motes of dust and dirt dropping steadily from the ceiling clogged the beam of it.

Despite the fact that he had to travel stooped over, causing strain on his back and stomach, Mooney made remarkably swift progress. Halfway through he was panting, out of breath, and drenched in sweat. The closeness and lack of ventilation made him feel as if he was about to suffocate. For a man who'd suffered one coronary in the course of his lifetime, he was almost cavalierly indifferent to the stress he was subjecting himself to.

Overhead, he was aware of the rumble of traffic. From time to time, he looked up at the seams and fissures in the clay ceiling down through which rained a thin but disquietingly steady shower of gravel and earth.

When he found him at last, it was just as Pickering had said. He was sitting on a ledge amidst a number of crates and boxes. Not sitting actually, but crouching like one of the larger primates in the zoo, confined to a cage too small for him. He had that resigned look. Mooney had the distinct impression that he'd been waiting there, expecting him — that he'd resolved to run no further.

The beam of the flashlight lit up the head, appearing to detach it from the rest of the body. The first thing Mooney was aware of was the smile he'd heard so often described. It was indeed crooked. On the street, with his black hair, Mooney was not at all sure he would have recognized him as the blond-headed, vague, and slightly discombobulated Ferris Koops he'd interrogated at the station house.

Declining to approach any further, the detective came to a dead halt some thirty feet off in the tunnel. From where he stood, he could see quite clearly in the beam of his light the broken teeth, the glinting eyes, and a six-

or seven-inch Sicilian fisherman's bait knife held up like
a torch before him.

"Hello, Ferris," he said and heard his voice ricochet
off the walls of the tunnel. "You remember me, Ferris,
don't you? We had a nice talk together down at headquarters. I spoke with your old teacher today, Mr. Armstead. He told me what a great kid you were."

Mooney was aware of the bogus affability in his voice
and hoped that Ferris wasn't. As Mooney spoke, Ferris
tilted his head sideways, as if the motion were an aid to
comprehension.

"I want to take you up now, Ferris. Outside, where
we can talk." Mooney stood there waiting, stooped over
in the tunnel, his neck and chest aching. Still no response came. The eyes gleaming in the beam of light
watched him. They appeared not to have blinked once.

"Ferris, come with me now. I promise no one will
hurt you."

Mooney waited. Still nothing, but in the next moment
the figure shifted as if casting about for a more comfortable position.

"My name's not Ferris," he said in a dreamy laconic
way. He gave the impression that he was dazed or in
some sort of trance, but the moment Mooney took a step
toward him the knife blade flashed.

"Oh, that's right. Your name's Warren, isn't it? Warren Mars?"

Mooney stood there crouched over, his neck starting
to cramp.

"Warren." He heard his voice unnaturally soft, pleading. "I promise. If you come up with me now, I'll do
everything in my power to help you. Come on, Warren," Mooney said, extending a trembling hand toward
him.

The knife flashed instantly. Mooney flinched, seeing
the crouched legs rise and start to uncoil, as if ready to
spring.

It was then that Mooney decided to let discretion be

the better part of valor. He turned slowly and began his retreat, not at all pleased about having to undertake it with his back to Warren. He wasn't too pleased about having to go at all, but he had resolved after nearly two years of a frustrating and humiliating search that he would bring the Shadow Dancer in alive, and for the moment, this was the only way he knew to keep that possibility viable.

Pickering was hovering above the drain opening when he got back outside. "Glad to see you're still in one piece."

"How long did you say this line's been sealed off?" Mooney snapped.

"Nearly thirty years is what the commissioner said."

"What was his name again?"

Pickering's brow creased, struggling to recall. "Merton. Frank Merton. Commissioner of Sewer Maintenance. What about him?"

"I want you to call him."

"At this hour? He won't be in his office."

"Call him at home."

"I don't know his number. I don't know where he lives. The guy at Deeds and Instruments spoke to him."

"Go call the guy at Deeds and Instruments."

"He won't be there, either." Pickering's voice rose in exasperation. "Who the hell do you think is still working at this hour? This is Christmas, for Chrissake."

Mooney stood there glaring at him, as angry as he was puzzled by that disclosure. If indeed it was Christmas, he couldn't have cared less.

"Go find me that Sewer Commissioner, Rollo." Mooney spoke softly. There was an ominous edge to his voice. "I don't care how you do it."

Pickering stood there fidgeting with the buttons on his raincoat. A wet, cold wind had begun to sough in off the river. "What am I supposed to do once I find him?"

"Ask him about the sewer line."

"What about it? It's sealed, I told you."

"Ask him if it can't be unsealed. Ask him if it can be
 oded."

"Frank." Pickering's arms rose in dismay. "It's been
 ut off for over a quarter of a century."

"Well, you ask Mr. Merton if it can't be turned on
 ain. Just for a little bit. Maybe it's a simple matter, like
 valve or a petcock somewhere. You go get Merton on
 e horn now. Those emergency 'Sewer Rats' are sup-
 sed to be on duty twenty-four hours a day. Before I
 ve to go back down there and shoot him in the legs, I
 ant to see if I can't just flush the fucker out."

 e final days of the year were dwindling to a close.
 ere hadn't been much snow, but the weather was cold
 ain and rainy, and that night there was sleet. A pale
 iver of moon rode between a flotilla of angry black
 ouds, scudding low above the river.

It was going on one in the morning. The footpath
 mps had gone off in the park, all at once as though a
 agic wand had been waved, bringing down a darkness
 dden and complete. Mooney sat huddled in creaky
 inwear, concealed in a clump of tall marsh grass. He
 as not more than twenty or so feet from the drain
 pening, which in that spare light loomed larger and
 arker than in normal daylight. From where he sat it
 ve the appearance of some mystical square afloat in a
 ark void. The heavy grating lay off to the side where
 ickering had let it drop.

Just behind Mooney and to his right, Pickering shiv-
 red behind a screen of cold, wet grass. The place and
 eneral discomfort made him think of duck blinds in
 hich he'd crouched and shivered up north in Maine.

Surrounding him was none of the pristine tranquillity
 f the Maine woods, however. Not more than twenty
 et from his back, the choppy, sullen river tide punched
 ast, lolloping hard up against the shore. Beyond that,
 oaked in murky dark, the low, huddled silhouette of
 e Jersey waterfront stretched north and south. Di-

rectly in front of him, through the tall blades of mars
grass, Pickering had a clear prospect of the lower Man
hattan skyline. In that bleak, cheerless hour, the tal
unilluminated shafts gave the impression of a ring
dolmens strewn about some old Druidic ruin.

"What's keeping your pal, Merton?" Mooney mu
tered through clenched teeth.

"I told you, Frank. He was making no promises. N
guarantees. He hadda go locate an old survey map . . .

"Sure, sure."

"You're lookin' for a valve maybe a century old, some
where in lower Manhattan. It's a needle in a haystack.

"I know. You told me that already."

"Well, don't expect anything then," Pickering sulke
"The man was not overjoyed, called away from his di
ner table seven o'clock in the evening."

"I got lots better places to spend my evenings, too,
Mooney snarled.

He sank lower into the grass and deeper into himsel
The thick mist crept like icy hands down the collar of h
coat and up about his trouser legs. The longer he sat, th
more he smoldered like old burning rags. "Where th
hell's this valve supposed to be anyway?"

"He wasn't sure. He was calling in to check. H
thought it might come off a big feeder line north
Nassau Street."

"He thought?" Mooney jeered. "He thought?"

"That's right. He thought. And even if they find it, h
wasn't all too sure they could get the water level up hig
enough in this line to flush the guy out."

"I don't wanna drown the son of a bitch. I just wann
make it unpleasant enough down there to make hir
wanna come out."

"Merton understands that."

"Good. Just so he understands."

Mooney had run out of things to complain about an
by that time he sensed that the two of them had reache

point of sharp mutual dislike. "Go get yourself a cup of coffee," he grumbled, making a stab at reconciliation.

"I don't want any. You get a cup of coffee."

Mooney sat there unmoving, glowering at the dark square afloat in the void. For the past three hours or so, pelted by sleet and a biting wind, his cramped legs aching, he had lapsed into one of his deep funks.

One minute past midnight. A new day. It may as well have been April Fool's Day. No one felt himself more the butt of some cosmic joke than he did, sitting there in icy grass and damp clothing, shivering hard by the riverside waiting for water to rise in an abandoned sewer line. That day in *Newsweek*, an exclusive story had revealed how the poor benighted police, after having the Shadow Dancer in custody, had released him. The New York press had begun to write funny editorials about the ineptitude of the N.Y.P.D., comparing them to the Keystone Kops, and Mooney and Pickering, though mercifully unnamed, to Laurel and Hardy. The commissioner was grinding his teeth and even Sylvestri, the wunderkind, was trying to distance himself from the investigation.

When, two hours later, the water started, he didn't even know it. Wrapped in gloom and feeling sorry for himself, he thought he'd been listening to the river. He paid no attention to the sound until he felt icy water seeping into his shoes and creeping up around his pant leg. The shock of cold startled him and brought him halfway up out of the grass until he saw at once that he was standing in the midst of a wide, dark, spreading puddle. "Hey, Rollo —"

"I see. I see." The voice came back at him in an excited whisper.

They had no time after that even to consider what was happening, because what happened, happened far too fast. Mooney had barely time to yank the .38 caliber police special from his holster when a dark shape borne on a tide of gushing water hurtled out from the center of the square.

Even as Mooney watched the dark outline emerg
from the drain, it appeared to crouch suddenly and the
leap forward, not at a run but at a charge, moving on
line directly at Mooney, as though the hunted kne
exactly where his tormentors lay.

From where Mooney hunkered low in the grass, he wa
certain he'd been detected. Now he was about to b
attacked. Rushing toward him, the black shape loome
larger and larger, gradually taking on human form. H
could hear the hard crunch of feet on gravel, then th
grunt and labored breathing of exertion quite near hin
Something like panic rose in Mooney's throat as he sud
denly stood up out of the grass. His mouth opened an
formed the word *Koops*, but no sound came. Nothin
came except air.

"Koops." This time he heard his voice boom and carr
across the vacant park. The onrushing figure shuddered t
a full stop. With a narrow band of spongy earth no mor
than ten feet between them, Mooney was still unable t
see the face. But in the stance, the quick tilt of the hea
sidewards, he could read puzzlement and surprise. A
they stood there, gaping at each other, each waiting fo
the other to declare himself, Pickering made his move

They heard him before they actually saw him. Th
fast, clattering steps pounding up the thawing earth
sounded like some large, frenzied animal.

"Grab him," Mooney shouted, then lunged forwar
himself.

The dark figure whirled just in time to step aside
gracefully as Pickering hurtled past. With his finger
only inches from Koops's ankles, Pickering hit the earth
settling down on it with a soft groan.

Mooney came next. He moved out of the grass with
the slow, ponderous motion of a man wading hip-deep in
water. His gun out, waving it above his head, for on
awful moment, he'd almost taken aim and fired.

By that time Pickering had scrambled back up onto hi
feet. Koops was now standing at a point approximately

equidistant between the two of them, looking back and forth from one to the other with a curious air of detachment. His trousers, sodden with sewer water, clung to his legs. There was a blur of motion as the three moved about in a slow, stilted dance, feinting and jabbing at the cold air like pugilists trying to get the feel of the ground beneath their feet.

"Grab him," Mooney snapped, then lunged again. Koops turned in time to see the other detective lumbering out of the shadows. Like a matador, he executed a graceful turn, then bolted.

With the two of them coming at him from either side, he could go neither right nor left. Directly in front of him was the short, steep slope into which the drain had been built. The only alternative route still open to him was the river, and he took it.

Too stunned to react, they watched him charge toward the water, then dive. They heard the splash without actually seeing it. Then came the sound of the first strokes, rapid and frantic. In moments they'd lost sight of him in the murky night.

"Good Christ, he's in the water!" Pickering shrieked.

Suddenly they were both clambering down to the river, shouting all the way, "Koops." Mooney stood at the water's edge, bellowing into the foggy night, the tips of his shoes sinking slowly into the mud. "Koops. Koops." The cold spray off the river hit his face, and he could feel the chill, wet sensation of water seeping into his shoes.

In the next moment, something dark and large hurtled past. There was a second splash. Mooney bellowed at the whitish trail plowing over the water. "Rollo! You goddamned fool! Rollo!" He started up the shoreline, waving his arms frantically, like a man with his clothing on fire. "Rollo! Koops! Rollo! Shit."

The police launch arrived shortly after sunrise. It glided noiselessly through the Arthur Kill and slid up abreast of Bridge Street, dropping anchor some fifty yards offshore, roughly opposite where they'd gathered near the drain outlet.

The wind had dropped and so had the tide. The water lay still and flat, gray as a sheet of tin. The wreckage of an orange crate and a few bits of Styrofoam litter bobbed dispiritedly on the surface. The launch anchored offshore enveloped in vapory mist had a rather ghostly appearance. Gulls wheeled and shrieked above it as if in anticipation of something about to happen.

From where he stood, Mooney watched the divers strap on cylinders of oxygen and adjust their face masks. For the past several hours, special units of men had been scouring the shoreline north and south of the drain cap where Ferris Koops had disappeared into the frigid river waters several hours before.

Mooney knew how scant the possibility was that they would find him. At that hour and in that churning mist above the river nothing would have been easier than for a man in the water to drift a hundred yards or so down-tide, scramble ashore, and vanish cleanly into the night.

No one knew that better than Mooney, or understood its consequences more fully. Not only had he headed the investigation that had apprehended the infamous Dancer, then incomprehensibly let him go; now here he was scouring the riverbank where only hours before the Dancer had been trapped out in the open between two seasoned detectives, literally inches away from capture, but had once again given them the slip.

Mooney tried not to imagine how that would play in the morning papers. Silently, he watched one of the divers in full wet suit hoist a leg over the taffrail, climb down the ladder, and slip without a ripple beneath the surface of the brown, oily water.

The search went on for several hours. New men kept coming out with new equipment. Additional small police craft continued to arrive until shortly a small armada of boats floated in a rough semicircle offshore. Four or five police dinghies powered by outboards had deployed themselves closer in toward land. They trolled up and down in long sweeps and ever-decreasing concentric circles, casting large dragnets out behind them and hauling them in almost at once. A police helicopter, like a large dragonfly, circled low overhead.

Up on the shore several crime site unit specialists were moving in and out of the sewer drain. With big, glowing lanterns atop their blue metal riot helmets, they kept bringing boxes and crates up from below.

Shortly after seven A.M., two network camera crews were setting up on the shoreline and already panning the site. The reporters huddled in their vans, squatting on coils of electrical cable and drank endless coffee out of paper cups.

The sun was by then full up. It glinted off the long steel arch of the Verrazano Bridge and spangled the waters of the Arthur Kill beneath it. Even at that early hour the commuter traffic from the Staten Island side had started to build, moving toward the city with a weary resignation.

Somewhere about 9:15, the head of a diver popped to the surface about seventy yards south of the launch. He raised his thumb out of the water and pumped it in the air several times. Mooney could hear the low throb of the diesels suddenly turn over and accelerate. He watched the launch's prow turn slowly like a needle on the face of a dial and nose its way slowly downstream toward the diver.

There was a noticeable stir on the bank, as if everyone there had sensed that something important was about to happen. In a single motion the crowd surged downriver toward the point where the launch had anchored. One of the crew on deck was leaning over the rail, the better to hear the diver talking to him from the water.

The launch made several short maneuvers while the dinghies, like small white ducks, had circled in noiselessly around it. The torso of the diver appeared to rise halfway out of the water then, with a barely perceptible flip, slipped back under.

Pickering stood beside Mooney but slightly to the rear of him. Together they waited. By that time, Pickering had been to headquarters, changed into dry clothing, and come right back. Joan Winger had come down from the M.E.'s office to conduct the initial examination of the body, if, indeed, there was to be one. To Mooney's small satisfaction, Sylvestri was not there. He'd been called to a triple homicide in Bryant Park, so he was spared the embarrassment of having to view the spectacle of the "Little Lieutenant" strutting and fretting his hour upon the stage.

Suddenly, the diver's head, sleek and smooth like that of an otter, reappeared on the surface. With one arm he waved, while with the other he appeared to be dragging something just beneath the surface of the water.

Three or four of the dinghies quickly converged around him. Men with long grappling poles stood in the stern and poked at a dark object trailing behind the diver. In the next moment, the diver appeared to detach himself from the thing he was dragging behind him and swam toward the launch.

Whatever it was he'd brought up from the bottom was now being towed toward shore by a pair of dinghies that had it firmly secured on grappling hooks between them. When the dinghy hulls scraped up along the bottom, near the water's edge, eager hands seized their prows and hauled them up onto the narrow strip of land. The crisp air was suddenly full of the sound of rock and gravel grinding beneath the aluminum keels. The dark bundle they'd towed in tossed and rolled with a slow, sullen motion in the shallow foam between them.

In water it appeared inoffensive enough — possibly a bundle of old discarded clothing. Once up on the shore, however, it took on an entirely different appearance. Parts of human anatomy began to appear from within the bundle, flashes of white — a hand, an ankle, a foot inside a sodden boot.

They turned the body over, causing the head to make a sudden sidewards pitch. In the next instant, the face rolled skyward, purple and twisted in the rictus of death. Beneath the dripping outer garments, the body had begun to swell with gases. Clots of hair plastered like worms on the forehead leaked tiny rivulets of black rinse onto the face and throat. Where the eyelashes had been dyed, the rinse had run down into the sockets of the eyes, ringing them in lurid black.

Joan Winger stood beside Mooney, gazing down at the object at her feet. She appeared numb and shaken. "Is that it?" she asked.

Mooney looked up, uncertain if the question had been addressed to him, or to some larger entity beyond themselves. "Is that all?" she asked again. There was an air of dismay about it, as though she couldn't associate the limp, bloated thing at her feet with all the fuss and furor of the past twenty-one months. All of that savage frenzy; a city fixated on rampaging violence, paralyzed with fear. And the cause of it all, this poor, sodden lump of inoffensive rags, trickling a thin blackish stream of hair dye down into the damp earth around it.

THIRTY-EIGHT

"SO THERE YOU HAVE IT."

"I guess so."

"I'd like to release it to the press this morning. Any problems with that?"

Mooney pondered a moment.

"You seem troubled," Paul Konig said. "Something still bothers you?"

They were in the M.E.'s big, cluttered office, overlooking the East River, where just then a bright red tug was plying upwind through the choppy current.

"I understand all of it," Mooney said, unconvincingly. "I mean, I think I do."

"The body you hauled out of the river yesterday is Ferris Koops," Joan Winger said. "Take my word for it."

"I have no quarrel with that," Mooney assured her. "You've got your blood types matched. You've got the bite impressions matched."

"We've even got the bridgework," Konig said expansively. He was in an exceptionally good mood that morning. "It was recovered from the apartment on Eighty-first Street."

"We've also matched fingerprints from Bridge Street with some of those found in the burned-out Mercedes up in New Hampshire, and on the pink Crayola we found in the Coles house," Joan Winger added.

"If that isn't enough," Konig glowed, "we can even match those boot prints we took off the face of the construction worker — what was his name?"

"Mancuso," Mooney murmured.

"Right. Mancuso — with the boots we pulled off this guy from the river." Konig chuckled. He seemed more pleased with himself than ever. "I get the impression something's bothering you, Mooney. Don't fret it. This is Koops. A hundred percent guaranteed."

Mooney flicked back and forth through his pad. Konig and Joan Winger watched and waited until he found the entry he was seeking.

"Way back, from the very start of all this," Mooney began slowly, carefully formulating his rebuttal, "you were both convinced we had a copycat situation."

"So were you," Konig reminded him.

"Granted," Mooney conceded. "At least, pretty well convinced. You remember that every blood and semen sample we were able to lift at a crime site was an AB pos. But we also had two different sets of bite imprints, one with busted front teeth, the other straight."

"We understand that now," Konig said.

"Granted. Ferris Koops had a removable partial bridge. But at the time, we didn't know that — and that was throwing me, too. Now we know all about that. But one thing here" — Mooney tapped the page of his pad with his pencil — "still points to the possibility of *two* different guys. Ferris and a copycat of Ferris."

Dr. Winger brightened noticeably. She started to laugh. "Oh, you mean the azoospermia?"

Mooney frowned. "Right. The two different sperm samples. To me that still says two different guys."

The point appeared to please Konig mightily. "You do pay attention, don't you, Mooney?"

Mooney's frown deepened.

"Dr. Winger. Will you kindly clear up this little matter and put the lieutenant's mind at ease."

The young woman pushed a fluttery hand through her disheveled hair, causing it to tumble in a wave along the line of her cheekbone. She looked almost pretty that morning. "You're absolutely right, lieutenant. The sperm samples we were able to retrieve from at least six crime sites were of two different types — one normal, one azoospermic. One fertile, one infertile. Sure, that was one of the principle reasons we all leaned toward the copycat theory."

"Then yesterday we did the autopsy," Konig said.

"Ferris Koops was a cryptorchid," Dr. Winger pronounced softly.

Mooney's gray, tousled head turned slowly to regard her.

"A cryptorchid." The young woman repeated the word slowly, with deliberation, as though she were spelling the word out for him. "Put simply, our autopsy disclosed that Koops suffered from a condition that's relatively rare."

"The frequency of occurrence is, roughly, one out of a thousand infants."

"What is it?" Mooney pressed him.

"It's an undescended testicle," Konig explained. "It can be bilateral. But, mostly, it's on one side."

"It's easily correctable at an early age," Dr. Winger continued. "Simple surgical procedure, and if done soon enough, the child suffers no testicular abnormalities in later life."

"Okay," Mooney growled, "but what does all this have to do with — "

"Let the girl finish, will you, Mooney," the M.E. snapped, then caught the disapproving glance of Dr. Winger. "I mean, let *Doctor Winger* finish what she started to explain."

There was an awkward silence while the young woman tried to recapture the thread of her thoughts. Then she was speaking again. "As I was about to say, if not corrected, however, the undescended testicle atrophies. Since sperm is produced by the testes, a male adult with only a single working testicle naturally won't have the same output of spermatozoa as a male with a full working set. While cryptorchids can produce fertile sperm with a single normal testicle, very often it's not as sperm-rich as that of the normal male. And it will take a cryptorchid longer to replace fertile sperm after ejaculation than it will a normal male."

Mooney kept his eyes riveted to the young woman's. "Meaning?" he inquired.

"Meaning, that it's not at all uncommon for a male afflicted with this condition to suffer periodic infertility. One of the findings of our autopsy revealed that Ferris Koops had this condition."

Mooney glared back and forth from one of them to the other. "Dark, sterile? Fair-haired, fertile? I don't buy that. That's a bit too pat."

Konig puffed amiably at his cigar. "I agree, and yet given the forensic evidence . . ."

"Fingerprints, dentition, serology," Joan Winger threw in for good measure.

" . . . there's not a chance in ten million that Koops and Mars aren't the same individual. But I agree with you, Mooney," Konig rattled on. "The amazing thing is that the periods of fertility and sterility coincide perfectly with the shifts in character."

"How can you explain that?" Mooney asked.

Konig grinned above the smoldering stump of his cigar. "I can't."

"Possibly the fact that he was far more sexually active in the Mars mode than he was as Koops," Joan Winger speculated aloud. "That alone could have made him more apt to be azoospermic during the Mars periods."

"Or possibly this is some aspect of his particular psychopathology." Konig scratched his chin while the other two regarded him questioningly. He continued: "The mysterious transforming power of the mind over matter. The force of self-delusion. The degree of self-disguise."

Something approximating doubt flickered in Konig's eye, then was gone in a trice. Once more he was all grins and affability. He wagged a stubby finger at Mooney. "But so far as pinning down your boy's identity," he went on, "the sperm's a relatively minor detail when stacked up against all the major ones we've nailed him on. Take my word for it, Mooney. This is your 'Dancer.' Him and him alone. No ifs, ands, or buts."

The huge grin on Konig's face widened as he watched Mooney try to absorb all that had been said.

"Does that answer your question?" Dr. Winger inquired.

For a moment it appeared it didn't, but then something in Mooney relented.

"I guess so," he sighed, tapping his pad and flicking it shut. "So much for Ferris Koops, alias Warren Mars, alias the Shadow Dancer, or whatever. I guess you can go ahead now and have your press conference."

Shortly after Mooney left, Paul Konig and Joan Winger stood about in her office. Konig pretended to busy himself by continuing to study the slides of boot prints stuck up on the light box. "Amazing," he murmured to himself. "You really did a remarkable job here."

"Oh, well, that . . . " She frowned, checking telephone messages left on her desk. It was her way of trying to discourage the type of conversation she both anticipated and dreaded would follow.

"Well, I just want to go on record as saying you did one hell of a job on this."

"Fine." She was glancing over a toxicological report and looked up at him over the rim of her glasses. "Thanks. I appreciate it."

She returned to the report, hoping he would go. But when it became apparent he had not yet finished, she looked up again.

"I really must apologize."

"There's no need to. We have a small personality conflict. That's perfectly normal in many professional relationships."

"No, no." He flung his hands up angrily. "The conflict was all on my side. My fault. You understand?"

"Okay. Fine." She wanted to stop him before he could go on. But there was no stopping him now.

"It's just that — that I look at you," he went on blusteringly, "and I see my own kid." He looked at her, trying to gauge her reaction. "Not that you resemble her at all. You don't. But when I look at you, I see her. You understand?"

She nodded. "I understand." Her reply was barely a whisper.

"I've been mean and bitchy to you." He looked around, casting about for words. "It's just that having you around here all the time is . . . "

She knew he was about to say "painful," but couldn't bring himself to utter the word.

" . . . uncomfortable," was the word he finally settled for. "I'm sorry. It wasn't fair to you. I haven't been fair. I've tried to make you feel that it was your overall competence as a pathologist that I was objecting to. That was a lie, Joan. My lie. I didn't know I was lying at the time. I do now. You're a superb pathologist. Crackerjack practitioner. I've given you nothing but grief since your appointment here, and I just wanted to say I'm sorry."

THIRTY-NINE

"CAPOTE'S THE BEST HORSE RUNNING TODAY."

"Who said? If you ask me, that colt was a two-year-old champion by default last year. He's never run in even mildly respectable time."

"Eight'll get you five, he'll be one hundred percent ready for the Derby off two races. If he runs like I figure he will in the Wood, finishes well and runs in the top three, that means he's ready."

"Ready for nothing. He was a seven to five favorite in the Gotham Stakes nine days ago and barely managed to drag his ass in fourth, nine and a half lengths out in his debut as a three-year-old."

The talk was loud and spirited at the bar that night at the Balloon. Patsy was shaking drinks and Mooney was surrounded by his old crowd.

The evening news had been full of the Shadow Dancer case. Clips of the river, Suki Klink, the Bridge Street house, the apartment on 81st Street dominated the screen. Over and over again with tireless obsession, they showed the picture of men in dinghies with grappling hooks towing the body to shore. The *New York Post* ran huge cover portraits of Ferris Koops in death, small black rings circling his eyes.

There was a rush to give interviews, particularly by people barely associated with the case, but all, nonetheless, eager to grab off some small patch of glory for its resolution. The mayor, looking more relaxed than he'd

oked in months, congratulated the commissioner, who
ongratulated the force in general for its "fine coopera-
ve effort." The networks trotted out one psychologist
ter the next. All of them lent their windy expertise to
1e enigma of the "multiple personality." Speaking spe-
fically about Koops, they illuminated his particular
sychosis in easy lay terms for the masses. It all sounded
stute and quite impressive, particularly from individu-
s who'd never spent a minute in Koops's company. You
ad to wonder why it had taken so long to bring the case
▸ a successful conclusion.

Paul Konig and Joan Winger were interviewed and
onfirmed that the body recovered from the river that
morning was indeed that of Ferris Koops and that known
hysical characteristics of the Dancer did coincide with
10se of the cadaver.

Sylvestri gave an interview on the six o'clock news, in
which, in all modesty, he implied that in the several
eeks' time he'd been assigned to the case, more
rogress had been made toward its resolution than in all
wenty-one months prior, when the investigation had
rst begun. But it lacked conviction, and several times
uring the course of the interview he gave conflicting
ersions of the story and seemed confused about key
etails of the case.

The interview that was shown most frequently was the
n-site one with Mooney himself. It had taken place that
1orning after the body had been retrieved from the icy
▸aters of the river. As the senior officer there, he was
ombarded with questions from news and television re-
▸orters, all clamoring for information.

Weary from his all-night vigil on the river, he fielded
juestions with his usual testy forbearance, then startled
veryone, including himself, by crediting Detective Ser-
▸eant Rollo Pickering with having broken the case with
uis discovery of the abandoned sewer line running be-
1eath the house on Bridge Street. He said nothing of the

fact that it was he who had sent Pickering up to the cit
registry and the municipal archives on the keen hunc
that just such a hidden passage might actually exist.

Instantly, Pickering became the man of the hour
Mulvaney, looking dismayed and uncomfortable, wa
interviewed at Police Plaza. He declared that Pickerin;
would be decorated for valor and, almost certainly, pro
moted to the rank of lieutenant.

On the six o'clock news, Pickering described the dis
covery of the tunnel, the long vigil of the night before, an
how he had dived into the icy water in pursuit of the
fleeing Dancer. Whether by oversight or design, he neve
once mentioned Mooney or any part the veteran cop ha
played in the resolution.

Mooney took all of that quite philosophically. Fo
him, it was reward enough to have deprived Sylvestri o
much of the glory of the final victory.

The phone had started to ring shortly after Mooney
arrived at the Balloon that evening. Everyone had seer
the six P.M. news and his interview on the river. The
calls were from colleagues on the force, old cops he'd
worked with, now retired, and beloved track cronies
Mostly, they were of a congratulatory sort. They kep
coming in. After a while, Mooney declined to take an
more, instructing Patsy to say he'd left for the evening
What he'd neglected to tell anyone that evening was tha
in accordance with his deal with Mulvaney, he'd ten
dered his resignation in a terse, but thoroughly civi
cable to the commissioner that day.

He took a quiet supper with Fritzi at an inconspicuou
rear table after the dinner rush. They drank a goo
bottle of Bordeaux and spoke little. She could see that he
was tired but still keyed up from the day's events. Bu
she couldn't say if the source of that excitement wa
elation or anger. She knew there was reason for both

"How did you figure it all out, Mooney?" she asked

"I didn't. Baumholz did it for me. He appeared in
dream and told me."

"So now you've become a mystic. Soon you'll want to o to church with me."

"That's not mysticism. It's old age and fear of death. t's only when you're thirty-five that you can afford the uxury of that good old American pragmatism."

"Are you pleased?" she asked and refilled his glass. "Is t a relief?"

He sipped his wine and thought a moment, then nod-led. He was more relieved than he could say. "Yes. But ot for the reasons you think."

"Not sweet revengè?" she smiled at him archly.

"I'd be a liar if I said it wasn't . . . but it's not that ntirely."

"Then it's about your retiring."

His jaw dropped. "Who told you that?"

"No one. I could see it when you came in tonight. It vas all over your face."

"How did I look?"

"A little on edge, but very happy."

They were both silent for a while.

"I'd been thinking about it a long time, Fritz." He :lung to her hand as if he were shaking it. "I figured I ust don't want to wait around another nine months for a ew extra bucks in my pension check."

"I don't blame you. Life's too short. I'd rather you spend that nine months with me. I don't care to share ny time with Mulvaney and Sylvestri."

"A marriage made in heaven," Mooney quipped. 'They deserve each other." Fritzi agreed, and suddenly they were both hooting wildly at the image of those two locked in poisonous embrace over the next decade.

"I don't mean I'm gonna sit around on my duff for a year and a half and just metabolize," Mooney went on. "I can teach at the police college. I can do consultantships for corporations. I can even become a private gumshoe." He grew excited at the prospect even as he spoke. She calmed him down with a firm pat on the back of his hand.

"Or, you could do nothing for a while, which would

suit me just fine. Why think about it now? We've go
plenty, Frank, and that means you have all the time i
the world to decide."

The notion of a world in which he had "plenty of time"
was one he'd never been in a position to entertain. As h
thought about it then, the prospect was disquieting. H
was prepared to live with a bit of uncertainty for a while
All he knew for sure was that never again would he wor
for anyone other than himself.

Later, he went out to the bar. The Christmas tre
and wreaths shimmered there festively. He joine
old friends for drinks. Track cronies — Billy Ange, Hy
Wershba, Teddy O'Malley. They drank stingers an
talked about great old champions: Sea Biscuit, Cannon-
ade, Foolish Pleasure, Gato del Sol, Spend A Buck —
the names rang down like thunderclaps. They spoke
of turf and odds and handicaps and legendary jockeys
Cordero, Shoemaker, Laffitt Pincay, Jr., and Pat Day.
They evoked days of past glory and shattering defeats,
the proud unconquerable spirit of noble mounts, sires
and dames, scions with class bloodlines who never com-
promised.

They were loud and raucous. They drank to the new
year and to Mooney's impending liberation. People
standing nearby at the bar watched them and eaves-
dropped on their conversation. Mooney laughed out
loud that evening several times, out of sheer joy. Out of
relief. The old dread, the vague, gnawing, ceaseless
discomfiture seemed past. Yet, the face of Ferris Koops
remained, still present in his mind's eye. It was not the
bloated mask with the grotesque ringed eyes he'd seen
that morning, but, rather, an image of the small outcast
child, cowering alone all by himself in a tony institution
for the unwanted offspring of the well-to-do, locked in
the basement of a derelict tenement in Hell's Kitchen,
and then the grimy little nomad, foraging with other
nomads through the trash baskets of Grand Central Terminal after some small scrap of survival.

That evening before he went to bed he lugged his old telescope and tripod up to the roof. With the 500 × power lens, he scanned the April night sky to make certain that the universe was still there, all intact. There was Cassiopeia up to the north and Draco trailing like a long snake directly overhead. Behind him, Boötes flew like a great kite with brilliant Arcturus glittering in its tail, and there the rainy Pleiades had risen behind him in the east. They had promised a shift in fortune, and they had delivered. Everything appeared to be in order. Everything was in its place, all of his coordinates and guideposts, the old tried-and-true friends of his troubled youth. They were all still there, shining down, timeless, imperturbable, scarcely deigning to note all the ceaseless fret and turmoil of mortal man below.

That night he slept the untroubled dreamless sleep of infants.

EPILOGUE

EIGHT MONTHS LATER, MOONEY HAD OCCA-
sion to be passing through Grand Central. It was at the
end of one of those dog-day August afternoons. The city
had sweltered under a blazing sun that had hammered
mercilessly down for nearly a week. Daily, New York
had suffered from hundred-degree temperatures, water
shortages, drought alerts, and brownouts from record
power demands.

Along with thousands of other limp and dazed commuters, Mooney descended the escalator, conveyed
downward into the churning inferno below. Before him,
a blur of stagnant motion shivered equivocally like a
mirage in the desert. His damp seersucker suit clung to
his back and the calves of his legs. His wet inner thighs
chafed as he walked. The air inside the terminal was sour
and suffocating. It smelled like the meaty breath of a
bear that had recently fed.

Mooney was not rushing for a train (he pitied the poor
beggars who were), but merely taking a shortcut through
the terminal out to Lexington Avenue. At the foot of the
escalator, his eye was drawn to a noisy flurry of activity
outside of Zaro's, where people lined up to buy breads
and rolls and fast foods to take home for supper. Somewhere toward the rear of that line, but clearly separate
from it, he glimpsed what appeared to be a dark, spreading stain just to the right of Track 28.

Whatever it was, it caught his eye and held it until,
from all of that welter of chaos, a form gradually

emerged. It was a person of indeterminate sex, perched atop a mound of odd bundles and packages.

At that distance, Mooney couldn't make out the features of the person seated there. Still, he was struck by a sense of unmistakable recognition. As uncomfortable as he was in damp clothes and with chafed inner thighs, curiosity drew him closer to the place. Sure enough, it was Suki Klink. She'd taken up her old hunting grounds again outside Track 28, where weary commuters lurched and staggered out to the platform for the 5:40 to Poughkeepsie.

Swaddled in layers of clothes in that suffocating heat, she appeared to be enormous. Far heavier than he'd recalled. The apple-red cheeks seemed to have inflated to the point where the eyes had sunk into barely perceptible creases just above them. Now, there were only the sparse eyelashes to indicate the place they'd once occupied.

She sat amid bundles and packages, shopping carts stacked with magazines, newspapers, deposit cans and soda bottles, all of the detritus of an "all-disposable" civilization. The impression she conveyed, however, was not one of squalor, but rather something regal, on a grand scale, rather like a pasha presiding over a vast desert kingdom. She was wearing dirty white anklets and her swollen ulcerous legs stuck out from beneath layer upon layer of voluminous skirts.

She scarcely deigned to look up when he greeted her. The second attempt he made, he leaned down and stared directly into her face. "How are you, Mrs. Klink?" he asked. This time she stirred. It was like waking a drowsing lizard. Her head rose, her eyes cracked open, and a red tongue darted out across her lower lip. The movement was immense and stately, like that of a slightly crapulous Buddha.

"Remember me? Lieutenant Mooney. I came to visit you over on Bridge Street."

The eyes embedded deep within the doughy flesh were bemused and shrewdly wary. "You a cop?"

Mooney laughed. "Used to be. Retired now. How've you been?" He glanced around at the assorted bundles. "Looks like times are pretty good for you."

"You the son of a bitch who got Warren?" Her voice was full of reproach.

"If it hadn't been me, it would've been somebody else. He was a naughty boy."

"I don't say he wasn't." She hastened to cover the impression she'd conveyed. "I don't blame you. Not one bit. I'm glad you got him. He was bad. Did bad things." Her great girth stirred and the bundles shifted beneath her. "That's not the way I taught him. I tried to teach him right."

Mooney nodded sympathetically. "Sure you did."

She watched him intently, as if trying to gauge the sincerity of his reply. In the next moment, the florid skin above the cheeks stretched into a smile. Yellow stumps of teeth showed beneath the rubber blue lips. She grinned. "You hear about me?"

"No. should I have?"

"Sold my place on Bridge Street."

"No kidding? To the bank? I know they were after it."

"Well, they got it."

"I'm sorry," Mooney said, and he genuinely was. He hated to see banks win anything. The notion of that old ramshackle hovel plunked right down smack in the midst of the financial district, like a huge wen on the smooth marmoreal nose of American corporate grandeur, pleased him mightily. "I'm sorry to hear that."

"Don't be." The yellow stumps grinned up at him. "They gimme eight million dollars for it and the land. Three acres, it was."

She must have caught the incredulity in his face. She started to cackle, and in the next moment, her red, edematous hand, like a lobster claw, ducked into a large beaded reticule and plucked out a bank book from the mounds of debris stuffed inside. She flipped it open and Mooney suddenly had a glimpse of a bank balance with more zeros parading out behind it than he'd ever seen in a passbook before.

"Looks like the number of light-years between Jupiter and the earth," he observed.

She gazed up at him blankly. "Eh?"

"Nothing," he said. "Just thinking out loud. What are they doing with the place, anyway?"

"Doing? They done it already. Ploughed it under. Bulldozed it. Putting up a new building there."

Mooney smiled knowingly. "Well, what else would they do?"

"I got me a new place," she beamed. "Loft building down on Varick Street."

"You living there now?"

"In one of the lofts. Rest of it I let out. Lots of artists and crazy people. They pay their rent, though. Prompt and regular. They wrote an article about me in the paper couple months back. You see it?"

"Afraid not."

The puffy red hand swept down into the bag again and rummaged about for a while. It reminded Mooney of one of those wax gypsies in the glass booths you see in the penny arcades on 42nd Street that tell your fortune with a little printed card. Then something like a magnetic claw pulls out a cheap plastic prize from a heap of trash at the bottom and pokes it at you.

At last she fished out what she wanted and poked it at him. "They call me The Landlord Baglady." She made an unpleasant gurgling sound when she laughed. Sure enough, it was Suki — a full cover portrait on the cover of *American Business Week*. There she was, in full baglady regalia, standing out in front of her loft in TriBe-Ca. Printed just beneath the picture in large bold print were the words, "THE LANDLORD BAGLADY — AN AMERICAN DREAM."

"They tried to steal it from me. Take it for nothing." She giggled with renewed zest. "But I got me my own lawyer. Made 'em pay big. Who they think they're kid-

ding?" She howled gleefully and so did Mooney, suddenly aware she was no longer looking up at him but at
a scruffy, diminutive figure that stood with a disquieting
stillness before her.

"Well, looky here," she trilled. "Here's the little
seeker now." She reached up and clasped a small child to
her. With a yielding that seemed more like resignation
and distaste, the boy, attired in a bizarre combination of
rags, allowed himself to slip lengthwise against her,
drawn into the smothering heat and copious folds of her
garments.

At the same moment, his head turned and he gazed up
at Mooney. It was the eyes. Something about the eyes.
It would not be sufficient to say they were old beyond
their years. The word *troubling* came to mind.

The old woman fussed over the boy and kissed him
wetly. To this, the child submitted with sullen apathy. It
was as though he'd been sedated, but by things far more
potent than drugs. Everything of life had been hammered out of him.

Suki looked up at the detective and read his thoughts.
She put a hand up to the side of her mouth and averted
her head toward Mooney. "Poor little thing," she whispered up at him. "Poor little tyke. Got no home. Lives
with me, he does. I'm teachin' him to read and write.
Ain't that so, darlin'?" She cooed over the child and
chucked him beneath the chin. "What have you brought
nice for old Suki? Have you brought old Suki a little
present, sonny?"

Mooney watched the grimy little fist, clenched tight as
a knot, slowly open. He could almost see it struggling to
overcome its own inertia. At last, the hand hung open,
limp and indifferent, to reveal in its palm a dirty wad of
coins and rumpled bills of small denomination. "Oh, my,
see what the little entrepreneur has here. You done
splendid, you little scamp." Clucking happily, she
scraped the money into an apron she had banded around
her middle. She lifted the apron, revealing beneath it a

change maker such as bus and trolley-car conductors used to wear. The coins vanished quickly into that. The bills went into a small purse she'd fished out of her reticule. Into the child's hand, which still hung limp in midair in the timeless attitude of the mendicant, she pressed two one-dollar bills.

"Now that's for supper, sonny. Go get yourself an orange juice and a red hot. And mind, if there's any change, bring it back."

Undoubtedly, the boy had come to the old lady via the same route taken by Ferris Koops years before, and just like Ferris, had been introduced into the unconventional domestic arrangements of the house on Bridge Street. How much, Mooney wondered, did the old lady really know of the part played by Ferris in the Dancer's nocturnal forays? At the time of the inquiry she denied knowing anything. Possibly that was true, Mooney thought. But, on the other hand, it very likely wasn't. Mooney had no way of knowing, and at his present juncture in life, he didn't much care. The matter by then was academic. All he knew was that the old lady was alive and thriving, much to the regret of the district attorney and the board of directors of the Amalgamated Mercantile Bank. Clinging resolutely to her former style of life, which simulated most closely some species of vermin, she'd become a millionaire many times over. Surrounded by her bundles and packages, installed within those mounds of undifferentiated rags and fuming debris, she was happy as a clam. She came and went as she pleased. She owed nothing to anyone. She fed off her foragings and had nothing to do but collect her rents. She'd beaten the system at its own game.

And, then again, there was the child. All of his various needs had now devolved upon her. He would require protection and love. He would have to be taught the ways of the world. She'd suffered her losses with Warren, but she had a new prodigy now. He was her future and that made all the difference.

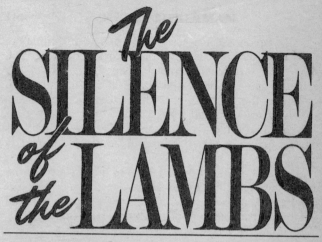

THE ELECTRIFYING BESTSELLER BY

THOMAS HARRIS

" THRILLERS DON'T COME ANY BETTER THAN THIS."
—CLIVE BARKER

"HARRIS IS QUITE SIMPLY THE BEST SUSPENSE NOVELIST WORKING TODAY." — *The Washington Post*